END OF PRIDE

BOOK ONE IN THE SOTERIA TRILOGY

L J DUNCAN

First published is Australia in 2020, by Duncan Press, Nairne, South Australia.

Duncan, L J, author.

End of Pride

Paperback ISBN: 978 0 6488501 1 3
E-Book ISBN: 978 0 6488501 2 0

www.ljduncan.com

This first one is for my wife, Linda. Thanks for the ongoing support. Thanks for the proofreading and the honesty. Above all, thanks for your patience.

CONTENT WARNING

This book contains scenes that some readers may find troubling. It is written for an adult audience and has elements of graphic violence, brutality, murder, sexual assault and rape.
Please be mindful of these elements, and other possible triggers if you choose to continue.

PROLOGUE

Union engineers had the artificial sunlight set to mild afternoon warmth.

The conditioned air hovered around twenty-three percent oxygen. Two Union soldiers paced down an illuminated Tier 2 corridor, making their way towards the Block 3 recreational chamber. They had simple instructions. A citizen had failed to attend his Lottery. This was a crime of the highest order, an act of defiant treason. Whether it was an unfortunate case of forgetfulness or a sign of civil disobedience made little difference to the soldiers. Their instruction was simple.

Execution.

As a loyal employee of one of the many sub-plaza medical facilities, the citizen fulfilled his employment requirements with positive review. He was always on time and always dutiful. His faithfulness did not matter. The rules were non-negotiable. Instructions couldn't be undone.

The taller of the two soldiers, referred to only as Four-Fourteen, stepped silently into the food court. He held an electrically charged taser cannon. Compact, powerful and accurate up to twenty metres, the taser cannon ejected a fatal bolt of compressed electricity. Less than a foot long and half the weight of an assault rifle, it was the weapon of choice for fast and effective firepower.

Four-Fourteen towered well over six feet in height. His Union uniform hugged his muscles like a second skin. The infamous red eagle emblem sewn across his chest was impossible to ignore. He evoked fear amongst the citizens.

The second soldier, Three-Sixteen, held a registration chip reader. Similar in size to the soldier's fist, the device located registered citizens by scanning the nearby area. It could home in on registration chips within a 100-metre proximity. Three-Sixteen entered the treasonous citizen's registration number. Within seconds, the device hummed as it locked in on its target. The screen flashed green.

Citizen 234-191 sat alone in a busy dining area. He ate a synthetic mushroom burger, lost in bleak thought. Slim and pale, he had bad skin and sunken eyes. He looked sick, as if he was already at death's door. That wasn't surprising. Whether above ground or below it, death's presence plagued the Empire. Citizen 234-191 wouldn't see death from the syndrome, though – he would see it at the hands of his oppressor.

With the synchronisation of a well-rehearsed dance routine, the soldiers positioned themselves behind the traitorous citizen. They rested the butts on their shoulders for accuracy and in front of a populated eatery they fired their weapons. The explosive impact sent Citizen 234-191 flying across the room.

Children shrieked.

Onlookers ran for cover.

Citizen 234-191 lay crumpled in an abnormally bent position, lifeless. The sudden impact broke his neck. His skin was charred black. Streams of putrid smoke began to fill the room.

Four-Fourteen and Three-Sixteen re-holstered their weapons and left the food court. They had been tasked with execution. Their job was done. Someone else would clean up the mess.

For those who witnessed the citizen's heartless execution, it served as a harsh reminder that despite God's presence, he would not be able help them. Faith and loyalty were superfluous. The Humanist Union was omnipotent.

ONE

WELCOME TO MY NIGHTMARE.

Thursday. Block 7's dosage day. *My* dosage day. While it was no different to any other Thursday, my thoughts seemed different – skewed, paranoid. Anxiety had reached an all-time high in my melancholic mind and I'd become too fatigued to fight it. I could no longer pretend that everything was all right. It wasn't. It never would be. It just couldn't be.

Normal for that stage in the dosage cycle, the synthetically conditioned air irritated the back of my throat and my eyes stung. Both symptoms showed that the previous week's Fosform Five dose had run its course. Either the air quality in the sub-plaza continued to deteriorate or I was developing immunity to the anti-corrosive drug. Despite a constant battle with hopelessness, I hoped it wasn't the latter. It's not as if my mundane and monotonous life filled me with joy but I didn't want to throw in the towel just yet. Depression was better than a painful death. But only just.

I stood patiently in line. Minutes rolled past and the long queue before me didn't seem to move. It's not like I had anywhere else to be. Over the years I'd taught myself to appreciate the time to think, to drift in and out of distant memories and hopeless dreams. It inspired thoughts of freedom and escape that I couldn't find within my sub-plaza reality. Over time I'd become better at it, zoning out as a means of masking my existence. And what a painful existence it was. My back hurt. My lungs hurt. Even my legs hurt. I could feel a piss coming on and I tried hard to ignore it. Standing in the dosage line always made me need to go. I convinced myself it was just in my head and I didn't actually need to. I didn't want to give up my spot in the queue.

The Union recognised the logistical difficulties of getting everyone in a numerical line based on their membership number, so they allowed us to be absent from work for the entire day when our Block had its scheduled dosage. That way, the citizens had no excuse for skipping their dose. Not that any sane citizen would go without the life-giving serum but the Union upheld accountability, sane or otherwise. So, for my fellow Block 7 residents and me, Thursday was our *day off* for the week, apart from Sunday, which was the Sabbath.

The line crept forward. I took two laboured steps then stopped again. The heft of my Union rubber boots dragged underfoot. I studied the three-dimensional hologram poster on the wall beside me. The Harbour Bridge and the old Opera House prior to the Artificial Revolution. The flawless blue sky and the sun's artistic reflection on the water looked so beautiful, so calming. Although I stood sixty metres underground and had no immediate desire to see the surface, I ground my teeth knowing it had all gone to shit.

It was approaching the end of Pride, the fourth month of the year. I kept thinking about the monumental milestone I was about to reach. I dreaded it more than anything else in my so-called life. It caused night after night of restlessness. My twenty-second year on this dying planet was coming to an end. Less than two weeks separated me from my milestone birthday.

A man's twenty-third birthday meant one thing within The Empire of Soteria: his Marriage Lottery. I feared the Marriage Lottery more than being fired or imprisoned or tortured. I dreaded the ultimate power The Union had over the rest of my existence. I struggled with the unknown. I struggled with intimacy. I always had.

I had dreaded my twenty-third birthday since the Lottery's introduction and now its frightening shadow towered over me, drenching me in unavoidable acceptance. So many nights I'd stayed awake fretting over its senseless domination, afraid of pulling the membership number of a complete and utter stranger. Would I fall in love with her? Would she love me in return? If I didn't like my soon-to-be wife there was nothing I could do other than grit my teeth and bear it – until death do us part.

Someone once told me that freedom exists in the mind. They told me that people are as free as they *allow* themselves to be. As a kid, I was naïve enough to believe them. There may have been a time when such idealism was close to the truth. There in that dosage line on the forty-second day of Pride, though, the aforementioned perception was not just overly optimistic, it was absurd.

This is Soteria: the land of safety and salvation.

Freedom did not exist. Humanity did not exist. Humanism and liberalism were just words mumbled among the older Millennial citizens. They had no real meaning in our refined society. The Union governed us helpless citizens in a way that even tenth-century barbarians would've called inhumane. In Soteria, under the strict rule of the Humanist Union, following your heart was about as realistic as drinking the river water or swimming at the beach.

Man, I hate the Humanist Union.

For fear of torture, I would never say that aloud, but that hatred grew stronger every day. Ever since they introduced the Marriage Lottery, it didn't matter if you loved your partner or even shared anything in common with them. If you drew their membership number on your twenty-third birthday you had to share your apartment with, conceive children with, and assign half your annual credit rations to that person until the end of your days. Just thinking about the twisted system made my blood boil and my heart rate increase with nervousness.

In thirteen days from that very Thursday, it would be my turn to draw a number and flip my life upside down. Justified as a rite of passage to becoming a compliant male citizen, the Marriage Lottery represented the step from adolescence to adulthood. Only men took part in the Marriage Lottery and picked the membership number of a registered female citizen between eighteen and thirty-five years of age. All male citizens of the Empire of Soteria took part in the Lottery. If female citizens weren't chosen before their thirty-fifth birthday, they spent the rest of their years alone.

Choice was a farce.

I would be forced to marry a complete stranger and there was no way out.

Divorce was outlawed. Adultery was outlawed. Homosexuality among registered men had long been a crime punishable by genital removal. Love became a long-lost fairy tale, a myth spoken about in stories and sung about in songs from before the Crusades. If that didn't indicate the lack of freedom in our *refined* society, then I clearly didn't understand the original meaning of the term freedom. If implying that freedom alluded to the ability to take your thoughts elsewhere, to daydream of a better, more hospitable existence, then I suppose that freedom existed in a melodramatic, metaphorical sort of way.

No one was free at all, though. We all served a purpose and if we no longer met the Union's expectations for that purpose, like all things obsolete, they discarded us and replaced us with another desperate citizen trying to survive.

Welcome to my nightmare.

TWO

It was well into the early hours of the morning.

Sweat dripped from Brie's dirty brow and the moist soil of the tropics clung to her stained clothing. The waxing moon lay on a bed of thick, poisonous clouds. The overgrown jungle was an ominous and forgotten place, no longer a region fit for humans. Especially not registered sub-plaza citizens.

Panting through her oxygen conditioner, Brie looked up at the towering wall above her, seeing it for the first time. Even through the heavy, black smog, the moonlight reflected off the gigantic concrete mass and illuminated the featureless ground beneath.

The wall itself was enormous. At a rough estimate, Brie thought it must be close to forty metres high and from the whispered rumours of the surface-dwellers she believed it was up to ten metres thick. It astonished her that the huge impenetrable wall surrounded the *entire* boundary of the Empire.

From the safety of the dense undergrowth, the top of the wall appeared to be free of guards, but replaced instead with a coiled labyrinth of intertwining razor wire. It proved to be a timeless yet effective security measure. Realisation became brutally clear. There didn't seem to be any simple way of getting over that impassable barrier. Although most people acknowledged this, it was a truth that Brie refused to accept.

As the birds began to chirp their morning tune, Brie adjusted the portable oxygen conditioner strapped to her face and took a few deep breaths. She continued crawling through the thick rainforest floor bordering the wall. Even after wearing the conditioner for weeks, she found it difficult to breathe through the carbon-fibre mask. She didn't like it at all. Having spent the previous three years in one of the Eastern Sector's finest sub-plazas, she not only forgot the foul taste of the outside air; she had never needed to use the mask. Unaccustomed to the mask's bulky design, the straps dug into the back of her neck and the seal rubbed on her cheeks. Friction burns, combined with the dirt and sweat from the tropical heat had become chafed blisters. The mask smothered her, increasing her agitation towards the oppressive heat. Despite this, she continued through the undergrowth one slow metre at a time. Freedom was so close. She had made it to the wall.

During her early childhood, Brie had battled with claustrophobia. Wearing an oxygen conditioner brought back those dark memories of helplessness and confinement. Given that there were only six hours of filtration left on her mask, she would soon be forced to discard the horrible thing, anyway. The fact it had lasted this long surprised her. It had been weeks yet her lungs still felt clear. She hadn't yet adopted a raspy, violent cough and her phlegm showed no signs of blood.

For close to three months Brie had been on the run, stopping for sleep only when she could find suitable shelter. Unfamiliar with the humidity and damp heat of the central tropics, Brie lost a considerable amount of weight through the lack of adequate food and constant sweating. Her exposed skin displayed a patchwork of cuts, grazes, chemical burns and insect bites the size of billiard balls. She was ill prepared for mosquitoes the size of flies and the acidic rain that fell daily. The absence of human influence and the constant hum of silence rattled her nerves. Brie feared that at any moment she might run into a squadron of irate Union soldiers seeking cold-blooded vengeance. As they had been trained to do, they would show her no mercy. Their power haunted her restless sleep. She remained constantly on edge.

Six weeks earlier, Brie found out her biological registration chip also served as a satellite tracking device. She took the most extreme measure to make sure the Union would struggle to find her. With a rusty scalpel and a pair of pliers, she took on the gruesome task of removing it from the back of her neck without anaesthetic. Her chip now rested on the sea floor somewhere between Queensland and the former country of Papua New Guinea.

Her rations were scarce. Concern rumbled in the pit of her empty stomach. Soon she would need to rely on the jungle for food. Due to the necrosis syndrome in both the air and the watercourses, many animals had become infected and therefore unhealthy to eat. Brie knew that hunting in the jungle presented a risk. Although the jungle provided enough plant life to eat, a large percentage of it caused violent sickness or powerful hallucinations. Brie couldn't afford either.

Because of her constant sweating, the self-inflicted wound on the back of her neck struggled to heal. Instead it became infected, weeping a mustard yellow discharge. If her body didn't fight the infection, blood poisoning would take her within the coming weeks. She pushed on through the undergrowth, trying not to think about the throbbing wound.

It was no accident that Brie had made it to the Northern Sector. She had planned it that way. The landmass of former Thailand was one of the few places within Soteria where there was land on the other side of the boundary wall. Other than parts of former New Zealand and Fiji, the rest of the giant walled barrier had water on both sides, making it almost impossible to get across the walls unnoticed. The ocean served as the world's largest natural moat, proving to be a very successful security measure for the Union. The wall wasn't so much designed to keep people out of Soteria; they meant it to keep the citizens in.

Given the lack of available Fosform Five in the Northern Sector, the previous decade saw Thailand, Malaysia and Indonesia fade into abandonment. Those that inhabited the once-tropical paradise fell victim to the syndrome. Over the years the region collapsed into an unoccupied jungle environment. Abandoned cities had become relics of the past.

As far as she knew, seven hundred kilometres separated Brie from any other registered law-abiding sub-plaza citizens. She sensed that solitude. That void in her life where human interaction once thrived had been replaced with introversion and paranoia. She hadn't had a conversation in weeks. Isolation had begun to take its toll on her sanity.

She diverted her eyes from the top of the impenetrable concrete mass to the thick jungle beside her. She came across a small rocky stream and stopped. Removing her oxygen conditioner, she took a large breath. Despite the flesh-eating heavy metals in the air, the coolish breeze blowing on her injured skin dissolved her claustrophobia. It provided brief relief from the mask's restrictions. She leaned forward and made a bowl shape with her filthy, callused hands and scooped water from the stream to rinse her face. She wanted nothing more than to drink from the stream, to plunge her head into the current and gulp huge mouthfuls but her desire to survive held her back. Instead, she filled a small plastic bottle from inside her pack and added two tiny Fosform capsules designed to filter tainted river water. After those two, only three more tablets remained in her supplies. Brie waited for the capsules to dissolve, until the water turned a faint turquoise colour, then gulped down a few mouthfuls. The Fosform made the water taste bitter but bitter was better than poison.

As the rising sun approached, the surrounding scenery became visible. The bluey-grey of first light started to show. Birds continued their morning song, sensing the impending sunrise. The sun meant a higher risk, a greater chance of being seen, hunted. Daylight also presented a greater chance of radiation burn from the sun's relentless fury. Brie re-fitted the mask and continued her slow traverse of the jungle clearing beside the wall. She followed the perimeter, keeping the wall to her right, searching for places to scale the giant concrete barrier. Having never seen it before, Brie didn't know what to expect, but she thought it would've been guarded with Union soldiers. She hadn't seen a single soldier since following the wall. Given the size of the walls surrounding the Empire, it would be impossible to have the entire perimeter guarded. That was *thousands* of kilometres.

The jungle's confinement got the better of Brie. She left the safety of the undergrowth to head out onto the flat, clearer land at the base of the wall to increase her pace. Despite the dangers, it was a risk she was willing to take.

The bare ground beneath her, cleared by machinery and infused with anti-vegetation toxins, should have allowed her to progress with ease. But the exposure in the open space between the wall and the jungle's safety increased her nervousness. Despite her growing anxiety, intrigue got the better of her.

Brie walked right up to the base of the wall and placed her hand on the daunting concrete mass. It was lifelessly cold from the darkness of night. So smooth and so tall, it was hard to comprehend how they had built the wall the whole way around the borders of the Empire in just ten short years. She marvelled at the structure, lost in a dream-like state. She stroked the cold concrete that restricted her from her freedom.

"Hey! I wouldn't do that if I were you."

Brie froze. The hairs on the back of her neck stiffened. She wasn't sure whether to turn and face the voice or to make a run for it. Stone cold acceptance hit her fast. There was nowhere to run.

Brie turned her head in the voice's direction expecting to see Union soldiers. Her heart hammered, her pulse pumped behind her rapidly observant eyes.

She saw nothing.

THREE

I LET MY MIND WANDER.

As I had trained myself to do, I made my thoughts leave the monotony of the dosage line. I thought about everything that fuelled my hatred. Trust me, there was an awful lot to think about. I don't know why I questioned everything. Maybe it was inherent in my nature. Maybe it was the way my parents raised me. For whatever reason, I couldn't just accept the cold, controlling truths of our shitty existence like everyone else. I just couldn't.

Often I wished I had the freedom to make my own choices. Often I dreamed of leaving behind my membership number and my registration chip to venture off and find somewhere better, somewhere cleaner and brighter and healthier and *real*. While I did my best to keep this optimistic longing alive, I had to accept the fact there was a high probability this other place, this utopia I longed for, most probably didn't exist. I hadn't even seen the Earth's surface in well over four months. The unbearable weather, the crime and the necrosis kept most prudent citizens below ground. The surface of the Earth in 2059 AD was not a place I missed.

I'd been in line at the dispensary for almost two hours. Based on the amount of Union doctors on duty, I would probably be in line for another two. I wouldn't be able to hold my bladder that long. The Union supplied public urinal bays outside the corridor of the medical precinct, but they charged a disgustingly high four credits for use. I held it out of stubborn principle.

Thirst made my mouth dry and my head thump. The long thermal lights running along the ceiling of the corridor seemed brighter than usual, uncomfortably bright. They contributed to the dull pain behind my eyes.

Stationed at ten-metre intervals along the walls of the corridor, Humanist Union soldiers stood in a textbook stance with their high-voltage taser cannons resting across their chests. Soldiers were always present at the Fosform Five dispensaries to enforce order. The Humanist Union Army comprised fiercely trained men only. They didn't permit women to join the defence force. It went against their morals, they said. The instructions were to shoot first, ask questions later. If anyone tried to compromise the distribution and administration of the formula, they received a taser blast to the face. The soldiers communicated with no one in the line and showed no emotion. They stood statue-still and just watched, waiting to deal with civil disobedience. It rarely happened.

The Union's slogan was stamped in large capital letters above the flowerbeds in the hall –

LOYALTY-UNION-SAFETY-SALVATION.

Oh, how I loathed those four bloody words.

They had been hammered it into me since my first years of school when the Union came into power. I was eight years old. I remember those days well. It was just before the months changed, just before *The War* started and just before the damn artificial sunlight ruined everything.

Alongside those four words the notorious soaring eagle, red, high and bold was printed along the corridor wall. The Empire's bird-of-prey logo angered me as much as their contradictory slogan did. You couldn't travel through a single block within the sub-plaza without seeing that red bird hovering above you on the walls, on soldier's uniforms, on almost everything, as a stark reminder that you were under the Humanist Union's watchful eye.

I hated that damn bird. It represented everything that was wrong with Soteria.

Progress in the line was slow but steady. I smelt the strong citrus acidic scent of sanitiser and anaesthetic. I knew I was getting closer to the injection booths. More images of the city prior to the revolution appeared on the walls. It flooded my thoughts with childhood memories. The city had transformed so much since I was young. I missed it every day. I missed the sun shining and the wind blowing on my back, the sand between my toes and the smell of the ocean air. Sure there was an artificial beach on Tier Two with white rubber flooring and crystal clear, chlorinated water but it wasn't the same. I missed the actual *real* world.

Although it was decaying and infected, the real world still existed in a physical sense. When Turner's Necrosis Syndrome (TNS) was first discovered in 2051, the Union began constructing subterranean cities, made possible because of the advances made in the Artificial Revolution of '45. Scientific breakthrough established the ability to source healthy doses of the required vitamins, radioactive energy and heat from artificial sunlight. They designed artificial air supplies and carbon reservoirs with synthetic oxygen conditioners. This therefore eliminated the need to live in Earth's tainted atmosphere in order to survive.

At that point, only the wealthy could afford to purchase apartments in the underground plazas. Nearly a decade after the discovery of the corrosive disease most of the lower class still lived on the surface, battling constantly to find Fosform Five doses or portable oxygen conditioners to stay alive. It was a battle they all ended up losing.

The Union completed building the 3rd Sydney West Sub Plaza at the end of 2057. They included me in one of the first consignments of citizen residents invited into the plaza as reward for the year I spent after graduation *volunteering* on the construction of the walls in the Pacific Ocean. I use the word volunteering lightly because they indisputably forced me into compliance. I did my bit for the good of the Union and that was my reward – safe, supervised and controlled housing in a sub-plaza apartment. The Union monitored my daily movements and recorded all audio from within my small apartment. Regardless, it was better than hustling to survive on the surface.

They designed the underground sub-plaza of 3rd Sydney West with seven underground tiers and seven blocks on each tier. Each block housed up to five thousand citizens. That meant that 3rd Sydney West Sub-Plaza could house 245,000 residents. Your socio-economic status determined which tier became your home. As a low-income earner I was allocated to the dull Navy-blue of Tier Three.

When 3rd Sydney West opened for public occupancy, there were already six other sub-plazas in the original Sydney metropolitan area and more being built on the Central Coast. They referred to this hub of civilisation as the Empire's Eastern Sector. There was talk of linking all the sub-plazas in the Eastern Sector by an underground train system. The Humanist Union would most likely persuade surface-dwellers to dig the tunnels with the promise of a sub-plaza apartment. To my knowledge they had made no progress on this underground labyrinth of trains. That didn't mean the digging hadn't started, though. I was a worker of no real significance. Although the Union paid my credits, I was not privy to anything more than public knowledge and believe me, public knowledge was scarce.

Sub-plazas in the Eastern Sector were self-sufficient. Once the Humanist Union entered your membership number into the residency list, you never needed to leave. Your apartment, employment, entertainment and recreation were all available within your plaza. Sports fields, botanical gardens, restaurants, cinemas, theme parks and brothels were all within the sub-plaza and you were welcome to utilise everything. Once in a sub-plaza most people intended on spending the rest of their days inside, confined to their safe and controlled life, in a way, biding time until death.

That's not to say they couldn't remove you, though.

If you broke any community rules, they not only banished you from the sub-plaza, they removed your supply of Fosform Five and left you to fend for yourself on the surface, trying to survive the TNS, the crime, the cannibalism and the poverty. That was best case. Worst case was a taser blast to the head. That thought alone frightened most modest citizens into civil obedience. Apparently with loyalty and union came safety and salvation.

What a sick joke.

They named Soteria after the Greek Goddess of safety, deliverance and salvation, despite the fact it was illegal to believe in the gods and demigods of Ancient Greece.

The Empire of Soteria Humanist Union and our propaganda-fuelled society apparently kept us safe by stripping us of all our freedom, choices and rights. The Humanist Union stripped us of everything that made us human.

Salvation and safety, they say?

The way I saw it is that we were prisoners in our own lives.

I wanted to break the chains.

FOUR

THEY MUST BE HIDING IN THE TREES.

As if synced with Brie's manic thoughts, two men appeared from the thick protection of the jungle. They walked forward and stood in the muddy clearing. Dressed in faded civilian clothing, Brie knew right away they weren't Union soldiers. Both men had short beards and short, dishevelled hair. Neither man wore a portable oxygen conditioner.

Although relieved, Brie remained guarded. They may not have been Union soldiers, but they were still strangers, armed with assault rifles, and they remained a threat. They looked hardened, dirty and rough. It crossed Brie's mind that they could've been *worse* than soldiers.

Caution kept her motionless.

"You look a little lost out here, sweetheart," said the older of the two. He had quite a distinguished eastern Australian accent. He grinned cheerfully.

Brie removed her oxygen conditioner to talk. "What do you *want?*"

"Well… I want many things, sweetheart. I want far too many

things to talk about this early in the morning. I'm more concerned why a young lass is walking around at the base of the bloody wall at the crack of dawn ready to get killed… You know this strip of land between you and me is filled with shock mines? Horrible bloody things. I'm amazed you got to the wall in one piece. Now, come on, nice and slow, let's get you back over here."

"Who are you?" Brie asked, her tone a strange mix of fear and hostility.

"Well, not that it'll mean much to you right now, but I'm Bruce and this is my buddy, Francis. Me and Francis are on night patrol."

Francis didn't say a word. He just stared at her with an unsettling look, nodding slowly. Standing alone beside the huge concrete wall, Brie was far too terrified to move.

"Night patrol? What do you mean 'night patrol'?"

"Damn, woman. You ask a lot of bloody questions."

"Well, I'm sorry but I'm a little *fucking* confused," snapped Brie. "I mean, other than you being Bruce and he being Francis, who *are* you and what the hell are you doing walking around the jungle with godforsaken guns…"

Brie surprised herself with her fiery response. She was only small. She had long, straight brunette hair, although tangled, and innocent, girlish features. She hadn't seen herself over the previous few months on the run but she knew she had thinned out, her dirty clothes hanging from her narrow frame. Now, dirty, nervous and alone, she would have looked like nothing more than a scared teenager.

"Okay, look. I'll explain everything when you get back over here away from those damn shock mines. If you step on one, Francis and I will pull metal splinters out of our arses for days. We aren't here to hurt you, okay? We're here to help. By the looks of things, you sure aren't part of the Union and anyone who's an enemy of the Union is a friend o' mine. If we wanted to hurt you, we would've put a bullet in your skull while you were embracing the damn concrete."

He had a point.

Brie didn't have many options, and she knew it. She walked on cautious tippy-toes towards her armed audience. She looked down at the bare dirt beneath her. There were no signs of mines. No metal. No wiring. Nothing. Almost afraid to breathe, Brie crept across the barren land awaiting a painful explosion. It didn't come. By the time she reached the safety of the trees she was sweating heavily, her heart hammering. She inhaled a mouthful of tainted, poisonous air and wiped the sweat from her upper lip.

Relief.

"Okay then sweetheart," said Bruce holding out his hand. "Now for the formal introductions. I'm Bruce Chadwick and this is Francis... Well, just Francis..." He cackled.

Once again Francis didn't speak.

"I'm Brie. Brie Kallas." Brie shook both their hands with her right, gripping her oxygen conditioner tightly in her left. "So, who are you guys? What are you doing out here and why don't you talk, Francis?"

More questions.

Francis opened his mouth wide, displaying to Brie an empty gaping hole where both his tongue and his teeth should be.

"Jesus Christ!"

"Yeah, the Union held Francis captive for about three years. They hammered out his teeth and cut out his damn tongue. Bloody maniacs those creeps are. He's been hanging out with me and the fellas up here in the jungle for almost a year now."

Brie nodded. "Look, I know you don't seem to like questions," she said, looking around hesitantly. "But I have many... What exactly are you doing up here in the jungle?"

Bruce looked into Brie's frightened eyes. He paused, inhaled then smiled an authentic, warm grin. "We're digging a tunnel," he said, pointing to the ground. "We're digging an escape tunnel under the bloody wall. There are thirty-seven of us all together living in our little community under the trees. We call the place Tunnel Town. Or just T-Town for short."

Hope returned to her weakened soul, energising her like a shot of Fosform Five. Escape might be possible.

LJ DUNCAN

"Oh wow… Is it finished yet?"

"Well think about that, sweetheart. If we finished it, we wouldn't be standing here talking to you, would we? We'd be free men on the other side, away from this godforsaken Empire."

Overwhelmed with the possibility of freedom, so many thoughts rushed through her frenzied mind. She paused and took a much-needed breath.

"I suppose you're right," she said. "Are you getting close?"

"We've been digging for about sixteen months and from what we reckon we gotta be pretty much under the wall right about now, so really we're only about halfway. The soldiers do random security checks about once a fortnight either from the top of the wall or along its base. They don't seem to venture into the jungle too far 'cause there's never anyone around here. The soldiers are bloody predictable. There're pretty much ten to fifteen days between their sweeps. They came past four days ago, which means we should be right for a week. Other than their fortnightly checks, they don't come up this way too much. The jungle's a dead zone. Anything north of Georgetown is left to the elements. Because the soldiers check the base of the wall, we started the tunnel about eight hundred metres back so the tunnel is almost a kilometre long and it's only halfway. Crazy, huh?"

"It sure is," said Brie. "Well I guess I'm lucky that you were on patrol when you were. Otherwise I might be splattered up against the wall right now."

She forced a smile.

These two deserters were complete strangers. Even so, Brie felt the safest she had since leaving Indonesia. Happy to find others with similar ideals and the same hostile distaste towards the Union, she sensed warm and alluring acceptance. Bruce was a little rough around the edges. That didn't matter. He seemed like a genuine and friendly guy. She felt refreshed and revitalised by conversation and hope. Still a little intimidated by Francis, Brie smiled at him and tried to swallow her uncertainty.

"So Bruce, how come you and Francis aren't wearing oxygen conditioners? Don't you get sick?"

22

"I used to wear one but some locals would go months without wearing them and they seemed fine. It seems the syndrome isn't as severe this far north. There're no bloody factories or power plants or sub-plazas round here. That's not to say that the syndrome won't get ya. If you spend over two months on the surface up this way your lungs and liver will bleed. It's happened to a few of me mates. Fortunately for us, we have a few pallets of Fosform Five we got from a supply train down in KL nearly a year ago."

Brie's eyes lit up. "No way. That must be worth millions of credits?"

"Yeah, well, it was. Ain't much left now. I'm sure it probably cost a few people their jobs, probably their lives too." Bruce sniggered. "It wasn't easy to get. Because the air's cleaner up here, we only need a dose every two to three weeks and we seem to be fine. At this rate the supply we have will only last us another month, then we're gonna head back down and try to get more.

"They bring the shipments up to KL from Darwin, across the train bridges, through the Central Sector. We've got an inside contact in Bali so he can give us a week's notice to gather our shit and head down there. Last time was tricky. We lost eight good friends, but like I always tell 'em, freedom isn't free, right? It comes at a price, if you know what I mean?"

Brie nodded. She knew that more than anyone.

"So how far is T-Town from here and is it all right if I come with you guys?"

"Well, sweetheart, it's not like me and Francis are gonna leave you in the bloody jungle! It's about three k's away. If we stick to the boundary clearing, it should take us about an hour. If you want anything to eat or drink, you'll have to wait 'til we get there. We travel light on patrol, just in case we come across any Union scum."

"No that's fine. I have water in my pack but my oxygen conditioner is on reserve supply. Is it even worth wearing?"

"Chuck that useless piece of shit in the bushes," Bruce said, smiling. "It'll do you more harm than good. Once we get back to T-Town, I'll give you a jab of Fosform and you'll feel the best you have in weeks."

Following Bruce's suggestion, Brie tossed the mask in the thick undergrowth then set off with her newfound accomplices through the jungle.

FIVE

THE LINE BEFORE ME FINALLY DISAPPEARED.

There were now only a handful of citizens between my much-needed dosage and me. I shuffled forward and took my place in a small, glass cubicle. When instructed, I stepped over the thick red line printed on the rubber floor beneath me. A middle-aged Injection Administrator looked up at me from his desk. He seemed as enthusiastic about the day as I did. There weren't many jobs more monotonous than being a Fosform Five Injection Administrator. It was a mind-numbingly repetitive task, but it had its merits. If you worked as an Injection Administrator you got a great sub-plaza apartment and an annually increasing credit ration.

My Injection Administrator was slim, pale and balding. He looked gaunt, almost unhealthy. He spoke to me with monotone indifference.

"Name?"

"Tyson Anderson," I replied, coughing to loosen the phlegm from my throat.

"Membership number?"

"636-124."

He typed my number into his touch-screen device and used a hand-held scanner to read the chip inserted into my flesh at the top of my spine.

"Okay, Mr Anderson, please step around the desk, sit down inside the yellow square and tilt your head to the left."

I followed his command. I knew what I needed to do. Each week they said the same shit, year in and year out. They had to. It was part of their job. Stick to the script, he would've been told. The Union was turning freethinking human beings into programmed machines.

I sat on the cold steel and tilted my head to the left, exposing the skin on the right side of my neck. The balding Injection Administrator inserted a pod capsule of the aqua-blue serum into an automatic injector gun and put it to my neck. The first few times getting the injection was uncomfortable, frightening even, but naturally after years of it, it became barely noticeable. Hearing the trigger press, I felt the cool liquid enter my vein. The Injection Administrator removed the injector from my neck and pressed a button on the gun, ejecting both the needle and the empty capsule into a large box-like bin on a conveyer-belt beside his desk. He typed something on his screen.

"Thank you, citizen. You're free to go. We will see you again next week." Not even a smile or any real sign that he acknowledged me as an actual person. "May the Lord Almighty be with you," he added as I departed. I clenched my teeth and walked away.

The Lord Almighty angered me almost as much as the Union did. I was told that you were as free as you allowed yourself to be yet you were forbidden to find faith in Allah or Buddha or the Hindu deities without facing surface exposure torture. Catholicism was the only accepted religion within the Empire and all its landmasses, even places that prior to the Union were predominantly Muslim. Even speaking about other religions in public was blasphemous. I only knew who Allah and Buddha were because of the modern-day Crusades, or what the Union referred to as *The Conversion*.

Towards the end of 2046, not even two years into its rule of the land, the Union wanted to show its unforgiving power and devotion to the Catholic Church. Funded with dirty money, it launched *The Conversion*. They considered this the pivotal point in history that triggered the start of the third world war and the true isolation of Soteria. The Union trained a ruthless Catholic Army and let them loose on a mission to convert or kill. The Conversion saw the largest mass genocide in documented human history.

By the start of 2047, the Union hunted down, tortured and killed over thirty-one million Muslims, Jews, Hindus, Buddhists and Atheists. Age and social stature were unimportant. A non-believer was a non-believer. In two shorts years the Humanist Union eradicated Islam from all cities within the boundaries of Soteria.

Within the Empire, Catholic propaganda was part of daily life. Every registered citizen with a membership number needed to attend Church every Sunday for Mass, zero exceptions. In Block 7 alone there were 23 churches, on Tier Three, 118 churches and in the whole of 3rd Sydney West sub-plaza, there were close to 1000 churches all built in honour of the Almighty Father in heaven. All built with dirty blood money.

It sickened me.

God sickened me.

The whole distorted view of the Union sickened me.

With my dosage injection complete, I walked down the exit corridor and out into the foyer of Block 7's medical sector. I made my way to the internal transporter tunnels taking me back to my apartment cell. I typed my apartment zone into the touch pad beside the navy-blue metal doors and felt the cell move gently beneath me. Eight seconds later and the door of the cell slid open. I was in my apartment zone.

Stepping from the cell, I turned the corner. The corridor was busy with Block 7 residents. I ignored them all and instead looked at the wall beside me, avoiding eye contact with my fellow residents. An attractive scene of a South-Pacific sunset covered the wall from navy-blue floor to navy-blue ceiling. The water rippled against the sand; the sunlight flickered off the moving waves. With three-dimensional light display technology, the images in the sub-plazas were surprisingly realistic. It appeared to be like looking out of a window, although Tier Three was sixty metres underground and a long damn way from the South Pacific. I strolled past the setting sun and made my way to my front door.

I placed my thumb to the sensor pad beside the door handle. After two seconds the sensor pad flashed green and beeped a long, low-pitch beep.

"Security code... step one... complete," spoke an automated female voice from a speaker built into the sensor pad. I then leaned forward and stared into a microscopic camera lens the size of a pinhead. A small globe above the camera flashed green and beeped a long, low-pitch beep.

"Security code... step two... complete," spoke the voice again as my automatic lock system on my aluminium front door disengaged. The retina scan was the latest in purchasable security systems. In such a controlled environment I found it pointless, but I purchased it anyway. Even in a sub-plaza they had citizens spending their hard-earned credits on products they didn't really need. Consumer culture still existed just as it always had. I couldn't talk, though. I was the same as every other sucker.

Upon entering my small room, motion-sensor down-lights came on and illuminated the main living area with the warmth of sunlight. I removed my boots and slid them into the shoe storage beside my front door. With bare feet on my alpaca-wool carpet, I walked over to my inbuilt media control system named Laura and switched her on, watching my wall screen awaken. Laura welcomed me home and told me the time and the following day's list of pre-programmed errands. As usual, I thanked her. At first I found it odd talking to artificial intelligence but like most things, conditioning made it seem normal after a short time.

I turned on the hologram remote control for Laura's hard drive installed in the ceiling beside the sofa and began searching through film titles. I slouched on the alpaca-wool recliner in front of my wall screen and stared at the wall beside me, lost in bleak hopelessness.

Was I a coward? Was I just behaving like a B-Gen brat?

I couldn't focus on anything for more than a few seconds. I kept thinking about the fact that in less than two weeks someone else would sit here on my alpaca-wool sofa set beside me.

What if she's ugly?

What if she's rude, obnoxious?

But wait…

What if she's unbelievably beautiful?

SIX

Brie kept pace with Bruce and Francis.

After forty-five minutes of consistent walking, Brie and her two new guides headed south through the thick woodland. "Make sure you walk a different path to me and Francis all right, missy? We don't wanna wear tracks into the forest floor."

Brie followed Bruce's request, walking to the right of her guides.

Thick, overgrown and intimidating, the jungle at that exact point along the wall had certain energy, a dark aura that Brie found frightening. It was mid-morning. The sun hung high but only small fragmented rays of sunlight filtered through the dense canopy above. After ten minutes of negotiating their way through thick bush, the three of them came to a clearing at the base of a tall tree. Thick buttress roots surrounded its trunk. Brie thought she could make out the smell of food cooking. Somehow, through the strange smells of the jungle she could smell fire and warmth and safety. After a month on the run, Brie learnt that safety had an aroma as distinct as the smell of death.

"Hey, guys. You seem to have increased in numbers. Where did you find *her*?"

Brie looked up. The voice came from somewhere above them.

She saw a small Asian man perched high in the tree holding what appeared to be a Union-issue taser cannon.

"You still up there, Evan?" Bruce called out. "Don't you ever bloody sleep?"

"Just coming down now. It's time I head inside for a feed."

"Well, come on down then, mate. This is Brie, Brie Kallas. We found her up by the wall wandering around with a bloody oxygen conditioner strapped to her face, about to get herself blown up. She's come up from the Eastern Sector, trying to find freedom just the same as us stupid bastards…"

Evan climbed down the tree with the agility of a primate. He leapt from a tree branch at least three metres from the ground and landed with gymnastic precision. Looking at Brie, he smiled and held out his hand to greet her. "Hey, Brie. It's nice to meet you. Welcome to what we call home."

"Thanks. I can't wait to see it."

Brie shook Evan's hand and introduced herself with a smile. She began a brief narrative of her story. Apparently it wasn't brief enough. Bruce interrupted her, cutting short her story. "Righto. You two can babble later. We gotta get underground. Follow me."

Evan rolled his eyes and smiled at Brie. "It's okay," he said with a welcoming chuckle. "You'll get used to Bruce's inviting personality."

Bruce entered between two shoulder high buttress roots and foraged through the leaf litter to produce a small cord. Pulling on the cord, he revealed the metal handle of a crude timber trapdoor under the leaves and dirt. Bruce lifted up the door and exposed a dirt and timber stairwell descending into the darkness.

Francis closed the trapdoor behind them. Brie could make out a dim light coming from the bottom of the stairs. Bruce was just a faint silhouette before her. She hesitated, and then followed the faint silhouette until she found flat ground. Needing to crouch to fit inside the entrance tunnel, Brie squatted down inside the darkness. Crudely made timber slats held up the ceiling along the length of the tunnel. On every fifth timber support a dated oil lantern hung to the side, producing a dull orange glow. "This is one of the entrance tunnels to T-Town," Bruce said to Brie. "We've got three other entrance points, just in case one is breached or collapses. Bloody cool, hey?"

"Yeah, I guess," said Brie. If she thought the oxygen-conditioning mask made her feel claustrophobic, then the tunnel was a whole new level. She felt trapped, uneasy. She felt nauseous. The tunnel began shrinking around her. She started sweating. Her breathing became short and erratic. Feeling light-headed, the tunnel began to close in around her. "I need to get out of here," she mumbled between erratic breaths. The dull orange glow began to swirl around her like a carnival ride. She panicked. Reaching out to Bruce for support, she fell forward.

Hitting the compacted dirt of the corridor, T-Town's newest arrival lay motionless. Bruce came to her aid, pulling her up to her feet and supporting her with an arm around her waist. "What's wrong with you then? Just relax, missy. Everything's all bloody right."

Between panicky gasps of air, Brie spat out broken words about claustrophobia and tight spaces. Francis, lacking sympathy, snickered at her response, cackling like a high school bully.

"Well," said Bruce as reassuringly as he could. "You're gonna have to get used to it 'cause T-Town is a maze of tunnels and caves built into the dirt. Now, take a few deep breaths, chill out and let's get you to the main quarters and get you something to drink."

Brie and her three guides stayed in the entrance tunnel for a few minutes while she lowered her heart rate and composed herself. Before long they continued along the tunnel, step by nervous step. The deeper they got, the wider the tunnel became. With each widening metre, despite the stale taste in the air, Brie found it easier to breathe.

The tunnel opened to a large cavern-like room lit up with electric lanterns hanging from eyebolts in the rock. The room had the homely aroma of boiled vegetables and spices and the warmth of quiet and friendly chatter. People gathered around the tables, men and women of varying age and race. Some were preparing vegetables and fruits around an old cast-iron stove, some were studying a map and others were casually playing cards.

As Bruce, Francis, Evan and Brie entered the cave, the residents turned their attention to the stranger. The chatter quietened. Brie's face turned a few shades darker as all eyes honed in on her. She felt intrusive. The silent stares showed that she wasn't the only one to feel it. Before the uncomfortable silence lingered too long Bruce introduced her and explained her story. They all listened with interest. Their stares turned from looks of caution to welcoming smiles as Brie spoke. After a quick introduction to everyone in the room, Bruce and Evan offered to show her around the rest of the bunker town, give her a well-needed Fosform shot and treat the wound on the back of her neck from where she had removed her registration chip. All the residents of T-Town bore the same scar.

Everyone in T-Town seemed so inviting. Accustomed to living within the sub-plaza system, where trust and honesty were almost foreign, she asked Evan why this was. His response made perfect sense. Everyone there had once been in the same position of desperation and despair as Brie had been. Every one of them had been the stranger in the room, the intruder.

The first room Brie encountered was just one of four communal rooms used for cooking and general recreation. Beyond the communal rooms were six sleeping quarters. The rooms were generous, with bunk beds built from jungle timber, stolen pallet racking and various bits and pieces from abandoned towns nearby. The bunks had foam mattresses and woollen blankets. Carpet mats covered the dirty floor and dream-catchers hung from the rocky ceiling. It wasn't the accommodation Brie had grown up with, but it was far more accommodating than what she had endured on the run.

Past the sleeping quarters were two storerooms for food, catering provisions, equipment and medical supplies. In the food storeroom, Brie saw entire pallets of Union-issue food. Twenty-kilogram plastic bags full of rice and grain, five-kilogram tins of powdered milk and dehydrated fruits. "Where on earth did you get all this food?" Brie asked, shocked. "How did you get it down here?"

"The same place we get the Fosform, missy. We get it from the bloody Union scumbags. We steal it from right under their noses."

From the catering store they took Brie into the equipment store. There, in the centre of the dugout room, she saw it. Through the glass cylindrical syringes the fluid glowed blue in the lantern light. It was a captivating, tempting sight. A metal pallet with the letters ESHU stamped alongside the red, soaring eagle emblem had all but a few rows of syringes left in the timber boxes on top. When full, the pallet must have held thousands of doses. Brie knew that the initials stood for: Empire of Soteria Humanist Union. She also read the slogan etched into the pallet. The very slogan she had heard her husband recite countless times:

LOYALTY-UNION-SAFETY-SALVATION.

After diverting her eyes from the invaluable blue liquid, Brie noticed a huge collection of guns, tools, ropes, torches and other weapons, both modern technology and pre-Union. The residents of T-Town had somehow acquired rifles, taser cannons, nuclear shock balls, splinter mines, oxygen conditioners and night-vision masks. Bruce noticed Brie's look of overwhelmed miscomprehension. "Bloody good supply, hey? If we ever need to, we'll put up a bit of a fight. Now anyway, let's get a dose in you. Lift up your sleeve and come 'ere." Brie obeyed and with the swift confidence of a Union injection administrator, Bruce shot the liquid into Brie's arm.

The cold rush of the serum coursed through her veins. Since her last sleep, everything had changed so much. A part of her thought she would just stroll up to the wall and climb over it, having never seen it, then walk off to find her freedom. Now it looked like she might spend an indefinite amount of time with these strangers, these criminals, in a dark hole under the surface of the Earth.

"Well," said Evan, standing in the storeroom's doorway. "Let's get that neck of yours cleaned up. Where did you leave your chip?"

"I removed it somewhere above the Northern Cape. That was three weeks ago, I think. Keeping time has been difficult."

"Well, shit, Brie. It's badly infected," said Evan, wincing. "First thing I will do is try to get as much puss as possible out of the wound, then I'll sterilize it, clean it and cover it. I'm not going to lie. It will hurt."

"I believe you," Brie said with nervous hesitation.

After a messy, painful and stinking ordeal, Evan had drained Brie's wound of the thick yellow puss, cleaned it with a saline solution then covered it with a gauze pad and bandage.

"Now I'll show you the rest of the place," said Bruce, smiling. "Wait till you see the bloody tunnel. It certainly is a sight!"

Led by Evan and Bruce, Brie left the equipment storage room and followed them deeper into the dim and dirty tunnel labyrinth they called home.

SEVEN

I woke to Laura's soft and flirtatious voice.

When I purchased her software, I could choose from hundreds of different voices and accents. After hours of indecisiveness, I made my selection. Now her voice had become a normal part of everyday life inside my apartment. From the speaker in the ceiling above my bed she not only bid me good morning, she told me the time and how much time I had, down to the seconds, until I needed to scan my registration chip at one of Block 7's churches. It was Sunday. Sunday meant a nine o'clock communal service at one of the many churches in the block.

After seeking my approval, Laura initiated daytime mode. An artificial image appeared of blinds opening across my wall, making the room come to life with an early morning glow. Although artificial, the light brought warmth to the room through ultra-violet radiation projectors installed during construction.

I rolled over. I didn't want to go to church. I never wanted to go to church. Like all the burdens of this so-called life, the thought of that damn Marriage Lottery still weighed me down, crippling me with endless uncertainty. The last thing I needed was to be brainwashed with contradictory bullshit and lies.

My Lottery draw was in ten days.

I couldn't seem to shake that feeling of constant unease. After lying in bed, lost in a vague zone of negative thought and pointless longing, Laura reminded me I needed to prepare for the day. She listed off the consequences of skipping a communal service. I didn't want to face those penalties.

I staggered into the small bathroom beside my bed and looked in the mirror. I looked dishevelled, sick almost. The lack of sleep had caused dark rings to appear under my eyes. My short, usually well-maintained hazelnut hair was messy from a night of tossing and turning. Despite not yet being twenty-three years old, there, in that moment, I looked thirty.

After a shave and a quick shower I opened the fridge to collect breakfast, which on Sundays comprised butter biscuits and a vitamin-protein shake. Kitchens didn't exist in most apartments in the sub-plazas. Other than the elderly, nobody cooked any longer. Not only was cooking a waste of time and money, cooking appliances took up valuable space in apartment cells. I had no intention of putting cooking appliances in my Block 7 apartment. Why waste the room when I had great, affordable eateries down the corridor in Block 6?

I had three small rooms in my apartment and I was thankful for that. I had a living room, a bedroom and a bathroom. That's it. My fridge was inconveniently shoved up against the side of my bed and was almost always empty. I did have a crate of vitamin- protein thick shakes. Always banana-caramel flavoured. I had raspberry flavoured loaves of butter biscuit and I always had frozen pepperoni pizza. I was a sucker for a frozen pizza.

After breakfast, I put on my work uniform. I stepped into my navy-blue canvas leggings, blue rubber boots and a navy-blue polyester collared jacket. Union uniforms had no pockets. They served no purpose. It made it easier for the Union Army to monitor any missing Fosform Five.

From my front door it was only a short walk to the closest internal transporter tunnel that took me to one of Block 7's churches, aptly named BC74 for Block Seven, Church Four. Even though I could scan in at any church on Tier 3, I always attended Mass at BC74. I guess, despite my hatred for monotony, routine became unavoidable. Like so many people, I was a walking contradiction.

Just after quarter-to nine and already the crowds had gathered at the large navy-blue entrance to the hall. Upon entering, I leaned over one of the many scanning booths attached to the wall and let the scanner locate my registration chip surgically inserted at the top of my spine.

"636-124, Tyson Anderson, welcome to church," an automated voice said from a speaker beside the scanning device. I stepped away from the wall and joined the crowd lingering in the aisles between the pews.

It didn't take me long to locate my closest friend, George Clarkson. George had been a friend of mine since before I moved into 3rd Sydney West. We met working out in the Pacific Ocean building the walls between Fiji and the Solomon Islands. Like me, he opposed the Marriage Lottery and the Union's methods of control. We were careful about speaking our minds openly though. If they heard us talking of such things in public, there would be severe consequences.

"Hey, George. Good to see you, buddy. You looking forward to another eventful Sunday morning session?" Sarcasm soured my words.

"Hey, Ty." He smiled as he shook my hand with a brotherly slap. "It could be worse, mate. Sitting here listening to the Father reciting bible verses is more tolerable than laying concrete out on those tropical islands. I'll be a happy man if I never see a tropical island or that damned wall ever again."

George had spent twice as long as I had working on the walls. He endured the backbreaking work for almost four years due to an apparent *glitch* in the volunteering process. His distaste towards the Union spawned from those four years of backbreaking work.

George and I took a seat in a pew near the back and waited for the service to begin. We chatted about trivial things until the lights dimmed and the organ came to life.

As the pressurised air drove through the brass pipes, the hum of chatter ceased and we all rose as BC74's resident Bishop, Father Nicholas Kassal arrived. Father Kassal was elderly and slow to get to the altar. He was a man of principle, forced to adapt to the unavoidable changes of the past fifteen years. He had been the resident Bishop at BC74 since before I moved into the sub-plaza and despite my cynical views towards the church and its ridiculous propaganda, I found him tolerable.

"Good morning citizens," he said before clearing his throat. "I'm happy to see you all on this glorious Sunday morning. As usual, a warm welcome to you all as we come together as one, in prayer and worship in the house of our Lord Saviour, Jesus Christ. As we prepare to celebrate the mystery of Christ's love, let us acknowledge our failures and ask the Lord for pardon and strength. Let us begin by reciting our penitential rite."

In a monotone and quiet mumble, the citizens in the pews read out the words written on the screens before them. "I confess to almighty God, and to you, my brothers and sisters, that I have sinned through my fault, in my thoughts and in my words, in what I have done, and in what I have failed to do. I ask Blessed Mary, ever virgin, all the angels and saints, and you, my brothers and sisters, to pray for me to the Lord, our God."

"May almighty God have mercy on us," Father Kassal bellowed from the altar, "forgive us for our sins and bring us to everlasting life."

I clenched my teeth. What a farce…

EIGHT

THE SERVICE CONTINUED MUCH IN THAT FASHION FOR A GOOD HOUR.
Father Kassal spoke about the Book of Romans, gifts, prophecies and other nonsense that made me disengage, unenthused. I began thinking about my parents. I rarely thought of them anymore. I'd trained myself not to. Mainly because it just made everything worse.

The last time I saw my parents was when the Union shipped me off to the Pacific at seventeen years old to help build the walls. They had just made Fosform Five commercially available, but it still wasn't affordable for most of the middle class. More people started getting sick. Because of my employment conditions, working on the walls' construction for the Union, I received free weekly dosage shots and access to portable oxygen conditioners but my parents were far from wealthy. They couldn't afford the drug's unrealistic credit price.

In the two years I spent away they got sick. By the time I returned they were dead and buried and the Union had sold their house, *my* home, at about one tenth of its value. The most fucked up thing of all was that the Union Officials didn't even tell me. I received no call, no message, no satellite video meeting, nothing. I returned home to find an empty patch of dirt where my family home had been. Over three months had passed since they died and I knew nothing. I was so shocked that I didn't even cry. That day was the day that I knew I loathed the Union. I hated those four fucking words. Loyalty-Union-Safety-Salvation. What a load of shit. With no siblings and no extended family to turn to for support, I felt pretty damn alone.

I came back to the present as Father Kassal wrapped things up. Brushing away the depressing thoughts of my kin, I blinked away the welling moisture. At the end of the service, the crowds began to disperse. Other than Thursday, Sunday afternoon was the only day off for Block 7 residents so it meant that all the department stores, restaurants, food courts and recreational facilities were busy. There wasn't a great deal of recreational opportunity on the whole third tier. Tier Two had all the theme parks, water parks, wave pools, rainforests and zoos. The finest restaurants and brothels were located on Tier One.

"What do you wanna do today?" George asked. "You wanna head up to Tier Two and catch some waves? I haven't been surfing in a month."

"That sounds perfect, man. A few waves will be just the distraction I need. I can't believe that in ten days I gotta draw a number and get married! I'm not coping with it at all."

"I wouldn't be." George gave me a glum grin and shrugged. "I've still got six months until the Lottery and I'm already stressing about it. I can't imagine how you feel."

"I feel like shit. I don't know if I should just accept it and prepare myself to live this horrible life down here with a random stranger or if I should escape it?"

"What do you mean *escape it*, mate? It's not like you have a choice. Do you want them to torture you, or imprison you, or worse? You can't escape it…"

"I dunno," I said, sighing. "A part of me just wants to scan in at work and then catch one of the transporter tunnels up to the surface and make a run for it. I've heard stories of people escaping this godforsaken place before."

George looked around, paranoid. "Tyson, watch what you say, mate," he whispered, a flicker of fear in his eyes. "If the wrong people hear you say that, dressed in your Union uniform, you could get tried for treason. You know what they do to the treasonous? They'll chop your damn balls off and leave you in a cage on the surface. If you ask me, I'd rather spend the rest of my days with an overweight and grumpy woman I have nothing in common with than get left to die in a cage on the surface."

"Well, you're you and I'm me, George. I just wanna be free. Is that so much to ask for? Spending my whole life with someone I'm forced to marry because of a ridiculous legislation isn't freedom. I refuse to give in. I refuse to be another part of the machine. I'm not saying I am gonna escape or anything, I'm just saying that I don't *want* to draw this fucking number next week! It's driving me crazy…"

"Well, I think you're kidding yourself. This is the world and these are the rules!"

"Fuck the rules!"

George looked around again. Fear oozed from his wide eyes. "*Shhhhhhh…* Look, man, next week is next week. How about we go get some waves and forget about it for the time being? Let's just focus on today."

I took a breath and gave George a discouraging nod.

We made our way to the main transporter tunnels between Tiers. There were seven main tunnels and each cell could hold a little over one hundred people but because church had just ended, the corridors teemed with pedestrians. We crammed into one of the seven cells and headed for Tier Two. After ten seconds, the cell doors opened upwards and the masses exited into the dark yellow pavilion.

Each Tier had a different base colour for everything. On Tier Three everything was navy-blue, so I still found it odd seeing everything on Tier Two lively and yellow. Even though I preferred the warm and welcoming yellow of Tier Two, I couldn't afford to live there. The apartments went for twice the price of Tier Three, and Tier One apartments went for twice the price of that.

George and I wandered the large yellow halls past rocky waterfalls and perfectly manicured garden beds into one of the main shopping malls. The mall had seven levels of shops, all accessed by rotating corridors and escalators. We stopped on the bottom level for a vitamin shake and some noodles at one of our favourite Thai stalls. I leaned into one of the scanning booths at the stall to pay for our meal.

Our biological registration chips that we scanned to sign in at work and church also stored our credit rations. Actual currency was no longer used in the sub-plaza. Instead, the credits you earned from work accrued in the system, which then transferred your credits onto your chip.

A short walk got us to an internal transporter tunnel that took us to Block 3 of the Tier. Block 3 housed the water theme park. A six-second journey in the cell got us there. The block had water slides and roller coasters unlike anything I had ever seen on the surface. Some went for over a kilometre, winding their way through the blocks of the Tier. There were pools, lazy rivers, water fountains and more. The entry price was one hundred credits per person, comparable to a day's work for the average income. To me, it seemed damn well worth it.

After changing into our swimwear and leaving our clothes and boots on an empty bench beside one of the lap pools, we headed to the surfboard stall. We grabbed a board each from a yellow rack mounted into a fake-rock cliff and made our way to one of the two wave pools. As expected, the conditions were perfect. The waves were clean, two to three feet and because of the horseshoe shape of the pool, the waves wrapped around the artificial point forming perfectly barrelling waves.

The wave pool didn't have a sandy bottom. Instead, it had a spongy rubber surface, the typical Tier Two yellow. The water was crystal clear, an inviting twenty-five degrees Celsius and to my surprise, the waves remained uncrowded.

We strapped our leg ropes to our ankles and began paddling out through the deep channel in the centre of the pool. Man, it felt good. Moments like these, I thought, living in the sub-plaza under the strict rule of the Union could almost be tolerable. George was right. For the first time in days I forgot about the damn Marriage Lottery gnawing away at my sanity.

George caught the first wave. It was an absolute ripper. He'd always been a good surfer. Hell, he'd always been good at every-thing. He was the guy that could pick up any skill and master it. I envied his abilities. He turned hard on the wave, sending a violent spray of water over the back of the wave. He repositioned and caught the wave all the way to the channel. I paddled hard for the next wave. As I attempted to stand up on the board, the wave threw me from the lip and pummelled me with breaking force. I came to the surface and gasped for breath, panicking. George laughed at me from the safety of the channel.

Over an hour passed and we shared the waves with other surfing enthusiasts from all tiers of 3rd Sydney West. After two or three good rides I headed in to relax. Fatigue seemed to grab hold of my tired muscles a great deal quicker than George.

Another twenty minutes later George joined me beside the wave pool.

"Sometimes," I said to George as he put his board down. "All you need is a bit of good old-fashioned fun to make things better, hey?"

George smiled. He said nothing. His smile was enough.

NINE

Several humid days had passed in T-Town and already Brie Kallas felt more accepted than she had in most of her twenty-four years.

In such a short time she became accustomed to the tight spaces, the musky smell of dirt and the humid darkness. She got to know most of the T-Town residents and felt a warm sense of acceptance she hadn't been familiar with growing up within the Union. It didn't take her long to find a place and purpose within the community, contributing to hunting, collecting water and preparing meals.

Of the other thirty-seven escapees, only nine were female, yet all the men appeared to be polite, well behaved and supportive of the women in the group. Most of the others came from the Australian continent, but there were a handful of Indonesian, Thai and New Zealanders amongst the mix. Because of Bruce Chadwick's fatherly stature in the group, Brie formed a quick connection with the man. That's not to say there weren't other T-Towners that Brie had taken a liking to. In particular, there were Michael and Remy.

Michael Butcher was tanned and muscular. Not muscular like a body-builder, but Brie could tell he kept busy. He measured six feet tall and didn't look a day over twenty-five. He didn't know his age or his birthday, having been on his own since his youth. His mum had died from leukaemia when he was only a child and the Union took his Dad to help build the wall and he never returned. They gave Michael no explanation of his Dad's whereabouts. Instead, they took him from his family home and placed him in the Humanist Union foster system until he reached adult age.

Brie melted into Michael Butcher's aqua blue eyes whenever she talked with him. She found him attractive, kind, real and approachable. Despite all the hardship he'd endured, he had a genuine sense of humour and a warm heart. He spent most of his days down in the tunnel digging, but he'd now spent two nights in the common room with Brie sharing stories. Michael was rapidly becoming her closest friend in the bunker.

Remy was one of the other nine females. Like Michael, she seemed to welcome Brie into their small community with open arms. A sense of warm comfort radiated from Remy's loving personality. She was calming. Brie sensed a connection with her right away, almost sisterly. Brie and Remy spent the first day together in the jungle. Remy took on the role of jungle tutor, educating Brie on what foods could be eaten and what foods harboured the syndrome.

Born in Thailand, Remy had the soft features and kind smile of a Thai girl but the accent of a misguided traveller. When the Humanist Union had come to power and launched the modern-day Crusades, Remy and her family fled south to escape the genocide.

Remy shared countless stories with Brie while out picking fruit in the jungle, yet Brie didn't go out of her way to speak about her past. It wasn't until she tired of Remy's persistent questioning that she decided to open up.

It was during Brie's fourth day at T-Town. They were sitting at a scenic waterhole where the creek widened, having a break between collecting fruits and root vegetables. According to Remy the water was safe to drink from and bathe in because it came from deep underground springs between the limestone bedrock.

Remy and Brie removed their shoes and waded into the water. After some silent relaxation, the prodding began. "So Brie, how come you seem to keep so quiet about your past? I've shared all my stories with you. You said you came from a sub-plaza, yes? Why would you leave the safety of the plaza and venture on such a dangerous journey on your lonesome? Something must have happened? Please, you can tell me."

"Well, life in the plaza isn't always what it seems, Remy. Do you know what it's like having to check in everywhere? Do you know how belittling it is to have to scan your chip in at work every day, and church every Sunday, at dosage every Friday?"

Remy looked at Brie, "No, I guess I don't know these things."

"Do you know what it is like waiting every day to see if your number will get drawn and you're forced to marry a complete stranger? And when you get drawn your life gets turned upside down."

"Well, no. But I worked out on the walls, Brie. And my team, my own colleagues abused me. To me, a sub-plaza sounds a lot more inviting than the walls, even if it is with a strange man. I mean, over time the strange man will no longer be a stranger, right?"

Brie's eyes trailed off into the distance for a moment, lost in tortured thought. She winced and pursed her lips, scarred by distant memories "Well, I guess we've both been hurt by someone, hey?"

She paused and took a deep breath.

"Look, I got drawn for marriage at twenty-two, just over two years ago. The man who drew my number, Peter van Bueren, was the nephew of a key Union Advisor based in a Brisbane sub-plaza. At the time, I was living in one of the cheapest sub-plazas in the Empire. Peter was living in Brisbane Central sub-plaza, the third biggest and most luxurious in the whole Empire.

"At first I thought it wasn't so bad. I mean, Peter wasn't over the top attractive but he wasn't a beast. He was wealthy and the apartment I moved into was about eight times the size of my previous home. Peter came across as a nice guy. He had a lot of money and a good group of friends and all that. But he had dark secrets. I did everything they had taught me to do to be a good, compliant wife but I know for a fact he wasn't that into me. He never wanted to be romantic with me. In the first few months he would fuck me because that's what's expected, but he would never look into my eyes or say nice things. He would never really kiss me. Passion would not even come close to explaining our relationship. A year into our new life together he started drinking heavily and soon after the drinking came the aggression. He was into some weird shit, Remy!"

"What do you mean? What sort of *weird shit?*"

Brie looked away, staring off into the thick jungle canopy, fighting the onset of tears. "I don't think I want to talk about it."

"Your secrets are safe with me, Brie. But if you don't want to tell me, I get it. Whenever you're ready, okay?"

There was silence. It was a comfortable silence, inviting and warm. Remy looked at Brie with a warm smile and rubbed her back.

"Well," Brie continued. "Peter would come home from drinking after work and he would tie me up and... He would rape me, Remy. After the sexual abuse he would beat me, telling me I deserved punishment for being promiscuous."

Tears welled in Brie's eyes. Remy placed her hand over Brie's for comfort, interlocking their fingers. "It's okay, Brie. It's all in the past. That prick can't hurt you here."

"You know what?" Brie said, wiping a single tear as it rolled down her left cheek. "Other than the Bishop, I've told no one that!"

"It's all right. Like I said, your secret is safe with me, Brie."

"So, after a year of this constant abuse I tried to speak to one of the Catholic Bishops at a church within our block. As soon as the Bishop found out who my husband was, he sent me away. Peter van Bueren was a powerful man, Remy. He couldn't be touched. I had no one to turn to. I put up with the abuse, each day becoming a little crazier, a little more withdrawn and a little more depressed. I thought about suicide, but I didn't want the scumbag to win. Finally, after reaching a certain tipping point about four months ago, I had enough. I waited for him to get home from work on a Friday. I knew he would be drunk. As he stumbled through the hall, I belted him across the face with one of his expensive bottles of whisky. I killed him, Remy. I beat him again and again in the face until the bottle shattered. It sent shards of glass piercing through his bloodied face."

Remy's expression didn't change. She held Brie's hand, gripping it tight.

"Well, it sounds like he got what he deserved. I hope you don't regret what you did…"

Brie didn't respond.

"Then what? What did you do? How did you get away?"

"I panicked. I dragged his body into the refrigerated storeroom, washed the blood off me and I left. I knew it was only a matter of time until they would catch me so I headed to the top Tier, purchased some supplies, a backpack, some rations, a portable oxygen conditioner and made my way to the surface.

"At first, walking the surface alone frightened me. In that first twenty-four hours I didn't stop. Fuelled by fear, I kept going until I could walk no further. I snuck into an abandoned house through a broken window, climbed into the roof through the manhole and I fell asleep in the rafters. Since then I've been running. I've bribed my way onto ferries and boats and car rides. Once my supplies ran short, I used my wits to get where I needed to." Brie chuckled to herself, her laugh heavy with guilt and self-loathing. "Whatever I've had to do, I've done it. Everywhere I reached, though, Union soldiers kept turning up. At one point, by chance, a crazed group of Northern Cape militia showed up and started shooting the soldiers there to get *me*."

Remy listened to every word of Brie's outlandish story, wide-eyed and supportive.

"It wasn't until the militia soldiers told me that my registration chip was acting as a global locating system that I knew how they kept finding me. I felt embarrassed for not knowing. I arranged an old petrol motorboat to take me north towards the islands but before I did, I used a pair of pliers and a scalpel from a medical kit on board the boat and removed my chip.

"I tell you what. It fucking hurt! But the whole time I was digging inside my neck with the pliers searching for the little chip I thought to myself, 'you know what, Brie, this is better than getting raped by a sociopath.'

"Since then I haven't seen a single soldier. I've hopped from island to island, keeping clear of the trains and the road bridges between the Central and Northern Sectors and, the last week, although lonely, has been easy going. Besides the snakes, the mosquitoes and the mutants, I've been very much alone."

Remy leaned forward and gave Brie a comforting, sisterly hug. It was the first real act of compassion Brie had felt in years. Resting her head on Remy's shoulder, Brie sat there and cried, embracing her new companion in silence.

Neither of them spoke. They didn't need to.

TEN

THE TWO GIRLS RETURNED TO T-TOWN AN HOUR BEFORE SUNSET
with sacks full of berries, root vegetables and citrus fruits.

Brie placed the two sacks of fruit and vegetables on the table
beside the stovetops and offered to contribute to the preparation.
Bruce insisted that she had done enough for the day. She sat down,
had a drink of coconut water, nibbled a few berries and watched her
new family work together.

After the Fosform shot she had received a few days earlier, the
wound on her neck had healed in just a few short days. What had
been a puss-ridden and infected wound had already scabbed up and
hardened. Despite the dark and depressing memories that she did
her best to forget, Brie walked around the communal bunker with a
smile. For her, a smile was as foreign as the other side of the walls.

The smell of the stew bubbling away must have travelled
through the dark, dank tunnels of T-Town because before long
Michael and the other diggers joined the tables in the main
communal room. They were sweaty and filthy. Dirt-stained faces
and blistered fingers made it clear they'd been working hard.
Michael sat next to Brie. Because there were several spare seats

around the table, Brie convinced herself it must have been on purpose.

She hadn't had these feelings in years. She'd only known Michael for four days and she was behaving like a lovesick teenager. She over-analysed every little interaction, every irrelevant gesture. If she caught his eyes around the table she tried to look deep into them, showcasing her cutest smile. If Michael told a story, Brie attempted to listen, to question him and to laugh at his humour.

Brie had always been a law-abiding citizen of the Empire. The system had never allowed her to be attracted to someone and do anything about it. Before the murder of her husband and her daring escape, to like someone was nothing more than a distant dream. The idea of love was something so rare and so foreign to most registered citizens they didn't appreciate what it meant. For Brie though, there in that bunker town, it meant butterflies in her belly.

Before long the meal was ready, steam rising from two over-sized cast-iron pots. With plenty of stew to feed the entire group of underground outlaws, no one went hungry. Brie thought it tasted great. It sure beat the raw vegetation she had been living off for most of her journey.

After they scraped the bowls clean and some residents began washing up, Bruce asked everyone to gather in the main communal room for a much-needed meeting. The thirty-eight of them crammed into the dirty cavern. It was wall-to-wall with dirty bodies.

"As you all know," Bruce said loud and clear, "our Fosform supply has been running short for a while and now we're getting pretty darn low. I've had a satellite text from my mate down in Bali and he tells me that there will be a train with a few shipments heading to Singapore, Kuala Lumpur and Georgetown. He said it should head across the bridge to Bali by Sunday, which means KL the day after. That gives us five days to get down there. We can use the hover-bikes we've stored in the back-up bunker, but that means I only have room to take five others with me. Who's willing to help?"

At Bruce's request, people started looking to the floor, shuffling back in the room, trying to become invisible. There were never many that would volunteer for a task like this, but given the casualty rate on the previous Fosform mission, it made people even less inclined to raise a hand.

"Look," Bruce continued. "I know that what happened last time might put you off but think about it, the time before that ran without a bloody glitch. Last time was just bad timing. The bottom line is, without the Fosform we're all gonna bloody die and all this work we have put in will be for nothing. Now who's keen to head down to KL with me and rob some bloody Union scum?"

Francis raised his hand. Francis always raised his hand. He'd been on every Fosform mission or patrol the residents had ever attempted. Brie thought a part of him wanted retribution for the horrible things that he'd endured from the Union. A high risk Fosform mission might be the perfect opportunity for Francis to inflict some cold-blooded vengeance.

Bruce nodded at Francis in approval. No one else raised a hand. "Come on, guys. All of you have acted out against your Empire and already committed treason. All of you have shown that you're not afraid to stick it to the system. How the hell do you think we're gonna survive if we don't take bloody risks?"

Bruce became frustrated with his peer's lack of commitment. Sweat beaded on his brow, his eyes widened and with every word his voice became a little louder, his tone a little more aggressive. Two others that Brie didn't know well put their hands up to volunteer.

Bruce smiled and nodded. "Thanks, guys."

Caleb and Milly had been teenage lovers living in Auckland. They committed to the unpredictable life on the road after the Marriage Lottery was introduced. Growing up in poverty they could never have dreamed of affording sub-plaza living, so they made their way to where there was less pollution, less sickness and less Union soldiers.

Before Bruce started up again with a rant about sticking it to the system, Michael Butcher raised his hand. "Okay, I'll go mate. It will keep me out of the tunnels for a week and give my hands a chance to heal."

"Thanks, Mike. You're a bloody champion. That means I just

need one more. Come on, guys. I got three hover-bikes. I need a team of six."

Brie's world swirled around her.

Why, oh why, did Michael have to volunteer?

Brie felt stuck. Faced with quite a decision, but quite a prospect. The butterflies in her belly flapped their wings with anxious opportunity. She never intended to go, but the thought of Michael leaving and not returning, just after she had started to bond with him, was a thought that seemed too hard to bear.

Could it just be a childish crush? Was it worth leaving the safety of T-Town to follow that crush into the danger zone? If she joined them on their risky journey south, she wouldn't remain in T-Town without Michael to ponder on his whereabouts and get sucked back into anxiety, depression and loneliness. It would give her the opportunity to spend more one-on-one time with him. She could really get to know him…

And potentially get killed.

Was the threat of capture and death worth some quality time alone with Michael? It was a question that Brie couldn't find an easy answer to. "Fuck it," she called out, drowning the quiet murmurs. "I'll go. I mean, if I want to use the Fosform what right do I have if I don't help get it?"

Bruce looked at Brie and smiled. "Thanks Brie. Don't you worry about a thing, okay? It'll be a piece of cake. Now can you five follow me to the storeroom? We're gonna pack and prepare. I want the rest of you to remember this moment so next time when we need dosage you might be more willing to help."

The residents dispersed amongst casual chatter.

Once in the storeroom, Bruce, Francis, Caleb, Milly, Michael and Brie huddled around a small timber table and studied maps and weaponry. As was the norm, Bruce had the whole thing already planned and more or less briefed the others on what they needed to do. While listening to Bruce's plan, Brie's palms became clammy.

Had she just made a terrible mistake?

ELEVEN

While most of T-Town slept, Brie lay awake in her bunk tossing with restlessness.

Her mind wandered, thinking of the unknown dangers that lay ahead. She had just battled her way north and now she planned to head back south again into a potential ambush of soldiers seeking retribution for her merciless act of rage.

Am I nuts!

Sick of staring at the dream-catcher above her bunk, Brie sat up, slid on a pair of shorts and wandered the dark corridor until she reached the second communal room. Expecting some solitude, she was surprised to see Michael and Evan sitting at the table conversing quietly and drinking from two dented, rusty tin cans. They turned around as she approached, her footsteps falling softly on the compacted dirt.

"Hey, Brie. What are you doing wandering the bunker at this time of night?"

"I can't sleep."

"No, we can't either. There must be something in the air, hey? Why don't you sit down and join us? You care for a round of *Whooze?*"

"*Whooze?* What the hell is Whooze?"

"Well," Evan replied smiling, holding his rusty cup and swaying it from side to side. "It's our home-brew concoction. It's white, and it's thick and oozy. Get it, white ooze – whooze!" He then giggled.

"We don't know why we call it that. They've called it Whooze since Bruce and the others first arrived. Some agree with Evan, others say it's called Whooze because it make you feel woozy," said Michael, a childish grin on his face. "It tastes horrible, but it makes you feel damn good." Michael chuckled.

"Yeah, sure, okay. I'll try it. But what is it?"

"It's a mixture of several juices from some poisonous plants in the jungle, mixed with a bit of water and milk powder to lower the potency. Here, have a taste."

Brie sat down at the table and accepted the cup from Michael. The liquid was thick and white. It smelt like floor disinfectant but fruitier. Without hesitation, Brie put the cup to her mouth and took a sip. She gagged. She struggled hard to keep it down. Her throat burned. "Jesus," she gasped, handing the cup back to Michael. "That tastes horrible!"

"It sure does. But good-horrible, right?" Michael said, laughing. "So, do you want one?"

Without waiting for an answer, he poured some into a carved wooden mug and slid it across the table to her. She was still recovering from her first encounter, eyes red and throat sore.

"Look, Brie," slurred Evan. "It grows on you, mate."

Evan was right. After half a mug of the white liquid Brie's mouth and throat were numb, and the Whooze was going down well. It must have been strong. Brie felt lightheaded before polishing off her first cup. It wasn't the usual drunken feelings one might get from whisky or vodka or synthetic rum. It was something different, something hazier. Something more relaxing.

"So, Michael, I wanna know what happened last time on the train. Why was it such a fuck-up? Why are people so afraid to go?"

"Let's not talk about it, Brie. It will only make you think the worst."

"I don't care. I wanna know what we could be in for."

"Okay, but it's not pretty…" Michael took a swig of his Whooze. "Bruce and Francis left with eight others and they were the only two to return. All ten of them got down through the jungle without harm. About sixty kilometres south of KL the train crosses a narrow bridge over an empty valley, right? Bruce and the others had placed a fallen tree over the track to block the train's passage, so it looked natural. On the far end of the bridge Francis rigged some explosives hooked in to a remote detonator in his pocket. The plan was to wait until the Union soldiers had moved the tree and then blow the bridge, hoping that the train would drop into the valley, but not with enough momentum to destroy the train and the Fosform inside it. With me so far?"

Brie nodded, taking another sip on the Whooze in her wooden mug. Evan sat in a trance-like state, listening to Michael, reliving the horror.

"When the train reached the bridge, everything seemed to go to plan. The train stopped right before the tree and six or seven Union soldiers got out and attempted moving the branch. But something was wrong. Somehow without using the detonator, the explosives triggered before they should have, sending a huge fireball into the air. It took everyone by surprise and with surprise came panic and then the whole plan went to shit.

"The soldiers knew right away they were in an ambush. Before retreating into the train they started shooting into the thick of the trees, hoping to hit whoever was out there. While most of their shots hit nothing but jungle, two of our residents, Danny and Andrea, weren't so lucky. Danny died on the spot with a hole in his head and Andrea took a bullet to the guts. She began screaming, giving away their position. Francis did what only Francis would do. He ran out from the trees and began shooting like a maniac. He's a bloody animal, Brie. He took out all seven of the soldiers standing beside the train, two of them as they climbed back on board.

"By that point others had appeared from the back carriage. They threw nuclear shock balls toward Francis, Bruce and the others. The jungle became a fire-fuelled death trap. It became a bloodbath. Two of the hover-bikes got shot to shit in the crossfire."

"Jesus Christ. You're not filling me with much confidence here, Michael!"

"I told you, didn't I? You asked for it."

"I did."

"Anyway… Bruce returned fire with portable gas grenades and took out most of the remaining soldiers. At that point only Bruce, Francis, Thien and Oliver remained. Andrea, Danny and four others were dead. The four survivors left their shielded spot behind the trees and approached the wreckage. If any of the fallen soldiers had a glimpse of life left in them, Oliver sprayed them with bullets, taking that glimpse away. They were intent on boarding the train and taking the Fosform. Retreating was not an option. They had lost too much."

Michael paused and took a large sip of his Whooze.

"They got onto the train and had a shootout with a few more soldiers. The train driver, Oliver and Thien were all hit, killed on the spot. Bruce and Francis were the last two men standing on the entire train. They knew that they didn't have much time before more soldiers arrived so they loaded up what Fosform and supplies they could, tied one bike behind another, made sure all their comrades were dead, said their goodbyes and got on their bloody way. They returned four days later filthy and bleeding, missing two hover-bikes and eight of our friends…"

Michael stopped talking and a powerful silence filled the room. Evan emptied his rusty mug and refilled all three.

"You know what," Evan said to Brie. "That was a terrible thing to happen. We lost some good people but like Bruce said earlier, without the Fosform, we're all gonna die anyway, so, well, yeah."

"Then why didn't *you* volunteer to go, huh?"

"Look Brie, I've almost been here since the beginning. I've been down there and come back with Fosform the first time. I've paid my damn dues. I'm willing to do my part for T-Town, but I'm not Francis! I'm not gonna go every time. You think I enjoy *killing* people? You think I like the *weapons*? The *violence*? I do it because I want my freedom. That's why we're all here. So don't even for a second insinuate that I haven't done my part."

"I'm sorry, I didn't know…"

"It's all good. I'm not pissed off. I'm just sick and tired of this place. I've been here too damn long and been drinking this damn Whooze too much. It rots the mind…"

Evan took a large swig and once again emptied his mug. "On that note, I'm heading to bed. If I don't see you in the morning, good luck guys. I hope you come back alive…"

After Evan stumbled off down the tunnel, Brie and Michael sat in silence. Brie noticed the effects of the Whooze now. She felt woozy, off balance, nauseous. It blurred her vision. Along with the woozy nausea, a strange sensation of invincibility came over her.

"Wow, this shit is *strong*," she said to Michael, grinning as she shuffled closer towards him.

Masked with a confidence unknown to her, she had an urge to tell Michael how she felt about him. Desire coursed through her drunken veins. She wanted to be touched. She wanted to do the touching. It had been a long time since Brie enjoyed the strong hands of a man's romantic embrace. Brie wanted to be wanted.

The Whooze took control of her timid and protective personality. Now she had nothing more than an insatiable, drunken animal instinct.

"So… Michael Butcher," she said, running her fingers through his short blonde hair, masked with the confidence of the Whooze. "If I were to tell you I haven't had a man in sometime, what would you say?"

Michael looked at Brie with a warm smile. "Where has this come from?"

"What does it matter where it's come from?" She leaned over and gave Michael a soft and playful kiss on the neck. "I want you and if we leave tomorrow and things end up like last time, I'll spend the rest of my days in Hell kicking myself for not doing what I'm doing right now. I want to feel you…" She kissed him again on the neck then whispered in Michael's ear. "I want to feel you… in me."

Without waiting for approval, Brie leaned forward and kissed him. It was a long kiss, a kiss full of emotion and passion and drunken confidence. Michael kissed her back and wrapped her up in his arms. Brie straddled Michael. She kissed his neck and began grinding his lap, rubbing herself against him with drunken desire. Through their clothes Brie felt him harden. In a blurry act of heated passion they removed each other's clothing and right there in the communal room of the bunker, on one of the food preparation tables, Michael entered Brie. She closed her eyes. As the blackness swayed with woozy euphoria, she let out a drunken moan of pleasure.

TWELVE

The saying is that sheep need a shepherd, right?

What happens when the shepherd is only using the sheep to achieve his own personal agenda? What happens if the shepherd is just leading all his sheep into an enormous furnace so he can cook his entire flock and make lamb stew? I'll tell you what happens. The Humanist Union happens.

Master Stephen Haynes was the shepherd that carried the naïve and ignorant masses from their pastoral safe haven of community and social justice to something far more sinister.

When the Union took over as the governing body of Soteria in 2044, we all had to adapt to radical changes. The original twelve-month calendar was replaced with six longer months of 52 days and one month of 53 days creating an improved seven-month calendar. I had no idea how the rest of the world recorded date and time. Citizens of Soteria were no longer exposed to that information. Anything on the other side of the giant concrete walls of Soteria was unknown; to all intents and purposes it was foreign and forgotten.

They named the seven newly appointed months Wrath, Greed, Sloth, Pride, Lust, Envy and Gluttony, named after the seven cardinal sins quoted in the Holy Bible. The Union chose these names to remind us every day of the importance and power of God and of the complete lack of tolerance to sin. All sins against the Humanist Union were punishable by torture, execution of surface exposure.

Without Fosform Five or an artificial oxygen-conditioning mask, the atmosphere would rot internal organs from the inside out. With constant surface exposure, humans couldn't last more than four weeks on the surface, animals even less. The liver usually gave up first, followed soon by the kidney and lungs. After a few weeks of constant exposure, the lungs and throat began to bleed and usually after around thirty days the brain haemorrhaged and collapsed.

The forever-increasing air pollution and carbon emissions caused the collapse of the ozone layer and as a result, the loss of the atmospheres natural filters. Shortly after the beginning of the Artificial Revolution, the demand on industry and manufacturing increased tenfold and the need for land for agriculture and livestock declined.

With the ability to grow crops and raise animals inside factories underground, free-range open land farming became a dying industry, replaced with the manufacturing of mega-structures, artificial lighting systems and indoor farming. No longer did vine growers or banana farmers fear losing their yield because of nature's cruel unpredictability. They could grow their crops in an artificial, therefore entirely controlled environment. For the fruit, grain and vegetable growers of the Empire there were no longer such things as a bad year or a low-yield season. The demand for construction, iron ore, steel factories, nuclear power and core-metal mining continued to increase. In the decade following the start of the Artificial Revolution, the Earth's atmosphere took a toll worse than in the previous two centuries.

Sulphur oxides, nitrogen oxides, carbon monoxides and volatile organic compounds began to suffocate the world in the form of exhaust fumes from factories and the waste product from the indoor artificial farms, permanently scarring the skyline. The atmosphere's natural mechanism for filtering air was on the brink of collapse.

The streets became unsafe. The air we needed to survive became unsafe. Asthma was prevalent in 85 percent of the Australian population and the average life span dropped daily. The evidence proved that the cause of these health issues was the pollution but it wasn't until 2051 that Doctor Patrick Turner associated the air pollution with internal necrosis and brain haemorrhaging, largely attributed to the levels of heavy metals, carbon and sulphur oxides in the air.

With the ozone layer dysfunctional, the metals and oxides didn't break down enough, making air itself a harmful poison to humans. Along with his research team, Doctor Turner created and introduced the Fosform serum. It took the Doctor five trial serums for the dose to prove effective without serious side effects.

Fosform Five built a barrier in vital organs, blocking the heavy metals and oxides from entering the bloodstream through oxygen transfer. It was only effective for a short amount of time. After six or seven days, the barrier weakened, and the necrosis began to rot your organs. This meant we required the dosage on a weekly basis.

The Union reassured the people that by building underground we would escape the syndrome. This was not quite the case. Even those living in sub-plazas required a consistent dosage cycle. Although the artificial oxygen conditioners were effective, tainted outside air found its way in through entrance docks above Tier One and through faulty oxygen systems, cracks in seals and even by leeching through the soil. We needed Fosform Five, and the Union knew it. Freedom was a faded dream. Freedom was a torn and tattered photograph on the bedside table of a dying old citizen.

Needless to say, I hadn't had a good few days. It had been over a week since I'd managed a good night's sleep. I seemed to lie awake in an uncomfortable sweat, dreading what life had become. Even Laura sensed something was amiss by my erratic heartbeat and constant restlessness. Through the speakers in the ceiling she asked me if there was anything she could administer to help. I ignored the robotic voice until she went back into hibernation mode. I was in no mood to talk to the damn ceiling.

Despite anxiety and depression's greedy claws tugging at my

soul, I forced myself to go to work. I spent most of my time lost in thought. For some inconceivable reason, I had an unusual urge to see the surface. I had an urge to see the old neighbourhoods I used to roam. I wanted to soak up all the negativity, to drown my sorrows in the harsh reality of our world. I thought it would make me feel better. Or maybe it would make me understand that what I had wasn't so bad.

I walked around the office from one tedious task to another, barely responding to people, barely operating on anything more than habitual discipline. Jonah ran into me on the way to the dosage production units. Even though Jonah and I never saw eye to eye in terms of religion and the Union, he was a kind-hearted human and the closest thing to a real friend I had in my office. He could tell something bothered me. "Tyson, what's with the glum face? Anything I can do?"

"Shit, is it that obvious?"

"Mate, you're walking around like a surface mutant, staring at the ground with a look of distress, or angst… Or both!"

"Well, you know what, Jonah? I have to pull a marriage number in a few days. It's all I think about. I can't sleep. I can't eat. Shit, I can't even masturbate. My mind is fixated on that one damned thing."

"Is that *all*?"

"Thanks for the sympathy," I replied, thick with sarcasm.

"I pulled a number over four years ago now, Tyson. It was the best thing that ever happened to me."

Just hearing Jonah say that angered me. Trust him to embrace the system. "Yeah, but what if I get the number of someone I'm not compatible with? What if I don't like her at all?"

"It's called sacrifice, Tyson. There are many things in life you may not like, but you do them anyway. It's about sacrifice and conditioning. When I first met Anong, it worried me, too. I'd never spent much time with girls, especially Asian girls. All of a sudden I had a random woman in my apartment, forced to communicate and share my life with her. She had different customs, different habits and different ideals to anything I was familiar with. I would never have said that I found Asian women attractive but now, to me, Anong is the most attractive woman in this sub-plaza. It's about conditioning. You will learn to notice their positive attributes. In time you will learn to trust and love whoever you pick."

"Shit, Jonah. I really hope you're right."

"Look, man. Remaining positive is better than freaking out about it. That won't make your time any more tolerable. Go into it with an open mind. If I learnt one thing from the Marriage Lottery, it's that it will happen no matter what. You can't change it. You can't escape it. So suck it up, stop moping around and make the most of an unusual social injustice that we have no control of."

"Well, thanks, Jonah… I guess. I'll try to keep that in mind."

His words resonated.

You can't change it. You can't escape it.

Make the most of an unusual social injustice that we have no control of…

It was all about *control*.

Fuck control.

After my shift at the Fosform office I returned home, got changed out of my navy-blue Union uniform and made my way to the main transporter tunnels. Jonah's motivational pep talk did very little to soften my anxiety. If anything, it made me more unsettled. I still had the need to go wander the surface. I felt claustrophobic in the sub-plaza. I wanted to know the tiniest inkling of freedom. The only way I could gain that was from standing on the foul and polluted surface. I wanted to appreciate what I had down in the safety of 3rd Sydney West. I sucked down a banana-caramel vitamin shake from a vendor beside the transporter tunnel, then made my way up to Tier One.

I hadn't ever really spent time on Tier One. Everything was a maroon red. The walls, the floor, even the Union soldier's uniforms. I liked it even less than the navy-blue from Tier Three. The maroon of Tier One looked so foreboding and evil. All it reminded me of was blood.

There were a few things I needed before taking the final transporter tunnel to the surface. I needed to purchase a portable oxygen-conditioning mask and enrol in a permission database to get access to the outside world. The cheapest portable oxygen conditioner had enough filtration for eight hours on the surface although I doubted I'd be spending over two up there. I made my way to the export office to find a small line of people waiting to enrol in the permission database.

After waiting, I entered my purpose for visiting the surface into the monitor. I stated that my intention was to visit the gravestones of my parents, a worthy enough excuse. I had no real desire to visit their graves. That would just fuel my depression and send me over the edge.

The export office granted me permission. I hurried through the triple seal chamber doors to the final transporter. With me there were four other citizens heading to the surface. They appeared calm, as if heading to the surface was part of their everyday lives. There's a good chance it was. Many people still worked in the factories north of Pittwater but returned each evening to their sub plaza apartments.

An automated voice recording began once the transporter tunnel seal rolled closed. "Please don your oxygen conditioners now. We will expose you to surface conditions in thirteen seconds." The voice then counted down.

I was nervous. Even though I'd spent most of my childhood on the northern beaches, it was now foreign. I began to sense anxious unease. I placed the mask over my face, adjusted the rubber straps at the back and turned on the filtration system. My first few breaths made the mask fog until the filter adjusted to my breathing pattern. As the automated voice reached zero, the chamber doors opened and sunlight made its way into the cell.

Real sunlight.

The artificial sunlight that we lived with every day was so pure and vibrant that when I felt the harsh glow of the real sun on my skin, I instantly went into goose bumps.

The sky was a filthy grey haze. The wind blew strong. The other four citizens left the cell and wandered off towards the exit. I hesitated for a moment, questioning my motives. Why had I chosen to enter this chaotic place of disease, death and crime? I guess I was searching for something. I just wasn't sure what the something was.

As with all the sub-plazas, Union soldiers guarded the perimeter zone around the entrance to 3rd Sydney West. People couldn't freely come and go, so before I could exit the compound I needed to have my registration chip scanned at the checkout. Ten armed Union soldiers guarded the checkout. The process involved passage through two sets of electronic gates surrounded by high-voltage electric fences with flame throwing turrets at the top of the fencing. Overkill, I know.

The surface soldiers stared at me without emotion. I smiled through my mask and nodded a friendly greeting. I received no response. Unlike the soldiers on each Tier of the sub-plaza, surface soldiers wore standard surface fatigues, a mix of light and dark grey blotches.

Outside the compound was busy. Cars, hover-bikes and pedestrians cluttered the roads. Most people wore oxygen conditioners. Those that didn't have a mask appeared sickly and thin. They were dead men walking.

I reached the hover-bike hire compound and scanned my chip to hire a small single person hover-bike. Mainly used on the surface, hover-bikes relied on indirect air-pressure being sucked through an electric engine and being forced out through small jets under the chassis of the vehicle, keeping it just over thirty centimetres above the ground. Powered by solar energy, with small panels covering the back half of the vehicle, hover-bikes ran forever providing the circuitry or the panels remained functional and that they had access to charge during daylight hours. The reason they introduced hover-bikes on such a large scale was that by the late thirties, on hotter days on the surface, car tyres had a tendency to melt on the hot bitumen.

I started up my hover-bike and drove out the gate past the surface soldiers, leaving the compound behind me. The air was warm. The wind was strong. Within minutes my shirt was wet with sweat. I made my way towards the motorway and joined the queue of other road users. The constant presence of Union soldiers was impossible to ignore. I couldn't seem to travel more than a few kilometres before I passed another squad of armed forces.

As I gained speed along the motorway, I noticed dead bodies and dilapidated buildings. More than I had ever noticed before. It had been months since I'd been outside of 3rd Sydney West and from my short drive it was evident that things had gotten a lot worse. Buildings beside me were nothing more than piles of rubble and dust, mere carcasses of former architectural pride. Human bones littered the sidewalks and roads. Old cars lay burnt out and stripped of everything, leaving behind blackened metal shells. The contrast between the architectural beauty and sterile cleanliness of the sub-plaza and the filthy chaos of Sydney on the surface was almost too much to stomach. A terrible wave of guilt came over me for taking my safe and clean underworld life for granted. Seeing the surface and all its chaos was a genuine slap in the face and I hadn't even made it across the bridge yet.

Blooms of algae had taken over the harbour. As I crossed the once illustrious Harbour Bridge I looked down into Sydney Harbour itself. Entire fields of green and brown slime covered the surface of the water. Rubbish and debris floated within the fields of algae and even through my oxygen conditioner I smelt the sickly stench of rotting vegetation.

I hope Stephen Haynes got what he wanted.

I parked my hover-bike at the once-popular cityscape lookout and took in all the misery. Perched high above the city on the quarried face of the hillside, the abandoned lookout used to be a popular spot for tourists and photographers. Now, graffiti-ridden and overgrown, the vantage point served as a stark reminder of societal collapse. Tourists didn't exist. Photographers didn't exist. As I stood alone, staring down at the hell that we created, I thought about the future. Not just my future, but also the future of our civilisation. Our kids. Their kids. What would life look like for them?

The city was in ruins. Humanity was in ruins. Life was in ruins. I stood there for ten minutes and let the dismal scene pummel any fleeting feelings of hope. I got back on my bike as negativity and hopelessness consumed me. I drove north.

Not long after leaving the lookout a squad of soldiers stopped me at a fortified roadblock. They had the road fenced off and were interrogating road users. I sat on the bike and waited for the vehicles ahead of me to pass through the checking station. It gave me time to think.

I thought seeing the surface would settle my nerves or make me reconsider my desire for escape, but I don't think it did. If anything, it heightened my unsettled anxiety. A part of me wanted to get onto the main northern express tunnel and keep driving until I hit the tip of the Northern Cape. Fuck this place off for good. Fuck everybody. Fuck the Union.

But I was a coward. An act like that required guts.

Two soldiers with Union-issue conditioners strapped to their mug faces walked towards me. They looked equipped for space travel with full-face helmet-like masks and oxygen cylinders attached to their backs. Unlike the civilian masks filtering the air from the outside atmosphere, the soldiers breathed fresh, synthetic, bottled air. Even though I'd done nothing wrong, something about the hostility of the soldiers frightened me.

"Name and membership number," the taller of the two soldiers barked at me.

"Tyson Anderson. 636-124."

"Lean forward, Mr Anderson. We would like to scan your chip. There have been deviant rogues in these parts lately. Unregistered surface scum have been out here killing registered citizens."

I leaned forward and the smaller of the two soldiers used a handheld chip reader to scan the back of my neck. Within seconds it beeped. Both soldiers observed the text that appeared on the touch screen.

It checked out.

"So, Mr Anderson, what's your purpose outside of your sub-plaza? Why have you crossed the harbour?"

"I'm heading up to the old Narrabeen community cemetery to see my folks. They were buried there when I was out on the walls back in—"

"Okay, that'll do Mr Anderson," the tall one bellowed, interrupting me mid-sentence. "We're not here to learn about your family history. Narrabeen is about twenty minutes in these conditions and you'll only need a short time to talk to your dead parents so we expect you heading back past here in an hour. Is that understood?"

"But what if I come back a different way, like along the Esplanade?"

"Well, you won't, Mr Anderson. You will come back past here within sixty minutes. This is not a negotiation. Now, for the sake of your buried parents, I suggest you get a move on or else we might change our minds and send you back to the 3rd Sydney West right now."

"Yes, sir. Sixty minutes."

I sped up past the Union fencing and drove up the empty road with nothing but hatred and resentment towards those stupid fucking soldiers.

THIRTEEN

THE FURTHER TOWARDS THE NORTHERN BEACHES I WENT, THE quieter the streets became.

People moved about here and there, but many of them were obvious surface dwellers: filthy clothing, mangy hair and cautious stares. I ignored them as I drove on by. Bodies lay in a pile on the sidewalk, stinking like sun-rotten death. Most of the corpses were naked, their clothing stolen by other surface dwellers.

I'd only been living in the sub-plaza for a little over two years and in that time, because so many people had either made the move underground or died, the surface had taken such a toll it was almost unrecognisable. It concerned me that in half a decade we wouldn't be able to leave our sub-plazas at all. What sort of Empire would the Humanist Union have created if no one could even leave their own little underground prison cell?

It was all about *control.*

I pulled the hired hover-bike into the old parking lot of the Collaroy surf club, right on the foreshore of Collaroy beach. The bitumen had cracks and potholes bigger than bathtubs. Weeds grew from the corners of the concrete gutters. The white lines separating car parking spaces were faint, barely visible. Because of climate change and the rise in the sea levels, there wasn't much beach left but the steep angle of the sand meant the surf club was still safe from the high-tide line. The building itself was decrepit and abandoned. The white walls, once a clean beacon of safety for beachgoers, were covered in spray-paint, dirt, blood and God-only knows what else.

A strong wind blew from the east, causing the sand to lift from the top of the dunes and fill the parking lot with tiny white granules. Sharp and prickly against my exposed skin, it felt good to feel something natural, something elemental. I knew it was hazardous to go to the coast, not just because of the syndrome but also because of the people who lived there. For some inexplicable reason I didn't seem to care. Depression was taking autocratic leadership. Survival was on lunch break.

Perhaps a part of me wanted danger? Maybe a part of me wanted to endure pain? Then at least I would feel something...

Standing on the top of a small dune, I looked down the beach. Because of the filthy haze, I couldn't even make out the point at North Narrabeen. That beach, right there, was the beach where I first learnt to swim. That right there used to be my backyard. That right there was now nothing more than a toxic cesspool.

I spotted a group of people about a hundred metres along the beach. They sat around an open fire beside a derelict shelter on the sand. I couldn't give you a reason, but I began walking towards them. I think I was so overwhelmed by my hate for the Union that I just didn't care what happened to me. I was numbed by something more powerful than me. Something drove me towards those people, towards that open fire, towards the unknown.

As I walked out onto the softer, non-tidal sand I heard something rustling in the bushes on the dune beside me. It caught me off guard. I froze. Out of the overgrown coastal wattle a young man... no, a child in fact, emerged from the shrubbery.

"I wouldn't go over to those men if I were you," he said with a cautious whisper.

I looked him up and down. He was a surface dweller. He looked homeless. Tattered and stained, both his jeans and grey shirt were falling apart. He looked no older than fifteen, skinny and malnour-ished. He had dark hazel eyes and hair colour to match. His hair was so filthy that it was hard to tell if it was his actual hair colour or if it just needed a good clean. He stared at me through bloodshot eyes.

"And why shouldn't I go over there?"

Again he whispered. "They're not nice people. I have seen what they do. They eat people!"

"They eat *people*?"

"I've seen it. They live there in that tin shelter. They go off during the night to steal Fosform and they bring people back, all kinds of people. Quick, get up here in the bushes before they see you."

Convinced by the kid's authenticity and frightened by the seri-ousness in his whisper, I followed his advice and ducked in behind the coastal wattle to watch the fire circle from our hidden viewpoint.

"Thanks, I guess."

"No problem. I've been observing these guys for about two weeks and I've seen them bring back men and women. They kill the men, cook them over the open fire and eat them right there on the beach, right off the body. The women, well they have their way with the women until they've all had a go then they cook and eat them too… People like you, people with masks on. Oh boy, they would cook *you* up in a minute…"

"Jesus Christ! Good thing I didn't go over there, hey?"

"Oh, they would have eaten you for sure," he replied with a strange grin.

My heart rate had increased. My palms were sweaty.

"Are you bullshitting me?"

"Why would I lie? Seriously, at night, this place is dangerous as hell."

"Why do you watch them? Where do you live?"

"Over on the esplanade."

"Like, in a house or on the actual *street*?"

At first the kid appeared cautious. I didn't blame him. He spent a few seconds staring at me, calculating. I guess he concluded that I was of no real threat to him.

"I live in a small bunker under a house on the esplanade. It's abandoned and boarded up, but I have an access tunnel behind the old chicken shop across the road. I think it's an escape route from an old bomb bunker, or even part of the original sewers."

"Right," I said. "And why do you watch them?"

"I watch them 'cause I watch everything, everyone. I have nothing else to do. I wander around here observing, listening and stealing… Waiting to die, I guess!"

"Bloody hell. That's morbid, isn't it?"

"Well, it's the truth. I'm lucky if I get a jab of Fosform once a month when I steal the odd dose here and there from dead people's houses. Sometimes I don't even have a needle and I've just had to drink the shit before."

"How old are you? What's your name? Where are your parents?"

"Eli. My name's Eli. I just turned fourteen last Tuesday, I think. Maybe fifteen. I can't really remember. I don't know where my parents are. One day I came home, and they were gone. It wasn't long before people took over my parent's house and I had to leave. They were mean people. Violent, angry, hateful people…"

"Shit, I'm sorry. I lost my parents too. How long have you been out here like this? I mean… Do you have anyone?"

"I have friends, I guess. Or at least I've *had* friends. But they keep dying. Everyone out here seems to die…"

I sat in silent shock. I was ill-prepared for a conversation of such magnitude. This homeless kid had taken me by surprise. It was heavy.

"You don't look like you're from around here," Eli said to me. "Besides the oxygen mask which is a dead giveaway, you look, well, healthy I guess. Where are you from?"

"Umm… I live in one of the sub-plazas out west. You know, underground?"

His eyes lit up in astonishment. "I've heard about the underground cities, the sub-plazas. Man, they sound great. I wish I could go inside one of them. It would be so much safer than out here trying to live day to day. How can I get in one?"

All my hate towards the lack of freedom inside the sub-plaza became so transparent the second Eli put things into such harsh perspective. He was out there alone every day, literally fending off death. I had my apartment block, my entertainment systems and my unnecessary purchases. I had access to breaking waves, cinemas, brothels, restaurants and most of all, safety. I'd been complaining about my subterranean life when compared to the surface dwellers, it was heavenly.

Eli's struggle on the surface helped ground me, if only for a moment. At the same time it made me feel like a self-centred coward when comparing my problems with his. It made me realise that my life could've been a great deal worse. My over-entitlement was unwarranted.

"Well, Eli, it's not that simple. You can't just *get in* one. The Union needs to invite you or you need to complete a lengthy application. It's just not that simple. I'm sorry, but it's the truth."

"Yeah… Well you know what… Um, I don't even know your name?"

"Tyson."

"Well, Tyson! Screw the Union. They did nothing for me. They kicked me out of my house and they left me on the street. They only care about the people with money, what sort of messed up world is that? The ones without money, the ones like me are the ones that the government should care about and should look after. One of the older guys that I see around the place, do you know what he told me? He told me that thirty, forty years ago, the government gave money to people who didn't have jobs. They called it welfare or something? Can you believe that? The government just gave people money! So where is my *damn welfare?*"

"You're right Eli, you are, but there isn't a thing I can do about it."

Eli seemed irritated.

"You know what, Tyson? You better go back to your underground world before it's too late. This place only gets worse when the sun sets. I need to find some food and get in my shelter before sundown or else I won't make it through the night. This is no place for an *underground* person."

And without even a wave or goodbye, Eli hopped up from behind the coastal wattle and began running off down the sandy slope and onto the empty esplanade. I didn't know what to do. The silence became overpowering. I didn't feel safe. I wanted nothing more than to be back inside 3rd Sydney West surrounded by the citizens I loathed so much.

Hurrying back to the hired hover-bike, I couldn't take my mind off young Eli. I was sure that I would never see that young boy again. Hell, he probably wouldn't even live out the week. It occurred to me that by chance Eli had stopped me walking down onto the beach and towards the derelict shelter, possibly saving my life.

Without knowing it, that young, homeless thief had one of the greatest impacts on my life to date. It was overwhelming. Oddly, I felt guilty. I felt guilty because I had what Eli wanted so badly. Despite the lack of freedom that encroached my daily life I still had consistency, I still had hygiene. In contrast to my guilt though, I felt remorse because in a strange twist of things, Eli had what I wanted. Eli lived day-to-day as he chose, even if it was a constant struggle. Eli had a choice, and even though it was dangerous and frightening, Eli was free.

FOURTEEN

Tropical rains had hammered down for over twenty-four hours.

Gale-force winds had turned the jungle into a sinister and eerie place. The ground above T-Town had turned into a clay-like slop. Despite the foul weather there didn't appear to be a single leak finding its way into the underground bunker.

Two nights had passed since Michael and Brie's intimate encounter and since that erotic moment neither of them had mentioned a word of it to the other residents. Brie found the secrecy just added to her pulsating desire.

Putting aside desire, it was time to act.

Brie, Bruce and the other four had packed their provisions and were waiting for the storm to pass. They grew impatient. Bruce raised the point that if they put off their departure any longer, they would possibly miss the train and miss their shipment of the life saving serum. The weather alone would make the trip far harder and a great deal slower. They could waste no more time.

Once they were ready to depart they said their farewells to the rest of the residents. Because of the previous mission's catastrophe, the mood in the bunker was as sombre as the dark howling rains above the surface. Hugs, kisses and tears of hope were shed before Brie, Bruce, Francis, Michael, Caleb and Milly made their way through the cramped service tunnel to the exit beside to the hover-bike bunker.

Crawling out into the mud they were filthy and wet within seconds. The waterproof suits served almost no purpose. A short dash through the soaked undergrowth got them to the bunker and once there they wasted no time. They stored provisions in the hatches under the seats, then checked the bikes for any mechanical faults. Once they completed the checks, it was straight into the harsh, tropical elements.

Three bikes, six people. Everyone doubled up. Milly climbed on behind Caleb. Francis and Bruce agreed to share a bike and alternate the driving, which left Michael with Brie. Brie hopped on behind Michael and wrapped her arms around his muscular frame. Even in the howling weather she found him warm, secure. Even just something as insignificant as wrapping her arms around him for transport caused an increased heart rate and butterflies in her belly. Michael looked over his shoulder and smiled. "You ready to ride?"

Brie nodded.

"Hold on!"

After a slow morning, the three hover-bikes came to a small opening in the jungle at the same moment the weather began to clear. For the first time in days the rain stopped and a few rays of sunlight found their way through the jungle canopy. With the sunlight came instant humidity. Steam rose from the wet undergrowth and the temperature increased.

"We've travelled about a hundred and forty kilometres. We're way behind schedule because of this shit bloody weather. Have a drink, take a piss, swap drivers and we wanna be moving again in five minutes. We need to travel well into the night, but we should reach the old border into Malaysia by sunrise. Once we get out of the thick of it, we can increase our pace by double."

The men wandered off to edge of the clearing to empty their bladders. Brie and Milly sat in the sunlight and did their best to dry themselves before they continued the journey. "Aren't you a little scared?" Brie asked Milly, breaking the silence.

"Of what?"

"Well, not making it back. Of failing, I guess."

"To be honest, Brie, we're lucky we've made it this far. We've been living as free souls up in T-Town. We have no chips to scan. We have no compulsory church on Sunday, no forced husbands and no Union soldiers. I'm happy that we've lived as long as we have as free souls. I don't fear death. I would rather face death than live like a slave under the rule of the Humanist Union. I'm content with how things have been so no, I'm not that scared."

"Oh, I wish I felt the same. I mean, I agree with all of that but there's still this heavy sense of uncertainty and fear that I can't seem to swallow."

"In time you will. You've only been with us for a week. I've been here for a year. Trust me, we'll be in and out before you know it."

"I hope you're right, Milly."

The rain remained absent for the rest of the afternoon. The three hover-bikes weaved their way through trees, undergrowth, hills and creeks. Frequently the team of T-Towners drove past makeshift villages, other free people trying to live off the grid. As they neared the dilapidated dwellings, dirty and thin people emerged from the treetops with weaponry. Just as fast as they raised the weapons, they lowered them. The T-Towners posed no threat.

The sun sunk over the mountainous horizon and darkness swallowed the jungle. Their pace slowed down to a crawl. Brie couldn't see more than ten metres in front of her. Tailing as close as she could behind Bruce and Francis, she often lost sight of their bike and had to rely on sound and instinct for direction.

Just before midnight Bruce called a stop. Even with alternating the driving, Brie's forearms felt like stones from holding the handlebars for hours on end. They placed the three bikes in a triangle-like perimeter and set up inflatable mats in the middle. Between the six of them they passed around some fruit, water and dry goods. There was little conversation. They were all exhausted.

Bruce pointed out that they were less than a hundred kilometres from the old border. This meant that they were a third of the way there. "Let's all get a bit of shuteye and we wanna be back on the bikes at six. Rest those muscles, massage those arse cheeks and let's hope for more sunshine tomorrow. We need night-watch rotations tonight. Who knows what's out there in the trees. I'll go first. I'll wake Francis at two. Francis can you do two till four?" Francis nodded in approval and grinned, exposing his grotesque and toothless gums. "Great. Michael, you wanna do four til six?"

"Well, it's not like I want to, but I will."

Bruce laughed in a deep grumble then stood up to grab his assault rifle from the side of his hover-bike. "Sweet dreams, sweethearts!"

FIFTEEN

BRIE WAS ASLEEP WITHIN MINUTES.

It was a deep, dreamless sleep. She slept straight through the change in watch and straight through the strange noises of the jungle. She stirred as Michael was being woken for his watch, only because she felt the warmth of his body leave hers. Somehow, in the subconscious world of sleep, Michael and Brie had found each other and nuzzled together for warmth. Something about that made Brie feel good. After falling back into a strange and vivid dream state, she woke up sweaty and restless. It was still dark, but the jungle was silent. She rolled over to see Michael sitting up on one of the hoverbikes, getting a better vantage point of the surrounding landscape. He noticed her restless behaviour and looked over. "Do you hear that?" Michael whispered.

"Hear what?"

"Exactly! The jungle has finally gone to sleep!"

"What time is it?" Brie asked while yawning.

"It's twenty-past five."

Brie stretched, got to her feet and walked over to Michael's position on the bike. She sat behind him and wrapped her arms around his waist, resting her head on his shoulder. "So," she whispered. "You found me in my sleep, did you?"

"Well, I wasn't asleep. You looked restless. You were making weird noises, like grunts or something. I thought you were having a bad dream, so I rolled over and put my arm around you. It seemed to calm you down. Do you often have bad dreams?"

"With a past like mine, Michael, dreams will haunt me for the rest of my days. But that's a conversation for another day."

"No stress. I'm not asking anything…"

"Look, about the other night. I don't want you to think I did that for no reason. I mean… I'm not usually the one to do something like that so fast, but… Well there's something I like about you, Michael. You seem so approachable and genuine and…"

"Hey Brie," Michael said, turning around to look her in the eyes. "I rarely do things like that, either. I feel something different with you, too. Something I like. I'm not saying that it won't happen again 'cause I'd like it to, but at least for the next few days let's keep distractions to a minimum."

With that, Michael leaned forward and gave Brie a quick and gentle kiss on the lips.

Brie wanted that beautiful moment to last forever, but as fast as the moment begun, it was over. "Now, it's time to wake these guys up and hit the bikes. We have a big day. Today we wanna get down past Georgetown. That means less jungle and more soldiers. We're gonna head south and—"

"I don't care how we get there," Brie said, cutting Michael off. "I'm just following instructions. You guys get me there and I'll do what I need to do."

She leaned forward and returned Michael's kiss. Just as he began to kiss her back, she pulled away and rested her head back on his shoulder. They both smiled in the early morning twilight. The butterflies of desire fluttered in the calming silence.

Breakfast comprised fruit, stale damper, stolen Union muesli rations and dull conversation. Without the fruit, the damper and muesli would have been inedible. Its chewy and glue-like texture made it flavourless and hard to swallow.

The weather had taken a well-received turn for the better. The cloudless early morning light and lack of wind provided perfect conditions to travel south. After crossing the old border into Malaysia, the three bikes began to pass more signs of life. Village folk, mutants, outlaws and law-abiding Christian communities all appeared through the clearing landscape. Twice, they came close to Union tanks patrolling the outskirts of Georgetown and hid amongst the forest canopy.

The three bikes turned further southeast and battled up the overgrown slopes to get high onto the mountainous ridgeline above. Passing the outskirts of Bentung, an old township thirty kilometres north of KL, the group sighted a well-used dirt track. Worn paths snaked their way through the shallow grass. Scattered rubbish lay in piles against the rocky slope of the hill.

As the team came over a small embankment, Bruce halted his bike, causing Caleb and Brie to slam to a stop behind him. There, in the middle of the makeshift track were four naked, bloodstained bodies hanging from the limbs of an overgrown trackside tree. All four bodies were female, Caucasian, and all four had severed throats. Blood ran down the length of their bare skin, dripping off their feet onto the damp dirt.

"What the hell is this?" Caleb said, reaching for his gun.

Panic.

"Calm down," said Bruce. "It looks like some warning, I guess. Or maybe a sacrifice to the pagan gods? Get off your bikes, guys. Grab your weapons and follow me."

Brie was scared. Brie had never fired a weapon before. Doing it would be hard enough. Pulling the trigger, while aiming it at a real person would be a great deal harder.

Sure, she had killed Peter van Bueren, but that was out of desperation and survival, pure animalistic rage. That was different to going into a gunfight. She felt sick with fear. Sweat clogged her dirty pores.

Within seconds they huddled up against the carved-out hillside with their rifles drawn.

"Look," said Milly, alarmed. "Over past the track. There's a timber platform just above the canopy. I think it's a lookout. Probably empty, though."

Brie began to shake. The intense silence caused nausea to rise from the pit of her frightened stomach.

What the hell have I gotten myself into?

Before Brie even acknowledged that the noise she could hear was gunfire, she felt the warm spray of blood cover the left side of her face. Caleb fell forward into the dirt, his torso riddled with holes.

Brie vomited.

It rained bullets all around them. From behind a concealed bunker, the gunfire appeared to be coming from ground level, over behind the hanging corpses. Bullets hit the dirt and stone on the hillside above them. Chunks of earth came rolling down on top of them.

In the only open positions to do so, Milly and Bruce started returning fire, spraying the direction of the bunker with bullets. Francis wasted no time going into combat mode. While Bruce delivered cover fire, Francis dropped to the ground and crawled through the dirt to reach the closest hover-bike. From the side compartment he pulled out three nuclear shock balls. He crawled back through the rain of gunfire and began activating them with a series of numerical codes.

Milly screamed.

Brie sat frozen.

Caleb leaked dark red blood.

"What the hell are we shooting at?" Bruce yelled through the chaos.

There was no response. Only gunfire.

Francis threw the first shock ball. It fell short of the tree line. The ground vibrated as the blast sent dirt, rocks and flames through the jungle. The hanging bodies had disappeared, disintegrated by the force of the explosion.

Wasting no time, Francis threw a second shock ball, this time a little further. It reached the trees then rolled out of view, dropping below ground level. Once again the ground vibrated. People screamed. Debris went flying and trees dropped to the jungle floor.

The gunfire stopped.

Silence enveloped the gruesome scene.

Once the smoke cleared, Francis and Michael began crawling forward, in a military-style approach with their weapons forward and their chins to the dirt. Brie had constant ringing in her ears. Milly leaned forward and grabbed her partner, checking his vital signs for life. No breathing. No heartbeat. Caleb was dead, the colour already drained from his expressionless face. Milly kissed him on the forehead and placed him back down in the dirt. Now wasn't the time to shed a tear. Mourning would get her killed. Instead, she kept her eyes set before her ready to fire upon anything that moved.

Brie watched Michael reach the bunker and inspect the scene before him. It was a bloodbath. Limbs, organs and tattered clothing were all that remained of whoever had been shooting at them. Francis joined him and together they walked the length of the bunker. Brie, Bruce and Milly keep a watchful eye from behind.

Brie still couldn't move. She sat up against the rocky outcrop, sweaty and pale and watched Michael and Francis pace with courage through the dwindling flames.

Past the bunker, Michael reached a fortified building. There was no noise. No one moved.

"Who the fuck is in there? Show yourselves or we shoot!"

After a short but intense silence, Michael heard yelling. Female voices, native Malaysian language. He didn't understand a word being said, but both he and Francis kept their rifles aimed at the small building between the trees. A rusted tin door opened and two naked women ran out with their arms in the air, screaming in Malaysian.

"Get on the ground," yelled Michael.

They didn't understand him. Instead, they continued towards him with their hands raised, screaming. Francis aimed his rifle low and shot the soil before their feet. They dropped to the ground and buried their faces in the dirt. Francis looked at Michael, presenting a crazed, toothless grin.

Bruce, Milly and Brie came forward. Bruce and Francis entered the building. After only ten seconds Brie heard more yelling, this time in broken English, then more shots fired. Another ten tense seconds passed with no movement. Then, with just one hand, Francis dragged a body out the door and dropped it beside the cowering Malaysian women.

He wouldn't have been taller than five feet. He had long black dread-locked hair and tribal tattoos. Francis had shot him in the shin. The man winced in pain. He started cursing the gods and whispering some kind of pagan prayer. He looked up at Bruce and stared him right in the eyes. "You're in trouble now, sinner. You've not only angered my men, you've angered the gods. They were expecting these two whores to enter their realm today. You cannot keep Them waiting."

"Shut your filthy mouth," Bruce yelled and gave him a solid kick to the ribs. "Are there more of you? Where are the others?"

"Of course there are more," the guy said between laboured breaths. "We are infinite. We are servants of those who are more powerful than man. We are everywhere—"

"Don't listen to this bloody idiot," Bruce interrupted. "I say we put a bullet in him and keep going. I don't have time to listen to this nonsensical bullshit! If there are others nearby, they will have heard all the gunfire and they'll be on their way here. I'm not sure about you guys, but I don't wanna be here when they arrive."

"You can't escape us. You can try. But They will always find you."

"Shut your god-fearing mouth, you murderous *dog*!" Milly yelled with such harsh hostility it brought fear to the eyes of the defeated man. Without a word of warning she stepped forward and placed the barrel of her rifle to the man's left eye socket and pulled the trigger.

The Malaysian women screamed.

Milly roared with ferocity.

Brie, now with an empty stomach, dry retched.

"Well, I suppose that solves that then," Bruce said with a comical smile. "Now for you two," he said, looking at the screaming women. "You either come with us or you scram now. What's it gonna be?"

For the first time since coming across the sacrificial bodies, Brie opened her mouth to speak.

"Bruce, they can't understand you, mate. Isn't that obvious?" She walked towards them and helped the two cowering women to their feet. She pointed off towards the track heading to the township to the east and began waving in that direction. "Off you go. Go on."

Within seconds they ran off into the thick of the jungle. Then they were gone.

"Was I wrong to do that?" Milly asked, looking up at her companions, searching for reassurance.

"No bloody way, Milly. If you didn't do it you know I was going to! Filthy god-lover got what he deserved. Now we need to get out of here. Quick smart."

"What about Caleb?" Milly asked, tears welling in her frenzied, over-dilated eyes.

"What about him, sweetheart? We can't take him with us. We don't have time to bury him."

"Please, we need to bury him. C'mon Bruce, it won't take long. We can't leave him in the open to rot. He deserves more."

"For Christ's sake… Okay, Milly, but we're out of here in five minutes. Got it? Let's bloody-well hurry!"

SIXTEEN

Eight minutes later and they were on their way down the overgrown track leading away from the smoking remains.

They dug a shallow grave with the butts of their rifles and a small trowel kept in the side compartment of one of the hover-bikes. The hole was only just deep enough to cover Caleb's body. Milly found a small round rock and engraved Caleb's initials into it with her knife and placed it over her lover's grave. It was the best she could do under the circumstances.

Milly shook with shock. She was in no condition to ride up front. Francis rode alone and Bruce shared a bike with Milly. Even with the hum of the hover-bike's electric engine purring, Bruce could hear the uncontrollable wailing of Milly sitting behind him. For the rest of the afternoon there was very little conversation.

As the sun set over the distant coastal horizon, the five of them made camp and prepared an early dinner. Upon arrival at the campsite Francis left to scout the area. He returned within fifteen minutes with a sack full of parrots and parrot eggs. He wasted no time in gutting and feathering the small birds before he shoved sticks through the flesh and prepared a small cooking fire. The meat was tough and gamey but once cooked all five ate their portions without a word.

"Look, I know today was unexpected and losing it was fucked up, losing Caleb…" Michael said, looking around the fire at his companions. "But we need our heads screwed on tomorrow to pull this off. Milly, I can't for a second pretend to understand what you're going through but come game time tomorrow, we need to be able to count on you. When we get back to T-Town, we can mourn and have a ceremony and all the rest but, well, you get what I'm trying to say…"

Milly moved her eyes from the hypnotic flickering of the flames and looked at Michael. She hadn't spoken a word since burying Caleb.

"You can count on me, Mike. It's not like I didn't know there would be the chance of failure. It's like, no matter how much you try to prepare for a situation, you can never really know how you'll feel until it happens… I knew… I mean I *know* that the life we all live in T-Town isn't peaches and cream. We're outlaws. We steal from the Union. I'm not stupid and I didn't think we would be invincible. It just sucks, you know? It's just shit. I didn't wanna lose him…"

Brie moved from her position by the fire. She sat down next to Milly and wrapped her arms around her.

"What I've learnt is that there's no point preparing for anything in life because life has a funny way of flipping you upside down just when you get comfy. Life is a bitch sometimes…"

Milly rested her head on Brie's shoulder as they sat together and watched the dancing flames.

By the time the timber in the fire was nothing more than glowing embers, Francis and Milly were fast asleep, Bruce had gone for a perimeter walk with his rifle and Michael had his arms wrapped around Brie.

"I can't wait for all of this to be over so we can be back in T-Town," Brie said, staring into Michael's spacey blue eyes.

"And why is that, Ms Brie Kallas?"

"So we can venture off into the jungle, get lost and truly find each other. I wanna know you again. I wanna feel your skin on mine. But we can't do that here. We need our heads screwed on, right?" She leaned forward and gave Michael a long and passionate kiss. He kissed her back. She pushed her body against him and pulled away just as felt his excitement growing in his jeans. "Sometimes waiting makes it even more enjoyable," she said as she rolled over to get comfortable beside the embers.

"I suppose you're right."

"Goodnight then, Michael. I hope I dream of you. Wake me up when it's my turn to keep watch."

"Okay, Brie. Sweet dreams."

———

THERE WERE NO SWEET DREAMS.

There was no pleasant wake up call, no birds singing in the trees. The noise of panic and fear pulled Brie from a dreamless sleep, disorientated in the darkness. The embers had burned down to a dull glow and Michael was missing. Goosebumps crawled over her body as she heard the distant screams of a woman.

Then gunfire.

Then silence.

What the hell was happening?

Flashes of light emerged through the darkness. The muzzles of rifles lit up as lead bullets projected from their chambers, making the jungle come to life with short, rhythmic flashes. Terror filled the air. Even though Brie couldn't see, she could *feel* people all around her. The jungle was alive. She got up from the ground and began running. She didn't know where to run but she ran regardless, dodging trees, plants and rocks. Before Brie had made it twenty metres from the extinguished fire, she tripped over something, flinging her to the moist soil. Her jaw hit the dirt. It forced her lower teeth into her tongue from the impact. She tasted blood. Terror consumed her as she looked down at what she tripped on. In the faint moonlight she could see it. It was Francis' headless body.

His head was nowhere to be seen.

Screw this!

Crippled by fear and unable to get to her feet, she half crawled, half ran through the undergrowth. Footsteps became louder behind her.

Voices.

Gunfire.

Fear.

A team of armoured soldiers blocked her path. They fanned out into a defensive semi-circle. Brie's heart sank. The high-power laser torches, the grey camouflage uniform, the all-black full-face portable oxygen conditioners and the Union-issue taser cannons pointed at her face meant one thing.

The Humanist Union Army had found them.

One soldier stepped forward. He was tall and well built, well over six feet in height. He towered above Brie like an adult over a small child. Through his black oxygen conditioner he began to talk.

"So, *Mrs van Bueren*. It looks like your luck lasted only for so long."

If Brie thought her heart had already sunk, it just dropped from the ocean floor down into an abyss and into the coldest, darkest, most formidable place imaginable.

They had found her.

"We almost caught you in Papua New Guinea. We nearly gave up there and left you to the necrosis, but you must pay for what you did. There are several people who will be delighted to have a chat with you, Brie. Your husband's death upset some powerful people."

"You can tell them to get screwed, you filthy Union scum," Brie screamed through clenched teeth.

Without a word, the soldier unclipped his taser cannon from his belt and struck Brie across the face with the butt of his weapon. The force of the blow sent her to the ground, yet she remained conscious. As she spat blood from her mouth, two of her front teeth fell onto the dirt before her. She tried to sit up as the soldier swung his cannon again, striking Brie across the jaw. She slumped to the ground unconscious. The officer leaned down and picked Brie up as if she were nothing more than a bag of linen.

"Load Brie van Bueren into the hover-tank. Kill the rest of them!"

SEVENTEEN

I walked down an empty Tier Three hallway.

It was unusual for the hallways to be clear of people, even in the earliest hours of the morning. I noticed the hologram posters on the walls seemed different to any I'd seen before. They frightened me. I found it odd that the posters contained horrific scenes, photos taken during the modern-day Crusades, photos of blood and gore and death. Photos of decapitated Muslims. Photos of torture victims. This was definitely not a block I was familiar with. It made me uneasy. I had a strange sensation of something stuck in my throat. I swallowed. It made little difference. I needed to get somewhere fast, but I didn't know where I needed to be.

I turned the corner, heading towards an internal transporter tunnel when the lights in the hall dimmed. With just enough eerie light for me to make out the narrow walls of the corridor, I continued forward. With each step in the dim orange glow, my anxiety built. Uncertainty filled the empty halls. The air conditioner seemed operational but sweat formed on my forehead. I wanted to wipe it away but for some indistinguishable reason, I couldn't. The dim light soon turned to total darkness.

I panicked.

In all my time within the 3rd Sydney West sub-plaza there had never been a power failure. The corridors had never been dark. The generators wouldn't allow it. Something must be wrong.

"Hello…?" I called through the darkness. My weak, trembling voice echoed alone through the steel corridor. "Is anyone else here? What's going on? Hello…?"

I knew I couldn't stand still and simply hope that the lights came back. Instead, I used my hand to guide me along the wall and continued heading towards the transporter tunnels. I wasn't positive, but I thought I could hear distant whispering, whispering in another language, a foreign language I had never heard, maybe a language from outside the Empire. Then I felt it. It sent me running through the darkness, no longer using the wall as a guide. I panicked. Without a doubt in my mind I just felt breathing on the back of my neck. Warm, moist, heavy breathing.

"Who the hell is there?" I yelled into the uninviting nothing. There was no response.

Taking me off guard, the lights suddenly flickered back on.

I screamed.

Two metres away stood a strange woman. She was short, shoeless and red-haired. She had her eyes closed. My heart skipped a beat as I took a few rushed paces backwards. I wasn't sure if I was frightened or concerned. She just stood there with a hostile expression. Her clothes were ragged and filthy. Her hands and feet were blood stained.

"Hey… Are you all right?" I asked, with caution. She didn't reply.

She opened her eyes. My indecisiveness vanished. I was frightened.

She had the blackest of black eyes. Oil-black. No, they were *death* black. There were no irises, no whites; just black, demonic eyes staring at me. I tried to move but my legs didn't seem to work. I couldn't get my brain to send instructions to my body. Those black eyes continued to stare, boring into me. Her brooding and emotionless look turned to an evil smirk.

"Hello Tyson," she said in a hoarse whisper.

"Who the hell are you? How do you know my name?"

"What do you mean, Tyson? You know who I am. Why wouldn't I know your name?"

Fear.

Confusion.

Panic.

The sweat that had formed on my forehead now covered my body. Drips rolled down my spine and collected at the waist of my pants. "Why should I know who you are? What are you talking about?"

She stepped closer and raised her bloodstained and filthy hands, reaching out towards me in desperation.

"Tyson, I'm your *wife!*"

EIGHTEEN

I JUMPED UPRIGHT IN A FRENZIED JOLT, ALMOST LAUNCHING MYSELF out of bed.

Laura sensed a disturbance in the room and turned on the bedroom lights. I winced. She asked me if there was something the matter. After a quick glance around and a few deep breaths I informed her everything was fine and that I wanted the lights turned off. As I had programmed her to do, she followed my command without query.

My bed sheets were soaked. I wasn't sure if it was sweat or if I had pissed myself. I walked to the bathroom and washed my face. Man, it had seemed so damn real. The woman's stare was still so visible. Those eyes flooded my thoughts. I tried to force away the image. The anxiety I'd been facing around the Marriage Lottery had now found its way into my dreams, turning my peaceful sleep into hellish nightmares. I just couldn't escape it. The draw inched closer. I had one free day to go.

"What time is it, Laura," I asked the room.

"It's 4:19am," she responded. "I set your alarm to go off at 6:45, giving you two hours and twenty-six minutes until you need to start the day."

"Can you please cancel the alarm, Laura?"

"Of course, Tyson, your alarm has been cancelled at your request."

Sleep wouldn't return. I was way too spooked from the creepy red-haired woman and I had too much on my mind. I lay in bed with my eyes wide open, staring at the off-white ceiling paint thinking about my life. Tears began to well in my eyes. I tried to blink them away. They rolled down my cheeks onto the damp pillow. I cried out like a pathetic child. Laura ignored me. This was not how I wanted my life to be. I knew I was a cynic and I had high expectations but this was not a life. There needed to be something more.

Maybe I was too entitled. Maybe I was selfish. I knew that I wouldn't be able to keep it all bottled up for much longer. Fear of discipline could only placate my reactions for so long. I felt ready to explode. I was on the verge of a breakdown.

Life had to have a greater purpose.

Pissed off with everything, I got changed into my uncomfortable navy-blue Union uniform and left my apartment cell. I wandered down the main causeway of Block 7 and slumped down at my local coffee centre. I didn't even need to order. Christie and Fay ran the shop. They'd been making me coffee for two years. Like my attendance at BC74, I was a creature of habit. They made a great latte. Double shot, no sugar. They were both in their late fifties and they had adapted remarkably well to the Union's radical changes. They were always in chirpy moods, always smiling. Under different circumstances their positive attitude was infectious.

Fay walked over with an inviting smile and placed the navy-blue aluminium coffee container on the table before me.

"You alright there, Ty? You don't look your normal self, mate... And what are you doing here so darn early?"

"Can't sleep at the moment. Got things on the mind, Fay."

"You wanna talk about it, darling?"

"Nah, not really. I'm just sick of all this!"

"All what?"

I melodramatically waved my arms around the coffee centre.

"All *this*… This whole place! This sub-plaza. This uniform. This *life*! Sometimes I wish things were like they used to be."

"Jesus, Ty. That's a little pessimistic. Better lift those spirits real quick. We can't have you carrying on inside the plaza, it might offend people."

"That's why I said I didn't wanna talk," I snapped, raising my voice.

"Fine, hun, fine. Just remember, if you need to get things off your chest you can talk to me, but civilly, okay. It's better than bottling everything up."

"Yeah, I guess. For the time being I need some time to think."

"Okay, darling. I'll leave you alone with your thoughts then. Don't forget to scan your chip as you leave, hun."

She gave me a comforting rub on the back and walked back towards the kitchen without another word. I guess she knew when people just needed space.

I finished my coffee and headed to work early. With plenty of data to enter I figured if I started early I might finish early. That depended on which supervisor was on duty. The plan was to hang out with George and Jonah after work for my final night as a *free* man. Don't worry; I use the term *free* lightly.

Work was quiet. Time inched by at a painful pace. By mid-morning, Jonah and I decided that lunch would be a more suitable option. Fortunately for me, our supervisor for the day was tolerable and, within reason, allowed flexibility. We both had extra hours accrued, so I sent George a digital alert and told him to meet us down at Tango BBQ Grill on Tier Four at 1:00 pm. I would need to catch up on work tomorrow with a few extra hours. I would worry about that later. It was time to go drown my anxiety. Tomorrow's problems could wait. Extra hours at work seemed trivial in comparison to what plagued my thoughts.

By the time Jonah and I reached the Tier Four restaurant, George sat at a booth table with several colourful cocktails, plates full of flame-grilled meat and three stunning girls – Tier Four prostitutes, I assumed. Dressed in short, leather skirts and loose singlet tops, their clothing left nothing to the imagination. All three had fake tits and God knows how many other surgical implants. George introduced them as Felicity, Sarah and Panda.

The Humanist Union permitted prostitution within the Empire but only for oral sex and manual stimulation, no insertion. Sex out of wedlock and adultery were both forbidden, but if you were not of Marriage Lottery age, then by all means, pay a woman for her oral services. The Union's lack of consistency was ridiculous.

Felicity looked the most attractive of the three, with jade green eyes, silvery blonde hair and caramel skin. The other two looked almost identical. They both had aqua blue eyes the colour of Fosform Five, yellow blonde hair, copious amounts of eye make-up and a smile that said 'I'll do anything for the right amount of credits.'

I slid into the booth beside Felicity and grabbed a tall glass of the bright orange drink before me. We all toasted to my last day without a wife. We toasted to my official arrival to adulthood. The six of us tapped our glasses together and all took swigs of the colourful concoctions. For the briefest moment, there at that table, I almost felt the warm grasp of happiness.

As the afternoon continued the cocktails flowed. George made a speech about my last night as a single man and the start of my adult life. He prayed for me, asking God to send me a beautiful, compliant young wife with a sound education and a raging libido. I laughed and questioned if women like that existed anywhere within the Empire.

I'd never been much of a drinker so before long I was on my way to full-scale drunk. I felt merry. Confidence grew. For the first time in a month, the anxiety hammering away at my conscience felt subdued by the false confidence of alcohol intoxication. False or not, I enjoyed the feeling.

The afternoon turned into early evening. Before we got totally out of control Jonah left the table to make his way home to his patient wife. You could tell by his apprehension to leave and his constant flirtatious remarks towards the girls he wanted nothing more than to take one of them into the toilet cubicle and have his way with her. Because of strict laws forbidding adultery, as much as Jonah wanted to utilise the services of the willing young escorts, he knew there was no way he could. If the Union caught him, they would banish him to the surface, or even worse, castrate him with no anaesthetic. Jonah bade us farewell and wished me luck in the lottery.

"I hope you pick a good one, mate. I hope you pick the woman of your dreams."

By nine o'clock my vision lost clarity. I looked over at Felicity and smiled. She said something about it being my lucky day. She moved closer and kissed me on the neck. I giggled with drunken delight. Right there at the table, concealed by the cover of the draping tablecloth, she unbuttoned my Union uniform pants and started to play with me. I grew in her hand and she began to rub it with the skills that only come from her line of work. Within seconds I was as hard as sub-plaza steel. George said something inaudible, his words slurred by the rum. I nodded and smiled. He raised his glass and laughed. Everything seemed so unreal, dream-like almost. It all became a blurred, fragmented display of images. I leaned back and let Felicity work her magic.

One of the other girls, Sarah maybe, but I wasn't sure, slipped down off her booth seat and disappeared underneath the tablecloth. I felt her hands on my thighs and her warm mouth around my shaft. Felicity stopped her handiwork as Sarah took over. I tried to keep a straight face at the table while my dick was being sucked in the middle of a family restaurant.

There in that moment the marriage lottery was the furthest thing from my mind. Despite the alcohol it didn't take long for me to finish in her mouth. She reappeared from under the tablecloth, smiling. She grabbed a glass from the table and took a big sip, all the while smiling at me with that same *I'll do anything* look.

My vision's clarity seemed to fade with each passing minute. Soon after Sarah's under-the-table surprise I began to lose memory. I saw the girls leave, but I didn't remember saying good-bye. I saw a pile of vomit on the table but I wasn't sure if it was mine. I saw fragments of images, nothing more. George pissing on a corridor plant by a transporter tunnel, a photo of the once infamous Uluru on the wall, more vomit, conversation with Union soldiers, then blackness. Spinning, wobbling, unease then undisrupted total blackness.

NINETEEN

CONFUSION WAS MY INITIAL REACTION AS I GAINED CONSCIOUSNESS.

Then pain.

My head felt like I'd been head-butting the corridor wall all night. I opened my eyes and the pain increased. I saw light, artificial sunlight. This meant morning had come. The artificial sunlight operated on a timer system and rose at about 6:45 throughout 3rd Sydney West. It felt like I was only at the table, only wandering the corridors mere minutes ago. I still felt drunk.

I took a few deep breaths, trying to keep down the contents of my stomach. It didn't work. I leaned over and vomited, bringing up thick yellow paste-like bile. Only then did I realise that I wasn't at home.

Then I noticed wind. Then I noticed the smell of rotten pollution. The stench of death filled my nostrils.

I forced myself up, wiped the bile from my lip and I looked around. It wasn't artificial sunlight at all. It was *actual* sunlight. Somehow, for some unknown reason I had gone to the surface. And without an oxygen conditioner! The shock sobered me right away. I spun around and spotted George about ten metres from me, asleep

on the concrete, drool cascading from his open mouth. He also wore
no conditioner.

For whatever reason we had fallen asleep in the vehicle hire
compound above 3rd Sydney West. People moved about, preoccupied with their morning errands. They ignored us. Without masks
on and with a pile of bile beside me, we must have looked like sickly
surface dwellers. I stumbled over to George and nudged him with
my boot. He didn't stir. I nudged him again, this time somewhat
harder. "Hey George, wake the hell up... We're on the surface...
George!"

He moaned and rolled over. Opening his eyes, he looked
around. He smiled. "What on Earth are you smiling about?" I
shouted. "We're on the *fucking* surface!"

"I know, mate. I know! Don't you remember last night?" He sat
up, yawned and wiped the crusted saliva from his chin.

"No, not at all. I remember nothing after leaving the restaurant
on Tier Four."

Even talking made my brain hurt more. My temples thumped
with swollen aggression.

"Well, after we left Tier Four, we figured, well, you figured it
would be a good idea to get some *fresh* air, so to speak. You
kept going on about wanting to see the moon one last time as a single
man or some romantic nonsense. I went along with you because I
haven't been up here in six months. It stinks like shit. It's a filthy
bloody place. I don't know why I listened to you. Up on Tier One we
ran into some soldiers. I went to school with one of them. We started
talking and they were this damn close to denying our access up here
until I explained to them you have to draw your lottery number
today and that it would be your last time as a single man to come to
the surface. Somehow that convinced them and they allowed us up.
We must have damn well passed out. Don't you remember any of it?"

"Not really. I remember getting my dick sucked."

George laughed. "Man, I hope you remember that. Those girls
cost me close to a week's worth of credits. I'm glad it was worth it!"

"Yeah, thanks for last night, George. I needed it. I feel terrible now, though. I need to sort myself out before I head to Tier Two and attend the Lottery. I can't go there like this, can I?"

"I don't see why it should matter, mate. I mean, you have dirt and vomit on your Union uniform and you stink like surface filth but so what…"

"I take it you're being sarcastic, George?" He looked at me with that cheeky grin that I had grown to know so well. "Anyway, I need water… And coffee. Let's head back down to Tier Three so I can have a shower, get a coffee from Fay and Christie then go *ruin my life*…"

"Righto, Tyson. Just keep telling yourself it could be worse. A lifetime on the walls or a lifetime with a fat, obnoxious woman…"

Again, I couldn't tell if George was being sarcastic. I ignored him.

After a long, hot shower and two double shot coffees, I felt almost human. My head still thumped. I got two Valdeine tablets from Christie at the coffee shop. They discontinued the manufacturing of the hybrid painkillers to remove addictive substances from the Empire, but Christie had a stash from a previous disabling injury. Given that it was my Lottery day, she seemed happy to help.

By mid-morning, the painkillers had worked wonders. Other than a coarse throat, probably from vomiting too much, I felt pretty normal. I had until 5:00 pm to make my lottery draw. There was no point procrastinating and torturing myself with apprehension any longer. I thought it would be best to make my way to the transporter tunnel, head up to Tier Two and get the whole disgusting ordeal over with.

I felt nervous. I felt sick with stress. I couldn't accept that it was happening. I couldn't accept I was about to draw a fucking number that resembled a person, a real person who could be in Melbourne, or Hobart, or Kuala Lumpur or Denpasar.

I felt dizzy.

Shit, I can't do this!

Hyperventilation.

Narrowing of the airway.

I gulped in synthetically conditioned air.

So many thoughts ran through my manic mind. Turbulent waves of emotion crashed against the shorelines of my sanity. Anxiety clawed at me with a vengeance. What could I do? I reflected on this life and the next. Would there even be a next life? Would it be a life better than this one? Was I going to throw everything away and settle down in 3rd Sydney West with a wife and some children and grow old working at the Fosform office until I retired and lived out my end of days in this underground prison? Is that even a life? It seemed so fucking pointless. I needed more. There had to be more…

Oh, to hell with all of this!

I don't understand what motivation drives people to make choices. I don't know what power compelled me to do the things I did, but somewhere within that motivation and power lay the essence of freedom. Somewhere there was something more powerful than rationale, more powerful than common sense. Something within me happened. I made a choice. Choice was exactly what the Union didn't want its citizens to make. Fuck the damn Union. Fuck the Lottery. Fuck Master Stephen Haynes. Fuck 3rd Sydney West.

I made a choice.

Instead of pressing the touchscreen for Tier Two, my subconscious desire for freedom took control. I pressed for Tier One. The steel doors opened and they greeted me with the dark and foreboding maroon that I loathed.

What on Earth are you doing, Tyson? You will not get away with this.

I hadn't planned on leaving the sub-plaza, yet my freewill refused to conform. The export office and the guards would notice that today was my lottery day. I needed to come up with something, and fast.

I purchased a portable oxygen conditioner and made my way to the export office. The line was small. The export office assistant was an old, thin, veiny woman. She had grey, wiry hair and large, thick-lens glasses. Her nametag read Mary-Anne.

Are you really going to do this, Ty? You will not get away with it.

Once at the front of the queue I registered for permission via the touchscreen beside Mary-Anne. She read over the information and looked me up and down.

"It's your twenty-third birthday today," she said in a peculiar tone. I couldn't tell if it was a question or a statement. I nodded. My heart pounded. "So I will assume you haven't drawn your Lottery number yet, Mr Anderson? I also have on my records you were only up on the surface this morning. Why is it you want to go back so soon?"

I hoped to the forbidden deities that I would pull this off. "Well, Mary-Anne... I have friends on the... um... surface, you see. One of them is a woman if you catch my drift. A woman I have been close with..." I forced a smile as sweat began to flood my pores. "As it's my duty as an obedient citizen to draw a number this afternoon and find myself a wife, I think it's only right of me to see this friend of mine one last time and say goodbye. As you can imagine... Once I have a wife I'll no longer be able to see this, um, this friend of mine."

I had always been a terrible liar. What a terrible excuse. I could sense her judgement through those thick lens glasses. After what felt like a solid minute of her intense stare she smiled, revealing crooked and stained teeth. Her smile showed that somewhere in that frail old mind she was reliving memories. Maybe once she had a young man calling upon her. Maybe she felt sorry for my made-up female companion and sympathised with her. Whatever the reason, it seemed to have worked.

"Okay, Tyson Anderson. You have two hours on the surface. My shift ends in three so I expect you back here before then. Understood?"

I smiled and nodded in compliance. "Thank you, Mary-Anne."

"Good luck."

I couldn't believe it had worked. I made my way to the triple seal chamber door and stepped inside the final transporter. The door closed and the automated voice spoke through the speaker docks. "Please don your oxygen conditioners now. We will expose you to surface conditions in thirteen seconds."

TWENTY

THE DULL AND STORMY SURFACE CONDITIONS WERE HORRENDOUS.

The rain indicator beside the checkout terminal stated that current rainfall was at twenty-seven percent acidity. The weather was warm, but the wind had an unusual stench to it. Even through the filtration system I noticed it. The conditions were far less hospitable than my previous journey across the bridge.

I hoped it didn't rain. With no rain protection suit twenty-seven percent acidity could mean burns if I had prolonged exposure.

After hiring a hover-bike and exiting the compound, I took to the back streets of the western suburbs. I had no idea what I was doing. Was I prolonging the inevitable or was I going to make a dash for freedom?

If I weren't back at 3rd Sydney West by nightfall, they would put out an alert that I had failed to draw a number. If I tried to escape and soldiers caught me, they would try me for treason. I'd be jailed, killed or even worse, tortured. How much was freedom worth? Was it worth risking my life?

The optimist in me screamed yes. The passive and compliant citizen said no.

I needed time to think.

Time was something I did not have. Without the time to execute decisions I was running on pure impulse. Impulse gave me an idea. For some unknown reason, with all the chaos going through my head I thought of Eli, the kid from the dunes at Narrabeen. Despite his age and his ignorance, I thought talking with the young surface dweller could give me some insight. He said he often roamed the area and that he lived under a house on the Esplanade. I wondered if I'd be able to find him.

I turned the hover-bike northeast and made my way through the dilapidated suburbs. The whole time I speculated about what life on the run might be like. I thought about all my possessions I would need to leave behind. That didn't bother me. I thought about the people that I would leave behind. George had been like a brother to me since working on the walls and if I made a dash for freedom, a part of me felt as if I'd be abandoning him. Would he do the same to me? Did he feel the same hate and resentment towards the Union that I did? Was true friendship worth a lifetime of misery?

Shit, I needed time.

Within twenty minutes I pulled into the Collaroy parking lot. The place was deserted. A strong wind blew salty spray off the ocean, making the visibility even worse than normal. The sea breeze did well to mask any undesirable odours coming from the land. The salt spray collected on the lens of my conditioning mask and every few seconds I had to wipe the condensed droplets off to see.

I wandered up the empty Esplanade looking for Eli. Black clouds lingered over the headlands of the beaches. An electrical storm approached. The mist and low clouds made it seem like nightfall, yet somewhere behind the pollution the sun remained high in the sky.

I felt uneasy. What if I ran into those cannibals from the beach? What if they caught me and cooked me?

What if I joined them and became a surface-dwelling cannibal myself, living from day to day off the charred remains of helpless victims?

Not a chance on this hellish Earth!

I called out Eli's name every couple of minutes as I walked the esplanade. I was cautious, making sure I didn't yell too loud.

Was I making a huge mistake? Should I just go back to the sub-plaza?

Doubt was trying to make me conform. Doubt was the enemy of hope.

Soon enough, through the wispy salt haze, I spotted an old chicken shop on the far side of the street. Cracked and peeling paint covered the facade. Pine palings and thick ply boards covered where the windows had once been. Eli mentioned an access tunnel behind the chicken shop that led to his bunker. I looked around to make sure there was no one watching me and I crossed the road. I had that strange, unnerving suspicion that I was being followed but the whole place looked as deserted as the former United States.

After climbing over a corrugated iron fence beside the chicken shop, I found myself in an overgrown yard. Piles of scrap iron, bags of rotten rubbish and a jungle of vines filled the block. Fear clawed again at my back. Fear and doubt were working together, trying to lure me back to the miserable safety of 3rd Sydney West. The only thing stopping me from running back home like a frightened child was control and conformity. I would not let them win. I just couldn't.

"Eli... Eli... It's Tyson. Eli, I need your help."

Nothing.

I called out again, scanning the overgrown yard for an entry point.

Still nothing.

In the battle between doubt and hope it appeared doubt had the better tactics. I turned to leave, walking back through the piles of rotten filth when I saw something, or someone, dart across my peripheral vision. I spun on the spot and saw Eli. He was wearing the same stained T-shirt and the same tattered, filthy jeans as our first encounter. He ran for cover behind two old rusted fuel drums.

"Eli, it's me," I said in a quick, forced mumble. "We met in the dunes the other day. Remember..."

Without even rising from behind the drums and showing himself, he talked. "Of course I remember. I'm not stupid! What do you want? Why are you here? Shouldn't you be underground?" His words were thick with resentment.

"Look. I don't know why I'm here. All I know is that I'm about to be a felon. I've broken, well… I'm breaking one of the Union's laws and they'll soon be after me."

Eli rose from behind the rusty drums with a look of angst on his dirty face. "Then what the hell did you come here for? I don't want any soldiers coming round here."

"I don't intend on staying here long, but I needed to talk to someone and I didn't know where else to go. It's not like I know people on the surface. In terms of living on the surface, you have far more experience than me. I mean, I haven't spent much time up here since I was seventeen."

The young boy's expression changed from one of angst to curiosity. There may have even been sympathy behind that cautious gaze of his. More than anything, Eli seemed happy that someone had thought of him. He probably hadn't had that in a long time.

"All right, Tyson. Follow me. But hurry."

From behind the rusty oil drums Eli took a few steps towards me and leaned forward, lifting a thick wire cable from within a pile of rubbish on the ground. Pulling the cable taut revealed a sheet of cast iron. It had dirt, rubbish and even grass growing on top of it so when slotted into place it looked like any other part of the yard. Eli dragged the sheet metal to the side, exposing a small, dark hole and climbed down inside.

I followed him, climbing in with more difficulty than the scrawny teen. Once inside the small, damp, foul-smelling tunnel, Eli closed the sheet metal back over the hole.

Complete darkness enveloped the hole before Eli pulled a spot torch from somewhere and lit up the tunnel before us. The torch was not much bigger than his pinkie finger but its power was unbelievable. Lit up like a Block 7 hallway, I could see everything in fine detail. The tunnel looked like part of the old sewer system. It smelled like that, too. It was wide enough to squeeze through, but the height of the concrete passage meant crouching or crawling was the only way forwards.

Eli crawled through like a seasoned animal, while I scrambled, trying hard to avoid old gas pipes and broken storm water outlets. After about twenty metres the tunnel opened up to a height where I could stand up with ease.

I didn't know what to feel. A part of me was kicking myself for being so difficult. Why couldn't I just put up with the crooked bull-shit inside the sub-plaza like everyone else? Why did my parents raise me to be so damn opinionated? The fact that I refused to conform now had me crawling around the sewers on the surface. I refused to let the human spirit die. As long as I fled, as long as I opposed the system, the flame of the human spirit still burned within me. That was something. In that moment, that was enough.

The access room led to rotten timber stairs. Three or four of the stairs had rotted through so I needed big steps to clear the voids. Eli bounced up them with the agility of a mountain goat. I tiptoed up the broken pine, the wood creaking beneath my steps.

At the top of the stairwell a doorway opened up into a large room. Eli reached up to the ceiling and turned on two battery-oper-ated lanterns. The room lit up with a bluish white glow. Once inside, I removed my oxygen conditioner.

There were stained mattresses sprawled in the corner with old, grey woollen blankets thrown across them. Other than the mattresses, the room seemed more or less empty. There were two buckets in the far corner, which I assumed were for toileting. Dirty clothing was scattered around the room along with a touch-screen home theatre unit, two laptops and a portable music dock. Eli noticed me looking at the electronics. "Yes, it's all stolen," he said. "But the houses I steal from are empty or the tenants are dead. I figure if they don't need the shit then there's no harm in me using it."

"I guess you're right."

Man, this was depressing. It was once again a massive slap in the face. Trying to keep a straight face seeing how Eli lived was hard. I kept asking myself how much freedom was worth. Living in squalor and being free or living in hygienic grandeur with a stranger for a wife and no freedom.

"So, Tyson. What is it you came all this way to talk to me about? What advice will I be able to give you? I'm just a kid."

"Well, you've survived this long on the surface by yourself so you must be doing something right."

He stared at me.

"Look," I continued. "I don't know how much you learnt about the Union and its laws but have you heard about the Marriage Lottery?"

Eli shook his head.

"Okay… So there's a law right, that on every male citizen's twenty-third birthday, they have to draw a membership number at random from, well, tens of thousands of numbers. The number that you choose is the membership number of a registered female citizen between eighteen and thirty-five years old from anywhere in the Empire. That person, that female you pick is the person you're *forced* to marry and you're not allowed to divorce them or cheat on them or anything. You're stuck with them until you die."

"Man… That sounds okay to me. I'd love a wife one day."

Eli's response took me off guard. It was not the response I wanted. "No, Eli, don't you get it? What if it's someone who's rude and vile, or someone that has nothing in common with you. The thing is you have no choice. It doesn't sound okay at all, it sounds absolutely not fucking okay!"

"I guess so. I mean… They shouldn't be able to force you into it. What if you already love someone else?"

"Exactly!"

"Anyway, what does this have to do with you committing a crime? What does this have to do with *me*?"

"Today is *my* twenty-third birthday. Today I'm supposed to draw a number and I refuse to."

"You refuse to?"

"Yeah, look… I'd rather leave my life behind than let the Union force me into such a controlled life… I think… I want to make my way out of this horrible place. I want to escape Soteria."

"You want to *escape* Soteria?"

"Yep."

"Are you mad? Where would you go?"

"I don't care. Anywhere. Europe. Asia. South America. There have to be places in the world that are still normal. Places free from the syndrome, places that aren't governed by power hungry lunatics."

"I guess. I've never thought about it."

"Anyway, I figured you'd be able to give me some advice. I thought you might have some information on where to go, on how to get out of the Empire or something…"

Eli paused for quite some time. "Look at me, Tyson. I'm a kid. I live in a cellar connected to the old sewers. If I knew how to escape the Empire, if I knew how to be free, don't you think I would have done that, instead of wandering the streets stealing and waiting to die from this rotten damn necrosis."

"You *are* free, Eli. You have no one telling you what to do."

"Yeah, well, freedom isn't all that it's cracked up to be."

"Well here it's not. But it could be amazing outside the Empire?"

"Or it might be worse?"

Silence.

I hadn't expected this.

The two of us looked at each other. He wasn't providing the helpful insight I had hoped for.

"Well, you must have some ideas? I mean, if you *wanted to* escape what would you do?"

"Dunno. I don't know the world that well. They never taught geography when I was at school. I grew up with the Humanist Union in power so I can't really help. I've spoken to others who've tried to do similar things. Some head north and try to get through the wall by land, like up in the Northern Sector. I hear that's a long way, though. Some try to cross the wall out in the ocean. I know that the first things the others have done so they don't get tracked is remove that thing in their neck."

"You mean my registration chip?"

"Yeah. I've heard that they're also used to track people. Like a satellite locator."

My face reddened. My heart rate increased.

Panic.

Doubt.

"Are you serious? How do I not know that? How did the others know that?"

"Dunno. People talk. The walls have ears, I guess. Anyway, they cut the chip out and crush it or bury it or something."

Shit. If I haven't been to the lottery draw by 5:00 pm, they'll be able to track me down.

My world just spiralled into madness. Reality was on the verge of changing shape forever.

This was the moment.

This was where I either committed to a life on the run or went back to 3rd Sydney West with my tail between my legs.

Screw it. I'm committing. I won't let them win.

"Okay," I said to Eli. "I need to get this thing out of me! Do you have a sharp knife? Or a blue torch?"

"What, you're going to cut your chip out? Now?"

I nodded. It was a slow nod weighed down with apprehension. "Yeah, I'm gonna need your help!"

"All right," Eli said, swallowing uncertainty. "I think I've got an old multi-tool. It's got two different knife blades on it, a pair of scissors and some other stuff. I have a click-lighter, not a blue torch. That will work to heat the knife, I suppose."

"Do you have anything to drink? Like something to numb the pain?"

"Do you mean like alcohol?"

"Yeah, something like that?"

"Tyson, I'm only fourteen."

"Yeah, okay, okay. There was no harm in asking."

I had one final thought about my apartment and my job, about Laura and her programmed habits, about George and Jonah and my banana caramel shakes and frozen pizzas. In my own strange way, with a melodramatic shake of the head I said goodbye to all of it. Removing my registration chip was a first-degree felony.

Removing a chip would send anyone, Union official or not, straight to the execution chamber.

If I thought apprehension was something I had already felt, then I'd been kidding myself. The thought alone of cutting open my neck and pulling out the tiny microchip was enough to induce vomiting. I needed to toughen up if I was going to survive the foreign surface world. I needed to erase the compliant conditioning of my underworld if I wanted a taste of freedom.

There was no more time to waste.

TWENTY-ONE

ELI OFFERED TO DO THE GRUESOME TASK FOR ME.

His exposure to death, violence and gore from surviving on the surface made him perfectly suited for the task. He heated the sharpest and largest of the two blades until the stainless steel glowed orange, as best as he could, sterilising the blade.

Once it cooled down, he asked me if I was ready.

"As ready as I'll ever be…"

The initial sense of the blade entering my skin made me flinch. I clenched my teeth and fought the urge to pull away. The noise of my flesh being torn was enough to turn most people's stomachs inside out. The wound squelched as Eli dug deeper into my neck. It only took a few seconds before I felt the blade hit metal. Eli pried the chip from the wound. I tried my hardest not to, but I'm pretty sure I screamed. With a bit of wiggling it didn't take long until I heard the small metal chip hit the concrete ground behind me.

Then it was all over.

The whole thing took less than ten seconds.

Even with the knife no longer in my neck the wound throbbed in succinct rhythm with my heartbeat. The warmth of fresh blood trickled down my neck. I felt light-headed and faint. I turned around and thanked Eli.

Stone cold acceptance hit me. I was now a felon. I was a treasonous deserter. There would be no turning back. Well, not unless I picked the chip up from the concrete floor and shoved it back into the wound. I turned around and stomped on the small electric chip. It crunched under the weight of my Union issue boots.

I am now a felon.

Two very different emotions overcame me. I felt an immediate sense of ease and relief, knowing the Union could no longer track me but realisation hit me like a baton to the chest. I would no longer be able to return to the sub-plaza... Ever. The life that I knew, the life that I loathed so much, was over.

Regret.

Opportunity.

Fear.

Nausea.

"You don't look too good," Eli said to me with a straight face. "But I suppose I wouldn't either." And he laughed.

I swallowed hard to keep my breakfast down.

"Shit, Tyson. It's bleeding a fair bit. I'm not sure what to do now..."

I knew what we needed to do, but I didn't want it to happen.

I'd already endured such pain. I told myself a little more would be bearable. "We need to burn the wound," I said. "We need to heat the blade and cauterize the wound to stop the bleeding. Here, pass me the click-lighter."

Once the blade glowed violent orange, I passed it back to Eli and took a few deep breaths. The anticipation seemed worse than the pain itself. Without warning, Eli pressed the glowing blade onto the bleeding wound. It was so hot that it felt cold. I roared. Without time to move, I vomited all over my uniform. I tried so hard to keep conscious but felt myself slipping into the safe and comforting blackness.

Blurred vision.

Distorted sound.

The pain eased as a blanket of nothingness smothered me.

I woke up disorientated and wet. A slight whitish blue glow swayed from the torch hanging in the corner. It only took a few seconds before the pain returned to my neck and everything came flooding back. Eli stood beside me with a plastic cup, empty. By the water dripping from my chin it was fair to assume that he had thrown the contents of the cup on me.

"How long was I out for?"

"Uh, about five seconds, I reckon."

"Five seconds! Why the hell did you throw water on me then?"

"Dunno. It seemed like the right thing to do, I guess. How do you feel?"

"Like shit! I feel like you've stabbed me in the neck and burned me and I smell like I've just vomited all over myself."

Eli smiled. "So, what now? Do you have a plan?"

It was embarrassing. I had absolutely no plan. I didn't know where I was going and I didn't know how I planned on getting there. It's not like I had woken up with a grand plan of escape. Everything had been based on impulse. The whole thing was far from premeditated.

"Let me think... Heading to the Northern Sector is too obvious. It's what everyone would do. I need to head east via the sea, then north up through the Pacific. What I need is a boat. I need to get up to the central coast and get a boat to head to New Zealand, or even better, to New Caledonia."

"New... what?"

"Never mind. It's an island out by the walls."

When I had dreamed about my escape again and again in my mind it had always involved me venturing off on my lonesome and triumphantly climbing over the wall I helped build to find freedom on the other side. Without putting it into practice, solitude suddenly seemed overwhelming. I wasn't sure if I liked it.

I looked over at Eli. His young, innocent, blood-shot hazel eyes caught mine. "I don't suppose you wanna come with me? It's not like you've got much going on here?"

"I don't know, man. It's a long way. What if we don't make it?"

"So what? At least we tried. What are you gonna do if you stay here in Collaroy and watch people? Think about it. If we get to the Solomon Islands or Fiji and get over the wall, we could head north to China. Imagine if we got there. Imagine not needing Fosform or not needing to live underground. Imagine being able to swim in rivers and breathe the air. Imagine being able to date girls and follow whatever religion you want to follow. Just imagine…"

"Yeah, but what if China is the same as Soteria? What if China has the same rules and same problems as here?"

Although he had a valid point, I refused to let the innocence of Eli's questioning ruin my dreams.

"There's only one way to find out."

"I guess."

"So, are you going to come with me or not? I could use the company…"

"Well, I need… I mean… Okay. Screw it. You're right. It's not like I have anything to lose. Let's do it."

"Okay great. You won't regret it, Eli. Now pack your stuff. Any food or Fosform you have will be helpful. We need to get out of here ASAP. If the Union track me, it will show here as my last recorded location. Somehow, we need to get across the Hawkesbury River unseen and head for Gosford. From there we'll get a boat and head northeast."

Eli sounded unsure, but he smiled a confident grin. "Okay, let's do it."

TWENTY-TWO

Brie didn't know how long she had been awake.

Confined to a small, pitch-black cell, she drifted in and out of pain-fuelled consciousness. She had no way of knowing how long it had been since they took her from the jungle campsite but based on her dry, cracked lips and rumbling stomach it had to have been several days. As time passed, Brie experienced broken sleep, waking from horrible nightmares only to realise she was living one.

She had zero visibility. From feeling around she worked out that her cell was solid concrete, little more than a metre wide. She was naked. The concrete was coarse and prickly, cold on her bare skin. There wasn't enough room to lie flat so she sat upright against the cold, uneven wall. She had to go to the toilet several times. As best as she could, Brie tried to use the same corner of the cell but during her restless sleep she continued to roll over into her own urine. Sitting there naked, bruised, hungry and helpless, Brie Kallas began to cry.

Her jaw ballooned out to the side, tender and throbbing. Her top two front teeth were missing and her ribs felt broken. Being hit over the face by a soldier was the last thing she remembered before waking up in the uninviting blackness of the cell. She wondered if her friends were alive. She knew Francis wasn't. Sparing a thought for Bruce, Michael and Milly, she prayed they somehow escaped the brutality and unforgiving violence of the Union.

Hours passed. Brie thought they had left her in there to die. Hunger had drained her energy. Thirst had drained her wits. She slumped in the darkness, plagued with deflated defeat. Suddenly the far wall of her cell opened up, flooding the darkness with bright, white light.

Out of instinct Brie covered her groin with one hand, her breasts with the other. The brightness burned her eyes. She squeezed them shut but opened them again just as fast when someone grabbed her. It was a man. A huge man wearing bloodstained grey overalls. He picked her up and threw her over his shoulder. Well over seven feet tall with arms the size of most men's thighs, a chest like a forty-four-gallon drum and a thick ginger beard, the man held Brie and left the cell.

As her eyes adjusted to the light, she observed her surroundings. She didn't have time to panic. She was far too lethargic to attempt resisting the giant. Resistance would've been futile, anyway. The giant carried her down the bright concrete corridor with ease.

At the far end of the hall a small group of Union soldiers huddled by a large fortified door. The paint either side of the door was flaked and faded. Wherever she was, it was old. Brie saw ventilation shafts in the walls below the ceiling. She concluded that she must be underground, somewhere within Northern Sector of the Empire. Eastern Sector sub-plazas had all been constructed with steel. The concrete was a dead giveaway.

As the large man carried her past the group of soldiers, they yelled foul insults and abuse. Like a bunch of rabid dogs they snarled and swore as she came within reach. Fear coursed through her aching veins. One of the soldiers came up and slapped her hard on the bare arse cheek. Another approached her face as she hung over the back of the behemoth's shoulder. He grabbed her by the hair, snorted phlegm and spat in her face, covering her eyes with sticky, putrid saliva. "You don't realise how fucked you are, you little whore," he said, laughing. "You're going to wish you were dead!"

The behemoth walked Brie into a bright open room. White fluorescent lights lined the ceiling and white tiles covered the walls. It stunk of disinfectant. Large iron drainage grates covered the centre of the concrete floor. Clumps of human hair and dried blood hung between the grates in the floor.

Fear.

Hopelessness.

The giant threw Brie down onto the iron grates. Pain shot through her wrists as she tried to break her fall. Two soldiers walked in holding high-pressure hoses and began spraying Brie's naked body down, removing the dirt, blood, piss and grime from her bare skin. She tried to scream. Her throat was so hoarse that nothing but an airy whisper came out. The high-pressure water stabbed her bruised skin like an onslaught of needles.

After several minutes, the wash-down stopped. It left her panting and exhausted on the floor, her skin tingling and red. Despite its brutality, the wash-down had provided Brie with the opportunity to swallow some water while being sprayed. It was the first liquid she'd ingested in days.

The behemoth walked back in, his huge black gum boots keeping him dry as he took enormous strides across the flooded floor.

"Please," Brie whispered. "Please don't hurt me. I'm sorry, please."

The behemoth didn't respond. Instead, he picked Brie back up, threw her over his shoulder and carried her out into the bright corridor, down a flight of steel stairs and into another cell. Although damp and mouldy, it had lights, a flushing toilet and a foam mattress. It was a vast improvement from her previous cell.

The behemoth threw her down on the worn mattress and turned to leave. As he did so, three soldiers entered and pushed closed the rusty iron door. The hinges groaned. Anything outside of the damp cell ceased to exist. Reality now consisted of Brie, alone and naked on a mattress on the floor, and three sex-starved soldiers. One of them was the man who spat in her face in the corridor. He adjusted his manhood in his pants as he stared at Brie.

"You know what happens to little whores who murder Union Advisors in cold blood?" He began unbuttoning his Union-issue trousers with a sadistic smirk. "Well, you're about to find out..."

Another soldier, short, blonde, with a greying goatee beard, leaned over the bed and grabbed Brie around the neck. She tried kicking at him. He grabbed her leg and easily overpowered her. With the malice of a starved predatory animal, the blonde soldier punched Brie twice in the nose. Two quick jabs. Her eyes welled with tears as blood poured from both nostrils, filling her mouth with the metallic taste of blood. Hysteria masked the pain. She knew what was about to take place. She had endured it before. It brought back scarring memories of her late husband.

Along with the short, blonde guy, a muscular dark-skinned man held Brie down while the first soldier, now semi-naked and erect, climbed on top of her and forcefully rammed himself inside her. She screamed. She pleaded for mercy. He hit her across the face and began thrusting. "This is what you get, you whore. You better damn-well like it!"

The dark-skinned soldier silenced Brie's helpless screams as he shoved a dirty, bloodstained rag deep into her mouth. Because of the thick blood clogging her nostrils, breathing became difficult. She closed her eyes to take herself away from the hellish ordeal. It was futile. The pain kept bringing her back. Like some kind of sick karma, they punished Brie for killing her rapist husband with the same inhumane abuse.

Once the first soldier finished inside her, the short, blonde soldier removed his pants and entered her. He proved far more violent. He belted her across the face as he had his way with her, moaning with sick satisfaction. Brie pleaded to God for it to end. It didn't. They forced her down onto the mouldy mattress as the animalistic thrusting continued. The blonde soldier ejaculated in her and swapped with the third, dark-skinned soldier.

Nausea came in ferocious waves as her manic heartbeat hammered. Tears blurred her bloodshot eyes. Blood dripped from her chin. Brie thought death might be coming. She hoped it did. Anything was better than living this nightmare.

The three soldiers flipped Brie over onto her stomach and held her legs apart as the last soldier entered her from behind.

"A real whore loves it in the arse," he said before shoving himself inside. Brie tried screaming through the rag. They were pointless screams. There was no one there to hear her.

The pain was intolerable. The trauma was crippling. The dark-skinned soldier grabbed Brie by the hair and continued to penetrate her violently. After a minute of torturous pain, he too finished inside her. He wiped his manhood on Brie's pillow, stood up from the mattress and spat on Brie as she lay shaking on the worn foam. "Next time you better be wetter for me!"

The three satisfied soldiers replaced their pants and exited the room, laughing. They left Brie on the bed as blood and semen leaked out from inside her. Far too traumatised to move, Brie shook uncontrollably with the rag still in her mouth. After a few minutes of semi-conscious shaking, she built up the psychological energy to remove the rag as she vomited violently on the floor.

Rolling over proved too difficult at first. Brie's face and ribs were bruised, possibly broken. Her groin throbbed, raw, torn and bleeding. In such agony and hopelessness, she wished to die. Right there, as she lay in a bloody, wet patch on the mattress she wished for it all to end. She curled up into the foetal position and cried helpless tears.

Brie drifted away, traumatised and shivering. She woke, startled, only minutes later to the sound of someone entering the room.

Expecting the worst, Brie opened her eyes to see the giant, red-bearded behemoth standing at the entrance to the room with a plastic bottle full of water and a bowl of slop. Whether the bowl contained thick soup or watery porridge, Brie could not tell. He placed both items on the ground and left the room only to return straight away with a pair of tracksuit pants and a ragged old woollen jumper.

"It'th the betht I can do for you," he said with a deep voice. He had a distinct lisp and a foreign accent. He walked over to the bed and handed Brie the clothing. "Put thith on tho you don't get thick. If you get thick in here, you will motht probably die."

The behemoth turned and left the room, sliding the steel door closed and locking it as he departed. Brie had conflicting emotions about him. He worked for the Union. He threw her on the ground as if she were nothing more than a bag of rubbish. He let the soldiers violate her, but somewhere in that strange voice Brie sensed compassion.

One small agonising movement at a time Brie pulled the track pants up over her waist and slipped into the woollen jumper. Both were too big for her and they smelled of someone else's sweat but it was far better than the exposed nakedness she had known for days.

She crawled over to the water and gruel in the middle of the cell. She sat on the cold concrete and tried to stomach as much as possible. The gruel tasted like stale and over-cooked oats mixed with something she couldn't quite put her finger on. It tasted acidic, metallic almost. Despite the bland and metallic taste and despite her lack of teeth and swollen, bleeding lips, Brie ate the entire bowl, even wiping the dregs with her finger and licking her finger clean. She took the water bottle, guzzled half of its contents in one go and carried it back to the mattress. She lay down exhausted and stared at the water-stained ceiling.

Fear was no longer an emotion Brie could feel. They had fucked the fear right out of her. She was so far past fear, now. She had been beaten, starved, tortured and raped. There was nothing else to be afraid of.

Lying on the filthy mattress she began to think about how many other people, people like her, had been tortured and raped in that very facility, in that very room, on that very bed.

Had someone died on that mattress?

She began to consider death. Would it be so bad? If they planned on keeping her alive to endure more torture and rape, she would embrace death with open arms. The morbid thoughts and dire circumstances brought on more tears. The thought of never again seeing freedom was too hard to bear. She had had such a short taste, a tease. She had only just found out what it was like to know true friends, true love even, and it had been taken away from her as quickly as she found it.

Her thoughts drifted from death and torment to Michael Butcher. She pictured his warm smile and strong muscles, his blonde hair and his hypnotic blue eyes. She wondered if they had killed him in the jungle. What if he had survived? What if they held him captive? What if he was in the same sub-plaza, in the same corridor? In the room next door, even? The tiniest spark of hope, like the last burning ember in a campfire, lifted her spirits.

TWENTY-THREE

THE AFTERNOON SUN RESTED ON THE OVERGROWN HORIZON IN THE jungle labyrinth of the Northern Sector.

The weather was cold for the tropics, even for late Pride. Evan and Remy sat high in the branches of T-Tree, the tall brown Salwood tree above the main entrance to T-Town. It was Evan's usual lookout post but for him it also served as a place of solace and comfort.

They began to worry. It had been seven days since Bruce, Francis and the others left and there had been no word of their progress. Evan knew that the team had satellite communications for emergencies, but he assumed the others had stayed off the satellite phone for fear of being tracked. He refused to think the worst.

In Bruce's absence, Evan had taken a leadership role in the outlaw community. He did his best to keep both morale and production rate high. There hadn't been enough digging going on; there hadn't been enough hunting, either. It seemed as if the T-Towners were waiting around the bunker for the return of their fellow outlaws with a big sack filled with Fosform Five.

It hadn't yet come.

"What are we going to do if they don't come back?" Remy asked Evan, breaking a long and drawn out silence.

"Don't speak like that, Remy. They will come back. If you think bad things, bad things will happen. We just need to remain positive and keep everyone else positive."

"Yeah, okay, I get it… But what if they *don't* come back? The Fosform we have will only last everyone another month, then we'll start getting sick."

"Look, I don't want to talk about it. We'll cross that bridge when we get to it. *If* we get to it!"

The day dragged on with little conversation.

The birds noticed it before Evan and Remy did. Their constant song changed its tune. At first it was barely noticeable, but it became louder as each bird fell silent. There was a distant hum. It seemed to get closer. Without a doubt in Evan's mind, it sounded like some kind of vehicle. It wasn't the sound of one of the hover-bikes with which the others had departed. That was certain. The noise was louder than a hover-bike, a higher pitch, more of a whine than a hum.

"Shit, do you hear that? It sounds like a motorbike?"

Remy looked at Evan. "What should we do?"

"It's coming from the south. Grab your rifle and get low."

Remy settled into a more secluded viewpoint. Tension filled the humid air around them. Uncertainty climbed its way up the limbs of the tree to their vantage point. The clacking whine of a two-stroke engine became louder as the two guards sat frozen, waiting for the bike and its rider to appear through the thick undergrowth. Evan's aimed his taser cannon at the ground beneath them.

A single motorbike appeared, an old, dinged-up dirt bike. At first one man was visible riding the bike. He wore what looked like a Union soldier's helmet. Evan placed his finger on the trigger, keeping the man in his sights. On the back of the bike, tied to the chassis appeared to be another person lying down. The bike came to a stop under T-Tree, right before the entrance to T-Town.

"What the hell?" Remy whispered.

Evan didn't reply.

The rider stepped off the bike, looked around and removed his helmet. Hope, desperation, happiness and fear all flooded Remy's thoughts in the single overwhelming moment the rider removed his helmet. It was Michael Butcher.

"Michael," Remy yelled out as she placed her rifle back down in its crude holster in the tree. She pounced down between the branches. Evan slung the taser cannon over his shoulder and followed her.

Michael looked exhausted. Dirt and dried blood covered his filthy face. His clothes looked like tattered rags, unrecognisable from when he had left only a week earlier. Evan noticed Bruce unconscious and tied to the back of the bike. Something terrible had happened.

"Bloody hell, Mickey. Here let me help you," Evan said, grabbing Michael by the shoulder. "You look terrible. Where are the others? What's wrong with Bruce?"

"Bruce isn't doing too well, mate. He's lost a shit-load of blood and I reckon he's lost his left hand. Shit got heavy down there. We lost the others. Let's get Bruce inside and cleaned up and I'll tell you all about it."

Evan and Remy carried Bruce down into the thin, dim tunnel and placed him onto his bed. His breathing was shallow and slow. His face was pale. Michael had wrapped his left hand, or what was left of it, in a blood-soaked rag. The resident medic, Gabbie, carried in a first-aid kit, some medication, some hot water and some Fosform and wasted no time in cleaning up Bruce's dirty wounds.

Word travelled through the bunker of Michael and Bruce's return. Everyone put their tasks on hold and met in the main communal kitchen where Michael sat with Evan, wiping blood, dirt and grime from his face.

All the T-Towners waited for Michael to talk. They filled the room with mixed emotions. The mood had lifted but at the same time, concern filled the small bunker. People seemed glad to see Michael and Bruce return, but it was also clear that from the original six, four people hadn't returned and they had no Fosform.

No Fosform meant serious trouble.

LJ DUNCAN

Michael took a deep breath, settled back onto the wooden back-rest of his chair and began. "So, we started off great," he said, looking around at his comrades. They crowded around like excited fans at a music concert, eager to hear his story. "We made good progress and we almost got to KL when we ran into some weird voodoo sacrificial offering. We met resistance there, not Union resistance but God-crazed maniacs. Surface dwellers. We lost Caleb straight away. He got shot and died right there in Milly's arms."

In unison, people in the room made a sigh of sympathy. Others muttered insults under their breath.

"We wasted a fair bit of ammunition there but we buried Caleb as best as we could and we got within a few hours of KL to set up for the night. Everything went fine. Well, except losing Caleb, you know? Francis took watch, Brie, Milly and Bruce slept by the fire and I was taking a piss when out of nowhere, with no bloody noise at all, they were on us. Union soldiers, armoured, dressed in their grey fatigues, shooting at us. I can't put my finger on it, but somehow they knew we were there. It's like they were waiting for us. I tried fighting but there were too many of them. I killed one guy. I stuck him with his own knife. I made a run to the bushes to the north, dropped inside a rotten tree stump and watched. I didn't want to flee, but I just followed my instinct. I'm not a coward or anything, there was just so much gunfire and blood and screaming and death…"

Michael stopped and wiped a lone tear from his left eye. He blinked, trying hard to subdue any more. "They killed Francis like a fuckin' animal. They shot him in the heart then cut off his fuckin' head. They got Milly too. They shot Bruce a few times, but he somehow pulled shock balls out and started throwing them in all directions, lighting the jungle up like fireworks on the last day of Gluttony. He killed a good half of the soldiers but one of the shock-balls exploded just as he threw it. I watched him get blasted through the jungle from the force, a good ten metres into the canopy of a tree. He hasn't woken since."

The other residents sat in silence with wide eyes. Some looked distressed, others looked furious, but every one of them listened intently.

"Anyway… Through the darkness, I watched them get Brie. They didn't kill her. They started talking to her. They *knew* her name. It's like they were hunting her or something. They called her Brie *van Bueren*… One soldier roughed her up a bit and then they picked her up and just left. They took Milly and Francis' bodies with them. God knows why. I sat in the tree stump for a good twenty minutes until I was sure they'd left then I found Bruce. He was breathing but bleeding badly. I wrapped him up then went looking around for our stuff. They shot our hover-bikes to shit. They destroyed all three—"

"Shit! What did you do next?" Seb, one of the older T-Towners interrupted.

"Well, I gathered what little food I had left into a rucksack, left Bruce under some large leaves with a note in case he woke up and I headed west down the hill to find something to get us home. After a few clicks I came across an old farming town. There was no one around. A bunch of old vehicles lay scattered through the yards. Not one of them started. I felt like I had just gone back in time. I mean, the most modern vehicle there was an electro-Hilux from the mid 30s. Its tyres were rotten and weeds grew out of the tray. The whole place spooked me.

"I opened up an old shed and found the motorbike underneath a canvas tarpaulin. The keys were in the ignition and somehow, after six or seven attempts to turn it over, it choked itself to life. I grabbed what smelt like unleaded fuel in a plastic container, duct-taped it to the side of the bike and went back for Bruce. I expected him to be dead when I got back, but he wasn't. He was still unconscious, still breathing. I threw him on the bike and duct-taped him to the chassis so he wouldn't fall off, then I just started riding. It's been three days since they took Brie."

"Why the hell did they take her?"

"Man, I wish I knew."

"How the hell did they know her *name*?"

"I have no idea guys. They killed the others, but for whatever reason they wanted her alive…"

Remy's face began to change a few shades darker. She felt her cheeks burn. She knew why. She knew what Brie had done, but had promised not to tell anyone. Remy was the only one there that knew the truth about Brie's past. Was it okay to break the promise now? The circumstances were now different.

Brie was long gone.

Brie could be dead.

If she wasn't, she was *as good as dead*.

Remy sat there for a minute, juggling her thoughts. She wanted to tell the others. She convinced herself that in the current situation telling the others seemed acceptable. Brie would have done the same thing. She cleared her throat.

"Brie was married to Peter van Bueren," she said, interrupting the concerned chatter amongst the residents. The chatter ceased. "In the Marriage Lottery, one of the Empire's most powerful Union officials drew Brie's number. He used to rape her and beat her."

"How do you know this?" Gabbie interrupted.

"She told me one day out hunting. According to Brie, Peter held influence within the Humanist Union. He could get away with whatever he wanted. She even tried going to the Bishop for counsel but he sent her away, saying the Peter van Bueren was untouchable."

"Jesus Christ," Michael Butcher said, angered. "What a sick bastard!"

"Anyway, one night Brie had enough and killed him. She beat him to death with a whisky bottle and left his body in their sub-plaza apartment. She left Brisbane and went on the run. This all happened in the months before she arrived here. From what Michael has said, the Union have found her. Peter van Bueren was a close friend, or at least an ambitious student of Master Stephen Haynes."

"Well, shit," Evan said, shaking his head. "She's as good as dead."

"I don't think so," said Michael. "The Union won't kill her.

They'll keep her alive as long as bloody possible and make her pay for her sins. Even more of a reason to find her and get her out."

In unison with a few others, Seb laughed. His tone thick with passive aggression. "Get her out?" Seb said. "What do you mean *get her out*? She's in an underground plaza somewhere, in a cell, being guarded by Union soldiers. And what? You're just going to walk into the place and take her. Yeah, righto, Mickey!"

"Well, I dunno. But I'm not gonna leave her there."

"That's how this works, mate," Seb said, raising his voice. "We're outlaws. We lose our comrades, our friends, our lovers. Milly and Caleb are gone. Francis is fuckin' gone. We can't just storm into the Devil's lair and take him on. Even thinking that is diluted stupidity. I mean she's a nice girl and all that but we only knew her for, like a week at most. She's still a stranger to most of us."

"I don't care. There's something about that girl I will not give up on."

"Well, then... Soon enough we'll be sitting around this table again mourning over your bloody death! It's stupidity!"

"Look," Evan interrupted. "One step at a time. Mickey, you're tired. Bruce is in a damn coma. How about we all get some rest and we can have this discussion when everyone is a little calmer? Brie is no doubt going to end up back to wherever she fled from. If Union officials want to speak with her, they won't travel north to KL, they'll send her south. Even if you wanted to go rescue her like a knight in shining armour, it's not like you're gonna get on a bike tomorrow and head to the Australian mainland. Everyone needs to chill out."

"You're right, Evan, you're right," said Michael. "I need some damn sleep. Step one is making sure Bruce is okay. Step two is getting the bloody tunnel finished so we can get out of here. I'm just tired, that's all. If you'll excuse me, I need to go lie down."

Most of the crowd dispersed as Michael left the communal bunker. He reached his sleeping quarters, lay down on his hardened mattress and without even the time to process the conversation that took place, sleep claimed him.

For Remy, the opposite occurred. Once in bed, sleep wouldn't come. She lay on her back staring at the dirt above her. She thought of Brie. She could only imagine what kind of punishment Brie would endure because of her treasonous murder and escape. She knew that they would endeavour to keep Brie alive until they had broken her. With the purest intentions, Remy hoped that Brie was dead and buried and free from suffering.

TWENTY-FOUR

It had just gone sundown.

The Army would be looking for me by now. I was a fugitive. I was a treasonous felon. The Union would search every nook of 3rd Sydney West for me. After that, they would be tracking my chip.

Good luck with that.

Eli suggested I leave the hover-bike at Collaroy. He wasn't certain but since removing my registration chip, paranoia had set in. He thought the Union might track citizens through sub-plaza hire vehicles. He had a valid point. I erred on the side of caution and abandoned the bike.

We found solar-cycles in a garage just outside Mona Vale. Solar-cycles had a period of popularity in the late-twenties, for teenagers and young adults. Their popularity waned when affordable hover technology became available. Generating enough silent energy to power the chain through solar power, there were no pedals. In their place were small foot-pegs and there was only one gear. The tyres were made from a compound but soft plastic, meaning the wheels would never go flat or require replacement.

We headed north through the outer suburbs without incident. TNS had left the streets deserted. Before long we reached the old

Barrenjoey Lighthouse at the top of the hill on the headland. The once-famous tourist attraction lay in ruins, covered in graffiti and vandalised. The large sandstone blocks that had stood for two centuries lay sprawled across the ground as if someone had knocked the lighthouse clean off its foundations. From the tip of the over-grown peninsula I looked out over Pittwater and the Hawkesbury River and made out the land on the other side. The other side of Pittwater, once a National Park, later became used in the Artificial Revolution to house massive factories and indoor farms. Silhouetted in the dull twilight, the enormous chimney stacks in the distance bellowed black filth up into the already tainted and poisonous air. Further north, across the Hawkesbury itself, our salvation waited.

Crossing the Hawkesbury River seemed like it might be easier than I had first expected. I had images of bridges lit up by huge flood-lights, guarded by swarms of armed soldiers. That was not the case at all. The banks of the river were silent. There, at the tip of the penin-sula guarding our freedom, was nothing other than foul-smelling, swamp-like muck. I feared that if I got any of the muck on me, I would get sick. Eli assured me that the river water, because of its prox-imity to the saline water of the sea, was no more harmful than the air. Judging by the overpowering smell, I wasn't sure if I believed him.

We found an old aluminium dinghy discarded and flipped beside a stretch of abandoned weatherboard shacks.

"I reckon we can use this to cross the river," I said as I flipped the small boat upright.

"Man, it's a long way. But I suppose it beats swimming."

"Here, grab the other side. Let's drag it to the water's edge."

The electric circuits had long since corroded away so the inboard jets wouldn't spark. Instead, we needed to use the boat in its most primitive form. We threw our rusted solar-cycles into the boat then began searching for whatever we could to act as oars.

We pushed the small boat through the muck and paddled out into the stagnant, black water. I used a fibreglass water ski while Eli used a weatherboard panel off the side of a fisherman's shack. Both items seemed to work all right.

In the darkness we guessed the river to be four hundred metres wide. Once out from behind the willow trees, I felt the boat move from underneath us. Out in the channel the current was strong, much stronger than near the shore.

"Shit," Eli said to me, his face almost invisible in the evening twilight. "The tide must be going out or something. The current shouldn't be this strong. Here, paddle hard."

We started putting in long, fast strokes to fight the current but our small vessel seemed to have a mind of its own, controlled by the moving water underneath us. I looked back. We had only got about one hundred metres from the shore but already the holiday shacks were over three hundred metres away, shrinking in the distance to nothing more than blurred shapes in the darkness.

Shit. At this rate it will suck us out to sea.

I started to panic. I paddled in unison with Eli, who, strangely, seemed a little too calm. I was freaking out. I stood up and put everything I had into the long, fast strokes. The boat rocked beneath us. It began to spin from the whirling water. All of a sudden the boat turned backwards. We changed position and began paddling the other way.

In the disorientating drama, it occurred to me that splashes of the foul-smelling sludge were landing all over me. I started to panic about the slop but somehow told myself I could only afford to panic about one thing at a time.

By the time we made it halfway across the river we were a great deal closer to the sea than I wanted to be. My arms burned with lactic acid. My heart pounded. I wasn't sure how much longer I could paddle with such ferocity. By the drop in the efficiency and power of Eli's paddle strokes it seemed he was in the same boat. No pun intended.

"Wait, Tyson. I've got an idea," Eli said, still calm but breathing heavily. "Let's stick our oars in behind the boat to act as rudders. That way we can use the current, not fight against it. If we put rudders in on the right angle, I reckon we'll be able to veer across the river."

"You know what? You're smart for a fourteen-year-old. I wouldn't have thought of that."

We put Eli's theory to test.

At first nothing appeared to happen, we just rocked with the current side-to-side, down towards the mouth and closer to the violent waves. My panic had not subsided at all. It increased with every metre closer we came to the mouth of the river. I changed the angle of the water ski, pushing it hard to the left and we seemed to glide diagonally across the channel.

I smiled in the darkness. "It's working!" I yelled. "Push harder Eli, it's working!"

The river mouth was only a stone's throw away. I could hear the waves crashing on the sandbar. I couldn't see them yet, but the noise brought chills to my bones. We kept veering until the northern shore of the river seemed within reach.

Hope still remained.

The current eased as we got in leeward of the land and we slowed down, starting to paddle at a less chaotic pace. I wiped drips from my forehead, unsure if it was sweat or infested river water. The last remaining twilight had left us; Eli and the shrub-covered shore-line were nothing but silhouettes. With each passing moment, the twilight turned darker. With so much smog in the sky and no moon-light, we would soon travel in pitch-blackness.

We left the vessel on the muddy edge of the tidal flats and continued around the peninsula towards the outer Gosford area. East Gosford housed the only sub-plaza in the Central Coast region so staying along the coast, while taking longer, would prove safer. At least that's what we hoped.

Once we reached the outskirts of deserted suburbia our pace increased, and so did my paranoia. TNS and rising sea levels had hit those neighbourhoods hard so, like most coastal suburbs, the resi-dents were long gone. It had only been half a decade since people had moved underground, but in that time, things had deteriorated so much.

Because of war, industrialisation, poverty and crime, the outer suburbs had become a forgotten and rotten environment. Electrical power, running water and gas was no longer supplied the outer suburbs, so we travelled along a once busy and well-maintained family friendly urban road in total blackness. Invasive weeds smothered the houses. Weatherboard panels lay rotting beside crumbled buildings. Every so often we passed an old boarded-up house and we could make out the faint flicker of candlelight or the glow of torchlight within. People were inside. I wondered what sort of people they might be. Most probably people like Eli, innocent victims of the changing world left to suffer. I didn't want to take any chances running into anyone in case they were not like Eli at all. They could have been people like the cannibals from Narrabeen, or worse.

"How are you feeling?" I asked as we cycled through the winding streets of the headland. "I reckon it must almost be midnight. If we keep up a pace like this, we should be on board a boat by sunrise."

"I'm okay, I guess," Eli responded. "A little tired... How do you feel?"

"It's all a little surreal," I said. "I mean, I've thought about my lottery for so long. It's haunted me for weeks, months even. I can't believe I cut out my chip and escaped my sub-plaza."

"Are you having second thoughts?"

I didn't respond right away. "No, absolutely not," I said. "I'm just a little scared, that's all."

Eli stayed silent. He processed my response and we continued to cycle through the quiet streets.

"Hey Tyson," Eli said after minutes of silence. "Do you know if the Union keeps watch over the water? Do they patrol the sea? Otherwise it would be too easy to grab a boat and leave?"

"Yeah, I'm sure there will be patrols. I'm just hoping luck will be on our side and we slip past them. All we can do is try, right?"

"Uh-huh... So how's your neck?"

"It feels like shit. It feels like TNS has found a new breeding ground," I said, smiling in the darkness. "Look, I get that you don't know me at all but I wanna thank you for coming along with me. Having to do all this on my own would have made things much harder. I don't know why I came to see you in the first place, but I'm sure glad I did."

"Hey, no worries. In the past four hours I've had the most excitement I've had in years, so you know what, I'm glad you did too."

Eli's comment made me smile.

As midnight flowed into early morning, the land before us began to rise. From our high point we could see west out over the Central Coast hub, and in particular, Gosford and its sub-plaza terminal. It didn't seem that far away. It was lit up for kilometres around it, high power lights marking the Union-controlled perimeter. I could make out the headlights of vehicles moving around in the distance. The place thrived with movement, even at the earliest hours of the morning.

Soldiers never sleep.

"Okay, let's stay along the coast from now on. If we get to Terrigal, we can steal a boat from the hydro-harbour there."

I knew about Terrigal's hydro-harbour because when working out on the walls, rations and supplies would come via hybrid boats and the crew often told me where they had come from. More than once the crew spoke of a harbour at Terrigal.

About a kilometre from Terrigal and a few hours before sunrise, Eli and I came across our first real challenge. Because of the damming of the Avoca River, the only usable thoroughfare between North Avoca and Terrigal was a bitumen road that climbed up over the headland. Perched on top of the craggy hillside sat a menacing steel and concrete Union fortress.

It had been built high on the headland, guarding the harbour we aimed for. It had pivoting spotlights on turrets close to fifty metres off the ground. The spotlights were unlike anything fathomable. They looked bright enough to burn holes through clothing at close range. It was as if mankind had extracted a part of the sun and was holding it within these giant light globes. Giant light globes that searched back and forth along the shore, into the massive hydro-harbour and out to sea. It was a devastating sight.

"Shit," I whispered. "This is *not* fucking good. There's no way

we can get into the harbour with that bloody light on us...
Damn it!"

Despair and doubt.

Doubt was the enemy of hope.

"We have a better chance trying to get a boat in broad
daylight," Eli said.

Hope.

"But we will be exposed once we get out to sea, I suppose."

"We're exposed out there either way. Look how bloody powerful
those lights are! The soldiers in that tower could see a damn plastic
bag floating five hundred metres offshore. There's no way we can
get in and out of that harbour. Not now, not in daylight, never!"

Doubt seemed to win.

"Well, what do you suggest?"

"Shit..." I stared at the massive concrete tower, chewing my
bottom lip. "We can't try to sneak around it. God knows how many
soldiers are up there watching. God knows what sort of artillery that
place has set up, aiming out of those turrets. We're better off
walking straight up to it, straight past it, like we do it every day. You
know, like, if we look like we're not doing anything out of the ordi-
nary then we can walk right past..."

"Really?" Eli said, doubtful. "That's the worst suggestion I've
ever heard. All they need to do is stop us and try to scan your chip,
see the wound on your neck and it's all over..."

"Yeah, but heaps of surface dwellers don't have chips."

"All I'm saying is that if they ask to scan you, we're done for."

Eli was right. That was a huge risk to take. That was stupidity.

"Okay, we have to go back then. We need to get a boat from
somewhere else."

"Back?"

I needed to remain positive. I had no choice. It wasn't like I
could just go home. I was on the run now forever. I needed to be a
leader. If I started doubting myself, then Eli would start doubting
me too. Eli had the ability to turn around and leave if he chose to. I
did not.

"We will swim," I said.

"Swim? What do you mean, swim? We can't swim to New Cale-donia. Are you mad?"

"No, don't be stupid. See those lights, right?"

Eli looked out to where I pointed.

"They're scanning the beach and the water but underneath the tower, at the base of the headland, there are the rocky cliffs sepa-rating the two beaches, yeah?"

"And…"

"So the cliffs act as a barrier to the light, right? Because of the angle of the hill, if we stick as close to the cliffs as possible, we might get into the harbour unseen."

Eli looked down at the cliff line below. Even in the darkness he could sense the power of the waves crashing against the weathered rocks, but he could see what I meant.

The steep angle of the headland restricted the lights' rays from reaching the water right at the base of the cliff line. There was a blind spot. The distance between the two beaches stretched a couple hundred metres. If we drifted out into deeper water, the lights on the tower would undoubtedly spot us. Alternatively, if we swam too close to the cliffs, the unforgiving fury of the swell would crush us into the rocks. We needed to stay right in the blind spot for the entire length of the cliff.

"I dunno, Tyson. I'm not the best swimmer. I mean, I want this as much as you but is it worth dying for?"

I squatted down and grabbed Eli by the shoulders. Even though I couldn't see his face in the blackness, I did my best to look into his eyes. I did my best to sound confident. "Eli, what did you tell me only a few days ago… You said that you were just waiting to *die*, didn't you?"

Eli shuffled beside me, but said nothing.

"So how is this any different? At least you now have a purpose. It's three hundred metres. That's not that far and I'm sure we can wade through the water for the most of it. If we get into the harbour, we can find a boat, get inside it and wait."

"Wait…"

"Yep. We hide, like a stowaway and wait inside a boat until the owner or driver or whatever leaves the harbour. We wait until we're well away from land and then we come out from hiding and…"

"And what? Are we gonna kill them? I don't know if I like your plan too much at all. I don't know if I want to kill anyone."

"We won't kill them. We'll just throw them overboard or something. Or make a deal with them… Look, I dunno. We'll work that out when we get to it. I never said this was gonna be easy, but it's better than living in the damn sewers *waiting to die*! Now come on!"

TWENTY-FIVE

WITHOUT WAITING FOR ELI'S APPROVAL, I BEGAN WALKING DOWN the steep slope towards the bay south of the fortress.

I abandoned my solar-cycle. The hill down to the beach was too steep to ride with any control. The hillside had once been home to timber bungalows and holiday homes but, like the rest of the region, residents had deserted it. Eli took a minute to think about things then swiftly followed suit, jogging down the hill behind me.

"Wait for me," he called through the darkness.

We weaved through the backyards of ruined houses, climbing over fences from yard to yard, staying hidden from the all-watchful lights of the tower above. I found it strange that such an extreme security measure existed on a stretch of the coast that seemed all but deserted. Other than the hydro-harbour there didn't seem to be anything else around. Why had the Union built a lookout post of such size? What was it protecting? What was inside that hydro-harbour?

By the time we made it to the sand at the northern tip of the bay, the rocky cliff top blocked the tower from view. I saw the sweeping lights going back and forth over the deeper black water. The daunting sound of the waves echoing off the jagged rocks deafened us. They sounded powerful, ferocious. Nausea rumbled against my throat. Doubt started to seep through the cracks.

Doubt was the enemy of hope. I needed hope on my side to win this battle. Hope was what the Humanist Union was afraid of. Hope would get us inside that harbour.

"Right. Are you ready for this, Eli?"

I didn't get an answer.

"We can do it, mate. Just stay near me and let's stay as close to the cliffs as we can."

"What about our bag? What about our rations?"

"Here, pass me the bag and I'll take it." I strapped the bag to my shoulders, tightened the shoulder straps and continued walking across the thick, wet sand.

In the darkness, drowned by the noise of the water crashing against sandstone, I entered the oily black water one apprehensive step at a time. The temperature was comfortable. I hadn't been in the ocean in years. With TNS so prevalent in the water at most of Sydney's beaches, the Union had outlawed swimming around the time I started high school. As I was on the surface without an oxygen conditioner anyway, I either needed a Fosform dose real quick or I would be dead in a week. I tried not to visualise my organs rotting and instead focused on the job in hand.

The extensive wall of rock to our left stretched all the way to Terrigal hydro-harbour. Maybe I underestimated the distance. In the darkness it seemed a lot further than three hundred metres. Doubt started paddling in the murky water beside me.

Doubt is the enemy of hope.

Eli stayed right by my side and before long, still wading, the first set of waves came rolling through. With the moon hidden by thick smog, visibility was low. We needed to rely on the sound of the waves to duck under them. They weren't as powerful as I first expected, but then again, we weren't beside the cliffs yet. Doggy-paddling to conserve energy, I paddled north, staying only metres from the rocks. I looked out to the east and watched the powerful beam of white light illuminate the water only metres to my right. The cliff only just disguised our approach. If we drifted any more than ten metres from the rocks, it would expose us, caught like a deer in headlights.

"Are you all right?" I turned and asked Eli.

"For the time being I am. I can still touch the bottom. But we've only gone about twenty metres, Tyson. Ask me again when we're halfway."

"Try not to swallow any water. It's bad enough that this water is touching our skin but if we swallow it we're as good as dead."

"I guess this is what living life on the edge is all about, huh?"

"Not if it's gonna kill us from the syndrome, Eli. Then it will all be in vain."

After another fifty metres I felt trapped, vulnerable. I wanted nothing more than to turn around, but knew I couldn't. If I was this damn frightened, I couldn't imagine how Eli felt. It was all the more terrifying not being able to see anything. I could hear the water between sets lapping at the jagged sandstone and I could hear the waves rolling in off the sandbar. I could hear Eli panting behind me. I could hear all these things but I couldn't see a damn thing. The darkness fuelled my fear.

Fear dampened all other emotions as I sensed a huge wave come rolling towards me. I tried to brace myself as it hit. I held my breath as it sent me rolling through the black water. After tumbling a few times I broke the surface with just enough time to take a few breaths, regain a sense of my surroundings then get hit by another, larger wall of water. It sent me upside down, spinning with its unrelenting force. My leg hit a rock, then my chest hit a rock and then I felt the cold, sharp surface of the cliff face.

As the water receded from the rocky ledge, it dragged me from the rocks and dropped into the deeper churning water. Coming up, I gasped for air, spluttering in the darkness. Despite the lack of visibility, I scanned the water for Eli.

"Eli, are you there" I called out between deep breaths. The waves had moderated between sets to smaller, manageable walls of white water. There was no response. The white lights of the tower scanned the depths a little further out. Panic rose with every gasping breath. "Eli, where are you?"

Choking. Sputtering. Splashing. I turned towards the cliff. Only metres away, nearer to the rocky ledge, Eli threw his arms around, lashing out at the surface of the water.

"Are you all right," I asked, swimming towards him, grabbing him around the shoulders and holding him up.

"I told you I was a shit swimmer," he said, coughing.

"Well, we can't stop now, let's keep going. We need to time our duck-dives with the waves, though. If we dive under them before they hit us, they'll just roll straight past. C'mon, mate. We can do this."

We got another hundred metres, maybe more, blindly duck-diving under the waves as they approached us. Our progress slowed. My muscles ached. The darkness of the sky turned into a milky grey. I could see the waves coming now from quite a distance. We had to hurry. The sun would soon be rising.

Another set rolled in, bigger and more ferocious. A huge wall of broken, furious white-water threw itself towards us. I heard Eli curse. Taking a deep breath, I dived under. The rolling power of the wave pulled me and dragged down deep, spinning and tumbling. I hit the cliff ledge again, hard. The impact knocked all the air out of me. I felt the backpack get torn from my shoulders.

Panic.

I didn't know which way was up.

All I wanted to do was breathe, but I knew it would kill me if I did. I fought the urge to inhale and kicked for the surface. Once I broke through, I faced a whirling, choppy, rocky torrent of moving water but at least I could breathe. Eli bobbed in the water five metres out, not caught by the grasp of the previous wave.

"C'mon, Tyson. Stop messing around," he yelled, his face only just out of the water.

"You think I'm messing around?"

Swimming was becoming harder. Fatigue increased in my aching shoulders. Each stroke added weight to my tiring muscles. Lactic acid burned. I knew I couldn't stop.

The cliff beside us began to degenerate into broken blocks of rock. The visibility was improving, the beam of light becoming less powerful, less obvious in the early dawn light. With the harbour only a hundred metres away, we moved into shallower water. To my surprise, I was able to touch the sand beneath me. Being able to rest my tired feet on actual ground had never felt so good. Eli stood next to me, panting and wiping water from his chin. "The last stretch," he said, grinning with a strange stare of determination in his blood-shot eyes.

Near the hydro-harbour, we faced a thick, razor-wire fence between the rocky headland and the outskirts of the harbour's southern end. The fence continued right under the water, secured by huge, steel pylons concreted to the sea floor. Inside the fence neat rows of boats filled the piers. There were sailboats, fishing boats, hybrid-boats and hover-boats, all secured to large steel docks. By water, the only entrance to the harbour was through a central channel blocked by large steel gates. Unless we had a combination code or a remote control for the gate, I didn't like our chances of getting through.

The sun hadn't quite shown itself on the eastern horizon, but I sensed it was only minutes away. We needed to be faster. Eli dived under water and appeared thirty seconds after on the other side of the fence, inside the harbour.

"What the... how the hell did you do that?"

"There's a small hole down by the rocks, the wire has rusted away. It's a squeeze, but you'll make it. Hurry."

I followed suit, diving under, seeing a small hole in the corroded metal. At first it looked no bigger than a turf-ball. Eli was smaller than me and I was doubtful that I'd fit. I bent the wire on the edges of the hole and pulled myself through, wriggling like an animal caught in a trap. After a panic fuelled struggle, I slipped through and came to the surface.

We're in!

The turret lights still scanned back and forth across the water. I watched the ray of light come hovering across the southern end of the harbour, past the boats closest to us and towards the cliffs. It headed right for us. We wouldn't have time to escape its path.

Just when the light came within metres of us, it veered in a sharp arc, following the fence line, leaving us unseen as we bobbed in the murky water.

"Man, I thought we were done for."

"Quick, see the yellow hybrid? Let's get to it. Now!"

Despite our aching and tired muscles we swam as fast as fatigue would allow. We passed several old sailboats, three new model hover-boats and a large, outboard fishing rig. I couldn't believe fishing boats still existed. Fishing in the ocean for food seemed like a laughable idea.

We reached the hybrid tucked between the jetty and the outboard fishing rig as the light swept back past. It followed the jetty, bright and all-consuming.

"Under!" I yelled.

We both dived under the water and held the bottom of the boat. Even under the gloomy water I saw the large light hit the fishing rig and the hybrid, lighting them up like daylight. It trailed off, following the line of boats north in a pre-programmed pattern.

I returned to the surface and gulped for much-needed air. Although tainted and poisonous, it was life giving nonetheless. I climbed the stainless steel ladder at the back of the boat and pulled Eli up. The hatch cover into the cabin didn't have a lock. I slid it open and we both dropped inside. For the first time since seeing that foreboding fortress on the headland, I felt somewhat safe. Exhausted, but safe.

Eli searched through every cupboard, container and drawer in search for water, food or ideally, some Fosform Five. Losing the backpack in the swim meant we had none of our rations. Already my stomach rumbled. He returned from the front room of the cabin with a stained plastic bottle and a packet of raw rice. "I think it's whisky, but I'm not sure," he said to me, shaking the bottle in his hand. "And the rice. Well, it looks old, but it's better than nothing. Who knows how long we will wait."

Eli was right. We could sit in the dull and damp cabin for hours, days, weeks even. All we could do was hope that whoever owned our stowaway boat would leave the harbour soon. I knew it was a long shot but I couldn't give up on hope. I'd come this far.

Since the pivotal moment when we cut out my chip this was the first time we had stopped moving. This was the first time I sat still, alone with my thoughts. Realisation slapped me in the face. I was no longer in a sub-plaza. I was no longer working for the Union. I was no longer a registered citizen and I no longer had to worry about marrying a stranger. But most importantly, I was no longer a slave. In a strange sense of the word in its most raw form, I was free. Someone once told me that people are as free as they allow themselves to be. I think I understood what they meant.

TWENTY-SIX

RESTLESS AND DEPRESSED, BRIE VAN BUEREN STARED AT THE BROWN water stains on the ceiling.

In her starved and delusional state she formed shapes from the stains, the way a daydreamer would make images in the clouds on a summer's day. Her whole body ached, the swelling and bruises now visible across most of her skin.

She could no longer cry. After the first few times they raped her, she cried for hours but after consecutive days of torment she had grown numb. The pain and emotional detachment combined to create a strange void in her soul, a dark empty place in her thoughts. Despite the horror, she wouldn't let it break her. She somehow held it together through each horrendous encounter. She knew that if she broke, then they would win.

Half a dozen times the lisping giant, who had since introduced himself as Liam, had entered the room with water and food. For two of those visits, he came in with stale, rock-like rye bread. Because of Brie's missing teeth and broken jaw, instead of chewing the bread, she tore off chunks of the loaf and sucked it until it dissolved in her mouth. Eating a loaf of bread took the better part of two hours. When battling hunger like she was, having to suck her food seemed just as torturous as the beatings she continued to endure. She had never known pain and suffering like this. She had never known longing like this. She had never known regret, fear and hopelessness like this. Most of all she had never known hatred like this. With each of her oppressor's thrusts and with each blow from their fists, hatred grew inside her. It incubated in her darkening soul.

In her semi-crazed and hungry state, Brie again thought of Michael Butcher. She wished he had never offered to go on the stupid Fosform mission. She wished she had never offered to join him. In her delusional state of despair she blamed him for her current circumstances.

The screech of the steel door sliding open interrupted her thoughts. Expecting to see the soldiers for their daily dose of sadism, she breathed a sigh of relief when Liam walked in, this time with no food and no water.

"You can walk with me or elth I'll carry you. I think you're leaving."

Brie fought through the pain and rose to her feet. The cold concrete numbed her bare toes. Liam looked at her. Through his grotesque and giant eyes she sensed shame.

Liam supported Brie by the shoulder and with his other huge hand he handcuffed Brie's wrists together with a carbon-fibre rod-like device. Because of her injuries her pace was slow as she followed him out of her cell, down the corridor and through a large concrete hallway into a sizeable, multi-storey room. It was the first time she had felt artificial sunlight since her capture. The warmth was amazing. Revitalising.

At the end of the room, men sat around a trapezium-shaped stone table. Two were soldiers that had frequented her cell daily and the other three wore Union Advisor uniforms, synthetic leather and latex. Liam left Brie at the table and walked off back into the pits of Hell where he lived. Brie was sad to see him leave. With him around she felt the tiniest inkling of warmth. With him gone she felt vulnerable and cold.

One of the three men stood up and removed his glasses. He was elderly, at least in his seventies. His wrinkled skin sagged, bulging bags pillowed under his eyes. He cleared his throat and looked at Brie with a burning gaze. "Well, look what they've done to you," he said with a strong British accent. "What a terrible waste. You had such potential, Brie. I don't know why you had to kill Peter and then try to make a dash for freedom. Such a terrible waste... Do you know who I am?"

Brie shook her head.

"I'm Eric van Bueren. I'm Peter's uncle. I'm also the closest associate to Master Stephen Haynes."

Brie looked at him with resentment. She refused to respond.

"If we are being honest, I wasn't shocked to hear that you killed Peter. I know what he did to you. His apartment, which my credits paid for, remained under video surveillance. I don't agree with his methods of treating women but who was I to stop him? Pity you got caught, I guess." He smiled a sinister, chilling smile. "Now, the Master himself wants to have a word with you. I understand he's curious about the company you kept during your short stay in the Northern Sector; the same company that has stolen Fosform Five from the Union. I believe he wants to get some information from you. I assume that you will be compliant?"

Again, Brie didn't respond. Van Bueren's gaze was icy, calculating. He stared at Brie, his expression thick with hatred or pity, or both. He was a powerful man, used to being listened to. As effortlessly as his aged body allowed, he left the table, picked up a black canvas bag beside the doorframe and returned to his seat. Still staring at Brie, his expression unchanged, he opened the bag and poured its contents onto the table. Two foul smelling, rotten human heads hit the table and rolled to a stop in the centre. Brie gagged. The soldiers laughed. Eric van Bueren stared. "I believe these are friends of yours?"

The stench was potent, unbearable. Decay had broken down the flesh, but Brie could still make out their faces. It was Francis and Milly. Rotting, pale, maggot infested heads were all that remained of her two friends.

She swallowed her fear and looked at van Bueren, expressionless.

153

"These two, and a few others were with you when my men took you. This one here," van Bueren said, poking Francis' face with his index finger. "Our security cameras caught this one here on two separate occasions stealing from our supply trains. They have been lucky in the past but no longer. Stealing Fosform is one of the most treasonous crimes one can commit, except killing a Union official, removing your registration chip and escaping to the jungle. Now Brie, you *will* come with us to Brisbane Central and you *will* tell the Master where these renegade friends of yours live. Won't you?"

Brie kept a straight face. She looked Eric van Bueren in the eyes.

"Does it look like your threats frighten me, *Uncle?* Your soldiers have beaten me, raped me, arse-fucked me and starved me! You're just as sick as that nephew of yours and these soldiers are just as sick as that cunt of a Master... Go bend your knee to him, you filthy, old, obedient DOG!"

Her outburst was invigorating, energising.

And stupid.

Van Bueren adjusted his glasses. His facial expression didn't change. "Look here, Brie. If you want the beating and the rape to end, then you had best be a little more helpful. I can leave you here with the soldiers and, as you can see, they don't get out much... So I suggest you watch your blasphemous tongue. You can stay here or I can take you with me to Brisbane to see the Master and if you are compliant, if we get what we want, we might offer you a quick and somewhat pain free death... It's up to you."

Brie's outburst had exhausted her. She wiped her swollen lip. "Fine... I will be compliant," she whispered, defeated. "I will tell you what I know."

"Splendid," van Bueren said, smiling. "Let's not waste another minute then. We have a jet waiting above ground. We should be there within the hour. Gentlemen," he said, looking at the two soldiers. "Give Brie some clothing and a shot of Fosform, burn the heads of her criminal friends and let us be on our way."

After a shower, some Valdeine, a dose of Fosform Five and some clean polyester and latex clothes, Brie felt somewhat better. The painkillers took the edge off the pain from her torn vagina, making walking more tolerable. Still handcuffed, they took Brie through a series of levels of the underground maze via a transparent elevator shaft. It allowed her to see everything. The place was a control station for the Union, including the surveillance centre for the greater part of the Northern Sector of the Empire. "Where are we?" she asked van Bueren, her voice coarse and quiet.

"We are in an old Union sub-plaza in Kuala Lumpur. Believe it or not there are over three thousand prisoners down below us, in far more horrible conditions than what you were dealing with... Well, besides the rape I guess." He chuckled.

Brie held her tongue. Insults and outrage wouldn't help her cause.

Reaching the surface level of the barracks, Brie looked out huge floor-to-ceiling windows to see actual sunlight. Dull and overcast as it was, it lifted her spirits. For a while, down in the damp darkness Brie thought she would never see sunlight again. She looked at the outside world to take her mind off the dungeon and the memories that accompanied it.

One of van Bueren's accomplices strapped a portable oxygen conditioner over Brie's bruised face and the four of them left the compound. They entered the poisonous elements and walked across the concrete yard towards an aircraft hangar beside the fortified fence line. The air was humid. In a peculiar way, the uncomfortable air was the most comfortable thing Brie had felt in a fortnight. They escorted her into the hanger and up an alloy ramp into the jet.

The inside of the jet mirrored the lounge room of a top tier sub-plaza apartment with a carpeted floor, leather couches and a spa bath, bubbling and warm in the corner. A marble-top bar displayed a range of foods and beverages, foods that Brie hadn't seen in years, foods that Brie didn't even know still existed. Eric van Bueren caught Brie eyeing up the delicacies and encouraged her to help herself, although he refused to remove her handcuffs. She opted for the fruit, as it was soft and easy going on her broken teeth and swollen jaw.

With a strained effort she bit into a fresh, ripened mango. After inhaling the mango she filled a steel plate with strawberries, raspberries and blueberries and took a seat on the huge suede couch to eat them. Compared to her dark and foul-smelling cell, she felt she had just entered Heaven itself. She wasn't stupid. She knew the plane ride wouldn't last long and all the pleasantries would soon be over. It was all just a big tease. It was a cruel jape. It was Eric van Bueren's sick way of fucking with her tortured mind. They wanted to pick her up only to drop her again. They wanted Brie to see what would have been hers if only she had endured her sick and twisted late husband.

Once the jet was airborne, Brie tried resting her eyes. Every time she closed them she saw those filthy soldiers, violent and erect, spitting on her and thrusting, moaning and laughing. She tried to erase their faces from her thoughts but they seemed imprinted into the blackness behind her eyes. It made her sick to the stomach. She tried hard to keep the fruit in her belly.

Van Bueren and his accomplices ignored Brie for most of the flight. She was a prisoner, not a guest. Within an hour the engines slowed and the jet came to a stop. Brie didn't even feel it hit the tarmac on landing. Van Bueren sat on the couch next to her, grinning his same sadistic smile. He was an arrogant, wealthy old narcissist. Brie despised his cruel smile. She despised his wrinkled face. She saw her late husband in his eyes. They had the same sadistic eyes.

"Well now, Brie," he said. "We will take you to the Brisbane sub-plaza penitentiary, the biggest in the Empire. There we will give you a cell. For the best part of your stay, our guards and soldiers will not assault you, but I cannot guarantee that the other convicts will not have their way with you. At least until the Master meets with you, until we decide on your fate, we will leave you in gen pop. It's quite a strange place down there. Let's hope you survive."

TWENTY-SEVEN

GEORGE KNEW WHAT MUST HAVE HAPPENED. HE WASN'T AN IDIOT. The abrupt departure troubled him, but even so, he wished Tyson the best. Although he wasn't confident of his friend's success, he prayed for it anyway.

He sat alone in BC74 listening to Father Kassal recite Bible verses the same as every other Sunday. His mind was elsewhere. Tyson could be dead by now. They could have him locked in a surface cage. He could face torture at the hands of the extremist Union.

The previous day, on Tyson's twenty-third birthday, George had finished work and went looking for his friend and his friend's new wife. He raced with excitement through the Tier Three corridors. George couldn't find Tyson anywhere. He searched for him at his apartment, at Christie and Fay's coffee centre, even Jonah's apartment cell. Something didn't seem right. After an hour of searching, it became clear to George that his friend had done the unthinkable.

There was only one way to make sure. After his search of Block 7, George made his way to Tier One to check the database of citizens leaving the sub-plaza. He waited in the line with frenzied thoughts, his heart rate an erratic mess, until an elderly woman greeted him, wrinkled and weathered. Her nametag read Mary-Anne. He put on a polite smile, despite the concern that ate away at him.

"Hi, Mary-Anne," he had said. "I don't suppose you can show me the sub-plaza surface departure log for the last twenty-four hours?"

Mary-Anne gave him an odd look of curiosity. She squinted through her thick lens glasses. "And why would you want to see that, young man?"

"I'm looking for someone. That's all. I'm sure you won't mind."

Mary-Anne was silent for a moment. She pursed her lips and brought up the recent log data on the screen before her. "I bet you're looking for the young fella who didn't draw a marriage number yesterday. Yeah, Anderson, I think it was."

At this, George's jaw dropped. "Well... Umm... The thing is—"

"I tell you what," Mary-Anne interrupted. "I gave that love-struck little brat a few hours and he never checked back in. Might have run into trouble up there on the surface. I tell you what, though. He missed his Marriage Lottery. When he checks back in, *if* he checks back in, he will be in a world of trouble. His Advisors will eat him up, they will. Now, young man, what's your membership number?"

Fearful of the repercussions, George spun around and left the checkout station. He knew he had already pried too much. The Union would most probably interrogate him. That's if they didn't get to Tyson first. His thoughts were a manic mess. His closest friend, the closest thing he had to family, had done the unthinkable. Tyson Anderson had abandoned him.

After the monotonous Sunday morning church service, George waited for the residents to disperse before making his way out of BC74. He wanted to be alone with his sombre thoughts. After most of the crowd had left, he got up to leave. George was forced to stop only ten metres from the scanning lobby. His heart skipped a beat.

Soldiers.

Three of them stood before him with weapons drawn. Navy-blue uniforms, taser cannons, emotionless stares.

"George Clarkson, 545-234," the tallest of the soldiers said. It wasn't a question.

George stood frozen. One soldier pulled a registration chip scanning device from his grey belt, stepped forward and held it to the back of George's neck. He didn't dare move. The device beeped, then an automated voice read out George's registration number. "545-234."

The soldiers didn't communicate. They didn't need to. The tallest soldier placed the device back onto his belt and withdrew a black canvas bag from his pocket. In a swift, well-practiced motion he pulled the bag over George's head, zipped it tight and smacked George over the head with the butt of his taser cannon. George winced in pain before being hit again.

A mask of darkness consumed him.

George regained consciousness as they removed the black canvas bag from his head. Bound to a small steel chair, he was naked and frightened. The young soldier who removed the canvas bag left the room without a word. A large steel door closed behind him. The room appeared smaller than most sub-plaza bedrooms. The walls were concrete, all white. George had never seen white walls inside 3rd Sydney West. All the walls in the entire sub-plaza were colour-coded based on their tier. He was somewhere else, somewhere different. Somewhere the registered citizens didn't even know existed. Bound to the chair by metal cuffs surrounding his wrists, ankles and neck, he was incapable of moving. While fear and uncertainty flooded his thoughts, so too did resentment. He was there, locked to the chair, helpless and naked because of Tyson's selfish actions. He loved his friend. But this was all Tyson's fault.

Hours passed. George fought thirst, hunger and a thumping headache. As pain and restlessness began to show signs, the door rolled open. A soldier walked in first and stood silently beside the white wall, his taser cannon resting across his chest. Then someone else came in. He was short, pudgy and pale. He wore navy-blue, the colours of Tier Three. As with most Union Officials, ego and authority oozed from his mannerisms. He stood beside George and pulled a small tablet touch-pad from the pocket of his synthetic polyester pants. He didn't introduce himself.

"Mr Clarkson," he said in a high-pitched, whining voice. "I understand you were close with citizen 636-124, Tyson Anderson. Is this correct?"

George nodded.

"Is this correct? Answer me, you useless peasant!"

"Yes! Yes, Tyson is a friend of mine."

"And do you know of his whereabouts?"

"No… I haven't seen him since yesterday morning."

"Are you sure?"

"Yes. I know the rules. I will not lie to you guys. Loyalty and union - I get it!"

The short, pale advisor stared at George.

"I have recorded video surveillance of the two of you heading to the surface and coming back the following morning. But the footage shows that you didn't leave the surface compound. Is there a reason you felt the need to leave the sub-plaza, but you never left the compound?"

"We were drunk, okay. Ty wanted to see the stars."

"And then?"

"And then nothing. I went to work. He went to work."

The short, pudgy advisor didn't like George's conceited tone. He balled his fingers into a fist and belted George across the jaw.

"The thing is, George Clarkson, we have tracked Tyson Anderson's registration chip to his last known location. North Collaroy. The funny thing is that we also recorded him going there a few days prior? Would you know why?"

It puzzled George. "To the same place? Collaroy? I have no idea why? He must have kept secrets. Even from me."

"Well… Some of my soldiers got there first thing this morning and found his chip *removed* from his neck, crushed and dysfunctional. They found it inside a crude underground dwelling, in the old sewers. It appears someone has been living there for sometime. Do you know anything of this dwelling? Who it might be?"

"No, no, I don't. I have nothing to tell you…."

"I'm not sure I believe you, Mr Clarkson. I want to know who he went to meet, and why?"

"Look," said George. "He spoke of freedom often. He spoke of his distaste towards the Marriage Lottery. That's all I know."

"Well, I want results. I want to find Tyson Anderson 636-124. If there are things you're not telling me, I think a day or two in a surface cage will re-jog that memory of yours."

"No! Please, I know nothing. Really, I don't!"

"Shut up, you pathetic swine. Be grateful I don't cut you to pieces right now. I will revisit in two days. Until then, I suggest you pray for clouds."

The Union Advisor left the room. The lone soldier stepped forward and replaced the black canvas bag over George's head. He felt the cuffs on his ankles, wrists and neck release as a low pitch beep sounded. The blood flowed to his extremities for the first time in hours. He knew where he was going. Two days in an open cage in the dirt. Surface exposure torture. For the first time since Tyson's departure, George felt hatred towards his best friend.

TWENTY-EIGHT

MICHAEL BUTCHER WOKE TO AN EMPTY ROOM AND A CLOUDED MIND.

Feeling refreshed, he climbed out from his pallet-racking bunk bed, stretched, put on his jeans and left the sleeping quarters. He was starving. He had no idea how long he'd been asleep. It could have been hours, days, or longer. His bladder ached.

After visiting the amenities, he walked down the dirt corridor to the communal room. Fellow T-Towners prepared the night's meal. They offered him water and some leftover lizard meat from the night before. He scoffed the tough meat, barely chewing the chunks as he gulped them down. He asked about Bruce, who had still not woken. According to Gabbie, Bruce had been mumbling strange things in his sleep, which was a good sign. She assured the others his condition remained stable. While it wasn't clear how long he would remain in a coma, she seemed confident he would live. Soon after Michael finished his meal Evan returned from patrolling the perimeter. He looked drained. He looked like the pressure of leadership was taking its toll. He approached Michael with a weary smile. "Hey Mickey, good to see you awake, mate. How do you feel?"

"It feels like I've slept for days."

"That's because you have, mate."

"How long?"

"You got back on Tuesday, and now it's Thursday afternoon."

"And I hear Bruce hasn't woken up yet?"

"Nah, it looks like he's in a coma. I don't know what to do. I mean he's stable and all that but he's pissing and shitting himself. We can't force-feed him forever. We don't have the things here we need like IV drips to sustain his life. He better bloody-well wake up soon, hey."

"Look," said Michael, taking a deep breath, changing the subject. "I'm not gonna give up on Brie. I just can't."

"C'mon mate. Are you gonna bring that up again? You gotta leave it alone. Seriously. She's gone, mate."

"I won't accept that. I felt something with her I've never felt with anyone. It could even be love!"

"Love… And is that worth dying for," said Evan, raising his voice. For such a passive person it sounded oddly out of character.

"Maybe it is, Evan. Maybe it is!"

"Mate, with all due respect, you're a damn idiot. You've worked your arse off digging this damn tunnel to get a shot at freedom and you're going to throw it all away 'cause of a girl you *think* you know. You don't know shit about her. Would she do the same for you? Or would she keep her eyes focused on that tunnel ahead of us on a chance to rid herself of this bloody Empire?"

Evan's harsh outburst silenced Michael. Evan was right. Michael knew that if they got under the wall and clear from this place that there would be countless opportunities to find love.

"Yeah, look. You're right, Evan, I know you are. The thing is, I can't stop thinking about her." Michael paused. "I need to go down in the tunnel and dig. Maybe it will take my mind off her."

"You sure you're ready for that? We have a good team down there at the moment."

"If I can't keep up, then I'll come back and chill out. I'll see you this arvo."

Michael was right. Once down in the tunnel, preoccupied with work, his thoughts didn't travel. He rid his thoughts of images of gunfire and explosions, of death and blood, of the short, attractive, tanned brunette he had grown so fond of. For the afternoon he stopped thinking about her perfect smile, her deep dark eyes, her flawless naked body and her beautiful soul.

The only tools the T-Town digging team had to use for mining were items they had stolen from the surrounding area over the course of the year, so the progress of digging was slow, especially when they hit rock. The digging team, comprising Seb, Alex and the two Toms, had been trying to cut through an enormous deposit of limestone blocking their path. In the previous two days the team hadn't yet dug three metres.

As the hours drifted past, the team chiselled away at the limestone until progress could continue on the other side. There was something therapeutic about digging. Michael didn't think about Brie, about Francis, about Caleb, about Milly. All he thought about was swinging away at the hardened dirt with his blunt gardening pick.

Before long the lunch break finished and the afternoon shift arrived, comprising two local Thai men, Robin and Krit. They looked identical, both short and thin with genuine smiles and thick black hair. In the previous six months Robin and Krit had contributed more to the digging than any other T-Towner, except Michael Butcher.

Krit squeezed down the tunnel where Michael swung his pick and placed a hand on Michael's sweaty shoulder. "Mickey, I have good news, yes," he whispered in broken English. "Bruce awake. He confused, but he awake. Evan with him now…"

"Thanks, Krit."

Michael Butcher put down his gardening pick, wiped the dirt from his face with the bottom of his shirt and left the tunnel. Walking into Bruce's room, he found Evan and Gabbie kneeling beside his bed, whispering. He knelt down beside the two and looked at Bruce. He was pale. His lips had cracked and he had lost a noticeable amount of weight. Cradling a metal flask of water, Bruce looked up at Michael and smiled. "Good to see you here, Mickey. I hear you dragged my sorry arse the whole way back? I owe you one, mate."

"You would have done the same for me, Bruce. I would not leave you there. Has Evan told you about the others? About Brie?"

"Somehow, and I don't know how, I remember most of it. I remember seeing Francis on the ground. I remember watching them shoot Milly right through the fucking heart." Bruce looked down to where his left hand would have been. Instead, all that remained was a scabby stump wrapped in a roller bandage. "I remember that happening, too. I felt the bloody thing explode and I thought, fuck me Bruce, you're gonna die. I don't remember seeing Brie, though. Evan just told me they took her alive."

"They knew who she was, Bruce. They were waiting for her."

"That's impossible. She removed her chip. They were just lucky, I reckon."

"Yeah, well, she was married to one of the most powerful people in the whole damn Union. Remy knew all about it."

"So I've been told. That would have been good to know before we took her with us. I've been lying here thinking maybe, just maybe, if we didn't have young Brie Kallas with us on our journey then the outcome could have been different. If it was Brie they were after the whole time then they might have been nowhere near us that night. But it also makes me think if she stayed here, they might have found T-Town and ruined it for everyone... In a fucked-up way I'm sort of happy they got her down *there*."

"You're *happy* that they got her?"

"C'mon mate, you know what I bloody mean. I'm happy it happened down there. Not here where there's an entire community of people..."

"Okay, Bruce. You need to rest," Gabbie interrupted. "You and Michael can talk tonight but right now you need to eat some stew and relax."

"Gabbie's right," Evan said, standing up. "Come on Mickey, let the man rest. We can talk with him later."

"No, it's all right, I'm bloody fine. What we need to do is work out how we're going to get more Fosform or we're all fucked!"

"Listen, Bruce," Gabbie said. "I watched my husband and both my sons die. I know when people need to rest and *you need to rest.*

165

You've got three holes in you and you're missing your damn fingers. Conversation can damn-well wait."

Gabbie was small and frail, in her mid-fifties. She had wiry grey hair and a weathered face. She was a respected senior figure in the T-Town community with the heart of an angel. She had been a nurse in her previous life. Out of instinct she had resumed similar responsibilities in their outlaw community. Gabbie had always been the silent and obedient follower and because of Bruce's position in the community. He was not used to being told what to do. Gabbie's stern instruction took him by surprise.

Gabbie took in a big breath and crossed her arms, almost like a strict mother. For a moment there was silence.

"With all due respect, Gab," Bruce said, trying to sit upright, wincing through the pain. "I wish there was time to rest, but there isn't. We need to organise a way of getting some dosage quick smart. There's no point me resting and healing if my organs are gonna start bleeding from the inside. There won't be a train for a while now, we missed our chance, so we're gonna need to do something far more rash, far more dangerous. What worries me the most is that we no longer have Francis. And I'm now about as useless as tits on a bull. If you don't mind, I need to sit with the lads for a while and work out what we're going to do. I can rest when I'm bloody-well dead!"

A look of discontent came over Gabbie's weathered face. She knew well and good that there was no point trying to talk sense into someone as stubborn as Bruce Chadwick.

"Bloody men," she muttered under her breath as she left Evan and Michael to talk with their leader.

TWENTY-NINE

The day passed uneventfully.

Through the salt-crusted porthole window of the cabin I watched the sun drift across the brown, hazy sky. I could tell Eli was restless. He'd searched every square inch of the boat at least three times. We tried eating the raw rice, but it proved terrible to chew and once swallowed, it expanded in the stomach and gave me horrible pains.

A few boat owners had entered and left the secure harbour, but I had only seen them from a distance through the blur, or heard the hum and rumble of their engines. No one had even come close to our side of the harbour.

I sipped at the whisky. I offered to share it with Eli but he had one mouthful, gagged and pulled a face of sheer disgust. Hour after hour passed. Soon the contents of the bottle had been consumed; our conversation became dull and exhausted. Although I refused to bring it up, the obvious and very realistic chance that someone may never board our stowaway boat lingered at the forefront of my thoughts. Hell, the owner of that hybrid could have fallen victim to the syndrome and would never come to sail us off towards the grey space of our uncertain future.

Nightfall came as hunger and thirst emerged. The back of my neck stung, the wound becoming infected already. The all-watchful lights returned and started scanning the harbour. The feeling of safety I had when we first made it inside the cabin had since been replaced with a sense of claustrophobic imprisonment. I felt trapped. I could see in Eli's eyes that he felt the same way. He sat motionless, staring out the porthole until he turned to me with an impatient, frustrated scowl.

"Look, we can't just sit here," he said to me. "I'll sneak along the dock to search for food in some other boats."

"Are you sure that's a good idea? If there are soldiers watching and that light lands on you, we're screwed."

"I've been watching that damn light for an hour now. It follows the same pattern. I can memorise it. You know what? I don't even reckon there are people watching. I reckon it's just there as an intimidation tool. Like a fake security camera."

"Well, it's a lot riding on what you *reckon*. Just be careful, okay? I'm gonna stay put."

Eli stood, crouched and alert at the back of the cabin, counting aloud until the light hit the boat next to our hideout. He then leapt up through the manhole and disappeared into the night. I heard a few quick, light footsteps across the fibreglass roof and then stone-cold silence. It was the first time since my journey north had begun that I had been alone. It only took a few minutes until the uninvited sense of longing hit me.

Emotions cascaded through my mind. Regret. Fear. Longing. Loss. By now George would've known of my disappearance. He would have been one of the first people interrogated. Man, I hoped they had inflicted no extreme measures upon him. That was a burden I didn't need. I would never know, though. I missed him already. Eli was better company than solitude, but George and I connected. George and I had spilt sweat and blood together out in the Pacific and he was like a brother, a brother I had abandoned. A brother I would never see again.

Anxiety increased with each lap the spotlight made of the hydro-harbour. Time was difficult to keep. Hunger had subsided for the time being, but thirst was making me lightheaded. I closed my eyes. If I could sleep, then I wouldn't feel the thirst or the anxiety.

Sleep didn't seem to come.

Footsteps above made my tired muscles stiffen. Eli, dripping wet, dived headfirst into the cabin just as the spotlight rolled over the boat beside us and landed on the deck of the hybrid. He smiled. No, he smirked at me like a giddy child. His hands were full.

"Jackpot," was all he needed to say. In one hand he held a canvas carry bag, in another, an automatic electro-pistol. He emptied the canvas bag and pulled out two tins of diced fruit, a bottle of water, four powder sachets of protein and a handful of dehydrated 'mariner' meals. After taking a big gulp, Eli handed me the water and I took a huge, refreshing mouthful. Life came alive within me. I felt the liquid line my throat. We wasted no time in opening the tins, devouring the peaches and pears from within, followed by one of the mariner meals. Energy returned to me, taking me from my zombie-like state of lethargy.

Eli still had a smirk draped across his face. "There's something else," he said.

"What? What is it?"

Pulling a folded and laminated sheet from his wet pocket, he passed it over to me. It appeared to be a timetable of some sort. It looked like a delivery timetable for a commercial shipping supplier.

"I found it in the freighter I boarded. Look at the dates. The boat is leaving here on the first day of Lust. That's in three days! We just need to wait it out for three days, get inside the freighter then we will be on our way. It's heading out to one of the security stations on the wall. Look, look, right there!"

"I am looking, Eli. I *can* read!"

This news almost brought tears to my eyes. Hope was over-whelming when doubt had the upper hand.

"Okay," I said. "We'll wait it out in here until the end of Pride, then we make the move, find a good hiding spot and wait for the boat to leave. Once it's well on its way to the security station we make our move and head north."

"Well, we're gonna need more food and water if we're gonna sit here for three days."

"Two days," I corrected him.

After the excitement wore off and the fruit and mariner meal settled in our stomachs, sleep came to both of us. I didn't stir until the gloomy sun pulled me from my dream state the following morning. That's when I started to cough. Not just a normal cough. It was a phlegmy, deep, lung-aching cough. I knew what it meant. Eli looked at me through puffy and sleep encrusted eyes. He, too, knew what it meant.

"Shit, man. We need to raid more boats. We need to find some Fosform. All that water and air has gotten to you."

"Well, why hasn't it gotten to you yet?"

"I think my body is more used to it. I mean, I go a month with no Fosform. From what you told me you get a jab every week."

"Not anymore," I said glumly.

"No, but that was your choice, Tyson."

"I don't think we can wander around in the daylight. If we're going to search more boats, then we need to do it under the cover of darkness. How long do you think I have? You know, until it gets real bad?"

"I dunno, man. I don't really know how it works with you lot who live underground. Your lungs aren't used to the air, I guess. I feel fine…"

Doubt came back. Hope's short and triumphant stint had quickly waned. Doubt seemed like the stronger warrior. Doubt was more suited to these difficult conditions. Hope was way out of its depth.

"Well, there's no point pondering," I said. "We need some Fosform and we can't get it until tonight. How about we have a protein shake or something?"

We passed the time with conversation. Meaningless in the scheme of things but conversation kept my thoughts from wandering. If I let my thoughts wander, I would convince myself I was dying. I hadn't left the controlled life of the sub-plaza to die only a few miserable days later.

I had left to find something real. I had thrown my life away to wake up each day proud and happy and free.

Death was not the freedom I searched for.

I asked Eli about his childhood and what he remembered. It sounded glum. I thought they controlled my childhood, but I still had my early years before the Union. I still had a few years when I was free to do what I wanted. Eli grew up with the Union and soldiers and the building of the walls. I told him about my early memories, about camping holidays up the coast. About learning to swim. About surfing and fishing. About sleeping in a tent. All of those things were foreign to him and just the concept of a holiday sounded like some amazing, far-fetched dream-like reward. He told me of his life, his schools, and his family. It's crazy how only seven years separated us in age, yet it was like we came from different generations, different times. Different worlds, even. As I sat and listened to his stories, I began feeling fatigued. My throat hurt. My eyes stung. I coughed violently, interrupting his monologue.

I could see the doubt and uncertainty in his eyes.

We needed to find some Fosform Five.

We didn't have two days.

THIRTY

Foul weather swamped the Brisbane skyline.

Bitter wind and thick, acidic rain hammered in from the ocean. Far from a welcoming invitation to her old city, two soldiers threw Brie into the back of a Union troop transporter truck, protecting her from the hazardous elements.

It wasn't long until the truck came to a stop. Brie was nervous. She had endured so much pain; she knew there would be so much more to come. She considered making a dash for freedom the second the back door of the transporter opened. She knew if she attempted an escape they would shoot her with a taser cannon. It would be a quick and painless way to end all the suffering.

The thought of her ending it all lingered, like the smell of hearty cooked meals inside the communal room of T-Town. It was comforting. The thought of finality soon evaporated, though. Something held her there. Something was worth the suffering. Was it the thought of recapturing that feeling of freedom? Was it the opportunity to find Michael Butcher again? Was he even still alive? His head didn't get dropped on the table in KL. Maybe he got away? Maybe he made it back to T-Town? She had got there before. She might find her way back. Was it just pointless longing? Hopeless hope? She

172

didn't know. She had had a small glimpse of freedom and maybe that small glimpse was enough to make her fight for it again. Death was the easy way out. Brie wanted more than that. She would endure whatever she needed to, to find salvation. She *would* find salvation.

The back doors of the transporter opened. Two soldiers in grey fatigues and full-face oxygen conditioners held taser cannons at Brie's face. The Perspex screens on their masks were reflective. She couldn't see their faces but in the reflection she glimpsed her own. It was the first time she had seen herself in weeks. She looked hideous, almost unrecognisable. Her jaw was swollen, bulging to one side. Her left eye-socket puffed out, purple and grotesque. Big, purplish rings hung under both eyes. Regardless, she stood tall, confident and firm. Despite the pain, the bruising and the broken bones she showed her captives a sly, toothless smile. She would not let them break her. Not on this day.

A third soldier entered the transporter truck and pulled a black canvas bag from the pocket of his fatigues. Without a word the soldier placed the canvas over Brie's head, zipped it tight around her neck and dragged her from the vehicle. She felt the rain soak through the canvas. It tasted foul. She heard muffled, inaudible voices. One voice was recognisable by the strong British accent: Eric van Bueren.

"Take her to G-Block," Brie heard van Bueren say. "Tomorrow we will take her to the Master."

Thrown on the back of a hover-buggy, the uneasy feeling of the unknown rode with her in to the correctional facility. G-Block. Brisbane Central. Brie had heard rumours of the infamous place. The buggy travelled a short distance then Brie was inside, away from the acidic rain, away from the wind and the toxic air. The hum of the hover-buggy echoed in the confined space. She imagined they must be in a transporter tunnel, going down no doubt.

Her journey came to an abrupt end shortly after the transporter tunnel. Brie heard a combination of typical sub-plaza beeps. A few sealed doors rumbled open. They ripped the canvas bag from her head. Brie stood with Eric van Bueren on top of a concrete balcony.

He smiled callously, victorious. Twenty-five metres beneath the balcony stood G-Block.

G-Block was a crowded, open arena similar in size to a turf-ball oval. Surrounded by a twenty-five-metre high wall, escape seemed impossible. It reminded her of a giant, gladiators' fighting pit. With little furniture, no walls and no guards in the arena itself, G-Block housed nothing more than a few hundred ragged, starved and angry convicts with nowhere to go.

Brie didn't think she could feel fear any longer. But she did.

"Put on her magna-jack then lower her down," van Bueren said to one soldier before locking eyes with Brie. "Now, Brie, *if* you last the night, we will collect you tomorrow to get cleaned up and meet the Master himself. I suggest you prepare yourself to be compliant. Understood."

Brie nodded, overwhelmed.

"Like I said," van Bueren added. "In here it's not my soldiers you have to worry about. It's everyone else."

Eric van Bueren, uncle of her late husband and loyal associate to the Master, turned and walked away. A soldier appeared holding a shiny, metallic vest. A magna-jack. They held her in place while two soldiers lowered the metal vest over her head and locked the device closed with a series of adjustable clamps. It gripped her tightly around her thin frame, uncomfortable and stiff. Claustrophobia once again set in.

"What the hell is this?"

"It's a magna-jack."

"And what in Satan's sub-plaza is a magna-jack?"

"It's a magnetic jacket. Do not attempt to remove it," the closest soldier said. He looked young, fierce, heavily built. "If you try to remove the device, it will sense disturbance and eject three small barbs into your abdomen. It will not kill you. Not right away, anyway. It will cause the highest amount of pain and discomfort. Please do not attempt to remove it."

Brie looked down into the crowded mass below. Everyone in the arena wore a magna-jack.

"What if someone else tries to remove my magna-jack?" Brie asked. "You know, by force?"

"Then the device will sense disturbance and it will eject three small barbs into your abdomen. I suggest you do not allow anyone to remove your device."

"But——"

"Now, stand inside the yellow circle, traitor whore," the young soldier said, pointing to a yellow circle marked into the concrete balcony.

Brie followed the command. Before she could register what was happening, she was lifted off the ground, sucked a good metre in the air by an enormous magnetic disc on a crane-arm. Helpless, she dangled from the robotic arm as it lifted her over the edge of the balcony, stuck to the disc like an insect stuck to glue. It lowered her down into the arena. Members of G-Block looked up at her, watching her descend. When she dangled about three metres from the arena floor, still out of reach of any aggravated G-Block inmates, the magnet disengaged and she felt herself drop.

Bang...

She hit the concrete floor hard, sending bolts of pain up through Brie's limbs. In agony, she lay on the floor as filthy, ragged inmates surrounded her. Brie scanned the eyes of those closing in on her. She looked for compassion, she looked for sympathy. All she could see was barbaric rage.

She gained her feet one slow movement at a time. She stood still, overwhelmed, unsure of what to do next. The surrounding masses closed in on her. Claustrophobia was setting in.

Helplessness.

A commotion caused the crowd to disperse. A lone woman pushed through the masses. Well over six feet tall and built like a man, she was muscular, hardened. She had short orange hair and the defined jaw-line of a soldier. "Don't worry," she said, a faint New Zealand accent. "No one will harm you unless I tell them too."

Brie was speechless.

"Welcome to Hell," the tall woman said, laughing. "My name's

Lucy, but in here everyone calls me Lucifer," she laughed wickedly. "You know, like the fallen angel?"

Brie nodded, her mouth open in confusion.

"I help keep this place in order. What's your name and what's such a pretty girl like you doing in a place like this?"

Hesitant to respond to the giant woman at first, Brie finally spoke. "I'm Brie," she finally said, quiet and intimidated. "The Union captured me up north. I escaped my sub-plaza."

"You brave bitch," Lucifer said. "Looks like someone has taken some aggression out on that pretty face of yours. I'll take a guess and say that soldiers did it?"

Brie nodded.

"Fucking scum," Lucifer said.

Again Brie nodded.

"Here, come with me. I'll show you around this godforsaken pit."

Apprehensive at first, Brie rubbed her aching knees and followed the giant Lucifer through the crowds. There were people of all ages, all races. Ragged clothes, long, matted hair, filthy beards. Some looked like they had been in G-Block for years, others looked frightened, as green as Brie. As they walked through the pit Brie looked around, taking in the menacing place. The arena's walls were smooth concrete. There was nothing to scale them with. They passed lifeless bodies. At first Brie thought they might be asleep, but no, the colour had drained from their skin, their eyes rolled back, lips lifeless and blue. Dead bodies left to rot amongst the living.

Some G-Block inmates were naked, except for their magna-jacks. Exposed genitals swamped her vision. She saw some men missing theirs, victims of genital removal, most probably homosexuals or adulterers.

"This place is horrible," Brie muttered through broken teeth.

"Sure is," Lucifer said, laughing again. "But in a way it's better than solitary confinement. At least in here you can socialise, fight and fuck! And I run the damn place!"

"How did you manage that?" Brie asked. "You're a woman?"

Lucifer studied Brie, attempting to gauge the newcomer.

"Look… I might have a pussy between my legs but I ain't no damn woman," she said. "I run this place because, young lady, no one has yet beaten me in a fight. No one…"

Lucifer laughed again.

They walked over to the corner of the pit furthest from the robotic crane. Lucifer had several mattresses and old pallets forming her own private quarters. A small group of hardened inmates guarded it. As Lucifer approached, the men nodded and stood to the side, allowing her to pass. They looked Brie up and down like the fresh piece of meat she was.

Lucifer sat down on a grey foam mattress and looked up at Brie. "Now, let's cut to the chase, Brie baby. If you want my protection in here, I want to see how well you can eat pussy!"

Brie's eyes opened, wide, shocked. "Excuse me," she said, startled.

"You heard me. People don't get a free pass in here, especially people as good looking as you. I'll make sure you're protected, but it isn't free. You gotta make me cum."

"Same-sex relations are outlawed in the Empire," Brie said, using whatever excuse she could conjure.

"Look around, sweetie. We *are* outlaws!" Without waiting for Brie to respond, Lucifer lowered her tattered pants, revealing her hairy crotch. "Ready when you are," she said, cackling as she spread her legs apart for all to see.

Brie's face reddened. She looked around. The hardened inmates watched, grinning like schoolboys. The soldiers above the pit looked on. Embarrassment rumbled in the pit of her stomach, a nauseous hum in her belly. The filthy soldiers of the Northern Sector had abused her daily. They had beaten and raped her. This couldn't be any worse. Brie was determined to survive. She *would* find her salvation. So, with no further thought or hesitation, Brie got down on her knees, wiped her mouth, swallowed nervously and paid for her protection.

THIRTY-ONE

THE WAITING GAME WAS NO GAME AT ALL.

Not when your lungs bled and your liver faced its final fighting hours. Over the previous years inside the sub-plaza my body had become dependent on my weekly dosage. My organs had lost all ability to cope with the harsh poisons of the surface. TNS was taking me faster than I could have imagined. Perhaps that was part of the Union's plan. Maybe the Union made people so dependent on the drug that when idiotic dreamers like me attempted to escape, they died in the damn process. I lay motionless, staring at the cracking white paint on the ceiling of the boat. I needed a solution. I would not lie here and just wait to die.

I had an idea.

"Hey, Eli," I said, coughing to loosen the phlegm. "Did you scout every boat in the marina?"

"Not every boat, no. Just the southern end of the complex."

"Do you think there would be any Union boats in here? Like Army boats?"

"Maybe. If there's a security post on the hill then I suppose there might be a Union naval vessel here."

"Surely there would be Fosform supplies in a Union boat. Like in ration packs or something? Surely?"

"I guess so. We will need to wait until sunset and go explore."

And that's exactly what we did.

We spent the afternoon talking about the future, talking about what we would do if we ever got out of the Empire, across the walls to our freedom. Eli said he would like to kiss a girl. He had never done that. I said I would like to go surfing for real. Not like in the sub-plaza with George, but surfing at a real beach with clean water, safe to swim and duck-dive and catch waves in the fresh air.

The sun set on the hills behind us. Cabin fever set in along with the syndrome's effects. I became agitated, sick of that damn boat. The small, confined, mouldy cabin appeared smaller and smaller by the hour. I needed to get out. I couldn't just sit there and feel my lungs get heavy. We waited for the giant, all-consuming security lights to switch on, then through the salt-encrusted port-hole we watched its pattern. To Eli's surprise, the lights followed a different pattern from the previous night. Once convinced we had memorised the searching light's route, we left the safety of our hideaway and made our way to the northern end of the marina.

It was terrifying. We ducked down between boats as the spotlight neared us, waiting for it to pass. We passed the ship where Eli found the rations and the electro-pistol the previous night. He was far more agile than me, skipping across the dock without a sound. His days on the surface, robbing, stealing and spying had made him good at going about unnoticed. I was the opposite, clumsy, loud and unsure on my feet. My lungs ached, the muscles in my legs throbbing like I'd run a marathon.

This better be worth it.

We came across a divide in the centre of the marina. A separate dock accessed the other boats to the north of us, only accessible by land. Rather than risk jeopardising our position, I suggested we swim to the other boats. Even though I knew the water would speed up the effects of the TNS rotting my lungs, I didn't see another way.

We entered the dark water. The cool change was revitalising. Despite the cold and murky depths, I felt safer, less exposed than up on the dock. A short swim got us to the other side of the hydro-harbour. We scaled the dock without difficulty. My head thumped behind my aching eyeballs. The boats on the north side all looked the same, various generations of sailboats, motor yachts, hybrid and hovers. The light's rhythmic pattern swerved past the perimeter fence, the daunting wire glistening in the glow, before the light hovered over a large hybrid boat at the northern tip of the harbour.

Bingo!

Clear as Fosform, I noticed the red outline of the Union's soaring eagle that I loathed so much, stamped at the front of the large, white hull.

"Hey, Eli! There!" I said excitedly, pointing towards the large hybrid.

He saw it, too. It had to be a Union boat. We dropped low and crawled along the wooden dock towards the back of the boat then climbed down into the back deck. The Union's infamous motto hung above us on the roof, looking down upon us with contempt. The light hovered over us again. I held my breath, frightened to move. Once the light hovered within metres of us and once more made its way to the southern end of the hydro-harbour, I tried the door. It was locked. I studied the lock. DNA detection.

"Dammit!"

Without the right DNA or retina scan, we wouldn't be getting through the door. We couldn't get inside. Defeat hit me like a kick to the ribs. Exhausted, I didn't think I had it in me to get all the way back to our little hideaway just to wait it out for nothing.

"I've got a plan," whispered Eli.

Rather than telling me, he leapt over the side railing and disappeared into the black water below without a word. I crouched alone in frightened silence, keeping hidden from the forever-present hovering light. My heartbeat hammered. Air wheezed past the phlegm in my throat, forced through laboured breathing. The silence worried me. The solitude worried me. Where the hell had Eli gone?

Minutes passed.

The light had hovered over me three or four times. I felt light headed. Nervous sweat beaded on my brow. Eli had been gone too long and I was a sitting duck. I started considering what I would do if Eli didn't return. I accepted defeat before it had even shown itself. Hope wasn't bringing its A-game at all.

I froze as muffled noise came from inside the vessel. My heartbeat went into overdrive. I held my breath, ready to dive over the side and swim for dear life. Someone or something was inside the boat. The first thing that came to mind was a taser cannon being shoved in my face. I saw visions of soldiers equipped with oxygen conditioners and weaponry. I couldn't move. Fatigue and fear glued me to the deck of that hybrid. Then the locking mechanism beeped twice. A small green light lit up beside the door and the airtight seal opened up with a *whoosh*.

In the darkness, Eli stood dripping wet with a huge, triumphant grin on his face. His teeth glowed in the darkness. I stood frozen in disbelief. "What the heck," I mustered up.

"Hurry up and get inside," he yelled.

Like an obedient sub-plaza citizen, I followed his command and stepped inside. He closed it behind me, the light flashing in three short bursts of red. The door sealed with a vacuum compression.

"How did you do that?" I said, amazed.

"Well, it's a good thing I'm so thin. I found the anchor chain and I climbed up the chain and inside the anchor room. From there the doors are all open."

"Really? You just climbed up the chain? It seems like a bit of a flaw in the security?"

"I only just fit. It was a tight squeeze. My ribs will be bruised tomorrow. There's no way a full-grown man would even consider it as a breaching point. Most people wouldn't even think it's there. I mean… It's underneath the boat."

"So how did you know it would be there?"

"Let's just say that over the last year or two I've broken into many places. Boats included."

"Well done, Eli. Man, am I happy to have you here with me. You're full of surprises. Now let's try to find some ration packs."

Finding the rations didn't take long at all. We found communal sleeping quarters at the bottom of the ship that housed eight narrow double bunk beds. The blankets and sheets were perfectly clean and folded. The Union was ever ready. Underneath the beds, small metal boxes, clasped closed but not locked, had been bolted to the floor. Each metal box contained a high-powered torch, an electronic distress blaster, some tinned food, some bottled water, a hand-held micro-taser and, yep, four small vials of Fosform Five. I smiled. Eli smiled.

We located an injector gun in the vessel's helm and without wasting time I grabbed a vial, inserted it into the gun and put the gun to my neck. As the cool liquid entered my body, life itself came back to me. My fight for survival was not over yet.

I administered the dose for Eli, injecting the serum into his neck. We gathered what we could into a waterproof dry bag, emptying the contents of the metal boxes. We had enough Fosform to last us a few months. We had enough food to last us weeks. All we needed to do now was get back to the freight ship and wait for the end of Pride. The first day of Lust was only two days away.

"Make sure we cover any signs of our being here," I said to Eli as we left the bunkrooms at the bottom of the ship.

"What, you mean beside the fact that the ration packs are empty." Sarcasm soured his words.

"Look, man. They're ration packs. The soldiers won't even open those boxes unless it's an emergency. This ship will be on the other side of the Empire before they realise that shit is missing and by then we will be a world away. We gotta clean up the empty vials and stuff. Take them with us and drop them in the water."

"Sure thing. It'll be like we were never here…"

We left the safety of the Union vessel, locked it closed behind us and made slow and silent progress through the dark water back to the freighter Eli had boarded the previous night. We needed to find a good spot to hide. Somewhere that provided relative comfort but where we could remain unseen until we wanted to be. I shoved one of the micro-tasers into the waist of my pants, swung the dry-bag over my shoulder and set off down into the bowels of the freighter to find that spot with Eli right by my side.

THIRTY-TWO

Bruce was finally up and about.

He was far from healed, though. The two Toms had helped put together makeshift crutches from carved tree branches. Being the proud leader that he was, he ignored Gabbie's pleas to rest. He wanted results. He visited the supply room, counting the amount of Fosform Five left on the pallet. With the current number of residents requiring a shot every fortnight, just two months' supply remained. The bad news was that a supply train wouldn't be heading into the northern sector of the Empire for another six months. They needed to find an alternative way to get the serum. Kuala Lumpur housed the closest sub-plazas to T-Town. Even getting inside one, let alone getting their hands on enough Fosform Five to accommodate the whole of T-Town and get it back through the jungle, was utter madness. For the first time since the digging of the tunnels began two years earlier, the sombre mood in their underground bunker was infectious. The whole of T-Town was slowly coming to terms with the brutal truth.

Time was running out.

Evan rallied the residents and called for a meeting. In the main room the whole group sat wherever they could find space. They were impatient, tired and anxious. They knew the reason for the meeting and they all knew there wouldn't necessarily be an answer. Bruce and Evan sat up on the main serving table, looking down upon their trustworthy followers. Despite Bruce's pain, he bit his lower lip and stood strong, enduring the ache. Now was not the time for weakness.

"We need to do something, quick-smart," he said to the group. "Hopefully something that doesn't involve getting more of us bloody-well killed."

"What about getting the tunnel done faster," Krit said aloud. A mix of mumbled chatter and varied responses filled the room.

"I wish it were that simple, Krit, mate. I really do. But it's taken a year to get this far. We can't finish it in a month. Even if we work day and night."

"Well, I've had an idea," Michael Butcher said once the chatter calmed. He stood up on the bench seat so his voice travelled better through the cavern. "The soldiers that patrol the wall, right? They must come from somewhere around here. They surely don't come up from KL every time they do patrols, right? We need to find wher-ever it is they're based and we need to break in there and take their supplies."

Uproar.

The T-Towners were unsettled, calling out remarks both for and against Michael's suggestion. Michael's belligerent attitude upset a few residents. This was the first time in the small outlaw communi-ty's existence that such a sense of disjointedness threatened their unity. The communal agenda seemed incoherent.

"Enough," Gabbie yelled in a deep and powerful voice. The room fell silent. She stood up on the table, overlooking her comrades and took a breath. "Friends," she said, inviting and calm. "All that is happening now is suggestions are being made. There is no need for outbursts. There is no need for anger or insults. Suggestions, whether they are realistic and achievable or otherwise, are nothing more than suggestions. Please allow each other the courtesy of speaking. If you do not show each other respect here, then you're no better than those Union dogs you ran from."

Silence lingered as Gabbie's words settled.

"Please tell us," Gabbie said, still standing on top of the table, "how you intend on getting inside a Union military barracks, *if* there even is one on the wall at all?"

"Well, it's not pretty. But desperate times call for desperate measures," Michael said. "What we need to do is find the patrol squadron and torture them or follow them to the location. Once we've done so, and this is the not-so-pretty part, we need to cut their registration chips out of their necks and insert them into our own necks. Stich 'em right back in there. Then take their uniforms and their oxygen conditioners. That way we can scan ourselves right through the front door and take it."

More uproar, this time louder.

"You want to *stitch* another citizen's registration chip into your own neck?" Alex asked, disgusted.

"If that's what it will take to get the Fosform, I'm willing to try."

"Are you fucking nuts?" Alex rarely swore. "What if they have the syndrome?"

"Well, I don't hear any better suggestions."

Bruce stood tall on the table, towering over the rest of the crowd. "Look, no one ever said this shit would be easy. It's like some of you cannot understand what we are. We're criminals. We're *against* the system. We are *outlaws*. Nothing will get handed to us on a silver bloody platter. We need to fight for it. I can only say this shit so many times… Michael's idea, although somewhat extreme, is not too bad an idea. I mean, I've heard nothing better."

"How about this," Michael said. "Let's have a day to think about it, to brainstorm how we will get some dosage. In that time if there are people willing to volunteer for a mission along the wall, let me know. I reckon it'll work 'cause it's the absolute last thing they'll expect, right?"

"Won't people inside the Union quarters, if there are even quarters, think it's odd, you know, a bunch of Union soldiers they have never seen before just show up? Their comrades go out on a patrol and a bunch of strangers return?"

"Well, that's something we will have to work around. We'll cross that bridge when we get to it."

"Fuck 'em," Bruce said. "The filthy pricks killed Francis. They killed Caleb and Milly. They took Brie away to fuck-knows-where. Why don't we use Michael's idea to get inside and then slaughter them all? That way we can just walk out with the dosage, leaving a bunch of dead Union dogs to rot."

"Enough," Gabbie said. "Michael's right. Let's all sleep on it. No one is committing to anything just yet. For the time being we need food and we need to dig. We can talk about Union dogs tomorrow."

With that, still disheartened and anxious, the T-Towners left the communal bunker and made their way off to their daily duties. Michael sat with Evan and Bruce. He was well aware of the danger involved in his proposed plan. He also knew that the number of T-Towners skilled in combat had declined. Most of them had died in previous failed attempts. The ones that remained were diggers, hunters and cooks. He wouldn't be able to storm the castle, so to speak, with a bunch of diggers and cooks. There was a lot of thinking to do.

"Is it too early for some Whooze?" Bruce asked, cackling.

"That depends on what your definition of early is," Evan said. "I've been up since three o'clock this morning."

Evan left and returned from the food storage room with a dented alloy bottle and a few crude cups. He poured the three of them a drink each. Bruce took his down in one gulp. "Pour me another," he said smiling. "It'll shit Gabbie right off!"

"So the last Union patrol came past about nine days ago," Evan said, swirling the cup of potent liquid in his hand. "That means we have anywhere between two and five days until we can track the patrol. The team we want needs to be small – small and stealthy. So we can take them by surprise."

"But once we get inside their barracks, we need enough fire-power to take them down. Two or three of us won't cut it."

"If we do it right, five will be perfect."

"Let's see what the others think tomorrow," Michael said, taking a sip of Whooze.

The afternoon rolled into the early evening. Michael and Bruce sat at the communal table, emptying the bottle of Whooze. Bruce was right; it did shit Gabbie right off. She had pleaded for him to take it easy. His response was typical of Bruce Chadwick. "I'll take it easy when I'm dead."

In silent reflection, Michael thought of Brie. He thought about her secrets, her past. Remy had known parts of it.

Why had Brie put that trust in Remy and not me?

He missed her. He knew she still lived. He felt it in his soul. If he succeeded in his outlandish plan, if he got a Union soldier's registration chip inside his neck, then he would become that soldier. He would become that registered citizen and go find her. He would scour the Empire in search of Brie Kallas. He didn't want to bring this up with Bruce. Not yet, anyway. He knew what his response would be. It would be logical. Michael didn't want to hear logic. Michael was in love. Love and logic were rarely fitting accomplices.

THIRTY-THREE

BRIE SAT INSIDE LUCIFER'S PALLET FORTRESS IN G-BLOCK.

The taste of woman still lingered in her mouth. Brie's commitment to the cause had pleased Lucifer. She said it had been the best oral sex she'd received in months. She said if it interested Brie, Lucifer would happily return the favour, which according to Lucifer was a rare gesture. Although flattered, Brie declined the offer. It was the first and hopefully the last time she would be intimate with a woman.

G-Block thrived on violence. From behind the pallets Brie watched the giant arena in sickening awe. Lucifer sat on her makeshift throne and watched Brie watch the madness.

"Where's the food and water?" Brie asked Lucifer, curious.

"Twice a day the guards drop magnetic boxes of food down. It's usually rice and bread. Leftover rations from Union soldiers. It's usually stale."

"Is it chaos? I mean, how is it distributed amongst the masses. Everyone looks so… so crazy."

Lucifer laughed a deep, masculine laugh. "Everyone down here *is* crazy, my love. My men and I distribute the food. At first there was resistance, but I've been in this fucking pit now for a long time.

I'm guessing a year now, but I don't know for sure. Now the others accept that I'm in charge. I make sure everyone gets what they want."

"Has anyone tried to take more than their share?"

"Every damn day! Look around, Brie. Everyone fights everyone. Death comes to most. The average life span in here is a few weeks, even less for women. This is the bottom of the world. The Union has dumped us in here and left us to rot. The magna-crane hovers over every few days, collecting dead bodies, but soldiers *never* come down into the Block. It would be suicide."

"What about dosage? How do people survive the TNS? Do you get injections?"

Lucifer cackled a sarcastic laugh, rich with bitterness.

"Yeah right! They put Fosform in the water supplies. It must do something 'cause I'm still here aren't I?"

"What are you in here for?" Brie asked, curious.

"I sodomized a Union soldier with a kitchen knife," she said, laughing an evil laugh.

"Jesus. Why?"

"He raped me. So I overpowered him, took a blade from the kitchen and shoved it up his arse until he was good and dead. Then his colleagues caught me, beat me and threw me in this pit to rot. I would've taken them on but there were four of 'em. And they had tasers. Weak bastards!"

"Wow," Brie responded, eyes wide and disgusted.

"What about you? You told me you escaped your sub-plaza. But why? And why G-Block? You must have upset somebody."

"Well… I was married to a Union Advisor. He would get drunk and abuse me so I killed him one night in our apartment cell." She turned and showed Lucifer her scar. "Then I removed my registration chip and escaped. I got to the wall, right up north, then the Union captured me and brought here."

"Man, men are such fucking pigs, aren't they?"

"So why did you come over and help me?" Brie asked, changing the subject. "Why didn't you just leave me to the pit, to the others?"

"Don't take offence, honey. It's a power thing. You're the freshest meat in here. I'm in charge, so the fresh meat belongs to me. And you're good looking and clean. I'll look after you as long as you give me what I want, and right now what I want is a good pussy eating now and then and a way to get out of this pit."

Brie's expression changed. Her eyebrows dropped, forming a dimple on her swollen cheek. "I can't get you out of this pit," she said, surprised by Lucifer's strange remark.

"I don't think you know what you're capable of, Brie Kallas. I have a feeling about you. There's something different about you. You will do good things. I can smell it on you."

"Umm. Okay, but I…."

"Don't over-analyse it, Brie baby. Just be happy you're in here with us, and not over on the other side of the pit, scared and alone."

The conversation came to an abrupt end as the magna-crane above the other end of the pit churned to life with an electronic hum. The masses became lively and loud from all corners of the pit.

Dinnertime.

The large magnetic disk on the crane-arm held a huge steel crate, similar in size to a hover-bike. The crane descended into the pit.

"Okay," Lucifer said, standing up from her mattress throne, towering above her trusty protectors. "Let's feed the animals."

Brie followed Lucifer and her three guards, Peter, Lachlan and Toby. As the giant orange haired beast made her way through the filthy masses, they parted, letting her walk casually through. She reached the container as it hit the stained concrete floor. Lachlan, Peter and Toby stood around the container, guarding the contents, gazing through the crowds, fists clenched and ready. Lucifer tore off the lid and looked inside. "Like I said," she called out to Brie, "rice and bread."

Close to a hundred loaves of bread filled half the container, the crust rock-hard and stale. Piles of fruit filled the other half. Apples and oranges, over-ripened, bruised and dirty. From the mass of filthy people an organised single-file line formed. The line made its way past the container, guarded by Lucifer and her three trusty men. As convicts passed the container, Lucifer handed each of them half a loaf and a piece of fruit. Brie was shocked that these people, these savages that would fight to the death put their differences aside to line up and receive their rations. It made little sense.

When a little more than half the line had received their rations, a green inmate, tall and tattooed, pushed in front of his peers and stepped towards the container. He looked at Lucifer, stepped around her and mumbled something inaudible under his breath. He went to help himself to the container. What happened next made Brie flinch. She had never seen someone act so swiftly, so agile and powerful, especially for her size.

In half a heartbeat, Lucifer stepped towards the tattooed man and before Brie could even blink she grabbed the man's head and snapped his neck in one swift motion. He lay on the ground with his head torn a complete 180 degrees. Blood spewed from his lifeless mouth. "Does anyone else want more than their share," Lucifer roared to the masses. "Come on, you weak cowards. Take your best…"

Silence.

A Union soldier whistled from above the pit.

The line remained compliant. No one else wanted to face the giant, orange-haired woman. No one else wanted to die before dinner. She giggled to herself. "That's what I fuckin' thought!"

Within ten minutes both the rations and the line were gone. Lucifer made her way back to her private quarters, followed by Brie, who held two oranges and a *whole* loaf of bread.

Lucifer bit into a bruised apple as she looked at Brie. Juice dribbled down her chin and formed small droplets before landing on her huge magna-jack. "Now, where were we? That's right. What you can do for me…"

"I don't really know…"

"I don't really believe you."

"Okay, if you want the truth, I'm only in here for the night. Then tomorrow I'm being taken to meet Master Haynes himself."

Lucifer stopped chewing her apple.

"Really, Master Haynes, huh? Interesting…" She paused, assessing her words. "Well, I want you to pass on a message to him."

Brie looked at Lucifer. "Okay, sure. What sort of message."

"You tell him I want a spot in his army... Yeah, I want out of this piece of shit pit and I'll serve him."

"Women can't join the Union Army," Brie said, doubtfully.

"Like I said before, Brie, I might have this beautiful pussy between my thighs but I ain't no woman. You tell him I'll fight any of his best soldiers. And if I beat 'em, I get out of this pit."

"Well, I can ask, I suppose."

Lucifer looked at Brie and smiled, chomping down the last of her apple, core and all. "I knew there's something about you," she said. "You very well might be my ticket out of the pit."

Brie took a piece of orange flesh into her mouth and nodded. "And you very well might be my ticket for surviving the night."

Lucifer winked. "Then I guess that makes us partners."

THIRTY-FOUR

I FELT LIKE A NEW PERSON.

The dose of Fosform was invigorating. I felt strong. I felt alive. My breathing was clear. My muscles seemed rested, ready for whatever came our way. Eli, accustomed to drinking the serum when he got his hands on it, was unaccustomed to full-strength dosage. He was a whole new person too. It was like he was high, adrenaline and dopamine coursing through his Fosform-fuelled veins. He paced back and forth with a grin matted to his face, his eyes wide, his pupils dilated.

"Man, I feel good," he said. "I feel like I could take on the world right now. You and me, Tyson, we will take on the world."

I smiled at my partner in crime.

"I'm glad you're so enthusiastic, but first we have to get out of this hydro-harbour. Then we can think about the world."

We found a spot down in the engine room. It was dark and moist but it presented the perfect hiding spot. Light leaked through a small window in above the battery units, designed to get large scale charging packs in through the side of the hull. Not much bigger than a Union office monitor screen, the window did provide fresh air to combat the dank.

The freighter itself appeared to be entirely electric. The battery pack itself was the size of a sub-plaza bedroom. The engines attached looked modern, more like computers than engines, but they powered the propellers beneath the engine room.

We hadn't even been in our hideaway for two hours when I heard distant sounds outside. Before long they weren't so distant. I peered through the small porthole window and spotted people at the entrance to the hydro-harbour. They wore the unmistakable grey fatigues of the Union Army. I felt my stomach tighten and my heart rate increase. Eli couldn't see, he kept asking what was going on. I ignored him until he started tugging on my sleeve.

"Just wait," I barked at him. He sat back in silent anticipation.

Four armed soldiers opened the gates to the hydro-harbour and stood to attention at the entrance. Despite the distance from our hideout, I could make out everything. They wore their usual full-face, reflective conditioners. A civilian vehicle reversed right up to the gate. I watched as six civilian citizens stepped out the back of the vehicle. They wore casual clothing and citizen grade, disposable oxygen conditioners. Once out, they removed three wooden crates from the back of the vehicle. I recognised the soaring eagle stamped on the outside of the crates. Whatever was in them was Union property. That much I was sure.

My initial thought was that the civilians were carrying something to the Union vessel we had raided the previous night. I began to worry. If that vessel left the harbour they might find something amiss. I wanted to be a long way from the land before any Union soldiers boarded that boat.

"What's going on," Eli said, growing impatient.

I finally gave him a response. "There are soldiers and civilians. The civilians are carrying containers of some sort. I reckon they're taking them to the Union boat."

Just as I voiced my thoughts the civilians turned left on the dock, towards us, and *away* from the Union vessel. Because of the viewing angle the small charging outlet offered, it meant that as soon as they turned left, they too had left my vision. All I could see was the four soldiers, statue still by the entrance to the harbour.

"Today is the end of Pride, right? Tomorrow's the first day of Lust?"

"I think so," Eli responded, eyes wide, pupils looking like they were about to explode out of his face.

"Shit, maybe we're wrong. We can't be wrong. Maybe they're early."

We sat in silent anticipation. Within a minute we heard movements above. Footsteps, muffled voices. I heard three distinctive thuds. They had placed the containers inside the very vessel in which we were hiding. I crawled back over to the charging window, my heart thumping like a hammer-drill. One civilian, short and skinny with long hair tied in a topknot, got into the driver's door of the civilian vehicle and moved it from view. He returned a moment later and said something to the soldiers. They nodded, lowered their weapons and closed the security gate, staying *inside* the compound.

"I don't like this," I whispered.

I hadn't had soldiers on my mind when I thought of commandeering the vessel. Soldiers could change everything. To add to my worry, the four soldiers, along with the short topknot guy made their way towards the freighter, out of view. I left the window.

"This is a commercial freighter, right?" I asked.

"Yep," Eli said, pulling the crumpled timetable from his pocket again and showing me the logo.

"So why the *hell* are there Union soldiers getting on board?"

Eli gave me a wide-eyed shrug. "Well, isn't everything owned by the Union?"

BRRRRRRRRR!

We both jumped as the electric motor beside us purred to life. It was loud in the engine room, unbearably loud. We didn't think that through when securing a hiding spot. The plan in my head was unravelling into something different, something more complex. Something dangerous.

"Follow me," I yelled over the hum of the engine. With no need to be told twice, Eli grabbed the dry-bag and crawled behind me to the other end of the engine room, underneath the ladder leading into the quarters above. Mildly more bearable, we were now far more exposed but less likely to receive permanent ear damage.

The hum stopped. I heard muffled voices. They became louder. Without warning, the door above us opened wide, flooding the engine room with gloomy light. Eli and I scurried behind a small shelving unit, scarcely big enough to conceal the two of us.

"Make sure the engine is at full charge," I heard a voice call out from above.

"Sure thing," said another voice, much closer.

The closer voice stepped into view. It was the topknot guy.

He began climbing down the ladder. Eli and I squished into the wall, scared to move, scared to look but too frightened to look away. My heartbeat thumped between my temples. It felt so loud within my brain that I was scared that the topknot guy would hear it. He reached the bottom of the ladder. He looked young. Not much older than me. Without looking around he made his way to the giant battery pack and pulled a small cover off the side. After flicking a few switches, a small digital screen lit up beside him. He nodded and whispered something to himself. He placed the cover back over the screen and turned to made his way back to the ladder.

"Ninety-eight percent," he called up. "Perfect."

As topknot grabbed the first rung, he stopped and looked in our direction. Something had caught his eye. I closed my eyes and wished myself invisible. He stepped back down and left the central platform, heading to where we had been only seconds earlier. My heart pounded against my chest cavity, about to rupture with anxious fear. I could tell by how hard Eli was grabbing my arm he was feeling the same thing. His fingers dug into my forearm, almost to the point of piercing skin.

Topknot leaned down and picked something up. It was a bottle of water – *our* bottle of water. Eli must have left it beside the engine mount. Topknot opened the lid, sniffed it, and then placed the lid back on. He shoved the bottle into the back pocket of his trousers and made his way back to the ladder and up, leaving the engine room. As he closed the door above the ladder, darkness swallowed us. It was wonderful, welcome darkness.

I took in a huge gulp of air, realising I'd been holding my breath the whole time he had been in the room. "Man, that was way too damn close," I said to Eli. "What's with the damn bottle? That could have given away our position."

"I'm sorry," Eli said, tears welling in his eyes. I don't think they were tears of sorrow, I think they were tears of relief. If they had caught us, it would have been an abrupt end to our journey.

"Hey, it's all good," I said, patting him on the back. "They didn't find us. Now we just need to wait it out down here. We're on the home stretch to freedom, my man."

Eli wiped away a lone tear and smiled. "Let the adventure begin," he said, laughing nervously.

"Well, if you think the adventure is only beginning now, I don't know what you call the last three days."

"I wouldn't call it adventure, I'd call it survival."

The engine hummed to life again. I heard some muffled yelling over the hum of the engine. Then the vessel moved. Even though the charging window was closest to the engine and its incessant noise, I wanted to see what was happening. I needed to. Looking out the small window I saw the dock getting further away. I saw the compound gates open before us. Nothing separated the freighter from the wide blue unknown before me. It occurred to me that this was the first time I had left the mainland since working on the walls. I had the same nervous feeling I did when I was seventeen and I had left my family behind to venture out into that same wide blue unknown.

There was something about the unknown that was alluring. My monotonous routine had been the same for two years. Every day was predictable. The same office, the same apartment, the same clothes and the same coffee shop. Hell, even the same pornography. The unknown, alluring Pacific Ocean we faced was electrifying. Monotony was a thing of the past. Monotony was what the Union wanted. As the freighter sailed through the marina gates, I kissed monotony goodbye.

Before long we were out of the hydro-harbour. As I looked back, I could make out the harbour getting smaller. I could make out the huge fortress on the headland, towering over Terrigal Bay. It looked small now, like a toy castle, nothing more. Through the small window, I breathed in the salty ocean air coming in off the waves. Despite its poisonous potency, it felt good to breathe it in. I felt a surge of hope flood through my veins.

Although I was trapped in the engine room of a vessel heading to God-knows-where, I felt free for the first time since leaving the sub-plaza. I was leaving behind 3rd Sydney West. I was leaving behind my Marriage Lottery. I was leaving behind Block 7 and I was leaving behind the all-powerful Humanist Union. It pained me to accept the fact that I was also leaving George behind. I shrugged away the uncertainty accompanied with everything I was leaving behind and I looked towards the blank canvas that was our future.

Bring it on.

THIRTY-FIVE

GEORGE DID HIS BEST TO BLOCK THE SUN'S RAYS FROM HIS FACE.

Despite his efforts, sunburn covered his skin. He had endured a whole day and night in a surface cage above 3rd Sydney West and now he faced the second day of sunlight. Even through the smog, the sun packed a potent glow. George was naked, thirsty, starved and fatigued. He tried rolling from side to side to limit the time he exposed his bare skin to the sun. It served little purpose. With each hour that passed he turned pinker. If thicker cloud cover didn't come soon, he would blister.

The cage itself was barely big enough for him to sit up straight. Cramped and confined to an uncomfortable crouching position, George's muscles ached. He didn't know how much longer he could endure the torment. He didn't know what else to do though; he had nothing to tell the Union that would aid in recapturing his closest friend.

With each burning minute, the resentment George felt towards his friend increased. Why did Ty have to leave? Why had Ty done something so selfish? A part of George wished he knew where his friend had gone, so he could tell the Union and be released.

George saw countless other surface cages varying in size alongside his. Some of them housed other sinners and some housed rotting, dead corpses. Others housed a handful of people, all of them naked, all crammed inside the same small, hot cell.

Damn the Union, George thought. Despite his bitterness towards Tyson, he could see what his friend had meant.

Wiping his cracked, dry lips, George looked up as he heard footsteps behind him. Two soldiers in Tier Three Navy-blue uniforms walked over to his cage. One aimed a taser cannon at George while the other inserted a combination code into the steel door. The door swung open.

"Come with us," said the soldier holding the weapon.

Trying to rise, George felt his stiff muscles give way beneath him. Fighting the pain, he crawled from the cage and stood. He barely had the strength to stand. One soldier led the way while the other followed behind, his weapon aimed at the back of George's head. Surely his punishment had ended. Thirty-six hours in the surface cage. Surely they would dock him a few credits and send him back to his apartment cell to rest?

Near the surface cages, built into a concrete bunker in the dirt, a small transporter tunnel existed for soldiers and prisoners only. If it had been where George had come from at the start of his surface exposure, he didn't remember it. He had woken up inside the cage with a throbbing head and no recollection of how he got there.

He followed the first soldier into a small transporter cell. They cuffed his wrists with a short carbon-fibre rod and placed a black canvas bag back over his head. He was becoming all too familiar with the canvas bags.

The soldiers escorted George from the transporter cell. He was told to sit. They removed the canvas bag and he squinted. The cylindrical lights above him seemed far brighter than usual. The room was like the one in which they had interrogated him prior to his surface exposure – all white, concrete – but it was not the same room. He could tell by the unusual brown stains on the floor and the steel chair's absence.

Without speaking, the two soldiers left the small white room and the short, pudgy Union Official who had interrogated George before entered. He wore the same Union clothing and flaunted the same arrogant smirk. He looked George's naked body up and down before speaking, admiring the severity of the sunburn. "Mr Clarkson," he said before a long pause. "I trust your time on the surface gave you some time to think?"

George nodded. "May I please have some water?" His voice came out as nothing more than a hoarse whisper.

"In due time," the Union Official replied. "I would like to know where Tyson Anderson 636-124 has gone. If you can give me some information, I will not only give you some water, I will pardon you for your crimes against the Union."

"My crimes against the Union? What crimes?"

"Mr Clarkson, we have security footage of you urinating in the flower bed of a Tier One hallway several days ago. That is an offence punishable by imprisonment. I want what's best for everyone, and what's best for everyone is you telling me what I want to know."

"I don't know where he is. I promise you."

"You will not play this game again, will you Mr Clarkson? Surely your time on the surface helped you realise the seriousness of my threats?"

"Look," whispered George, breaking as tears welled in his fiery eyes. "Tyson hated the Union, okay. He feared the Marriage Lottery. He didn't want to conform. He didn't want to live in these conditions. And I can't blame him. This is a disgusting excuse for a Union. He's gone, okay. Just forget about him. Go find someone else to pester, you stupid bastard…"

Shocked, the pudgy, greasy-haired Official stepped forward, his face only centimetres from George's. His putrid breath was warm and stale.

"Look here, you little *peasant*. I gave you a choice. You should thank me for that. We rarely give citizens choices and this is why. It's because you always make the *wrong* choices. It's a shame, too. I would have enjoyed tormenting you but you'll learn the hard way instead."

The Official stepped back and pressed a button on the small

screen attached to his wrist. Within seconds a soldier walked in with a long, sharp, crescent-shaped blade. He looked at his fat commander, grinning like a spoilt little child. The Official nodded. With no further direction required, the soldier stepped toward George and in a single, perfectly executed motion grabbed George's genitals with his free hand and sliced from thigh to thigh with the curved blade, taking George's manhood off, testicles and all. George screamed a horrific, blood-curdling cry. The fat Official cackled. The soldier, still holding George's private parts, threw them on the floor and walked out.

Pain and shock riddled George's manic mind. Unable to grasp what had just happened, he screamed through cracked lips as blood gushed from his groin. He looked down on the floor to see his own body parts, his own manhood in a bloody, shrivelled heap. It was the last thing he saw as he slipped into blackness.

The pudgy Official brought his wrist tablet to his face and compressed the digital microphone. "We need medics in here, now. I don't want to lose this one. He is the perfect body type for our needs. Send him straight to Terra Carcerem."

THIRTY-SIX

Brie woke up startled.

She sat up, unaware of her surroundings, her body clammy and wet. For a moment she thought she was back in her underground cell. To her relief she saw Lucifer sleeping beside her on a filthy mattress. Even as she slept, the giant woman looked intimidating.

Lachlan stood beside them, watching the masses stir in the pit, most of whom slept. Brie heard the odd conversation throughout the giant arena, echoing off the concrete walls.

"Can't sleep?" Lachlan asked, looking down at her with a sly smile.

She looked up at him and nodded. Lachlan stood six feet tall. Compared to Lucifer, he appeared average but he towered over Brie. His bicep and chest muscles bulged through his faded shirt. His short black hair, in contrast to his green eyes, gave him a dark aura.

Despite Lachlan being in G-Block for mass murder, Brie sensed a compassionate twinkle in his eye. She couldn't write him off purely because he had killed another. She had done the same thing, and worse.

"I'm not used to all the sounds, I guess. Or all the people, either. I spent a long time in solitary…"

"Yeah, the pit takes some time to get used to. Sometimes the lack of privacy gets to you. Especially the first time you take a shit…" He laughed.

Brie hadn't thought of that.

The two strangers conversed until the roof over G-Block glowed with the mild artificial sunlight of morning. 7:00 am. They talked about nothing in particular, nothing of any substance anyway. How long he'd been in the pit. Why he did what he did. What he would do if he weren't in the pit. Trivial conversation, while lacking substance, still let Brie know that she was amongst real people. Trivial conversation helped mask the trauma that still haunted her thoughts. Her time in solitary was still very much present in her mind. Every time she closed her eyes she relived the horrors of that mouldy cell. The relentless ache in her vagina reminded her of it all, but speaking with real people about real things helped numb her discomfort.

As the light intensified, so did the surrounding noise. The convicts began to wake, talking, yelling blasphemous insults at the guards above.

"God, I'm thirsty," Brie said, to no one in particular.

"The taps are over there," Lachlan said, pointing to the other side of the pit. "Here, I'll go with you. Make sure no one brings you trouble."

The two of them made their way through the waking mass of people. No one paid them any attention. On the wall, about waist height, seven taps lined up in a row, about two metres apart. Lines of thirsty convicts gathered in front of each tap, waiting to get their fill. As there was nothing in the pit to fill-up, one had to drink straight from the tap as it spewed from the concrete wall.

The water tasted bitter, similar to the river water Brie had in the jungle with the Fosform capsules in it. She ignored the bitter-ness and took several large mouthfuls. Despite the taste, it was much needed and refreshing. Because of the inconvenience of lining up and waiting every time she was thirsty, she thought better just to fill her belly now.

Looking to her left, roughly ten metres past the last tap, seven shower heads came out of the wall with crude holes in the floor beneath them. The showerheads spewed different water to the drinking taps. Tainted brown. Lachlan told Brie it came from an underground bore. It was undrinkable. Several convicts showered, naked, except for their magna-jacks, which clung tightly to their upper bodies, the water glistening off the slick metal.

Time proved hard to gauge, especially as the artificial lights never altered in intensity after 7:00. Close to an hour after lining up for a drink, the magnetic crane hummed to life. Lucifer stood, expecting the crane to be carrying a container for breakfast. It wasn't. The crane was empty. It hovered across the pit on its hydraulic arm, humming rhythmically. Once above Lucifer's pallet barriers, directly over Brie, it descended.

"Looks like you're out of here," Lucifer said to Brie, winking. "Don't forget to speak to the Master for me. I'll take on any of his best soldiers. If I win, I want out."

Brie nodded, preoccupied, watching the giant crane hover down to meet her. When it hovered a metre above her, dangling in mid-air, the magnetic attraction pulled her up, sucking her almost from the security of solid ground. Her feet lifted then before she could even let out a gasp it sucked her up onto the huge disc.

Helpless, Brie dangled from the crane, the magnetic power holding her firm. She looked down at Lucifer, who looked right back up at her. Before long the residents of the pit were nothing more than a crowd of dirty faces. The robotic arm moved Brie up and over the railing and back onto the balcony floor. The first thing she noticed once up and out of the pit was the change in smell. The pit had such a potent smell of sweat and sex, shit and piss that now up on the balcony, the scent of clean metal and lifeless concrete was a godsend.

Eric van Bueren waited on the balcony with several armed soldiers. He wore his thick lens glasses and a grey latex suit synonymous with the highest-level Union Advisors.

"Good morning, Brie," he said, smiling, articulating his words with his thick English accent. "It appears G-Block didn't eat you up and spit you out. It's an unusual place down there, is it not? So much damn violence."

"Your solitary cells are worse," Brie said, spitefully. "At least it appears some convicts in the pit have souls. That's more than I can say about your soldiers."

"Well, Brie. We don't pay soldiers to have souls. We pay soldiers to teach bratty little murderous whores a lesson. Now, it would be insulting to present you to Master Haynes looking like a ragged little pit-slut so we will get you cleaned up and give you some new clothes. Would you like that?"

Brie stared at him, indifferent.

The soldiers removed her magna-jack with the unusual, octagon shaped key. It beeped three times and released the locks. Brie took one last fleeting look down into the chaos of the pit before the soldiers escorted her away. Apprehension followed her down the sterile corridor. Despite the dangers of the pit, in the company of Lucifer and her men, she felt safe. Now she made her way back into the lion's den to meet with the leader of the pride. Alarm bells were ringing.

The cleaning this time was a little more graceful. Rather than being stripped and hosed down like a muddy piece of machinery, they sent Brie to a military shower block used by Union soldiers. Two of the armed guards looked on as they forced her to strip and enter the water. It was warm. She hadn't felt warm water in months. Not since abandoning her sub-plaza apartment the night she killed her late husband. It revitalised her. The hot pricks of water caused tingling sensations over her bruised and swollen skin. She washed away the grime and piss, the rape and the beatings. She washed away the residue of Lucifer's womanhood from her chin. She washed away the trauma. She looked at the soldiers standing idle beside the wall, half expecting them to behave like a pack of savage animals. They didn't appear to be interested. They stood still and waited, as instructed, until Brie finished her shower.

After her shower they gave Brie a towel and a set of female

Union uniform leggings, boots and a synthetic jacket. They were all grey, the neutral colour between sub-plazas. Only higher priority Union staff wore grey. Peter, her late husband, had worn grey. The clothing hung from her frame, a little too big, more so because she had lost a substantial amount of weight in the month prior but she didn't care. She was out of the filthy, bloodstained rags she knew so well.

Brie felt like a new woman. Eric van Bueren and two soldiers escorted her into a large transporter tunnel. The door opened to a spacious conference room with grey walls and matte-black polished flooring, devoid of people. A large marble-top table was positioned in the centre of the room with an abundance of foods and beverages, displayed not dissimilar to the banquet dishes on Eric van Bueren's flight.

Roast lamb lay in the centre of an oven tray, still steaming, with whole stems of rosemary resting on the flesh. Potatoes, pumpkins and tomatoes, baked and caramelised crowded around the lamb. There were fruits of every variety, platters of rock melon and watermelon, loaves of warm rye bread, raspberry butter biscuits and more.

Before being given permission, Brie wandered trance-like towards the table. Her stomach churned. Her mouth watered.

"Would you like some food, Brie?"

"Is that a trick question?"

"No, not at all. Please be my guest. We often find that people are more compliant, more helpful, when they have a full belly. Half of it will go to waste, anyway. Please, dig in."

Brie didn't need to be told twice. She paced across the room and began digging in with her hands, not concerned with manners. She sucked on a huge slice of lamb, the juices flowing down her chin. She could not chew the tender meat. Her jaw still ached, but she fought the discomfort and she inhaled the hot lamb flesh. She hadn't had hot, roasted lamb in six months, longer maybe. While filling her stomach with top-tier gourmet foods, it made her loathe the Union all the more. There were people in G-Block that were fighting for their lives to get a loaf of stale bread. Here, in this room, on that one table, would have been enough food to feed half the pit. It was sickening.

Regardless, despite the loathing, Brie stuffed her face.

After washing the meal down with some guava juice, van Bueren escorted Brie to a small seating area at the far side of the conference room. The seating was common for sub-plaza styling – grey, hard and uncomfortable. Van Bueren sat across from Brie. He stared at her callously, his skills in intimidation proving successful.

"Are you going to be helpful, Brie?" he asked, pulling a built-in tablet screen from the side of the chair and typing something with his fingers.

Brie nodded.

"Just remember, I brought you here because you would help. I could have left you in KL with the lads. I could have left you there to rot, but I didn't. Please don't let me down."

She nodded again.

Brie was battling her inner demons. She didn't know how she would play this. They wanted the truth. They would get the truth. They would beat the truth out of her if they thought she was lying. She didn't want to give up the T-Town location and ruin her fellow T-Towners chances of survival, of freedom, of life. But she didn't know what else to do. Her conscience was heavy. Sweat beaded on her brow. Indigestion caused pains in her gut. Would giving up T-Town's location be the easiest thing to do? Would that be too selfish? Would they have done the same to her?

Van Bueren finished typing and placed the tablet screen back on his armrest. As if on cue, a small door rolled open beside them. Two grey-clad soldiers walked through followed by a man, whom Brie could tell from pictures of government propaganda, was none other than Master Haynes himself. He was tall, skinny for someone of the highest importance. His hair was grey, thinning. He had a well-manicured beard, darker than the hair on his head. More like a gunmetal grey. He sat down beside Eric van Bueren and stared at Brie with sunken eyes. He forced a smile.

"Ah," he said. "Brie van Bueren. I've heard remarkable things about you."

THIRTY-SEVEN

Oh, how reality had changed.

Only a few weeks ago Brie had found salvation. A few weeks ago she never would have guessed that she would sit across from the Master of the entire Empire. The very person who had single-handedly built up Soteria and contributed to the destruction of much of the western world now sat with her, radiating arrogance and self-worth. Reality had been picked up, spun around and thrown on its arse. Brie sat with the one person who represented everything she hated.

Master Haynes had said a few things but Brie hadn't registered. She was lost in thought. She struggled to come to grips with what she intended to do, and what she intended to do was rat out her friends. Evan, Remy, Robin, Krit, Gabbie, Tinker, all of them. If she did what she thought she was about to do, then it would be the end for her fellow diggers. The past year of digging would be in vain. Her information would lead them all to slaughter.

"Brie, are you listening to what I am proposing?" Master Haynes' question brought her back to that reality. Despite the cruel world that he created, his voice came across as calm, confident. Supportive, almost.

"Sorry. I was just having a moment. Please continue."

The Master looked at his friend and colleague, Eric van Bueren.

"The thing is, Brie. I created a system. You defied that system the second you killed your husband. I designed the Marriage Lottery for simplicity, for productivity. Prior to the Marriage Lottery people wasted far too much time and energy looking for mates, for sexual partners, for fun. Did you know that prior to introducing the Lottery, when I still allowed people to make the choice, over fifty percent of marriages ended in divorce?" He raised his hands in a gesture of despair. "So, what on earth did they marry for in the first place, I ask you? The bottom line is that people are incapable of making choices, of executing a decision and sticking with it. That's why I have stripped people of that freedom to make choices. Why let people make the wrong choices when *my* Union can make the right choices for them? Huh?"

"With all due respect, Master, my husband would beat me, and rape me, and assault me. You speak of making the right choices but who is that right for?"

Master Haynes looked at Brie. He noticed her swelling, her bruising and her missing teeth. "Now let me ask you this, Brie. What has been more traumatising for you, being taken advantage of in your own household by your own husband or being raped by my soldiers in a KL dungeon?"

Brie didn't answer. She pursed her lips and looked at the floor.

"Exactly my point. My Marriage Lottery gave you a house, an apartment bigger than most in the Empire. My Marriage Lottery gave you food, shelter, Fosform Five and security. And you threw it all away."

"Life's not worth living if you're living in Hell," Brie responded.

"You haven't seen Hell yet, Brie."

"Everyone has a different interpretation of Hell, Master. Mine was in that Brisbane apartment."

"So, you killed one of my senior Advisors?"

"I did."

"And did it make you feel better? Did removing your chip and becoming a treasonous outlaw make you feel better?"

"It did."

Master Haynes looked at Brie, his emotions unreadable.

"Well, there's no point obsessing over the past. What's done is done. It shames me you felt compelled to do so, but I cannot change it. What you do now will have an enormous impact on your future. Think long and hard about your answers." Master Haynes paused, letting his words sink in. "The men we caught with you in the jungle have caused us disruption in the past. We have caught two on our cameras looting from Union trains. Not just looting food and supplies, but *Fosform.*"

He was silent again.

"How can I be the leader of the greatest Empire of human history if I have surface-dwelling outlaws stealing the most powerful item on the planet? I could have had Eric here interrogate you himself. I'm one hundred percent confident in his abilities but I demanded to hear the answer myself. To this day there has not been a soul who has taken such large quantities of my serum and these fuckers, *these fuckers*, have stolen it twice!"

That was the first time Brie heard The Master raise his voice. That was the first time she heard him swear.

"I don't care who they are," he continued. "I want you to tell me where they have been hiding out. I want you to tell me how many more there are and what their purpose is. I'm all for free people wandering my Empire until the syndrome rots their lungs, but I'll be damned if I let some ruffians threaten the safety of my hard workers. If shipments of Fosform Five due to reach my Northern Sector don't get to their destination, I have a potential pandemic on my hands. My soldiers, my staff, my citizens need that Fosform. Do you understand the severity of these crimes? *Your* crimes?"

Brie had a thought. The all-too-clichéd light bulb just lit up above her head. She thought of the barbaric sacrifices they had found on the Bentung ridge on their way south. She thought of the crude little shelter, the man with the dread-locks, the hanging women. If Brie could convince the Master that shelter was her hide-out, *their* hideout, she might keep the Union soldiers away from T-Town. When the soldiers got to the god-fearing voodoo camp, all they would find is rotten bodies and a burned down hut. Those bodies could be anyone, Brie thought to herself. Even Evan, Remy and the others as far as the Union needed to know.

Brie wiped her dried and cracking lips and looked at the Master, then at Eric van Bueren. "I will tell you," she said. "I will tell you where they're based and how I found them as long as you promise not to torture me anymore. Please. I will serve the Union. I will do whatever it takes. I will spend the rest of my days in G-Block if I must…"

"Rest of your days? Who said anything about rest of days? No more of my soldiers will have their way with you, but I might just send you to a surface cage to die. I said nothing about letting you live. It all depends on how beneficial the information you provide is. I want details."

"Okay."

This was the moment.

Honesty would be easier but it would not be noble, it would be cowardly. If Brie told Master Haynes a stone-cold lie and he learnt of her dishonesty, he would put her in a cell with savage soldiers. They would happily rape her to death. If she were honest though, she would condemn her peers to slaughter.

This was the moment.

The Union had already broken her. She couldn't be mended. Fuck the Union, she thought. Fuck Master Haynes and his pathetic requests. Nobility or not, Brie would not rat on her friends. She couldn't bring herself to ruin their hard-earned dreams.

It was now or never, and never wasn't an option.

"I stumbled across them by accident," she said, looking at the Master. "I was on my way towards the wall to see if I could get across the thing, to see if I could get out of Soteria."

The Master sniggered.

"When I made it just north of Georgetown, maybe by half a day, I headed up onto the mountain ridge to the north-east to stay out of anyone's way. I came across their camp. It's a small shelter, two or three huts hidden in the trees up on the ridge. They took me in and promised me food and shelter and Fosform."

"In return for what?"

"In return for nothing. They just wanted to help. They were nice people."

"Was Francis Balding a *nice* person?" The Master asked. That was the first time Brie had ever heard his surname.

"How do you know his name?"

"Brie, this is *my* Empire. I know more than you can ever fathom. That is why I want your honesty. My soldiers held Francis Balding captive for several years. If I remember correctly, we discharged him for aggressive behaviour towards his colleagues. When he talked back to his commanding officers one too many times, we had his tongue cut off, and his teeth hammered out."

Brie was confused. "What do you mean *discharged?*"

"Did you not know? Francis Balding used to be a Union soldier. He served in Indonesia during *the conversion*, or as the citizens like to call it, the *modern day Crusades*." Master Haynes sniggered again. "Francis Balding alone would have murdered over one thousand innocent people, just because of their Muslim beliefs, just because we ordered him to. Hence my question, was Francis Balding a nice person?"

"To me he was. He didn't talk, mind you, obviously. But he never came across as hostile or cruel to me. He sort of kept to himself."

"So, would you be able to show me on a satellite image of the region exactly where this camp is?"

"I think so. I could take your soldiers there if you'd like?"

"Unlikely. I don't know what sort of ambush you might lead my men into. How many outlaws are there in the camp you came from?"

"Umm, about six," Brie lied, her face flushing.

"Now, Brie. Think long and hard about the truth. If you lie to me once more, Eric here will cut your tits off. Why on earth would your friends need pallet after pallet of Fosform if there are six of you in hiding? A single pallet would last six hostile outlaws years. I ask again. How many are there? And don't test my patience."

"I swear there are only six, and me. I can give you their names if you like. Francis and Bruce took the Fosform and traded it with other surface dwellers. They swapped it for food and weaponry, vehicles and girls. That's why they needed so much. I promise."

For someone lying through her teeth, Brie sounded convincing. She remembered Michael's story of the Fosform mission on the train, of the huge number of casualties. She continued with her story. "There were more of them before I got there," she added. "But they died at some train bridge disaster. When I was there, there were only six. I would not dare to lie to you, Master."

Master Haynes looked long and hard at Brie. "Get me an SLD," he demanded, turning to one of his guards. The guard returned with a small tablet screen and handed it to the Master. He pressed down on a small green button on the tablet's edge. "Georgetown, Northern Sector," he spoke at the device.

"Georgetown, Northern Sector," an automated female voice spoke back from a small speaker inside the tablet. Master Haynes handed the device to Brie. "Show me where your hideaway is," he demanded.

Brie slid her finger across the screen, locating the ridgeline where they had met their resistance, where Caleb had been killed. It didn't take long for her to locate the small, over-grown road and the crude tin-roof of the shelter. Even from the satellite image on the screen, the shelter was easily distinguishable. The image quality was unbelievable. It was as clear, if not more so, than the human eye. Brie watched as people moved about, walking from the shelter to the small timber lookout above the trees. She swiped her fingers, zooming in on the image. She could almost make out the facial expressions of the people. "How long ago did this footage get recorded?" Brie asked.

"Recorded? That is live satellite footage, Brie. The delay is about thirty seconds, no more."

Brie face reddened.

Uncertainty.

Doubt.

They had left that place a burning tomb. And now already, only weeks later it seemed rebuilt, it seemed lively and littered with people. She recalled what the dread-locked man had said before his death. *Of course there are others. We are infinite.* It appeared he told no lies. The fact that the pagan shelter had been rebuilt would work all the more in her favour.

Brie handed the tablet to Master Haynes and pointed to the shelter, to the surrounding encampment. "There it is. That's my home, my freedom." She tried to sound saddened because she had given it up. She let out a false sigh of defeat.

"Thank you, Brie. Was that so hard?"

Brie didn't respond.

"I will send a squadron right away to destroy all those who inhabit that rudimentary little shelter," the Master said, his eyes still focused on the screen before him. "I will leave one alive for interrogation. I will also expect to see evidence of Fosform and Union-issue food and weaponry. Shouldn't I?"

Brie swallowed, her mouth dry. "I expect you will. It was there only two or three weeks ago," she lied.

"For the time being, until I'm happy with your information, until I've had closure on this tedious and time-consuming problem, I'm sending you back to G-Block. You can wait there until I hear from the soldiers up north. If we destroy the outlaw scum and I get back some of what belongs to me, you will have served your purpose. Not a second before. If I find out you have been untruthful, you will know pain like you have never known before..." He looked at Eric van Bueren. "Now take her back to the pit..."

"Wait," Brie said. "Speaking of the pit. There is a woman in there who has a proposition for you."

The Master laughed. It was an arrogant cackle. "A proposition for *me*? A convict pit-whore has a proposition for the Master of Soteria? Okay, humour me, Brie van Bueren..."

"She wants to join The Union's Army. She is as fierce a fighter as I have ever seen."

"That's ridiculous. Women don't serve in my army. What a stupid proposition."

"She has offered to fight your greatest soldier. She said if she wins, in one-on-one combat, that she should be taken from the pit and given a position in your army. She said she would serve you loyally."

"And what is this whore's name? What is she in the pit for?"

"Her name is Lucy. They call her Lucifer in G-Block. She controls the pit. They sentenced her for killing a Union soldier."

"Well, this sounds somewhat exciting. I'll think about it. If I engage in this offer, the fight will take place in the pit. If she survives, which I highly doubt, then I will consider taking her from the filthy den."

Without another word Master Haynes stood up, patted his colleague on the shoulder in a gesture of kinship and left through the same door he entered.

"Okay, Brie," van Bueren said, standing. "Let's take you back to the pit."

As they escorted Brie to the transporter tunnel, she thought about why she had lied. She didn't have an answer. She just couldn't bring herself to give up the true location of T-Town and destroy the hopes of so many hard-working friends. She wouldn't carry that burden.

Their chance for freedom, their chance of success was worth more than her life alone. She knew that. She knew, too, that it was only a matter of time until they revealed her lies.

Her heart thumped underneath her grey Union clothing. She had just dug herself a hole far deeper and far more dangerous than any G-Block pit. And she knew it was too late. The lie could not be untold. As she stepped inside the transporter tunnel cell, she fought off tears. She knew what would be coming.

The end.

It was only a matter of time. And the end would be far worse than death.

THIRTY-EIGHT

DESPITE GABBIE'S INCESSANT NAGGING, BRUCE REMAINED HELL-BENT on going along the wall with Michael and the others.

Despite his limping, his crude crutches and his hand still being a purple and scabbing mess, he refused to stay behind. Gabbie gave up trying. She knew her words fell on deaf ears. Bruce Chadwick and stubborn had always been perfect partners.

With expected resistance from some, Michael gathered a group of willing and ready T-Towners. It hadn't been easy but realisation became apparent over the previous days that without the Fosform Five, the syndrome would soon start showing its effects.

Michael, Bruce, Tinker, Robin, Krit and one of the Toms had all agreed on going. Evan and Gabbie would be in charge of T-Town once again. Alex, Seb and the other Tom would be in charge of digging. The group's departure caused mixed emotions within the bunker community. There was doubt and uncertainty, but they all knew above all there was necessity.

The six men gathered what weaponry, food, Fosform and supplies they could carry in backpacks then said their sombre farewells. It was early in the morning, only a little after sunrise. The breeze was light and the smoggy black clouds hung high and thin. They planned to get to the wall and walk west, hoping to come across a unit of soldiers on patrol and steal their identity. The whole mission relied on chance. It was a big gamble and the whole team knew it. There was quite a sound chance that there wasn't an outpost this far north at all. There was quite a sound chance that they were walking west for nothing.

Evan hugged his friends goodbye, reluctant to see them go. It was the second time in a month he'd had to watch Michael and Bruce leave. He wiped a tear from his cheek, blaming fatigue rather than sorrow.

Once gone, a void presented itself in the T-Town bunker. The place felt emptier than ever. The usual hum of warm conversation was missing. The laughter, the jokes and the humble comfort of family had been replaced with anxious unease. Evan needed time alone. He left the bunker and made his way up into his usual position in T-Tree overlooking the main entrance. To his surprise, he found Remy up there already seeking similar solitude. For an hour they didn't speak; they didn't need to. They sat perched above the jungle floor, listening to the noises of the forest. They listened to the birds sing. They listened to the wind through the leaves. Both of them prayed for their friends' safe return. If they didn't, they knew it would be the beginning of the end for all of them.

IT TOOK THE TEAM OF SIX NEARLY TWENTY MINUTES TO REACH THE base of the wall. Bruce's pace slowed them down. Once in the clearing at the base of the concrete monolith, Michael looked up. He hadn't seen the wall since he first arrived at T-Town months earlier. He forgot how threatening it was. A sense of apprehension overcame him simply by standing beneath it. It made him feel inferior, insignificant.

Michael and Bruce had taser cannons slung over their shoulders. Bruce would find it hard firing anything else with only one functioning hand. Tom and Tinker carried assault rifles and Robin and Krit carried the supplies and food in weathered canvas backpacks. Even with Bruce slowing their pace, they remained on schedule. Bruce was not only the oldest and least fit of the six. He was recovering from near fatal injuries. Because of his position in T-Town's hierarchy it would have been impossible to make his stay behind but a part of Michael wished he had. He loved the man like a father, but only an hour into their journey and Bruce began sweating, slowed by fatigue.

As the day dragged on and the hot sun arched across the muggy grey sky, the scenery barely changed. The conversation was sparse and broken. All six had things on their minds. All six were apprehensive about what they might run into. Bruce and Michael knew what it took to kill another man, but the other four had never taken a life. They had never needed to.

By the time they finally stopped, the weakening sun hung over the western horizon in front of them. The shadows were long and drawn out, the glare bathing their faces. Following the wall meant that the terrain was flat and clear. And fast. As long as they didn't venture more than a few metres from the tree line, the six would stay safe from the splinter mines. They walked either in single file or two abreast.

Robin and Krit seemed enthusiastic. Despite the dangerous nature of the mission they hadn't left T-Town in almost a year, except for hunting, so the mission had an element of adventure.

As Robin whistled melodic tunes Michael Butcher drifted, letting his mind wander to places and times worthier of daydreams. That olive brown skin, that thin, dark hair, those hazel brown eyes, those soft, sexy lips. These were the things that occupied most of his thoughts. He didn't think it possible. Michael had only known Brie a little more than a week, yet he felt drawn to her. He felt it was his life's duty to save her, to barge into the enemy's territory and walk out a triumphant hero with Brie Kallas hanging over his shoulder. He was well aware how stupid it sounded, but stupidity or not, Michael felt compelled to try saving the woman he loved.

Bruce pulled Michael from his thoughts of Brie with a harsh whisper. "Robin, shut the hell up," he hissed, ducking behind the thick foliage beside the track. The other five followed suit. Michael, switching back on from his vague dream state, didn't know what was happening. Bruce aimed the taser cannon forward, crouching like a jungle-cat.

At first it was faint, almost inaudible, but then distant, muffled murmurs came from up ahead.

"This is it," Bruce said. "It has to be them. Robin, Krit, get your bloody pistols out. We have to take them out, fast. No messing about!"

As the voices became louder, so did Michael's heartbeat. His sweaty hands felt loose around the rubber handle of the taser cannon. He looked at his peers. Robin and Krit looked frightened, the colour drained from their faces. Tinker, despite his tall, muscular build, looked the most terrified of all.

From behind a tall wattle tree leaning into the canopy above, a grey-clad Union soldier stepped into view, pursued by four others. Unlike the six T-Towners, the soldiers did not care for silence or stealth. The soldier in front clumsily placed a foot on the fallen leaf litter, crunching the debris under his Union issue boots. They wore full-face, oxygen bottle conditioners, standard for surface patrol.

Great, Bruce thought. Having a nine-kilogram bottle strapped to their back would make them slow.

"Wait," he whispered to the others.

Robin felt faint, nauseous and frightened. Michael had rage pulsing through his veins. He wanted retribution. He wanted blood. He could smell it. His finger rested on the aluminium trigger of the taser cannon. He grew impatient.

Lured into a sense of complacency by the constant lack of excitement on patrol, the soldiers paid little attention to their surroundings. They had done the same patrol loop hundreds of times and rarely, if ever, came across hostile activity. Their complacency would be their downfall. Just because they had a towering mass of concrete beside them didn't guarantee their safety, not when

Bruce Chadwick and Michael Butcher hid in the bushes beside them seeking cold-blooded vengeance.

The time had come.

Bruce stepped forward in a swift motion. Despite his wounds, he bounced up with his weapon drawn. Standing only a metre in front of the first soldier, he fired a taser round into the soldier's face. The Pyrex-plastic lens of the mask melted as the close-range electric shot burned a hole through the soldier's surprised frown. Before the other four soldiers reacted, Bruce aimed at the second soldier, right at his throat, and fired again. The soldier fell to the leafy ground below, his head hanging on by nothing more than his spinal cord and a string of tendons.

Despite the momentary shock, the other soldiers reacted, diving behind nearby shrubbery and rocks. Michael and Tinker rose to their feet. Tinker aimed his assault rifle at the small, dense shrubs that concealed one soldier and held the trigger down. Compared to the quiet surge of the taser cannon, the *clack-clack-clack* of an assault rifle was ear piercing, as was the horrific squeal that came seconds after from behind the bushes.

Orange-blue bursts of electric charge shot back and forth. Dried leaf litter caught on fire. There was yelling, screaming, swearing. Through the foliage, Robin and Krit had crawled forward on hands and knees with old-fashioned pistols at the ready. Robin watched the soldier at the back draw a satellite-communication tablet from his breast-holster and bring it to his mask, presumably to request back up. Robin had never fired a pistol before. He cocked the hammer back and started firing in the soldier's direction.

The first few rounds flew past the soldier, the third and fourth caught him in the chest. The soldier fell forward, burying the communication-tablet under his dead weight.

Two remained.

Krit jumped from his position in the trees and shoved the barrel of his pistol up under a short soldier's jaw. He pulled the trigger, sending chucks of brain and gore spraying through the trees.

One remained.

Tinker rushed forward, a surge of over-confidence flooding his actions. Holding down the trigger, he wildly sprayed the assault rifle, stepping into the open. As he did, he felt a burning, crippling pain rattle him. He looked down at his left thigh. He had caught a taser cannon blast to the leg. Smoke rose from the gaping wound on Tinker's upper thigh. It seared a hole the size of a fist into his leg, charred flesh, tendon and bone all visible. Collapsing under his own bodyweight, he looked up as the remaining soldier held his taser cannon to Tinker's face and, pulling the trigger, took his head clean off.

"We need one alive," Michael yelled over the chaos. "We need the last one alive."

Acting on pure adrenalin, Michael leapt over Tinker's lifeless body and in one swift, athletic motion, sprung onto the chest of the remaining soldier. He aimed his taser cannon at the soldier's hand that clutched his weapon and fired. The weapon, along with all the soldier's fingers, fell to the ground. The soldier roared in pain. The smell of charred flesh overpowered both men. Before the soldier could draw his back-up weapon from his belt, Michael aimed at the soldier's left hand and fired, taking the whole hand off at the wrist. Again, the soldier roared in agony. Michael roared in triumph.

The soldier, looking down at his missing hands knew he was defenceless, beaten. "Mercy," he yelled, tears of pain welling in his frightened and bloodshot eyes behind his mask. Bruce stepped forward and kicked the injured soldier in the stomach.

"*Mercy*? Would you have shown me mercy, you little bastard? I bet you wouldn't. So why should we show you a bloody inch of it?"

The soldier was young, still in his early twenties. He barely had facial hair. Michael ripped the full-face conditioning mask from the frightened young man and aimed the taser cannon at his groin. The soldier shuddered. He looked around. Four men held weapons pointing straight at him. He knew this was the end.

"What do you want?" he said, his lower lip quivering.

Michael shoved the barrel of the cannon hard into the soldier's groin.

"We want to know where you've come from. Have you got a base nearby? Where is it?"

The soldier, despite his obvious fear, sat silent.

"Where is it?"

Silence.

Without a word Michael lowered the taser cannon's aim to the soldier's ankle and pulled the trigger. More screaming. More charred flesh. Sweat formed on the young soldier's brow as he winced in agony. The colour drained from his face. If need be, the interrogation could continue much in this fashion until a vital organ was hit.

The electricity from the taser blasts cauterised the wounds so there was very little blood loss. The Union designed the weapon that way so their enemy would stay alive long enough to feel every little ounce of pain. The soldier was well aware of this.

"Okay, okay. I'll tell you," he said, panting. "About twelve clicks to the west of here we have a wall bunker. There is a door on the wall. A grey door. There's a code."

"And what's the code, young friend?"

"Each solider has a different code. It needs to coincide with your registration chip. My code is 0032."

"You wouldn't be telling me lies, would you?" asked Michael, raising the weapon back to the cowering soldier's groin.

"I'm not, I'm not. I swear it."

"And how many are inside this bunker? Beside the six of you."

"Another twenty. We come and go. There's a flight-pad on top of the wall. There are stairs up to it from inside the bunker. I promise you I'm telling the truth. Please, just kill me now."

Bruce stepped forward and pushed down on the soldiers sweating forehead with his boot. He towered over the panting soldier, crushing the young man's temple into the damp soil. "Look here, you little Union dog. We will kill you when we're good and ready. We're not done yet. Is there Fosform in this bunker of yours? Are there vehicles?"

The soldier hesitated, but only for a moment. Non-compliance was pointless. It would only lead to more pain. "Yes, there are ration packs stored in the sleeping quarters. There are Fosform injectors in the ration packs. Not much, though."

"How much?"

"Maybe one hundred doses in the whole facility."

Bruce looked at Michael. "Okay, mate. Let's do this."

One handed, Bruce held his taser cannon to the soldier's throat. Awaiting his fate, the soldier closed his eyes and mouthed a prayer. Bruce pulled the trigger and sent the bolt of electric energy right through the soldier's neck and into the damp soil below.

THIRTY-NINE

IT WAS ONLY AFTER THE CHAOS THAT THE SILENCE SEEMED SO inviting.

The smell of sweat, death and charred flesh tainted the peaceful aromas of the jungle. There were patches of burnt grass, singed and blackened from the taser blasts. It was only after the last soldier's execution, only in that comforting silence, that the T-Towners realised Tom was missing. Robin and Krit left the clearing and backtracked through the thick undergrowth. They found Tom with a gaping bullet wound to his chest. It was fatal – right through the heart. Dark red blood soaked his faded sweater, giving it a slick black appearance. The wound was clearly from a .30 calibre hollow-tip bullet, not a taser cannon. The only person who had been firing those was Tinker.

"Christ Almighty," Krit said in his thick Thai accent. "Tinker must have shot Tom."

The two Thai men, despite their small build, were surprisingly strong. They dragged Tom's limp, lifeless body back towards where Tinker lay. The four remaining men looked down at their two companions. After fifteen long seconds of silent reflection Michael was the first to speak.

"So, should we bury them?"

"Sure, but we gotta be quick about it," said Bruce. "We don't know what time they expect this patrol back. The last thing we need is more of those fuckers coming out looking for us. Surprise is what's gonna win this for us. We *need* the element of surprise!"

Robin pulled a small shovel from his equipment pack and right there, in the cleared land beside the wall, he began digging a shallow grave.

The mood was sombre as he dug. Losing two was better than losing four, but it was still a hard, distressing thing to swallow. What made the mood even more dismal was that all four of them knew what came next. Michael had framed it up well before they left the safety of T-Town. The four would need to become Union soldiers. If they planned on getting inside the sub-bunker without raising suspicions, they not only needed the dead soldier's clothes, they needed their registration chips.

While Robin dug, Krit and Michael removed the dead soldier's uniforms. Although these dead men represented everything he hated about the Union, it felt immoral to remove their clothes and leave them sprawled naked in the dirt. If God existed, he surely wouldn't approve.

Michael pushed his guilty thoughts to the side as he piled up the clothing, the weaponry and the oxygen conditioners into three neat piles. Luckily four masks still functioned. A taser blast had maimed the other one inoperable, melted through.

Conversation was scarce. The stench of apprehension filled the air. Robin and Bruce pushed their lifeless friends into the crude grave and covered them over. Robin said a prayer in his native tongue.

Hesitation clawed at the four comrades. They knew what they had to do next, but they prolonged it for as long as they could. It would be a gruesome task, far harder to do than strip a lifeless body of its clothes. Bruce looked at his peers. He could smell the apprehension, the fear. "I hope you lads have the guts for this... and the balls too."

Pulling a knife from a sheath on his belt, he flipped over one of the dead soldiers and sliced opened the back of his neck. He put the knife down and began sifting through the bleeding flesh with his fingers as calm as if he was gutting and filleting a fish.

"Bingo," he said casually as he pulled the small metal chip from the wound. He placed it on a rounded limestone boulder beside him, then reached for a bottle of river water and rinsed the blood and flesh off the tiny device. "One down, three to go."

Keeping the registration chips separate, Bruce repeated the process on the other three soldiers. Once all four chips rested on the bloodstained rock, he looked up at his peers with a wicked smile. "So, who wants to be 0032?"

"I'll do it," Michael said. "This was my idea, so I'll go first."

"Shit, I don't know if I'll be able to do this," said Robin, sweat beading on his face.

"You don't have a choice now, mate. Now get the sewing kit from your pack and lets get on with it."

Taking in a deep breath, Michael sat on a small round boulder and leaned forward, exposing the back of his neck to Bruce.

"This is gonna hurt, mate," Bruce said. Sadistic excitement soured his words.

"Jesus, Bruce. You sound like you'll enjoy this?"

"It's been a while since I've butchered somebody."

"Well, don't bloody-well butcher me, mate. Just do it."

Michael felt the blade touch his neck. Then the pain tore down his spine as he felt his skin rip open. Feeling a trickle of warm blood cascade down to the hollow of his back, he cringed, breathing deeply.

One handed, Bruce grabbed the closest registration chip. It glistened in the tropical afternoon sun. Its brief encounter with the outside world had come to an abrupt end. With about as much delicacy as a digger in the tunnels, Bruce shoved the small device deep into the open wound. Michael roared in pain.

Then the worst was over.

Bruce applied pressure to the wound. Robin shook off his ambivalence, stepped forward and began stitching the bleeding mess. The others looked on in anticipation. The only thread Robin had was a dark green nylon, used in their bunker home to mend clothing. It stood out dark against the pink of skin, almost comical. Only five minutes later and Robin had completed his crude surgery. It was far from precise but it held the skin closed and concealed the chip. Robin grabbed a dose of Fosform, cracked the top off the vial and poured some serum across the wound. "That should slow any infection," he said, then patted Michael on the back. "You're all done, mate."

"Thank fuck for that!"

After fifteen minutes of blood and gore, several aggressive outbursts and some lightheaded T-Towners, all four sat beside their friends' shallow grave with throbbing necks. They all had registered chips inside them. According to the Union's database they were now officially other people, with names, titles and credit rations. It also meant they could now be tracked.

They replaced their clothing with that of the dead soldiers, leaving the corpses sprawled naked in the undergrowth. They rigged up the oxygen conditioners and began to march, heading west beside the endless mass of concrete. Bruce looked at his peers and couldn't help but laugh. They looked like the real deal. As far as anyone would know, they were Union soldiers. Union-issue grey fatigues, Union boots, belts, weapons and full-face oxygen conditioners.

"Who'd have thought," Bruce whispered to himself, smiling.

According to their dead informant they had twelve kilometres to go. With less than two hours of daylight remaining, the group knew they would reach their destination in darkness. That made it even more difficult. It would be easy to miss a grey door in a grey wall of concrete, especially in the dark. Krit fidgeted in the pocket of his Union jacket. He pulled out a small electronic device the size of a chip reader. "Hey," he said. "What's this?"

Michael knew right away. "It's an SLD," he said. "A Satellite Location Device." He had seen one before. During his flight for freedom across the harsh desert of the Nullarbor Plains he had come across an abandoned Union vehicle. Inside the vehicle he had found rations, a weapon and an SLD. An SLD had a small touch screen with a satellite image of the entire Empire of Soteria. The device would pinpoint its exact location, accurate down to the centimetre.

Michael took the device and pressed a few buttons. "It'll now beep twice when we get eleven kilometres from our current location," he said to the others. "That way we will know when to keep our eyes peeled."

"Brilliant! Now let's go…"

When the SLD finally beeped twice, a barely visible new moon had replaced the sun. It was a dark night, still and quiet. The group had kept a consistent pace and taken close to three hours to walk the eleven kilometres.

Before they fitted their masks again they readied their weapons, gathered their wits and kept their eyes on the concrete wall. No more than ten minutes after the SLD had beeped Krit came to a stop. His peers stood behind him. He raised his hand in a gesture to halt then pointed to the wall, and more importantly, a heavily reinforced steel door at the base of the monolith.

The wall around the door was almost bare. To the left, at about shoulder height, was a chip scanner, similar to most within the Empire except housed within a steel cage, presumably for protection from hostiles. Above the door was a spy-eye camera. Hardly bigger than a child's fingernail, anyone who had spent time in sub-plazas knew that spy-eye cameras were far more powerful than they appeared to be. The image they captured was more powerful, more perfect than human vision. Even in darkness.

Michael looked up to the top of the wall to see if he could locate the helipad of which the dead soldier had spoken. Above the door, high on the top of the wall, perched on the edge of the concrete like the nest of the Union's all-watching eagle was a manned lookout. Even in the darkness Michael could make out the silhouette of two soldiers looking down on them. Michael waved casually up into the darkness. One silhouette waved back.

"Don't all look up," he whispered. "But there are soldiers on guard atop the wall. They're watching us. Act casual. It's now or never."

"Shit… Do you think they'll notice there's a soldier missing from our party?"

"Let's not stand here long enough for them to work it out."

Nerves and heart rates increased. Apprehension ran high through the outlaw team. Michael led the way, trying as hard as he could to show false confidence. He got to the door with the other three cramped behind him. He could hear the rapid panting of Robin over his shoulder, even from inside the oxygen conditioner.

Studying the door, Michael located the touchscreen underneath a steel flap in its centre.

"Here goes nothing," he said, inhaling deeply.

He leaned forward, exposing his neck to the scanner. It beeped and flashed a green light. "Officer Hawke, welcome back," spoke the generic female voice from a speaker within the scanner. "Please enter your security code."

Michael lifted the steel flap. The hinges creaked with friction. His palms were sweaty. For whatever reason, he hesitated.

"Hurry the hell up," Bruce whispered behind him. "Let's fucking get this over with!"

With his heart about to launch out of his chest, Michael pressed in the code: 0032.

Nothing.

Uncertainty crippled Michael as he sensed the eyes of the soldiers in the darkness above him. All four T-Towners held their breath and clenched their teeth. What had gone wrong? Had the dead soldier lied? Had he given them the wrong code? Right now they stood trapped, defenceless and with nowhere to run. Had this been the dead soldier's plan all along?

Then the touchscreen glowed green, beeped twice and the heavy steel door swung open.

Relief.

The open door revealed a dim corridor, concrete, cold and uninviting. At the far end was a stairwell and another set of doors. The four outlaws, donned in dead men's uniforms, stepped inside the corridor and closed the door.

FORTY

Silence echoed down the dim concrete corridor.

Michael's heartbeat thumped beneath the dull mask of silence. Beneath the grey uniforms of the most feared and disciplined soldiers in the world were four courageous outlaws.

He led them down the dim corridor one precarious step at a time. He had his taser cannon raised, his finger resting on the small alloy trigger. He knew it was only a matter of time until they would face combat. That was their purpose. He knew they would be heavily outnumbered. Despite his agnostic views towards the Catholic Church, Michael prayed for their success.

Breathing deeply, Michael reached the set of steel doors at the end of the corridor with his three companions close behind him. They were in too deep now. There was no retreat. He leaned forward and exposed the roughly stitched wound at the top of his spine. The chip-scanning device beeped twice and the steel door creaked open.

I am now Officer Hawke.

Adrenalin coursed through Michael's veins as he led his team up a concrete stairwell. They would fight blind. They had no idea what to expect. They had no idea where the stairs would lead them. It

231

could be an empty barracks. It could be a dining room with fifty fiercely trained soldiers eating their broth. Surprise would be their ally. Surprise was their secret weapon.

The four outlaws reached the landing at the top of the stairs. They entered a large communal room. It was lit with typical Union-manufactured cylindrical lighting. Artificial sunlight brought homely warmth to the room. At the far end was a recreation area. Six off-duty soldiers sat in grey fatigues on alpaca wool couches, watching a family comedy series. They laughed playfully. They were complacent within their quarters. A breach of their barracks was the furthest thing from their minds.

As the T-Towners entered the room, one soldier turned and looked at Michael and the new arrivals. He waved and welcomed them back, thinking it was his colleagues returning from patrol. Michael waved in return, baring a friendly grin. Preoccupied with the television, the soldier returned his gaze to the wall screen before him.

Michael's plan had worked.

"Let's bloody well get 'em," Bruce whispered as he stepped forward and raised his weapon.

Defenceless, off-guard and ill prepared, the six off-duty soldiers were sitting ducks. By the time Bruce fired the first round from his taser cannon, ripping a hole through the closest soldier's face, it was too late for the other five. Michael, Robin and Krit also began firing, tearing holes in the soldiers, the couch, even the concrete wall behind them.

Within seconds the six soldiers lay dead. Blood and charred flesh, chunks of brain and muscle were scattered around them, tainting the area with the foul smell of death.

"Well, then," Bruce said, cackling. "That was easier than I expected."

The T-Towners lowered their weapons.

A single moment of complacency, a single second of triumph was all it took to level the score. From a balcony above the communal room bright blue blasts of condensed electricity came firing down on them. Taser cannon blasts tore shards out of the concrete behind them as they ran for cover. A taser blast hit Krit in the stomach, tearing open his lower abdomen. Krit died before he hit the ground.

"Cover me," Bruce roared over the noise.

Robin and Michael leaned out from behind the kitchen bench and fired blindly up towards the balcony. As they did, Bruce, with his one functioning hand, ripped a nuclear shock ball from his vest, typed in the arming code and flung the device with the enthusiasm of a top-tier Turf-ball athlete. The shock ball cleared the balcony railing and disappeared from view. Less than a heartbeat later, powerful white light engulfed the balcony. Bruce and his peers ducked as fragments of glass, concrete and body parts came raining down on them, the explosion swallowing the whole level above.

Silence and smoke.

Michael pushed aside a soldier's leg, severed from the hip, as blood still spewed from the femoral artery. There wasn't time to think. There wasn't time to assess possibilities. Success relied on pure instinct. He ran as fast as his legs would allow. He reached the stairs, the level above him masked in thick, grey smoke. Not taking chances, he began firing blindly into the smoke, the blue blasts disappearing into the hidden confusion before him. Robin and Bruce joined him on the stairwell. Exhaustion slowed them down. Robin's forehead bled heavily. Fatigue gripped their tiring muscles.

The top balcony looked like a war-zone. Body parts, blood and furniture destroyed beyond recognition. There were no survivors. Apprehensively, they entered the smouldering death-zone and looked for access to the roof.

Robin wiped the blood from his head and dropped his weapon, replacing it with a dead soldier's micro-taser. Despite the poor visibility, he located a transporter tunnel built into the back of the room. The door opened, revealing a transport cell. Robin studied the transporter tunnel map. They could go down to a basement level or up towards the roof. Robin pressed the small icon to lead them to the roof, to the lookout on top of the wall.

"Wait," Michael called from behind him, panting, gulping in air. "If we cram into the cell and head to the roof, the second that door opens they will slaughter us. There's no doubt the soldiers on lookout have just heard the explosion. They'll be waiting. It'll be a death trap… I've got an idea. Grab one of those bodies."

Michael stepped over burning furniture and picked up the remains of a Union soldier. He was missing his arms, his head barely hanging on. As he grabbed the lifeless body, blood gushed from the gaping neck. He handed the body to Robin, who, because of his size could barely hold up the dead weight. Michael then grabbed the remains of another body, this time, little more than an abdomen with arms, entrails dangling from legless hips.

"We will use these as shields," he said. "Once the door opens, if we're fired upon, these bodies will take the brunt of it. Then we can throw the bodies out of the cell. They should distract the soldiers up there long enough for us to shoot them. Got it?"

Robin and Bruce nodded.

All three squeezed into the small transporter cell along with the dripping, stinking half-corpses. They barely fit. The smell was over-powering. Even someone as seasoned in death and gore as Bruce cringed from the potent stench. Robin leaned forward and pressed the icon for the roof. The door rolled closed and they felt the cell move beneath their feet.

Michael held a corpse. Robin held a corpse. Bruce stood at the back with his taser cannon in position. Blood pooled on the floor. Apprehension flooded the tiny metal cell as it reached its destination. Michael clenched his teeth. With a faint hum, the door rolled open. Before it was even half a metre wide, shots were fired from outside, impacting against the charred corpses. Michael had been right. They held the bodies firm, using them as shields as bright blue blasts burst against the charred flesh.

On cue, Robin and Michael threw the bodies forward and ducked.

Running on instinct, the aim of the two soldiers followed the thrown bodies, firing at the lifeless chunks of human flesh. As they aimed away from the transporter cell, Bruce stepped forward and with the rage of a caged primate, fired his taser cannon at the first, then the second soldier.

Both dropped to the concrete with burning, fatal wounds.

The three T-Towners emerged from the stinking, blood-covered cell. They stood triumphantly atop the wall. Bruce cheered. Michael and Robin roared with adrenalin. They were, possibly, the only people in the Empire of Soteria other than soldiers and wall-workers that had stood atop the boundary wall.

It was a moment to be written into the books of history.

"Well bloody done, lads!" Bruce yelled, patting Michael and Robin on the shoulder. He looked at Michael and smiled. "Who would've thought your bat-shit crazy idea would've worked?" He cackled. "Now let's go find some Fosform and get the hell out of here."

"Hold on a minute," Robin said as he walked away from the lookout tower, towards the northern edge of the wall. The other two followed. They cast their gazes north, looking out at something none of them had ever seen.

Freedom.

They looked out at what they had been digging for a year to reach and now it was right there in front on them, teasing them with its proximity. In the darkness it looked the same as the south side of the wall, thick jungle, nothing more. But the three of them knew it was far more than that. It was the land beyond the Empire. It was a sight that no other citizen of Soteria had witnessed. It was the rest of the world. It was the great unknown. It was freedom.

"There it is, lads," Bruce said, smiling, staring out across the darkness. "That right there is our legacy. That right there is what all of this is about."

There was a moment of silence. They let the scene sink in.

"Does any part of you want to just get down there now?" Robin asked. "I know it's wrong, but a part of me thinks we're this close, we might as well go for it…"

"No," Michael reproached. "The others put their trust in us. The others are waiting for Fosform, and then together we can all go. Not like this. We can't abandon our brothers and sisters…"

"You're right, Mike. I wouldn't be so selfish but a part of you has to think it, you know? It is tempting…"

"We will get there, mate. We've made it this bloody far. Now let's get that dosage and get home," Bruce said, breathing in a deep sigh of poisonous air. "This place will swarm with Union dogs in no time."

They lingered for a moment in silence, admiring the view, dreaming of their escape. Dreaming of their liberty. It was so close they could smell it. Reluctantly, one at a time, they turned away from the one thing that they fought for.

We will be back, Bruce thought to himself.

We will be back.

FORTY-ONE

SWELL HAMMERED AGAINST THE SIDE OF THE FREIGHTER.

Cold, salty water sprayed our stowaway location through the small charging window. During my time working out on the walls, boats had been my main mode of transport. I became accustomed to the sea, to the constant rocking, to the rising and falling. My stomach became seaworthy. Eli had never left the northern beaches of Sydney. His first real encounter with a boat was when he crossed the mouth of the Hawkesbury River with me four days before.

He sat behind me, pale faced and nauseous. As the vessel rose over rolling waves Eli would heave, bringing up our previous night's snacks in a filthy pile beside the hull. At first, I thought his retching might attract attention from above, but the sound of the waves smashing against the boat seemed to drown everything out.

Hours had passed since departing the mainland and I knew we had to act. We had to do something, but I just didn't know what. Or how. Eli's seasickness didn't help our cause. I ran various scenarios through my mind, scenarios that seemed plausible with a bit of imagination, but when put into practice in the real world, these scenarios seemed a little more fitting for films I had grown up watching.

I looked over at Eli. He looked back at me and wiped vomit and drool from his chin. He forced a smile.

"We need to do something soon," I said, my voice weak and disheartened. "We don't know for sure where this vessel is taking us. It could go anywhere."

"But the delivery schedule. The one in my pocket…"

"It might be wrong, Eli. They're also a day early. If the schedule is out by a day, it could also go to a different location. It might head to New Zealand, or east to the wall even? I can't sit here any longer."

"Okay, I'll be fine. Let's do it. We didn't come this far to wait in the wet darkness. What else do we have to lose?"

"Are you capable of what we need to do, Eli?"

He looked at me, unsure. "I guess so. It's not like killing someone frightens me. I've seen more death than most people. I know that smell better than anyone living in those underground cities. I can do it. *We* can do it. We didn't come this far for nothing…"

My young accomplice was right. Five days ago I never would have thought I would be out in the South Pacific Ocean, leaving behind the world I knew. I had taken a leap. I had got this far. We had got this far. I had pushed through the barriers of what I thought I could achieve, but now I needed to push more.

I pulled the micro-taser from the waist of my pants. It felt light and powerless. I had never fired one, but I hoped it had a similar effect to the full-sized taser cannons. Hope was the enemy of doubt. Doubt came crawling into my thoughts. Doubt that the micro-taser would be sufficient. Doubt that we could beat the soldiers. Eli stood, the other micro-taser held firm. He nodded, a look of grim determination on his face. And then he made his way to the ladder.

It was now or never, and never wasn't an option.

I knew there were about ten people on board. I had counted four Union soldiers and six civilian sailors when I watched them through the window. As I climbed the first rung of the ladder I hoped that the six civilians were unarmed and unskilled in combat. Taking on four Union soldiers would be hard enough. Surprise would be our ally. We would need to strike before they even knew what hit them. Standing at the base of the ladder, it occurred to me that I would have to take another's life. Until that point I had managed not to think about it. Now the thought was unavoidable. If we wanted to live, ten men would die. Was I capable of killing? Was I capable of stone-cold murder?

I was about to find out.

I opened the hatch ever so slightly. To my misfortune, it creaked open, the rusty metal singing a horrendous tune. I held it firm, frozen with fear, unable to open it or close it again. I heard Eli sigh beneath me, frightened by the creaking metal. Peeking through the small gap, I saw most of the room. No movement. The room seemed to be empty. Keeping the hatch open a few centimetres, I looked down at my trusty accomplice. Man, I was thankful that he was there with me. I would not have had the courage to do it all alone.

"Thanks," I whispered to Eli. I could tell it was the last thing he expected to hear.

"What do you mean, thanks? Thanks for what?"

"Thanks for coming with me. It means a lot."

"No worries, Tyson. Like I said, this is the most excitement I've had in, well, ever."

"I couldn't have done this alone," I whispered.

"Thank me when it's over. Let's just not get shot."

"Okay, once we're up there, stay within a metre of me. You cover left side, I'll cover the right, okay?"

Despite the fear in his eyes, he nodded.

Then I went for it. Faster than a Tier Two adrenalin ride, I bounced up from inside the ladder shaft, scanned the room and pulled Eli up from below. Frozen, we stood in the middle of the carpeted room.

Silence.

The three Union crates I had watched them load at the harbour lay stacked in the corner. Instinctively I crept towards them, Eli right by my side. I ripped the lid off the closest crate. It was just as I had suspected.

Fosform Five - hundreds of vials of it. Presumably being sent out to Union workers on the wall. Eli's eyes opened wide. For a surface dweller, seeing that amount of the serum was like seeing Jesus in the flesh.

I ripped the lid off the second crate, expecting to see more Fosform. I didn't expect to see what I saw next. Computer chips of some sort, intricate and detailed. Woven webs of wiring weaved around the small devices, all stored meticulously in the crate. While Eli scanned the room with his micro-taser, I pulled a small device out of the crate. It was the size of my palm, with gadgets and multi-coloured wires hanging from it. On the side in tiny engravings was the Union motto, then the word *Bestia* with a six-digit number after it. I pulled out another chip that looked identical to the first. It had the same engravings, the word Bestia and a different set of six numbers. "What are these?" I whispered.

Eli just shrugged.

"What the hell is *Bestia?*"

Again, Eli shrugged.

We could worry about that later.

With the stealth of a trained soldier, I crept, one slow footstep at a time into the next room. My heart pounded. My eyes were wide with terror. I was about to face what could be a quick and painful death yet I felt the most alive I ever had. Life, freedom and fear coursed through my veins.

FORTY-TWO

WE LEFT THE CARPETED ROOM WITH THE CRATES AND STEPPED UP the stairwell.

I saw three civilian men sitting at a small plastic table at the far end of the cabin. They talked among themselves. Our position on the bottom of the stairs meant we could see them clearly, but they would struggle to see us. I lay on the stairs and crawled up one by one until I lay just below the carpeted floor of the room. I pulled out my micro-taser and aimed it forward. Eli lay right beside me, mimicking my movements.

It's now or never and never isn't an option.

I took a breath and aimed the small weapon at the closest man. He was overweight with long matted hair and a scruffy beard. I pulled the trigger. A blue ray of condensed electricity shot forward and struck the man in the chest, tearing open his fat flesh. In the same second his associate looked up in shock, Eli shot at him, catching him in the face with a condensed ray of power, killing him instantly.

Then it got noisy. The third man dived from view, screaming as he did so, sending with him a table full of cutlery, shattered glass and food. Running on instinct, I raced up the final few stairs and started firing at the man. I missed twice. The third shot caught him in the stomach. He shrieked in dying agony.

Our position was compromised. As I ran to the far end of the room, I sensed Eli only a pace behind me. I kicked open the door to find two soldiers and two civilians standing in the centre of the helm, looks of astonishment on their wide-eyed faces.

The civilians sat frozen in awkward terror. The soldiers, trained for situations of this nature, rolled to either side, drawing their weapons, subconsciously reacting to perform exactly how they got paid to perform. By rolling either side they separated the target, whereas Eli and I stood side by side in the centre of the doorway, exposed and inexperienced. As one soldier fired his full sized taser cannon in my direction, I lunged forward, just as the electric bolt made impact with the metal door, tearing a hole through the steel.

It was chaos. There was screaming, shooting, murderous insults. My throat was raw with fear. Sweat pooled in my eyebrows, dripping down the length of my nose. I roared as I aimed carelessly and fired my tiny weapon. I needed accuracy and I needed to choose my targets. If the weapon drained its charge, it would no longer fire. Thinking rationally was not high on my list of priorities, though. I just needed to survive.

I clenched the trigger, sending bolts of condensed electricity in all directions.

From the corner of my eye I watched Eli fire at the frightened civilians in the middle of the room, taking both of their faces off with short, accurate blasts. They slumped down dead, chunks of charred brain leaking from their skulls. Then it occurred to me during the chaos that with those two civilians dead, no one was left to steer the boat.

"Tyson," Eli called out over the noise. "Left…"

I spun to the left as another soldier leaned through an open porthole window and fired a micro-taser. Pain tore through my forearm. A burning sensation more severe than any fire could provide radiated up to my shoulder. I screamed. I dropped my weapon. Just as he fired a second shot, I rolled towards him and hid underneath the windowsill. I looked down at my forearm. Nausea hit me. There was a charred and burning hole, half the size of my fist, bored deep into my arm, exposing my blackened bone.

I will not die today!

With my functioning hand I pulled Eli's hunting knife from the sheath on my belt, pounced up like a Jack-in-the-box and stabbed the soldier in the throat. The blade went in smoothly, all the way to the hilt. As I pulled the knife from his punctured windpipe blood sprayed through the open window, covering me in the dark, warm fluid. He slumped down outside the window.

The two soldiers inside the room defended themselves well, hidden behind the structure of the helm. They had positioned themselves with a soldier's logic.

"In the name of the Soteria Humanist Union, surrender your weapons," one of the soldiers called out.

"In the name of the Humanist Union, go fuck your sister!" Eli roared.

I looked over at Eli. His eyes were wide. He looked driven, like an animal hunting its prey. He grinned fiercely. I didn't want to leave him alone in the room, but I needed a weapon. A hunting knife would not do against trained soldiers with taser cannons.

I pulled myself up and leaped through the open window, landing on top of the dead soldier. Blood pooled around him on the deck of the vessel, leaking from the severed hole in his throat.

I picked up his micro-taser.

More taser cannon blasts erupted in the helm. I hoped that Eli was still in one piece. Staying low, I crawled around the front of the helm, to the foredeck entrance to the inner helm. The fourth soldier stood in position, weapon raised at the door, waiting to ambush us if we exited from the room. Before he saw me in his peripheral vision, I shot at his thigh. As he slumped forward, I shot at his heart. The stench of burning human skin made my guts churn. I fought the nausea as I put my micro-taser to the soldier's temple and pulled the trigger, just to be sure.

I wanted to finish this. I *needed* to finish this. I dropped my micro-taser and picked up the dead soldier's full sized taser cannon. It was far heavier. I pulled open the door of the helm, coming in behind a soldier, again trying to use the element of surprise to my advantage. As if expecting my approach, he fired. Then I fired. We both missed our targets. I fired again and hit him in the shoulder. He dropped his weapon, clutching the bored hole above his heart. The last soldier stood to my right and lunged toward me. He was twice my size, bulky and strong. He swung his weapon at me like a club, belting me across the chest. I dropped to the floor, no match for the bear-sized soldier. I brought my taser cannon up to face him. He kicked it out of my weakened and sweaty grasp with little effort. I was without a weapon, defenceless, tired and aching. I looked up at my killer.

"This is the end for you, you treasonous little thief," he said as he pointed the barrel of his weapon at my face. "I hope it was worth it."

As I stared down the barrel of the electric weapon I thought of life and death. I thought of my parents. I thought of all the pain and injustice that consumed our world. Then, out of nowhere, Eli dived over the steering panel, weapon forward, mouth wide, roaring ferociously. He landed on the back of the giant solider and held on, like a child being piggybacked. Before the soldier had time to react, Eli shoved the small barrel of his micro-taser up against the soldier's ear and pulled the trigger. The small, blue ray of condensed energy shot out the other ear, taking fragments of burning brain with it.

The giant mass of dead muscle slumped to the floor, sending Eli sprawling across the ground behind him. I blinked. It had happened so fast. I thought I was facing the end. I thought we had failed.

Panicking, I grabbed my weapon and rose to my feet. The soldier up against the wall with a hole in his shoulder was still alive. I walked towards him, weapon raised.

He looked at me. He began laughing. "What do you think you will accomplish, boy?"

"Well, your death, for starters," I fired back.

"My death is as meaningless as my life. *You* cannot stop the Humanist Union. The world cannot stop the Humanist Union. We will be unstoppable. Once the Bestia program goes live, it's game over…"

He pulled a serrated knife from a sheath on his belt and with the strict confidence only a Union soldier had, he tore open his own throat, his blood pouring out hot and dark onto his stomach, staining his grey uniform dark black.

"Jesus," Eli said as he took to his feet, looking at the room full of death and gore. "That escalated quickly, didn't it?"

I looked at my young accomplice and smiled. He smiled back. I dropped the weapon, pulled Eli towards me and I hugged him. He hugged me back, strong and emotional. I hadn't hugged anyone in years. Not even George. Not even a woman. Not since the day I left for the wall when I was seventeen, the last time I saw my parents, had I hugged another human. I hadn't felt like it. They didn't deserve it. That day, though, there in that blood-soaked cabin, Eli deserved it.

I let go of him, patted him on the back and took a step out onto the foredeck. The wind blew strongly off the swell. The sun hovered low on the western horizon. Despite the charred hole in my arm and the crippling feeling of guilt, I smiled. I smiled as tears of joy and fatigue welled in my eyes. Freedom was so close. I was the closest to freedom that I had ever known. There was nothing now separating me from the great unknown.

Eli joined me as we stood in silence watching the sun set in the west. We were both panting. We were both covered in sweat and blood. We both laughed.

Someone once told me that freedom exists in the mind. Someone once told me that people are as free as they allow themselves to be. Standing there on the bow of that freighter with Eli and a bunch of corpses I finally understood what they meant.

FORTY-THREE

THE PIT WAS ALIVE WITH IMPATIENT HOSTILITY.

Several painstakingly slow days had passed since Brie's meeting with the Empire's ruler, yet she remained in G-Block. With every passing minute Brie waited for the magnetic crane's approach, for it to pick her up and take her from the relative safety of the pit and leave her to face her brutal and unavoidable end.

Anxiety gnawed at her, making it hard to eat, difficult to sleep. She sat there in the filthy convict cesspool awaiting her fate. She knew it was only a matter of time before they discovered her lies. And when they did, she knew what would come. She had lied to save her friends. She battled with her conscience, trying every minute to convince herself she had done the right thing. The self-persuasion hadn't yet worked. She had lied to Master Stephen Haynes himself. It was not the sort of thing that people got away with. It was the greatest act of selflessness one could commit. Yet for some unknown reason, Brie felt guilty.

After breakfast on the fourth day since Brie's meeting with Master Stephen Haynes, a group of soldiers gathered on the balcony surrounding G-Block. On a normal day soldiers stood every

246

twenty metres around the oval-shaped arena observing the writhing chaos below but now, on this morning, over one hundred Union soldiers swarmed the balcony.

Brie spoke with Lachlan, whom, unlike other G-Block residents, she had formed a bond with. Lachlan looked up at the increasing mass of armed soldiers.

"Something is happening," he said, a cautious expression morphing. "I've never seen that many soldiers surrounding the pit. Ever."

"Maybe it's Lucy's fight," Brie said, turning to look at her protector.

"I think you might be right."

Lucifer clenched her fists. Brie watched her triceps flex. She stood a good foot taller than the average male. She was solid, frightening and dangerously quick for her size.

"Bring it on," she murmured through clenched teeth.

A man stepped forward on the concrete balcony amidst a mass of grey-uniformed soldiers. He had thinning grey hair and black-rimmed glasses. Dressed in the typical polyester and latex suit of a high-powered Union official, to most of the pit he was just another Union leader, pure heartless scum. To Brie though, he represented much more than that. To Brie, Eric van Bueren was the uncle of her late husband. He was the thorn in her proverbial side that had caused much of Brie's pain.

Van Bueren stood forward, leaned over the railing and spoke into a condenser microphone attached to the latex collar of his jacket.

"Convicts," he said. His voice carried to all corners of the pit through micro-speakers built into the concrete. "We have put a proposition forward. A request has been made by Master Haynes himself."

Confused murmurs filled the pit.

Only Brie, Lucifer and Lucifer's close companions knew what van Bueren referred to. Never had Master Haynes had any involvement with G-Block.

"Silence!" Van Bueren yelled through the microphone. The masses followed his command as the pit quietened down. "A certain G-Block convict, Lucy Harding, has offered to fight the Union's most powerful soldier. The Master has stated that if this convict, this *woman*, is victorious, then she will be the first and only female admitted into the Humanist Union Army."

Uproar came from the pit. A mix of blasphemous insults and cheers of support bounced off the concrete walls. Right away, convicts knew what the outcome meant. Either way, the dynamics of the pit were about to transform. If Lucifer were victorious, she would leave the pit. If she were not, she would be dead. It only occurred to Brie at that exact moment that either way she would no longer have a protector. Without Lucifer in the pit to provide structure, it would once again turn into murderous, uncontrollable chaos it once had been. Suddenly Brie wished she had never made the proposition to the Master. She needed Lucy in the pit. She needed her protection.

Once the uproar quietened down, Eric van Bueren continued. "The fight will take place in the pit. If any of you filthy convicts try to interfere, I will ensure that we take you to the surface and leave you in a cage to rot. I trust you all understand. Now please, clear the centre of the pit. Lucy Harding, step forward and show yourself."

The masses of ragged and dirty convicts pushed backwards. A sea of moving bodies compressed against the walls. A large clearing emerged in the centre of the pit. Two dead bodies, exposed and bloodied lay lifeless in the open space, victims of the previous night's quarrels.

Lucifer looked at Lachlan, Peter and Brie. She winked then laughed her deep, masculine chuckle. "Time to go kill a Union dog," she said as she entered the clearing.

Beside van Bueren on the balcony, a large soldier stepped forward. He was a monster, at least seven feet tall. With arms thicker than the average man's thighs, he looked oddly out of proportion. Bald on top, his head glistened with sweat. His jawline looked like it had been chiselled from marble, his shoulders looked like blocks of stone.

"I welcome Officer Harvey to the pit," said van Bueren, smirking. "He has never lost a fight."

The pit roared with excitement.

As soon as the Union Advisors located one big enough, Officer Harvey donned a magna-jack and waited for the magna-crane to hover above him. The crane struggled to lift him from the balcony. Its hum increased into a high-pitched rumble, struggling with the weight of the man. Every convict and soldier alike looked on in silent anticipation as the crane lowered Harvey into the stinking pit below.

For Brie, the anticipation was crippling. She began thinking about the foul things that would happen to her after Lucy's departure. Lachlan might protect her. But then again, Lachlan was a mass murderer. He had no loyalty towards Brie. He owed her nothing.

Uncertainty joined Brie in the pit. She wished more than ever to be back in the safety of T-Town, back with her friends, Michael, Bruce, Evan and Remy. A wave of thoughts flooded her mind, pointless thoughts of hopeless longing. She had learnt over her time in captivity that remaining positive served little purpose. Hopelessness was all-consuming. She tried it nonetheless.

By the time Harvey reached the concrete floor the crowded mass went wild with cheers. It was the first time that any G-Block convict had seen a Union soldier inside the pit. It was clear on several faces they wanted nothing more than to run over and tear the man to shreds. Only the one hundred charged taser cannons aimed into the pit stopped anyone from trying.

Lucifer stepped toward the giant soldier. She stood tall, yet compared to Harvey she looked of average size. Both had crazed scowls, anger and determination oozing from their narrowed eyes.

Lucifer made the first move. She had learned through her training as a youth that eight times out of ten the person to make the first move came out victorious. She leapt with agility, swinging a clenched fist at the giant's face. The connection echoed off the concrete walls of G-Block. In unison, the masses let out a gasp. The power of Lucifer's single blow would have knocked another man unconscious, but Harvey stood still, barely acknowledging the hit. He massaged his jaw and laughed a deep, monstrous bellow.

He rushed toward her. Although the ground was solid concrete, the whole pit seemed to shudder as he ran. Lucifer dashed to Harvey's side and swung up with an open palm, chopping the giant in the throat. He halted, rubbed his neck and laughed again.

Lucifer doubted her abilities. Her confidence waned. This man, this giant, seemed unbeatable. Harvey swung, connecting with Lucifer's magna-jack. The force of the blow sent her to the ground, coughing and sputtering. She was breathless. A normal man would have broken his knuckles from the blow, but again, Harvey looked undeterred.

"Screw you," Lucifer called out to the behemoth between gasps. "You ugly piece of Union scum…"

She rushed forward and gave the man two quick uppercut punches to the groin, then with every fragment of strength she could gather she swung at his face, connecting with his nose.

Blood spewed from his nostrils.

Harvey grabbed Lucifer and picked her up, throwing her across the empty concrete. She hit the floor hard, tearing the skin off both elbows.

Both fighters were panting. The crowd cheered. Even the Union soldiers above the pit roared words of encouragement to their colleague.

Driven by something more powerful that rage, more powerful than hope or desire, Lucifer ran at her opponent. She envisioned the soldier that had raped her. She envisioned everything that embodied her captivity. Driven by pure hatred, Lucifer jumped at Harvey, straddling him and locking her legs around his waist.

With one hand she grabbed his jawbone, tearing it down with every little ounce of hatred, dislocating his mandible. With her other hand she made a fist and buried it deep inside Harvey's throat. She kept pushing until half her arm was down his throat. She grabbed at whatever she could and in one horrible, spine-chilling action, she ripped Harvey's larynx out from inside him. Blood gurgled out of his mouth like a dark, red rupturing volcano and he fell forward into a lifeless heap on the stained concrete.

The masses in the pit roared with excitement. The soldiers on the balcony stood in disbelief. Harvey had never lost a fight and his loyal comrades had just seen him beaten by a *woman*. Lucifer stood, still clenching Harvey's bloody larynx in her hand. "Is that all you've got," she roared to the soldiers above. "Is your entire Army a bunch of pussies?"

Silence.

Frightened murmurs.

Eric van Bueren stepped forward on the balcony. The masses quietened down to hear him speak. "My dear Lucy," he said bitterly. "Harvey was just a warm-up."

"That's horseshit," Lucifer yelled. "I agreed to one fight, one fight against the Army's best. And I beat him, fair and fucking square."

Van Bueren looked down into the pit below. Behind his black lens glasses he narrowed his eyes to a slit. He pursed his lips, assessing his response. He chose his words carefully. "Who said anything about *fair and square*? You are a convict, Lucy, a pit whore. Our Union owes nothing to a rotten criminal like you."

"Come down here and say that!"

"Unlikely. But you *do* have another chance. As I was saying prior to your insulting interruption, Harvey was just a warm-up. I now give you your next challenger…"

The soldiers cheered, stomping their Union-issue boots in unison on the concrete balcony.

A man stepped forward, shirtless and muscly. Not a gram of fat on his chiselled body. He looked down into the clearing in the centre of G-Block, locking eyes with Lucifer. The man was of average height, nothing like Harvey's size. He stood a good few inches shorter than Lucifer. He had yellow blonde hair and a chin as hairless as a child's. He looked calm, confident. There was something unsettling about his composure. The calmness that radiated from him was disconcerting. Lucifer spat on the ground before her.

"Come and get me, Union dog," she roared as she flung

Harvey's larynx up towards the balcony. It fell short, hitting the concrete wall and leaving a dark red smear on the blank grey as it dropped to the dirty ground below.

Lucifer's new opponent wore no magna-jack. Instead of waiting for the crane, he stepped forward and in a swift and confident leap, jumped over the railing. The crowd froze, awestruck as he leapt the twenty-five metres into the pit below with nothing to break his fall.

Suicide, Lucifer thought.

The masses held their breath.

Her new opponent landed on both feet, barely bending his knees. He looked at Lucifer and winked. The audience gasped in unison. They had just watched a man jump twenty-five metres onto solid concrete. That defied physics. No man could survive such a feat.

Impossible, Lucifer thought. *This is no living man.*

Her challenger rushed towards her, running nimbly, his feet barely contacting the ground. She readied herself, standing sideways, fists up. The blonde man reached her and ducked her punches. He ran a lap around her, toying with her.

Without wasting time, without even letting her swing a punch, he grabbed Lucifer by the neck and, with one hand, without an expression on his face, removed her head clean from her shoulders. Blood bubbled out as her headless body hit the floor. She didn't even have time to scream.

The pit was silent. The masses stood frozen, petrified. What had they just witnessed? That man, that shirtless, blonde baby-face was no human. The soldiers cheered from above, stomping their feet in synchronised rhythm.

Brie felt sick. Uncertainty rose from the pit of her stomach. She was in a world of trouble. She looked over at Lachlan. He too looked terrified.

"What the hell *is* that thing?" he whispered, astonished, overwhelmed.

Lucifer's opponent dropped her head on the dirty concrete floor and walked towards the wall under the main balcony. Terrified convicts cleared the way for him. He stood beside the wall and waited, eyeing the cautious crowd around him. The magna-crane hummed to life, hovering down towards him. When it hovered just above his position it picked him up, lifting him from the stained and filthy concrete. Without a magna-jack there didn't appear to be anything magnetising the soldier to the giant magnetic disc, but he clung there, magnetised, dangling over the pit, smiling down on the masses.

Impossible, Brie thought. *That is no living man.*

FORTY-FOUR

DESPITE THE HEAVY METALS AND TOXINS IN THE AIR, THE OPEN ocean was like a freedom I had never known. It was peaceful. Rewarding even. My life inside the confines of the sub-plaza was now nothing more than a distant nightmare.

I no longer had to check in to BC74 and listen to Father Kassal's mind-numbing rambles. I no longer had to wait in line at dosage on Thursdays. I no longer had to comply with the Union's deceitful, sadistic propaganda. Instead, as the Captain of our freighter, I just steered our boat northeast towards my hopes and dreams with Eli right by my side. If everything went to plan, soon enough we would leave Soteria behind for good.

After we had commandeered the freighter, which for our own triumphant purposes we re-named the Wife on account of the Marriage Lottery draw that I never took part in, we threw the dead bodies overboard, cleaned the helm and taught ourselves how to drive the damn thing. It wasn't hard. With a modern electronic engine, providing the battery always charged itself, it was fool proof to operate. There was a throttle and a power steering shaft. That was it.

We took turns at the helm, stopping at night to rest. The first night I hadn't slept at all, paranoid that the Union and its ruthless soldiers might catch us. Upon inspection of the crumpled delivery schedule Eli still had in his pocket, it became apparent that scheduled voyage would take a week. Therefore, we had a week before the disappearance of the ship would raise alarm. My paranoia settled. I planned to be in New Caledonia in half that time.

The wound on the back of my neck healed fast. It must have been the excess amount of Fosform we had access to. In three short days the wound had scabbed and hardened, with no sign of infection.

The wound on my forearm was more severe. After the excitement and adrenalin of our shootout had waned, the charred hole in my arm had been crippling. Even Eli, comfortable with blood and gore, had turned away when I showed him the visible bone. We had soaked the wound in Fosform Five, shoved a gauze pad in the blackened flesh and wrapped a silver-infused bandage around the length of my arm. The Union medics often used silver in wound dressings to prevent infection.

Despite the hole in my arm, I felt the fittest I had been in years. Judging by Eli's constant energy, I sensed he felt the same. With welcoming weather on our side, we headed peacefully into the great unknown. I suppose that is exactly what defined freedom. I didn't know what the next day held in store for me but that lack of knowledge, that grey space beyond the present, was why I had given up my previous life.

That grey space was the closest thing I had known to freedom.

It didn't take long for Eli to find his sea legs and grow accustomed to the rhythm of the water. Despite its ferocity, his seasickness only lasted the first few days. I didn't admit it to my young accomplice, but I found the aftermath of his uneasy stomach comical.

We had found food, weapons, alcohol and even sex-robots stored in various compartments inside the vessel. Upon inspection it wasn't just the Fosform and strange computer chips that were being transported. It was also weaponry and machinery. We found whole crates full to the brim with taser cannons, enough for an entire squadron of soldiers. We found power tools I had never even seen before. Crates filled with ultra modern machinery that, to me, looked like something from another planet. Eli suggested they may be for wall maintenance, but I had my doubts. I had worked on the walls for a year and I had never seen tools like these. There were socket-drills the size of a grown man's leg, alloy plated with seven different function buttons. There were carbon-fibre arc-welding devices, electronic and lightweight. They resembled micro-tasers, but they had a discharging solder cylinder and a fist-sized blue-torch. I took one from a crate, thinking it might come in handy.

Eli grew on me. He was a likable person, authentic and quick humoured. More and more I thanked myself for going back to find him. Doing all of this alone would have been infinitely harder.

On a whole, the days passed uneventfully. After our daring dash up the coast and our shootout to gain control of the freighter, we embraced the uneventfulness. I hadn't known relaxation since I was a child, since before they shipped me off to the wall but there, on the Wife, in that first week of Lust, we attempted to relax. There wasn't much else to do.

———

THE WIND BLEW COLD AS I STOOD ON THE BOW OF OUR GETAWAY vessel.

I could feel the change in weather coming. I pulled up the anchor on our third morning out and started up the electric engine. The black clouds were thicker, more severe than the previous few days. Thick clouds usually meant higher acidity in the rain. High acidity meant it would be a day stuck inside the pressurised helm. That didn't bother me too much. I was content. I was accustomed to sub-plaza living. Confined spaces had been part of my everyday life. I could tell though, through Eli's mannerisms, that he felt trapped inside the cramped space. He had spent his days wandering the northern beaches and inner suburbs looking for food and Fosform. He knew freedom and open spaces. In the bridge, only nine square metres, he behaved like a caged animal. He didn't like it. His fidgeting and constant roaming irritated me. I did my best to ignore him but as the minor irritations grew I felt ready to snap.

"Eli," I said, turning my attention from the choppy, dark waters before me to my over energised accomplice. "Calm down, man."

"I'm bored," was all he replied.

"You drive, then. I'll be happy to sit down and relax."

I stepped away from the steering column and let him take my place. I turned my attention to the vast expanse of nothingness before me. Rolling swell and open poisonous air. The Wife looked so insignificant compared to the vastness of the ocean.

Hypnotised, I watched the rise and fall of the waves. It made me think about the oceans on the other side of the walls, the oceans outside of Soteria. If everything continued to plan, it wouldn't be long before I would see those oceans for myself.

Thunder rumbled as bolts of lightning tore through the sky. I felt the boat vibrate as lightning contacted the surface somewhere port side. With the ominous rumbling came the downpour of hazardous, poisonous rain. It looked thick, unyielding.

We headed right into the guts of the storm. The consistent grumble of thunder, erratic flashes of electric light, heavy rain and increasing swell made for frightening conditions. I shot a quick glance at Eli. He held the steering column firm, but he looked afraid.

"I don't know about this, Tyson." Eli said.

"Well, it's not like we have a choice, man. We can't just turn around and head back with our tails between our legs…"

"Tails?" Eli looked confused. He didn't get the expression.

I didn't bother explaining.

The dark rain hammered down as the day dragged on. It showed no signs of easing. The raindrops were the size of fists, smashing down on the foredeck, hammering the windscreen with unforgiving fury. The black clouds seemed to get blacker as we ventured further northeast.

Visibility was terrible. We couldn't see more than a hundred metres in front of our vessel. From my previous thoughts about the insignificance of the Wife, about the vastness of the ocean, it became apparent to me how alone and vulnerable we were out there.

Relying on our satellite location and digital compass, we pushed on. The engine hummed and the colour drained from Eli's face. I looked into the torrential downpour, the heavy rain glimmering like analogue static. I stared into it, imagining shapes and objects in the blur. I could see ships, buildings, people even. They were all just figments of my overly active, Fosform-fuelled imagination.

Then I saw it. It was nothing constructed in my mind. It was real. Towering up out of the choppy ocean was a mountain of rock. Shaped like a jagged spike, threatening and black, at first it resembled a giant, rocky shark fin. My initial thought was that it might be a tower, not dissimilar to the one at Terrigal, a fortress in the middle of the ocean.

Fear rose from within. If it were a lookout post, or a security tower, we might be in big trouble.

Uncertainty and doubt returned for the first time in days.

As we neared the jagged monolith, I saw the ferocity of the waves smashing against its rocky base. Close to two hundred metres high, the thing rose out of the water like something from an adventure movie. I studied the mass. It became apparent that it was nothing built by man. I felt my heart rate subside.

"Eli," I yelled. "Steer clear of that thing, man. There could be rocks underneath the surface."

"What *is* that thing?"

I walked over to the SLD built into the dash and looked at our location. I had never heard of the tall mountain jutting out from the water, but the satellite device knew what it was.

"Balls Pyramid," I said to myself, reading the screen.

"Balls what?"

"Balls Pyramid. It's an island, apparently. There is another, much larger island just to the north. It's called Lord Howe Island. According to the SLD it's now uninhabited."

"How far away is it?"

"Not far. Not even fifteen kilometres."

Silent thought.

"Should we shelter there from the storm? Let it pass?"

I thought for a long, silent minute before answering. "We could. If it's uninhabited, we'll be okay."

Eli looked at me, pale faced. He forced a smile. I could tell there was only so much more of the chaotic rise and fall of the angry ocean that he could endure.

"Okay, fine. Let's do it. There better not be anyone there, though... Head north-northeast but don't get too close to that giant rock mountain."

"Sure thing, Captain."

FORTY-FIVE

THE STORM INTENSIFIED.

The colour of Eli's face changed from off-white to a light shade of green. My previous belief about Eli finding his sea legs was perhaps a little premature. Waves hammered into the side of the Wife. A few times, as the large freighter rolled sideways, I thought we would go over. Thankfully, she had been built for those conditions.

With Balls Pyramid now nothing more than a faint silhouette on the dark horizon behind us we could make out distant mountainous shapes before us. According to the SLD, the island was about eight kilometres long, shaped north to south somewhat like a banana. With the weather howling in from the east, the plan was to get onto the western side of the island, in the lee of the land.

Within half an hour of passing the monstrous rock pyramid we were a stone's throw from the southern tip of Lord Howe Island.

Anxiety built in my belly. I knew that we needed to seek shelter from the raging storm, but I also knew that land meant people and people could mean the Humanist Union. With surface conditions so fatal, I convinced myself that any Union citizens had abandoned this tiny little island and left it to nature's control. Despite rational thinking, despite logic, with each metre we got closer to the land-mass towering before us, my heart rate seemed to double.

The shape of the island sheltered the water to the west from the howling wind. As soon as we came around the western side of the island, the swell dropped off and for the first time in a good few hours the constant swaying ceased. The calmness of the flat water made me dizzy. I had grown so accustomed to the rolling rise and fall that I still felt like I was rocking. Eli couldn't take it. He mumbled something inaudible before running from the steering column and vomiting all over the side of the hull. He turned to me, embarrassed. All I could do was laugh.

I took the controls and lowered our speed. We followed the western coast of the island for five minutes, maybe a little more. The terrain was mountainous but the further north we travelled, the lower and flatter the land became. There were no signs of life. No buildings, no houses, no power lines; nothing other than wild, sub-tropical vegetation. It was overgrown, thick and lifeless.

I veered the Wife through a gap in a rocky reef shelf and into even more sheltered waters. The rain still hammered down, but the wind was non-existent. It seemed like as good a spot as any to drop anchor and wait for the black clouds to pass.

Putting the throttle into neutral, I found a leather coat to shelter myself from the acidic rain and I ran to the bow of the boat to release the anchor chain. The rain was heavy, bitter. I could smell the poison in every drop. Concealed beneath the coat, I dashed back inside the safety of the bridge. I didn't get a drop on me. In such a ferocious storm, even a few drops of that rain could cause festering blisters.

It was now time to wait.

Hours passed and the storm didn't seem to ease. We sat in the mess room, eating for the sake of it. We had enough food for an entire crew so there was no harm in overeating. Boredom made the time pass slowly. I could tell that Eli had something on his mind. He was distant, distracted.

"You alright?" I asked him.

"Yeah, I'm just a little blown away, I guess. It still doesn't feel real, man. I mean, if you hadn't come and found me I would still be in the sewers, eating rotten food and drinking expired Fosform. I never would have thought I would be here, now, on our way to God knows where."

"Well, Eli, I'm sort of in the same boat." I laughed. "No pun intended."

I'm not sure he got my humour. If he did, he didn't react.

"What I mean," I continued, "is that I never thought I would be here either. But you know what? I'm glad that we are. Our life has a chance now, a purpose. We're so close to freedom. It's lingering just out there." I pointed to the east. "It's just there over the horizon and soon it will be ours."

"Well… thanks, Tyson."

"For what?"

"For coming back for me. I haven't really had anyone to talk to for a long time. I haven't had company. I haven't had… well, a friend."

The impact of that statement hit me like a taser cannon blast. It became apparent just how lonely his life must have been. And just how selfish I was. I did have friends. Well, I *had* friends. I had George. I had Jonah. And I had abandoned them. I threw them away the second I cut out my registration chip. Here was a young kid who had nothing and no one, and he put his faith in my dreams, my hopes. His act of selflessness made success even more important. I owed it to Eli.

"Thanks, man. I'm glad to call you my friend."

Eli's face reddened, uncomfortable with the emotional nature of the conversation. I changed the subject to ease his unwarranted embarrassment. As the blushed pink drained from his cheeks and he returned to his normal self, we heard the constant patter of rain-drops on the roof begin to soften.

From the starboard side window of the cabin we could see the storm weakening. A thick blanket of white cloud replaced the evil clouds that had, until now, swallowed our view.

Gaps appeared in the clouds. The sun's harsh rays penetrated between them, bringing colour to the previously dull landscape.

With the light, the visibility improved. I looked towards the island, signs of human influence now visible. Albeit rundown and overgrown, there was evidence of a once thriving holiday community. I could make out old hotels on the beachfront. Tall, elegant and once proud, vine and moss covered the old buildings. They appeared menacing, uninviting. I could make out old boats, washed up onto the beach in storms. Some still intact, others nothing more than rotten planks of wood and torn hulls.

While it looked like there was a time when humans had inhabited the island, it appeared the SLD was correct in stating that the place was uninhabited. I looked at the dashboard of the helm to get the time. We still had four hours of sunlight left. I looked over at Eli. He was sucking on a chunk of peach. I could tell he was thinking what I was thinking. It was stupid, far too risky.

"So," I said, a mischievous grin on my face. "You want to explore the island?"

"Do I ever. Let's get off this damned boat for a bit. I can't wait to touch solid ground."

"Ok, cool. Let's get some stuff together and go see what we can find."

"After you, Ty."

While I gathered some items for our exploration, Eli rigged up the small RIB safety vessel at the back of the freighter. RIB was an old term for Rigid Inflatable Boat. It was an aluminium-infused rubber boat with an inboard digital engine, typical of life rafts in the latter half of the 40s, typical for Union wall builders.

I left with a taser cannon, a torch, some drinkable water and that funny-looking welder I had found, all stashed into a black latex rucksack. I flung the bag over my shoulder and stepped over the gunwale. Eli already had the small boat in the water. It bobbed every so slightly as I climbed down the steel ladder and jumped in.

"Let's do it," I said with a grin.

Eli removed the ignition cover and pressed down on the ignition lever. With almost no noise, the engine purred to life and we started our smooth trip through the shallow tidal zone towards the desolate and lifeless beach.

"You know what's funny," Eli said, holding the steering column like a seasoned voyager.

"What?"

"I had never been on a boat in my life, of any type. Now, with you, this is the third boat I've been on this week. I'm starting to like it."

"That's what you get when you're trying to escape a place surrounded by water."

"Yeah, I suppose you're right. Still, it wasn't what I had imagined when you asked me to join you on your quest. To be truthful, I didn't know what to expect. This is the furthest I've ever been from my family home."

Other than working on the walls against my will, it was the furthest from home I had ever been too. I grew up in Union-controlled Soteria. Travel was not something I had ever experienced.

"Bring on the grey space," I whispered towards the unknown.

Eli slowed the throttle right down as we neared the sand. The water became shallow beneath us. It glistened, almost the colour of Fosform, aqua and inviting. About a metre from the edge of the water our life raft came to a stop. Eli switched off the engine. I stepped out of the boat, placing my feet into the shallow water. It was warm. Eli followed – far less elegantly, mind you – and jumped from the back of the boat, sending a torrent of water my way.

We both laughed.

Standing alone on the beach woke the fear in my belly. The gloomy nature of the island was potent. Distant birdcalls interrupted the silence.

I looked both ways along the stretch of white sand.

"Here, take this," I said to Eli as I handed him the small taser cannon. He took it without apprehension and shoved it into the waist of his trousers. I held the odd welding device. From our violent gunfight we instigated when we commandeered the Wife, it was clear, through nothing more that luck, that Eli was a far better shot than I was. Therefore, if we came across something hostile, I felt safer knowing that the responsibility rested on him.

"Left or right?"

"Hmmm." I placed my free hand behind my back. "Guess how many fingers I'm holding up," I said. "If you guess right, we go right. If you guess wrong, we got left."

"Okay... Three."

I pulled my hand out from my back, with three fingers extended. "Right it is..."

I looked to the right. A little over two hundred metres away was a deteriorated old hotel. It looked frightening. Suddenly I was second-guessing our need to explore. I wanted nothing more than to be back on the boat.

Doubt.

"Are you sure you want to do this?"

"Don't be a wuss, Tyson. We didn't come this far to turn back now."

With the confident stride of a Union soldier, Eli marched off up the beach. It didn't take long for me to follow. The sand looked so barren, so pristine. I could make out the small footprints of birds, so light they barely left an indentation. As we neared the old hotel, I froze in my tracks. "Eli," I said, looking down before me. "Look."

Right there, leading from the water's edge to the front of the hotel were footprints.

Human footprints.

FORTY-SIX

BRUCE CHADWICK TOSSED AND TURNED ON HIS SLEEPING PALLET, plagued with restlessness.

It had been two days since he and Robin had returned to T-Town with a little less than one hundred vials of Fosform Five and a gripping story. There were mixed emotions within the group. Their return skewed the morale. While the outlaw group had a new lease of life with a fresh batch of the anti-corrosive serum, Tom, Tinker, Krit and *Michael* had not returned. Bruce battled constantly with his own demons. How had he let it happen? How had he not talked Michael into changing his mind?

He wondered where Michael was now.

"Bloody fool," Bruce whispered to his empty room as he tried to reposition himself on the hard mattress.

After the gruesome raid on the barracks at the wall, Robin, Michael and Bruce had found the vials of Fosform Five in the barracks. Officer Hawke had been honest. They found all the serum and their accompanying injector guns in metal crates underneath the bunk beds in the barracks.

They found a supply of canvas travel bags and grabbed what

they could carry, including all the Fosform Five, some nuclear shock balls and a range of much needed medication. Once packed, they got out of the eerie, death-ridden barracks. Outside, back in the humid evening air, Bruce recommended that they remove the registration chips crudely implanted in their necks.

"It's bloody-well done," he had said. "Now let's rip these fucking things out and throw 'em in the jungle."

Robin nodded in compliance. He reached to his belt and removed his knife from its sheath.

But Michael had hesitated.

Lying on his sleeping pallet, sweaty and uncomfortable, Bruce played back the moment again and again and wished he had been more assertive, more convincing.

"I'm not going to take mine out," Michael had said, stern and serious.

"What you mean, you not take out?" Robin asked in his broken English, awestruck.

"I mean, guys, that this is my ticket to find Brie."

"Brie?" Bruce said, shocked. "Brie is dead, mate. Brie's gone!"

"You don't know that, Bruce. The Union doesn't kill all its prisoners. She is somewhere in some filthy cell and with this chip in my neck I can gain access to pretty much anywhere in the Union. I'm gonna find her and bring her back to T-Town."

"That, mate, is by far the stupidest fucking thing I've ever heard. You'd be walking into a death trap."

"Maybe so. But maybe not? I can become Officer Hawke. I'll blend right in. I'll ask around and I'll do what it takes, or die trying."

"Was she that bloody good, mate? This is madness…"

"I'm sorry, Bruce. You won't change my mind. There is something I felt with that girl I have never felt with anyone. I can't explain it. I'll search these barracks for a vehicle and I'm leaving. End of story."

Bruce stared at Michael, long and hard. Moisture welled in Michael's eyes. He looked away before the moisture became a torrent of tears. Robin stood by in silence. He knew no amount of pleading would change Michael's mind. He could see love-sickness glowing from behind Michael's sunken eyes.

"It's been real," Michael said, leaning forward and giving his friend a powerful bear-like hug. "Good luck, my friend. Now finish that fucking hole and get to safety. I'm going to go get Brie. I know I'll find her. I can feel it."

Bruce clenched his teeth. He shook his head.

"Be safe, friend," he said. "Thanks for bringing me back from the dead, too. I owe you one."

"I'll remember that."

And that was it.

Michael Butcher had turned, left his two comrades and re-entered the barracks.

Bruce and Robin ventured back to their bunker home in miserable silence. In the two days Bruce had been back in T-Town, he hadn't left his sleeping pallet. The digging was consistent, Gabbie and Evan were doing a splendid job at keeping productivity and morale up but without Francis and Michael, Bruce felt lost, like a stranger in his own home. Depression's greedy claws gripped him tightly. Gabbie checked on him from time to time, bringing him flasks of warm tea and daily rations of food, but she knew what Bruce needed was space and time. That's exactly what she gave him.

He will come back around, she had said to herself. *He's Bruce Chadwick.*

I AM NOW OFFICER HAWKE.

Alone and frightened, yet clouded by desire, Michael had re-entered the dark concrete corridor and searched around. He was brisk with no intention of lingering. The smell of burnt flesh and blood was already filling the narrow walkways. He found a charged taser cannon in the common room and a smaller, user-friendly oxygen conditioner with a handful of carbon-fibre filter spares.

Michael refused to think too much about what he was doing. The thought of not seeing his T-Town comrades again was a hard burden to bear. They were his family. And in a selfish act of love, Michael was abandoning them. Not to mention that the more he analysed his plan, the more it sounded like a ridiculous suicide-mission.

He blocked out reason. He blocked out logic. Love and logic would never be fitting accomplices.

Shoving some food and clean bottles of water into a ration pack, Michael continued his search, finding a vehicle garage under the far end of the common room. Inside the garage were half a dozen Union-issue hover-bikes, pristine and barely used. He jumped on the closest one, typed in the ignition sequence and secured his ration-pack on the back of the bike. After the ignition countdown proved successful, the solar-powered engine purred to life. An extensive search of the garage walls resulted in Michael finding a scanner beside a gap in the concrete. He scanned the dead soldier's registration chip in the wound above his spine and the concrete wall started groaning to life.

Michael watched the wall open right up, revealing an angled concrete rampart. He saw the faintest twilight glow at the far end of the ramp and felt the natural blow of a cool breeze gusting down the tunnel, filling the stale room with fresh, though poisonous air.

It must be a secret vehicle entrance, thought Michael.

He climbed onto the vehicle and throttled up and out of the darkness, leaving the wretched smell of death behind. Once on the surface he appeared from a small entrance underneath the thick cover of ferns. Running on hope and fear, he swung a right turn and began heading west along the wall, putting a greater distance between T-Town and himself. If he kept a consistent pace, he figured he would reach the coastline a little after sunrise.

Closer to sunset the next day, with the sun hovering above the horizon, Michael sighted the ocean at last. It glistened a yellowy-gold. The sun's reflection danced off the rise and fall of the ocean, its shimmer giving Michael a glimpse of hope. He sped down the clearing beside the huge concrete wall until he came to a guarded compound. The silhouette of the Union's wicked red eagle stood proud, wings spread, above the fortified entrance. The sight of that bird sent shivers down Michael's spine. In gunmetal grey stencilled letters, high above the compound gates were those four words:

LOYALTY-UNION-SAFETY-SALVATION

Followed by the name of the fortress:

AQUILONEM.

For the first time since leaving his friends at the barrack-bunker, Michael came across soldiers. For the first time since beginning his mad search for love he felt terrified.

He refused to let it show.

Two soldiers stood alert at the entrance to the compound, armed with taser cannons and fitted with full-face conditioners. As Michael approached, they raised their weapons and watched him with caution. Despite Michael's grey Union-issue uniform, it was obvious from their defensive reaction that it was not common to see a soldier come flying down the rocky hillside on a hover-bike.

"Officers," said Michael, pulling up beside the closest soldier, fighting the nauseous fear.

"What business do you have here, soldier?"

"I'm Officer Hawke," Michael said with false confidence. "I need to report to an advisor, now. There has been a breach of our barracks. Everyone is *dead*!" With each word, Michael's voice increased in volume. He yelled his last words with false hysteria.

"Barracks? Dead? Which barracks?"

Michael didn't have an answer. He stalled. The soldier looked cautious, uncertain.

"My *damn* barracks! What does it matter to you? Scan me inside now. I need to report to your advisor. I didn't come this whole way to speak to a fucking guard. I'm tired, dirty, sore and we have a damn slaughter to deal with."

Both guards looked wide-eyes as Michael yelled. Despite their apparent equal rank, they moved aside. The second soldier, the one yet to talk, removed a chip-scanner from its mount on the wall and scanned the back of Michael's neck. Luckily for Michael, the collar of his Union-issue jacket covered the seeping and poorly stitched wound. After a second, the scanning device beeped green, with Officer Hawke's identification code appearing on the small screen.

"Okay, Officer Hawke. Come on through."

The heavy steel door opened without a sound as Michael and one guard entered the compound. The other remained in position. Once inside, Michael removed his oxygen conditioner and looked around. The place looked like a fortress, all steel and concrete, bland and uninviting. Not dissimilar to the barrack-bunker he had just come from but it was far grander, far more opulent and wonderfully engineered.

Bright white lighting flooded the corridors. Tinted glass windows allowed natural light to creep in, bathing the concrete walls with warmth. Following the guard, Michael walked along the lit balcony overlooking the ocean through thick windows. Beneath him was a dock, equipped with cranes and ship construction machinery. To the far end of the dock was an air-dock housing three stationary helicopters and a handful of small aircraft. Soldiers, dressed the same as Michael, hurried from place to place, running errands and performing tasks.

What in Hell is this place?

At the far end of the balcony, the silent guard led Michael into an open room perched above the maintenance field below. The room was round, with a curved floor to ceiling window taking up half the room. From inside, one had an unrestricted 180-degree view of the dock and the shipyard. Aside from several latex couches and a hardwood desk, the room was under-furnished.

At the desk sat a tall, mid-forties man of African ethnicity. He wore the typical latex and polyester jacket and leggings of a high-ranking Union advisor. He looked up from his tablet screen as Michael and his guide entered.

"Can I help you two?" His voice was stern, direct.

Expressionless, the guard looked towards Michael and nodded, insinuating that it was Michael's responsibility to respond. Michael clenched his teeth and swallowed. This was the point of no return and he knew it.

"Good evening, Advisor. My name is Officer Hawke and I've

just come from—"

"I know exactly who you are and exactly where you're stationed," the advisor interrupted. "As soon as you scanned your chip on entry, my database told me everything about you. You are serving two months patrol duty at Gate Eight. Why have you left your post, soldier?"

"There has been a breach at Gate Eight, sir," said Michael, using the correct name of the barracks. "Outlaws have attacked the place and killed everyone. I'm the only survivor. I escaped by hover-bike before they could get me—"

"And who are *they*?"

"I don't know, sir. Surface dwellers. I'm unaware of their purpose."

The advisor stood. He was tall, towering over both Michael and the silent guard. He looked over towards the guard waiting beside Michael.

"Soldier, you can return to your position. Hawke, take a seat." Michael sat on the latex sofa. The advisor sat opposite. "My name is Saviour. You may call me Sav if it pleases you. I am the commanding advisor here at Aquilonem, the north dock. I find it odd that you show up here unannounced. Why didn't you call from Gate Eight first? Why didn't you activate the panic button? Why did the alarms not trigger?"

"I'm sorry, sir. It all happened so fast. I fled. I wasn't thinking…"

Sav gave Michael a distrusting glance. "Why do you insist on calling me *sir*? You are a ranking Officer. My name will suffice."

"Just manners, I guess. It's how my parents raised me."

"Interesting… I also find it interesting that Master Haynes put out a high-caution alert for a gang of thieving surface dwellers for the Northern Sector only two days ago, and now here we are. I will inform the Master's people in Brisbane of what has occurred. Did you get a look at any of the outlaws? Did you bring any of the external camera hard drives with you? This timing is surely more than a coincidence…"

"All I saw were taser blasts and dead bodies. They were dressed in black. They were local. Thai, I think. That's all I know. Look, Sav, I haven't stopped in two days. If you could provide me with quarters to rest, tomorrow I will provide a detailed account. Right now, some food and water would be helpful."

Saviour looked at Michael. There was something distrusting in his glare. His large dark brown eyes were intimidating. "You are aware, Officer Hawke, that this is the first time in the Empire's successful reign that outlaws have tried, let alone got inside a gate post and killed all but one Union soldier? This is no small feat!"

Michael nodded.

"We cannot leave this without a series of detailed reports and an analysis of the event. I will contact Master Haynes himself and a thorough report will begin tomorrow with your assistance. In the meantime, you may have your food and your rest, but you will stay here at Aquilonem until we have the report complete. Is that understood?"

"Sure thing. Thanks Sav."

"You may be excused, Officer Hawke. You will find the mess hall at the far end of the southern corridor. I will have someone meet you there and show you to your quarters."

"Great, I appreciate it."

———

As Michael left, Saviour watched him.

He wasn't a superstitious man. He wasn't a paranoid man either, but there was something about Officer Hawke that didn't seem right. His posture, his use of language, even the way he walked didn't look like the comings of someone who had undergone years of Union training.

"I need those hard drives," Saviour whispered to himself through clenched teeth. "I need to see what happened."

Acting as efficiently as they had trained him to do, Saviour contacted one of his Officers stationed on the dock. He ordered the

Officer to put together an extraction team of four soldiers and use a standby helicopter to get to Gate Eight and locate the hard-drives that stored all surveillance footage. "I want you back before morning," Saviour said. "Do not fail me."

Michael Butcher hurried down the southern corridor. His heart hammered. Sweat had gathered in every little crevice on his body, making the dead soldiers uniform cling uncomfortably to his clammy skin.

The short conversation with Saviour had been terrifying. Michael was in the lion's den. He doubted the rationality behind his decision to enter Aquilonem and now he wanted nothing more than to be back inside the comforts of T-Town.

What the Hell am I doing? I must be nuts. She'd better still be alive.

The mess hall was all but deserted. Except for a quiet group of soldiers sitting at the corner table under the dull-glow of artificial sunlight, Michael had the place to himself. A few of the soldiers noticed his arrival but continued in quiet conversation. They seemed disinterested in his presence. Maybe the comings and goings of strangers was common in Aquilonem, Michael thought.

He grabbed a plastic tray and made his way to the servery where a huge array of hot meals awaited the dinner rush. He piled onto his tray a steaming serving of lasagne, then pasta salad, crusty bread and what appeared to be a roast vegetable stew. He hadn't seen food like this in years. It was hot, hearty, *real* food. His stomach churned and gurgled as the aromatic smells attacked his nostrils. It was a welcome sight after a year of eating bird stew and lizard meat.

Michael took a seat alone on one of the centre tables. Only one mouthful into the rich lasagne and he heard a call from one of the Officer's behind him. "Hey soldier," the voice called out in thick accented English. "Why you sit alone? Come join us…"

As much as Michael didn't want to interact with the Union scum that he despised so much, he didn't want to draw unnecessary attention. He sighed, picked up his tray and cutlery, clenched his teeth and turned to join the table in the corner. As he approached, two of the soldiers stood to welcome him. One of them, short,

Asian ethnicity, shaved-head, grinned and put his hand forward in a gesture of welcoming. "Hello, soldier. Welcome to Aquilonem," he said. "What's your business?"

Michael took a deep breath.

I am now Officer Hawke.

FORTY-SEVEN

WITHOUT LUCIFER, THE FIRST EVENING IN THE PIT BROUGHT A whole new atmosphere to G-Block. There was no longer an alpha. There was no longer anyone in charge.

Brie sat huddled behind the makeshift pallet walls with Lachlan, Peter and Lucy's other trusted companions as they listened to the sounds of violence and death. She was frightened. The fighting had increased. Understandably. The dinner food drop resulted in a huge, viscous brawl where very few people got any food. Lucifer's headless body still lay slumped in the centre of the pit. Sticky, semi-dried blood oozed from her gaping neck.

Convicts were tearing at each other's magna-jacks, forcing the self-destruct mechanism to kill those who were incapable of defending themselves. It was outright chaos. In the few short hours since Lucifer's death, the pit had lost a third of its population.

"Before Lucy entered the pit and created relative peace," Lachlan said to himself as much as anyone else, "this was the norm in G-Block. I don't want to be the bearer of bad news, but we are in serious trouble." Lachlan looked over to Brie, who sat wide-eyed with concern. "Especially you, Brie. You are still the freshest meat in here. I wish I could truthfully say that we could protect you but I don't know how true that is. We all need to watch our backs."

Only four minutes later, as the deathly screams continued throughout the pit, the magna-crane above the arena hummed to life. It was well past feeding hour and there was nothing attached to the magnetic disk itself.

Brie repositioned herself to watch the crane hover slowly into G-Block. Her initial thought was that it might collect some of dead bodies that lay sprawled in the pit to rid the place of the stench of death. This was not the case at all. The crane hovered past the two corpses in the centre of the pit and began making its way towards the pallet fencing where Brie sat in hiding.

"Shit," Brie whispered to herself. "It's coming for me."

With her heart rate on the rise, Brie moved sidewards, past Lachlan and the others to gain a more concealed position against the wall. As if the crane was a living organism with all-watchful eyes, the metallic disk followed her path, groaning as it made its way towards her.

"Shit."

Brie knew that they had discovered her lies. On the tiniest of plus sides, she would escape the pit at a very convenient time. Despite her warranted fear there was a touch of relief knowing she would not fall victim to the murderous chaos. The place was ready to implode. It was only a matter of time before people needed sleep and when they did, they would be vulnerable.

Brie took a deep breath and stood tall, defiant and proud as she awaited the magnet's powerful force to lift her from the filthy pit. This was about much more than exit from the pit. She stood defiantly as she awaited her death. She could taste it.

The magnet's force pulled her from the ground, sucking her into the air. Hanging from the magna-crane, Brie looked down at Lachlan and waved. Tears welled in her bloodshot and swollen eyes. She knew this was the beginning of the end. She mouthed goodbye to Lachlan. He looked up at her in helpless desperation. He would be lucky if he survived one more night in the place for he, too, had just faced the beginning of the end. He looked frightened. He looked defeated. Brie looked down at him. His expression gave her courage. It fuelled her defiance.

That's what the Union wants, she thought to herself.

They want people to feel defeated.

They will not defeat me.

As the crane lifted her up and over the concrete balcony, a handful of grey-clad soldiers grabbed her. One stepped forward and pulled a black canvas bag from the pocket of his fatigues. Without a word, without even a change in his facial expression, he slid the bag over Brie's head and zipped it tight around her neck.

Blindfolded, they dragged her through a series of corridors, through transporter tunnels and down stairwells. Even through the thick canvas, even with her breath lingering inside the bag, it was a well-received change from the stench of the pit she had grown accustomed to.

After ten minutes of travel through the sub-plaza prison, they stopped and tore the black canvas bag from her head.

Brie squinted, adjusting to the harsh synthetic sunlight. She once again stood before Eric van Bueren and Master Stephen Haynes. They both sat cross-legged on a latex lounge in a communal conference room. Van Bueren wore his typical advisor uniform, grey and lifeless. Master Haynes wore typical attire for the upper class- nylon leggings and a plain, polyester-latex shirt. They both looked displeased.

They ordered Brie to sit on the lounge opposite the two men of power.

Master Haynes nodded at a soldier standing beside Brie. The soldier clenched his fist into a tight ball and backhanded Brie across her nose. Blood flowed. Eyes watered. Despite the pain, Brie did her best to sit defiant. Refusing to wipe her face, Brie let the blood drip down her chin and onto her shiny metallic magna-jack.

"Now Brie," the Master said, clearing his throat. "I'm sure you know why you deserved that."

She didn't answer.

"We gave you the benefit of the doubt and you lied to us. How dare you think you can try to manipulate me? Lie to *me*? This is *my*

Empire. I understand that you have a certain loyalty, albeit miscon-strued, to these surface-dwelling vigilantes but how long did you think it would take for us to discover the truth?"

"Long enough," she replied quietly.

"Long enough? Long enough for what?"

"Long enough for them to find their freedom."

"Would you care to elaborate?"

"Fuck off."

"I see." Master Haynes nodded at his loyal soldier and again the soldier belted Brie across the face. More blood. More defiance.

"How long do you think you can endure this, Mrs van Bueren?"

"I'm not a *van Bueren*," Brie roared, looking across to her uncle-in-law, who up to this point had not yet spoken.

"Well, Brie, your registration chip states otherwise."

"I don't have a registration chip, you stupid old bastard."

"Enough with the insults! It serves no purpose." The Master raised his voice. His temper had run thin. "I no longer have time to waste on you and your unjustified arrogance. You will tell me where these surface dwellers are, or we will send you off to Terra Carcerem today. And once you are there, things will get a lot worse for you… This is your last chance, Brie *van Bueren*!"

Brie thought about Michael Butcher once more. She thought about Bruce, about Robin and Krit and Evan. She thought about Gabbie and Remy. She refused to give them all up. She couldn't. Her eyes welled with tears. Her chin trembled. Their lives were worth more than hers alone.

"I suppose you better send me then."

Eric Van Bueren shook his head. "You're a damn fool, Brie. You're throwing your life away for a group of outlaws."

"There is nothing you can say to sway me. These people you call outlaws are *real* people with passion and ideals. Real people, who want to make their own decisions, not follow decisions they're *forced* to comply with. These *outlaws* are people who want one thing, and that's to *live*!" Brie spoke with a fierce passion. "Now take me away!"

Master Stephen Haynes smiled. "Well, Mrs van Bueren, the

next time I see you will be under different circumstances. I look forward to it. Your time in Terra Carcerem will treat you well."

Master Haynes stood up to leave, followed obediently by Eric van Bueren. They both towered over Brie, looking down at their prisoner. "By the way," Master Haynes said. "My Northern Sector advisors informed me this morning that a team of surface dwelling vigilantes raided one of our barracks, Gate Eight on the northern wall."

"There's video evidence of the intruders. It seems we're closer to catching your friends than you may think. We plan to incinerate the northern jungles today. That should clear out any unwanted vermin lingering near the wall. Your friends are doomed. We will flatten the entire uninhabited stretch of jungle within fifty kilometres of the northern wall. There will be no survivors..." The Master cackled with sadistic self-worth as he left the conference room. Just before exiting through the remote sensor doorway, he turned back and looked at the soldiers standing beside Brie. "Send her to Carcerem. I want her in the operating theatre by the end of the week!"

Master Haynes and van Bueren left. Silence enveloped the room. Brie looked over towards the three soldiers. One of them, his grey uniform tag reading Garrett, stepped forward and pulled a Fosform injector gun from his belt. He removed the vial of aqua-blue serum and replaced it with a smaller vial of a dark purple liquid.

Brie flinched, pre-empting what was about to occur. "What the *hell* is that?" she yelled, leaping from the couch and making a short and futile run to the corner of the room.

"This is just a little something that will make your journey to Terra Carcerem a little calmer."

"I don't want it."

"What you want is not of importance."

With taser cannons raised, the three soldiers surrounded Brie and encroached on her position. She roared her last defiant scream. Garrett laughed.

The two flanking soldiers lunged forward and held Brie firm around the upper-arms. Garrett stepped forward and held the injector gun to her neck, pressing down on the trigger. Brie felt the cool liquid course through her blood. Within seconds the room spun. Noise became unusual, fragmented and static. Nausea crippled her, intolerable and sharp.

"Am I dying?" Brie asked, her words slurred and echoing. "Is Carcerem... *Death*?"

Garrett didn't respond.

FORTY-EIGHT

GEORGE CLARKSON OPENED HIS EYES.

Crusty, dry and matted together with a glue-like paste, he had to force his eyelids apart. His vision was blurry. He felt groggy, distant, almost out-of-body yet surprisingly strong, calm even.

Strange memories flooded his cloudy mind. He wasn't sure what was memory and what was a twisted nightmare. As his mind sifted through the warped images, he vaguely remembered his final conscious moments, or at least, what his mind was telling him were his final moments. He thought he should be dead.

He recalled Tyson's disappearance. He recalled the surface exposure torture, the interrogation, and the *castration*.

Panicking, George reached down to feel his manhood nestled between his legs, where it had been since life began. To add to the rising panic, his fears were precise – there was nothing there. Where his penis had been his entire life, along with the rest of his reproductive organs, was nothing more than a smooth, healed, scar-free, hairless patch of skin.

"What the *fuck*?"

Nausea consumed him. His face flushed yet his heart rate remained calm. Trying to sit up, he discovered that they had strapped him to a steel table by thick nylon tape at the neck, waist and ankles. He tried looking around, wiping the paste-like crust from his eyes.

Once he wiped his eyes clean, he studied the room. He could see with such clarity. His vision was impeccable. Everything looked so defined, so sharp and in focus. George had always had slightly inferior eyesight. Not enough to warrant eye-surgery or permanent contacts, but still the difference was instantly noticeable.

George was in an empty room less than ten square metres. The colour of the walls was a light shade of blue, almost aqua. The colour of Fosform Five, he thought. George had never seen a Tier with Fosform coloured walls. He was confident he was no longer in 3rd Sydney West.

How much time has passed? Where in Hell am I?

Despite the fear and the crippling aroma of uncertainty, George found his heart rate calm, subdued almost. He had no pain. Once the groggy mask of confusion deteriorated, George felt no hunger, no thirst. He felt powerful.

What have they done to me?

FORTY-NINE

ELI AND I STOOD FROZEN ON THE BEACH.

I bent down to inspect the footprints. They were barefoot, large, and surely male. They looked fresh. The tide had gone out that morning and the footprints snaked their way below the high tide line. My heart rate increased. Frantic thoughts raced through my mind.

"We need to get back to the boat. Now," I said, my voice laced with authority. It was not a question.

"Hold on a minute," Eli said. "This is not necessarily a bad thing. I mean it could be someone just like me. Only two weeks ago my appearance would have frightened you. Only two weeks ago I was some hostile surface dweller to you. Just think about it. The footprints are barefoot, right? Union soldiers will not be walking around barefoot. It's probably a surface dweller. They're most probably more frightened of us being here then we should be of them."

I wasn't convinced. "Yeah, but Eli, we don't know if it's just one person. There could be a whole colony of dwellers in there. They could be mutants? They could be cannibals? Like the ones on the beach back at Narrabeen."

"Stop being such a wuss, Tyson. Living underground has made

you soft. We're armed. We're the dangerous ones. Now I say we follow the prints. They might lead us to food, or help. You want to escape Soteria? You want to make a dash for freedom? It won't be easy. It *hasn't* been easy. It's not like we can just walk away. It will take courage. It will take wit. And willpower!"

I felt belittled. A fourteen-year-old kid was talking down to me. I felt inferior, embarrassed. Survival was my priority. I didn't want to get this far only to get caught by some island dwelling mutant cannibals. I didn't want to escape the grasp of the Union's greedy claws only to get chopped up and thrown into a stew. Then again, Eli was right. It wasn't ever going to be easy.

"Okay fine, but you've got the taser so you're going first."

We inched our way across the sand, heading towards the menacing and dilapidated hotel. The silence was deafening. I could hear Eli's breathing. I could hear my heart hammering.

The footprints led to a once elegant archway entrance to the foyer. Vines and weeds covered the tiles. Dust, dirt, grime and spider webs covered every little nook and surface. We entered the foyer. Weeds grew over the windows, making the place dark and foreboding. The front doors, once motion-censored sliding doors, didn't function. They lay beside the doorframe, smashed and gaping open.

I let my eyes adjust to the darkness before taking another step. Eli seemed fine. Spending his days scouring the northern beaches for food and Fosform had made him far more courageous than me. It terrified me. The place smelt stale. A tinge of familiarity tainted the air. I knew the smell, but I couldn't put my finger on it. It wasn't a nice smell.

From the foyer, several overgrown corridors led to different parts of the abandoned hotel. None of them looked inviting, but I knew standing around in the foyer served no purpose.

"So, what now," I whispered to Eli.

"I dunno," he whispered back. "Let's try to find the kitchen. Who knows what might be in there?"

As I took another step I saw the faintest rush of movement to my right. Nothing more than a quick blur, moving shadows. I spun on the spot, holding up the welding device in front of me for protection.

Nothing.

Maybe it was paranoia. Maybe I was losing it.

"Did you see that?" I asked, my voice unsteady. Eli shook his head. "Man, I swear I just saw something there."

Entirely at random, Eli chose the corridor closest to the reception counter. I kept within a metre behind him as we both went deeper into the overgrown darkness. Whether it was paranoia or whether I was losing my mind didn't matter. There was something amiss. I was always a person to follow my instincts. My instincts had gotten me this far. My instincts had gotten me out of 3rd Sydney West and safely off the mainland and now my instincts told me to flee. I would ignore them no longer.

"This isn't right, man. We're being watched. I can feel it."

"Shhhhh…"

"What do you mean '*shhhhh*'? I'm leaving, with or without you."

Before waiting for Eli to comply, I turned and began walking back toward the foyer.

I froze in my tracks. The silhouette of a figure stepped across the entrance to the corridor, blocking our escape. I went into panic mode and ran away from the foyer, deeper into the dim corridor. Eli, sensing my uncontrollable fear, ran right beside me. We turned the corner only to find a mound of rubble, debris and a labyrinth of vines.

We had walked right into a dead end.

How could we have been so stupid?

"To hell with this," Eli said with false aggression, raising the taser cannon and aiming it down the corridor, waiting for the figure to come into view. He fired a warning blast towards the wall, letting our assailant know we were armed.

Painful silence.

"Wait… I mean you no harm." A voice came from the silhouette near the foyer. It was deep, hoarse, a slight European accent of some sort. He sounded old. Eli kept the weapon raised. I held the welding device but knew it would have little effect.

The silhouette raised both his arms in the air as a gesture of peace. "I mean you no harm," he said again. "You can trust me. I am not here to hurt you. I needed to make sure you meant me no harm. I wasn't sure if you were Union or not. I can see now that you are not."

"What makes you so sure?" Eli yelled back along the corridor, his young voice echoing through the tunnel-like hallway.

"Because you're only a child. Now, are you going to come out from there or will we continue to talk from opposite ends of the hall?"

We didn't respond. I looked at Eli. He looked at me and shrugged.

"What do you think?" I whispered.

"Sounds like some old bloke. I *guess* it will be fine."

"You just keep that damn taser cannon aimed at his face, okay? Let's go."

One tentative step at a time, we ventured back towards the light. As we got closer to the foyer, the silhouette before us became more than a black outline. We could see clothing, white hair, a dishevelled beard and wary, cautious eyes. He still had his hands raised.

"You don't need the taser aimed at me," he said calmly. "I am not your enemy. In fact, I am quite excited to see you. I haven't seen another human in well over a year now."

We entered the foyer. Eli stood beside me, the weapon aimed at the stranger. We kept our distance from him. Whether he meant us harm was one thing, but what if he was mutated, or contagious with some surface-borne illness?

Other than the scruffy, unkempt appearance he looked to be in relatively good health. He was thin, but not malnourished. His skin was tanned golden brown and his feet were bare. His snow-white hair was wavy and matted. His beard, similar in colour, was long and dread-locked. What struck me were his eyes. They were emerald green and inviting.

My heart still hammered and sweat beaded on my brow but the tension in the air had dissipated. I could sense kindness and warmth in the stranger's facial features. He looked harmless. Eli was not so accepting. He refused to drop the taser.

"What are you doing here?" I asked the old man.

"I could ask you the same thing," he said, grinning with stained yellow teeth. "Seeing as I have spent a year here without guests, the question is better suited to you, as you are indeed the intruders."

"We pulled into the bay to shelter from the storm."

"I noticed the boat coming in well before you came to shore. I have seen that boat before. I have also seen its crew before. How did you get hold of it?"

"You've seen it before? We are… we… Anyway, why are *you* here?"

I didn't want to tell the stranger our story. Not just yet anyway.

"You're a pushy young man aren't you," he said, grinning again. "I am here because I'm a deserter." He paused, then inhaled and exhaled a cowardly sigh. "That's the truth of it. I abandoned my job, my life, my Union. I could no longer live with the inhumane tasks they ordered me to do." He turned around, exposing the white scar tissue of a healed wound at the base of his skull. "I intended on suicide, but I didn't have the courage to commit. I abandoned my post out east and I've been here ever since. Carter is my name. Professor Augustus Carter."

I was confused.

"East? You mean west, right?"

"No young man, I mean *east…*"

"But there's nothing east from here except the Pacific Ocean and The Wall. I've been out there. I helped build that damned thing."

"Well, young man, I can assure you there are facilities all over Soteria that wall-builders and middle-class citizens know nothing about. Places that exist on no maps; on no GPS satellite images or SLD's. Places that even advisors and certain Union officials know nothing of."

For the first time Eli lowered the weapon. "What places?" he asked, a youthful innocence in his voice.

"I have come from Terra Carcerem. It's a laboratory facility on what was once referred to as Norfolk Island, some seven hundred kilometres east of here. I fled one night, using a Union submarine. I scrambled the circuitry, so the vessel was untraceable and I ended up here. I anchored the submarine close to where you have left your boat. Underwater, of course."

"Why?"

"Why what?"

"Why did you flee? Why did you want to commit suicide?"

"Because, young man, the Union has been busy. The Union has been creating what will no doubt bring on the end of the world. Not just the demise of Soteria, but the *world*! The Union has created the ability to send our race into extinction and I was a monumental part of it. I could tolerate it no longer. The things we did I wouldn't even wish upon animals, let alone human beings. These are dark times we live in."

Augustus Carter looked ashamed, saddened.

"Anyway," he continued. "Enough of my dark past. Why are you two here? This is not the place for two young citizens."

Eli and I told Augustus of our great escape. I showed him my neck. Scabbing as it was, it was still a visibly fresh wound. I spoke of the Marriage Lottery and my sub-plaza blues. I spoke of my distaste towards the Union. I spoke about my life, the friends I left behind. We shared a similar burden. We were both deserters.

Eli embellished our story of escape a bit, going into great detail about crossing the Hawkesbury River, about swimming around the point, about our stowaway in the marina. I let Eli tell it his way. He told stories well.

Augustus Carter seemed impressed. He said he admired our courage. He said he envied me for having the courage to do what I did at such a young age. He regretted not doing what he did sooner.

After a lengthy introduction, Carter led us through the back of the foyer and down the stairwell into where he had been staying. He had converted the laundry into relatively comfortable living quarters. He had food supplies, water supplies, even Fosform vials. He offered us both water. Tainted brown, we drank it regardless. Carter assured us the tannins from the eucalypt leaves caused the odd colour but that it was safe to drink.

"Welcome to my home," he said openly.

"One thing I don't understand," Eli said, wiping water from his chin, "is why you have stayed in the Empire. Why haven't you tried to escape for good, like over the wall? That's what we're going to do."

"Are you now?" Scepticism soured his words.

"Yep. Tyson and I will get out of this place for good."

"And where will you go?"

"Wherever the TNS hasn't affected, I guess. There has to be somewhere clean and safe. Surely?"

"Well, Eli, you may be right. There might be places beyond the confines of Soteria that are safe and clean and liveable, but I don't believe these places will remain liveable for too much longer."

"What do you mean? Why not?"

"You see, boys, during my time on Terra Carcerem I helped create a hybrid soldier; a hybrid human, really. We created artificial organs and bone structures that we surgically implanted into human subjects. We created an immortal and obedient soldier. Bullets cannot kill them, their own self-doubt and guilt cannot influence their actions and most importantly, they are entirely immune to the syndrome. The Union intends on wiping China off the map and then destroying what's left of Europe. I'm sorry boys, but that freedom you search for outside of our walls will not exist for much longer."

I didn't know what to say. Eli stood in silent shock, his mouth open in disbelief, shaking his head from side to side like a sideshow alley carnival clown.

"We can't let it happen," I said. "We must stop them."

Carter laughed. "Stop them, you say. Stop the Humanist Union? Now I don't want to dampen your fighting spirit, young man, but how do you intend on stopping them? It's a force more powerful than any empire before it since the beginning of human civilisation. A force that made the conquest of the Romans look like child's play."

"Romans?"

Carter looked at Eli and smiled. "Forget about the Romans. They educated me prior to the Union written curriculum. Just know this, the Humanist Union is omnipotent. They are unbeatable."

Carter's words resonated.

They are unbeatable repeated in my mind. Doubt was back. For the first time in days doubt's unwelcome existence was haunting, duelling with the inspirational feeling of opportunity.

"What do you call these hybrid human machines? Do they have a name?"

"We named them Bestia – *the beast.*"

"Bestia?"

"Yes, Tyson, Bestia. The Beast is the unstoppable soldier. The Beast will conquer China. The Beast will conquer what remains of Russia."

I looked at Eli. His eyes lit up at the name. We had seen Bestia before.

"On the boat we stole," I said, excited. "It has parts, electronic parts and circuitry and stuff in boxes. The parts have Bestia written on them…"

"This does not surprise me. That boat was most probably on route to Terra Carcerem. They are making more soldiers."

"So in our boat we have the parts to make these… these beasts?"

"Yes, I suppose you do."

"Well, that's it then. Let's sink the Wife. Let's take her out to deeper water and sink the bitch with all the Bestia parts."

"Yeah," Eli said, bouncing on his toes, suddenly as excited as I was. "Let's sink the fucking thing."

"That will not stop Bestia, boys. It might slow down the process but they will just send more, probably by air. It will be like throwing a rock at an artillery tank. It might put a dent in it but nothing more."

"Well, it's a start. What have we got to lose by doing it? Nothing! No offence, Augustus, but I refuse to just sit around on a deserted island for the rest of my existence. I will find my freedom or die trying to stop this disgusting system that controls us. Don't you get it, Augustus, you're not free? You're in hiding. The Union still controls you. The Union still keeps you stuck on this island because of fear of capture. The Union runs this whole fucking Empire on fear. Without fear what have they got?"

"Umm, they have robot soldiers, Tyson," Eli interrupted.

"Shit, Eli, don't ruin my big speech! What I'm trying to say is what's the purpose of escaping the Empire if the Union will scratch at our heels with hybrid fucking cyborgs. We will forever be running. At some point we need to stop running."

"I admire your spirit Tyson," Carter said. "You remind me of myself when I was younger and more naïve. Unfortunately, I was on the wrong side of the war. Look, I agree with much of what you have said but let's just take one step at a time. Let us eat and sleep, and tomorrow we can sink your boat. How does that sound?"

My own emotions had exhausted me. I had worked myself into a semi-hysterical tizz with my motivational pep talk. Suddenly all I wanted to do was absolutely nothing. The beauty of hiding out in an abandoned hotel is that there wasn't much to do other than absolutely nothing. The Wife would have to wait. But tomorrow she would see her final hours.

FIFTY

MICHAEL BUTCHER SHARED AN AQUILONEM BUNKHOUSE WITH SEVEN other Union soldiers.

As Officer Hawke he had entertained the soldier's conversations, but he was in a constant state of caution. Only twenty-four hours into his rash plan and all the lies had drained Michael of his wits. The anxiety would kill him if the Union soldiers didn't do so first.

Michael got little sleep that night. His mind wandered. He thought of Bruce and Francis. He thought of the legacy he had left behind at T-Town. The tunnel would be well over a kilometre long now. He thought of Brie, her smooth skin, her beautiful smile, and her broken heart. He missed her.

Since that night in the jungle when Brie was taken, Michael felt a void he hadn't known before. He felt a longing and a need to be her knight in shining armour. Michael knew that his plan was stupid. He knew that it would lead to nothing more than violent incarceration or perhaps death, but a part of him that was okay with it. He was content knowing that he had tried.

Just as Michael drifted into a panic-plagued sleep, Devereaux, the young soldier beside him pulled him from slumber. "Hey

293

Hawke?" He had to say it twice. The first time Michael didn't even register that the soldier spoke to him.

I am now Officer Hawke.

"Yeah, what?" Michael said, rolling over to look at the young solider sitting up on his bunk.

"I'm thinking, right? I'm running your Gate Eight scenario through my head and I can't understand a few things."

"Yeah, okay," Michael said, sensing a discussion he would not enjoy. More lies. More anxiety.

"So were there guys stationed on the wall above the entrance?"

"Yeah, two soldiers up top. Standard protocol."

"So how do you suppose these outlaws even got to the door unnoticed, let alone get inside it?"

"I don't have an answer. I was relaxing on the sofa and before I knew it, these *traitors* started shooting. If I knew how they got in, I probably would have stopped them."

"Wow, man. I just can't believe it," Devereaux said, shaking his head in disbelief. "Did you take the hard drives? Did you watch the footage?"

Michael hesitated. *Footage?* "Nah, I didn't have time. I just got the Hell out of there."

"Hopefully, when Pasquale returns from Gate Eight with the footage it will all make a little more sense, hey? Man, that's just the craziest story."

"Pasquale? What's Pasquale doing?"

"Didn't you know? Pasquale is leading the recon. They left by chopper about four hours ago to collect the hard drives. They'll be back by sunlight. With over thirty cameras inside the facility it should give us a good sign of who the outlaws were and how they infiltrated the wall."

Michael couldn't respond. Fear silenced him.

Oh shit, I'm a dead man. How could I be so damn naïve? It's the most advanced and paranoid military establishment on the planet. Of course there are fucking cameras! There's probably a camera on me right now.

"Excuse me for a minute, Devereaux. I need to visit the amenities."

Michael left the dormitory and made his way down the quiet corridor to the amenities room. Someone occupied the shower stall at the far end of the room, but other than that the clinical, white-tiled room was empty. Steam bellowed from the far corner. A cloud of moisture hung beneath the ceiling, giving everything in the block a damp touch.

Looking in the mirror, Michael was pale, clammy. He needed to wipe the condensation from the glass to get a proper look at himself. Fear radiated from his panicking eyes. Nausea hit him. Leaning over the sink, he vomited.

"This was a stupid idea," he whispered to himself, wiping spew from the side of his mouth. "This is absolute madness."

Michael knew there was no way he could stay in Aquilonem. He knew that as soon as they saw the footage he would condemn himself to death if he stuck around. It was time to leave the North Dock. Without returning to the dormitory, Michael hurried down sweeping corridors as fast as he dared without drawing attention.

Keeping his head down, he hurried past the mess hall and passed the general meeting area. Aquilonem seemed to sleep. Compared to his arrival, the place was deserted. For Michael, this was not a bad thing.

Struggling to get his bearings, Michael followed corridor after corridor, weaving through the massive fortress, trying his hardest not to break out in a panicked dash for escape. Thankfully, he hadn't come across a single person.

After what felt like an eternity, Michael came to a steel door blocking his path. Stencilled into the steel above the door was the words AQUILONEM and GARAGE.

Bingo!

Sweat trickled down Michael's temples. He felt his pulse throbbing behind his eyes. Officer Hawke's stolen uniform clung to him. He was fatigued yet he knew he needed to create as much distance he could between himself and Aquilonem before the sun rose and Pasquale returned with the evidence.

Rest would have to wait.

Michael leaned toward the registration chip scanner. The device beeped twice, flashing a small green light of acceptance. The door hovered open, revealing a huge warehouse with vehicles parked bumper to bumper. There were artillery tanks, jeeps and hover-trucks. There were hover-bikes and hybrid RIBs. Michael saw vehicles he had never seen before. Amazing state-of-the-art technology with wheels twice the height of a man, wings spanning ten metres and inbuilt rows of taser cannons above the front windshields.

"I'm in way over my head," he whispered to himself.

Wiping the sweat from his forehead with the grey sleeve of his stolen Union uniform, Michael crawled between vehicles, searching for something that he would know how to operate. He found a jeep nearer to the front of the warehouse. Michael checked to see if it was unlocked. It had a gunmetal-grey paint-job and enormous puncture proof tyres. Michael needed to climb up a small steel ladder just to gain access to the driver's seat.

It's now or never and never isn't an option.

Sitting in the oversized seat Michel compressed the ignition lever and held his breath.

Nothing happened.

As defeat set in, the electric engine purred to life.

Yes!

Wasting no time, Michael drove the large vehicle through a small gap between two artillery tanks. He followed the yellow arrows marked on the stained concrete floor towards what appeared to be the main vehicle entrance. Searching the touchscreen dashboard before him, he found an orange button with the words GARAGE EXIT across the screen.

He pressed down on the orange button.

The huge roller-door came to life. It clunked and groaned loudly as it raised itself to the full height of the garage. Michael could see moonlight. He could see nearby trees bending in the tropical wind, bathed in the milky grey of the half moon.

Hope.

Relief.

Escape.

"Time to leave the lion's lair!"

As Michael sped up through the giant steel roller-door, the compound lit up like midday. Huge floodlights switched on, aimed directly at the jeep. As quickly as the lights turned on a sea of armed Union soldiers appeared from the darkness, stepping forward in unison, all aiming taser cannons at Michael's getaway vehicle.

"Oh *shit!*"

FIFTY-ONE

GEORGE HAD BEEN ALONE IN THE SMALL, AQUA-COLOURED ROOM FOR hours.

Eventually he heard distant murmurs from outside, bringing the endless silence to a close. Footsteps. An electronic doorway glided open from floor to ceiling, revealing a light blue hallway. Standing in the middle of the hallway was a short man, middle-aged and over-weight. He wore an outfit George had never seen before. It resembled a trench coat. It was a large aqua-blue jacket with a comically large collar and a tail flap hanging down to his ankles.

The man stepped forward, entering George's small cell with confidence.

"Good morning, George Clarkson. I see you are alive and well... Splendid."

"Where in God's name am I? What have you done to me?"

"You will have all the answers in due course, Mr Clarkson. The first thing we need to do is finish the process. We need to update your software so you can begin your training."

"*Software*? Training? What are you talking about? I want to know what you have done with me. Why am I still alive? Where the *fuck* am I?"

298

The scientist ignored George's questions. "Hmmm, they always have such a temper before the software update. Always." He spoke more to himself than to George.

He sighed.

"Okay, Mr Clarkson. My name is Doctor Wells. After today you will refer to me as 'sir'. Now, before I remove you from your restraints I need to access your influx portal, located beside your registration chip. Can you be a helpful young man and tilt your head to the left? It won't take long."

"I'm not doing a damn thing until I get some answers. This is insane! Why do I feel the way I do? How has my wound healed so quickly? Why is there no pain?"

He sighed again.

"Fine, then, you impatient swine. You would like to know what we have done? Fine! You are no longer George Clarkson. You are no longer a registered citizen of Soteria. You are now the property of the Humanist Union. The reason you feel no pain is that reinforced titanium now makes up sixty percent of your skeletal matter. We have cauterised all your nerve endings and we have strengthened your neuromuscular junctions with an adhesive. You can no longer feel pain. Your body no longer operates with a beating heart. Instead, you run off a nuclear battery we have installed. You no longer require oxygen to maintain homeostasis."

"Jesus! This can't be real?"

"I can assure you, it most certainly is. Your muscles engage through electronic impulses charged by your nuclear core. Therefore, you will no longer fatigue. You will no longer suffer from TNS. You are a product of Soteria. A soldier. As soon as we update your software your loyalty will be limitless. You will follow commands without question. You will understand only what you need to know. To all intents and purposes, George Clarkson is dead. You are now Nine-Thirteen. Bestia Nine-Thirteen. Now, like I requested, tilt your head to the left so I can access your influx portal."

"And what if I say no?"

"My dear man, often new units try in vain to slow the process. It serves no purpose. If you resist any further, I'll release your plutonium drain. If I release your waste drain without you being connected to the refuge station, you will suffer radiation poisoning, which even for a Bestia will be the worst experience you have ever endured. Not physical pain, which is now not possible for you, but psychological pain. You will take a month to die. Before you do, you will go deaf and blind as your remaining flesh rots. You will be stuck for weeks inside your own rotting mind. Insanity will claim you before God does. Eventually, toxic shock will take you from this place. Now, for the last time Nine-Thirteen, tilt your *fucking* head to the left!"

George stared at the Doctor. He didn't have a choice. He accepted defeat. Despite such defeat, he didn't feel too deflated. His emotions seemed dulled, almost non-existent.

"This is Tyson's fault," George whispered to himself as he tilted his head to the side, exposing the back of his neck to Doctor Wells.

Without wasting time, the doctor turned on a large digital apparatus built into the wall. It had a small screen next to a series of keys and colour-coded buttons. Extending from the apparatus was a cord, not dissimilar to a power cord with an auxiliary plug on the end.

Doctor Wells leaned over George's restrained body and lifted a flap of reinforced skin at the base of his neck. Inside the flap were two metallic sockets. One was the influx portal for software updates and new training programs. The other was the plutonium drain.

The Doctor plugged the long auxiliary cord into the influx portal and started the update.

George's vision dulled, then it disappeared entirely. For a moment George saw black emptiness before a white light ruptured inside his mind.

The process took about ninety seconds. In that time he had shaken within his restraints, almost like the convulsions of an epileptic seizure. When the apparatus on the wall beeped three times, the software upload ended and George's shaking ceased. It took him several seconds to wake from the exercise.

When George finally opened his eyes, his pupils were unusually dilated, almost unhuman. Jet-black emptiness consumed most of his iris. He noticed Doctor Wells standing beside him but said nothing. The Doctor was the first to speak.

"How did the update feel?"

"It felt wonderful, sir."

"Can you tell me your name? Can you tell me your purpose?"

"My name is Nine-Thirteen, sir. My purpose is to serve the Humanist Union. My purpose is to do whatever you require of me for the good and longevity of Soteria."

"Wonderful…"

Doctor Wells typed a short code into the mechanism controlling George's restraints. After a series of beeps, they retracted, loosening their grip.

George was free to move yet he remained motionless. The Doctor had not yet given him a command.

"Okay, Nine-Thirteen. Please remove the cord from your influx portal and stand up beside me. We will test your loyalty."

"My loyalty is without question, sir."

"We will see. Now, come this way."

Nine-Thirteen stood up and did as he was told. He felt perfect. Not an ache in his body. Not a fatigued muscle. Not a rumble of hunger. He followed the Doctor out of the small cell-like room and into the aqua-blue corridor. At the far end of the hall he noticed two soldiers standing still, holding weapons that Nine Thirteen had never seen before yet somehow knew how to operate. His recent upload made him a capable soldier, expertly skilled in the use of all Union weaponry.

Doctor Wells turned into another small cell. Nine-Thirteen followed him. Unlike Nine-Thirteen's previous cell, the room was empty except for the room's tenant.

It was a small girl. Maybe ten years old. Her face was dirty. She wore ragged clothes and had matted and filthy, long dark hair. She had been crying. Fear filled her cautious eyes. She flinched when Doctor Wells and Nine-Thirteen entered the cell.

"Okay, Nine-Thirteen. We caught this girl breaking the law. She is a villain. She is a treasonous thief and she must be killed. Execute this citizen for the good of Soteria!"

"Without question, sir."

The small girl screamed and ran to the corner of the small room.

It was purposeless. She had nowhere to run.

Nine-Thirteen stepped forward. As the child attempted a dash to the other corner of the cell, he took three lightening-fast paces and grabbed her by the hair. He picked her up with one hand without so much as a change in facial expression.

In a swift movement, exactly how the software had trained him to do, he placed one hand on her shoulder, locking his thumb into her clavicle. He grabbed her by the jaw with his free hand and as effortlessly as opening new appliance packaging, Nine Thirteen removed the girl's head.

Blood spewed from her neck as the life flowed out of her. Her spinal cord, still attached to her skull at the Atlas vertebrae, was torn from her back. The young girl's thick red blood covered Nine-Thirteen from head to toe. He dropped her head as the body hit the floor.

He looked at Doctor Wells, expressionless.

"What next, sir?"

FIFTY-TWO

I woke up in a sweaty panic.

It took me a moment to remember where I was. I wasn't in 3rd Sydney West. I wasn't waiting to die in the hydro-harbour. I wasn't even on the Wife any longer. I was on forgotten soil and I didn't need to answer to anyone. Eli was fast asleep in the corner of the dim room, his deep breathing in a vexing rhythm. The place in which Augustus Carter had slept the previous night was empty. For a moment I felt the powerful claws of uneasiness as I noticed our strange new companion was not with us.

Had he set a trap for us?

Was he contacting Union officials and informing them of our escape?

Shit. Was he a Union spy?

Paranoia's a strange thing. The more uncertain I felt and the more fear accumulated within me, the more paranoid I became. I tried to shake it off. Why would the old scientist be living here in derelict conditions if he were in fact a Union spy? It just made no sense.

I got up and tried to shake off my unjustified paranoia. I was thirsty.

The old resort had its own desalination plant out the back of the kitchen, so getting filtered water was a Godsend. I guzzled a full bottle of chlorinated water and I left Eli asleep in the corner.

It wasn't long before I found Augustus Carter up in the overgrown reception area of the hotel. He had a tool kit, a range of various power tools and a box of strange objects I didn't recognise. He didn't notice me approaching.

"What are you doing?" I asked sleepily. Carter jolted as he let out a little squeak of surprise.

"Sorry, Tyson. I guess I'm still not accustomed to other people's presence. Solitude is all I have known for some time… You said you wanted to sink that ship, that Wife of yours, didn't you?"

I nodded.

"I am creating a simple charge and detonator with some good old-fashioned plastic explosives and some Bestia circuitry. It shouldn't be hard. We will plant the charge inside the hull of the vessel and the detonator should have at least a 300-metre range on it. I don't want to create an explosion big enough to see from Brisbane, I just want to sink the thing."

I nodded then stood in silence as I watched Carter tinker with the circuitry. It looked like a coiled mess of coloured wires and copper endings. It was confusing yet fascinating to watch him in his element. He hummed to himself as he stripped a few green wires and used a small soldering torch to attach the exposed copper to another, thicker black wire. Then he inserted the black wire into a small alloy cylinder and closed the lid.

"That should do it."

"Great, when do we do it?"

"There's no time like the present, my boy. Now before we turn the boat into part of the reef below, is there anything we can salvage from your boat? Any food, weaponry, Fosform?"

"Yeah. Come to think of it, there's a shit-load of food and supplies. And weapons too. We can take the RIB out there, load it up and then sink that bitch. I'll go wake up Eli. I know he's exhausted, but he wouldn't miss this for the world."

Thirty minutes later, Eli, Carter and I were sitting in the inflatable life raft as it purred its way through the balustrade style gaps in the reef. Despite Eli's excitement, he was apprehensive about sitting in the RIB with the explosive device resting on the floor beside him. Carter had assured him it was impossible for the device to detonate without a digital code sequence yet every little ripple we bounced over caused Eli to flinch, as if he were bracing himself to be blown to smithereens.

We reached the Wife and secured the RIB along the starboard side. The plan was to place the explosives inside the hull underneath the waterline. This way the explosion wouldn't be visible from abroad. The outcome, Carter said, was to tear the steel hull, allowing the boat to take on water. I think when the idea was first discussed, Eli and I pictured some enormous mushroom cloud of fire and destruction. I was a little deflated when I found out I would see little more than our boat swaying and shuddering, and then slowly sinking from view. Fire and destruction or not, it was still a win for us. It was a middle finger in the face of the Humanist Union.

Once on board, we gathered fresh weapons, straight out of the box. Our supply totalled three taser cannons, two badass combat knives, a micro-taser and three Union-issue full-face oxygen conditioners. These were unavailable to most registered citizens. Attached to eight-kilogram oxygen bottles, these full-face conditioners limited any exposure for Union soldiers patrolling the areas of high toxicity. They might come in handy later.

Eli emptied the cupboards in the mess and collected a substantial supply of tinned food, random tools, all the Fosform Five and a curvaceous blonde sex robot clad in flattering lingerie. Struggling back to the RIB with a balancing act of tins, he placed the canned food down inside the small boat along with the weapons, the dosage and the cybernetic girl. The gunwale of the small life raft was twenty centimetres closer to the surface of the water than it had been on the journey out there. Once the three of us climbed aboard, with the added weight of the supplies, I was hesitant the small vessel would get us back to shore. The thought of swimming back brought back unsettling memories from the previous week, getting pummelled by the waves against the high sandstone cliffs at Terrigal.

Carter returned possessing a grin of youthfulness. I could tell it was the most excitement he had had in some time. He climbed into the RIB beside Eli and me.

"Well, lads. That should do it. Once we're back within the safety of the reef, I'll enter the sequence of detonation and Bob's your uncle!"

"Bob's my uncle?" Eli asked, confused.

"Never mind! Once we're far enough away from the boat, to use Tyson's appropriate wording, we will *sink the bitch*!"

I steered the inflatable with caution, dodging the heads of coral poking out of the turquoise water. Once we reached a safe distance from the large rusted freight ship, I turned off the engine and allowed the RIB to float between the rocky inlets in the reef, moving rhythmically as the tide swirled around the reef.

"Can I do it," I asked Carter.

"Can you ever. Here," he said, passing me the detonating device. "The code is one-eight-one-four."

I didn't hesitate. I didn't pause for a moment of reflection. Instead, I typed the four digits into the small hand-held device and I waited.

The three of us sat motionless. I don't even think I breathed.

Suddenly there was a loud roar as the glass blew out from the porthole windows of the helm. The Wife shuddered as fragments of glass came raining down into the still water around the boat. The shock and rocking of the explosion caused a wave to form, close to two metres high. We watched in silence as the wave came rolling towards us. It lost its power and size as it rolled across the shallow reef. By the time it hit us it was a broken mound of white water.

There were no flames. There was no giant fireball. It had gone to plan just as Carter had said it would. After the wave had dissipated, the Wife groaned in disappointment and she began taking on water. We watched as the gunwale inched closer to the surface of the water. It wasn't long before the water started flooding the deck and in a matter of minutes, the Wife, my faithful chariot of escape, had gone from view.

"Well, that was exciting, wasn't it?" Carter had such enthusiasm in his words.

Eli and I didn't respond. We spent a moment staring into the bubbling wash of water. I thought this act of defiance would make me feel a sense of accomplishment. It didn't. It just made me loathe the Union all the more. It only fuelled the fire, when I guess it was intended to fight it.

"It's not over," I mumbled to myself as much as to Eli and Augustus Carter.

"What's not?"

"This, Eli, *this*! Don't you get it? Carter was right. Sinking that damn boat will do nothing to the Union. It won't change anything. They will just send more Bestia parts, by air next time. We need to do more. We need to fuck their shit up!"

"One step at a time, Tyson," Carter added as the voice of reason.

"You're right, Carter. That *was* the first step. Now it's time for the second step."

"And what do you propose the second step will be?"

"We're going to Terra Carcerem! We're going to flatten that place. And Carter, you're going to help us…"

FIFTY-THREE

MICHAEL BUTCHER WOKE TO A HIGH-PITCHED NOISE AND A throbbing headache.

Disorientated, the first thing he noticed was that he was naked and that they had bound his hands and feet. It was pitch black. He let out a defiant roar that echoed against the walls. It was to no avail. His defiance was met with stone cold silence.

Michael replayed his failed escape attempt over and over in his mind. He had made it out of the garage and the soldiers surrounded him right away. Somehow, they had known he was there. Under the watchful eye of trained killers, Michael had stepped out of the jeep with his hands raised. Saviour confronted him. They exchanged words but Michael's manic heart pumped with such ferocity he struggled to remember what they said. He thought they would execute him there and then. He was wrong. Saviour mentioned something about Terra Carcerem and soldiers, something about human donations.

After that conversation, a soldier stepped forward and every-thing went black. Michael had no idea how long he had been unconscious. He was cold and thirsty. His bare skin on the rusty steel made for an uncomfortable journey.

Not long after regaining consciousness, Michael heard the high-pitched noise change for a moment, becoming more of a brief echo before going back to the original whine. He concluded that he must be on a train heading somewhere.

In the hours of uncomfortable solitude that followed, they left him alone with his own sense of failure, frustration and hindsight. Looking back at it now, his plan seemed unrealistic from the beginning. A large part of him wished he had stayed with Bruce and returned to T-Town to claim their victory. His impulsive decision to chase Brie across the Empire was childish. Like Bruce had told him, it was a suicide mission. He had just been far too stubborn to listen.

Then he thought about Brie.

He wondered where she was. He wondered what sort of torture she had endured. He wondered if she were even alive. He thought about her smooth olive skin. He thought about her intense and captivating eyes. He thought about their lovemaking in the communal room of T-Town and the way she had kissed him. She had kissed him like the world was ending. She had kissed him like nothing else in the Empire mattered. For the first time since their victorious overthrow of the barracks at the wall, Michael felt a deep sense of regret.

Drifting in and out of pain-fuelled sleep, Michael woke as he was soiling himself. Unable to move, he continued until he had emptied his bladder on the rusty steel. He tried rolling over several times to escape the encroaching puddle of his own urine but he found the bindings restricted his rolling, holding his ankles firm. Defeated, he lay in his own piss and for the first time since his capture he began to cry.

He woke again as the consistent, high-pitch hum came to a stop. Despite how smooth the train ride felt, he noticed that the forward momentum had also ceased. He froze, listening in the darkness, and waited to hear movement outside of his pitch-black chamber. With his heart rate increasing and his naked body encrusted with dry sweat and piss, an electric roller-door opened with a *beep* as real sunlight came flooding in. Michael closed his eyes. After total darkness for so long, the light was intolerable. One eye at a time, he opened them to a narrow slit to see what was occurring.

"Get up," he heard someone say, still adjusting to the brightness. Michael didn't respond. "I said get up, traitor!"

"Well, that will be a little difficult as they bound my ankles, smart guy."

The soldier stepped forward and stomped on Michael's stomach with his Union-issue combat boot. It wasn't hard enough to break ribs but hard enough to prove a point. Michael was powerless.

"Who's the smart guy now, traitor? You have five seconds to get up or I'll leave you to rot on the surface…"

Michael used his bound hands to lever himself up but found he couldn't get the purchase he needed to stand. He struggled to his knees, doing his best to be compliant. That much was obvious. Without a word, another soldier stepped forward while the first aimed a taser cannon at Michael's face. He grabbed the bindings around Michael's wrists.

They dragged Michael Butcher forward by the steel bindings. The soldier dragging him seemed to have inhuman strength. With one hand he dragged all of Michael's eighty kilograms of dead weight through the sliding door of the train cell and onto an empty sterile platform. Noting his surroundings, Michael looked left and right. He was in another strange Union facility. The weather was different to Aquilonem. Colder. The air had a different smell. He looked backwards. It became immediately apparent that he hadn't been on a train at all. He had been captive in some kind of aircraft.

The soldier that hauled Michael from the craft stood still, as if waiting for instruction. Michael watched a short, plump man approach. He wore a strange coat that Michael had never seen. Aqua-blue with a high collar and a bird-like tail flap almost dragging on the concrete walkway. The man looked down at Michael with a callous grin. "Welcome to Terra Carcerem. The final stop for your journey."

"*Terra*— what?"

"Shut your mouth, swine. Our associates up north have informed me of your treasonous actions. How utterly foolish of you.

Not only did you murder Union soldiers, you then drove yourself to Aquilonem. Could you be any more pathetic? You inferior humans are so stupid! Luckily once we're done with you, we will not require you to think."

"Where have you brought me?"

"I said *shut up*! You will be told nothing, you murderous, treasonous, insidious insult to the Empire."

The plump man looked at the soldier waiting beside Michael. "Nine-Thirteen, grab this swine and take him into the Induction Cell."

"Right away, sir. Without question."

The soldier stepped forward with a small octagon shaped key and inserted it into a lock in the restraints beside Michael's left ankle. The device beeped twice and the carbon-fibre bar connecting both ankles retracted telescopically. Michael Butcher could stretch his legs for the first time in days.

"Stand up, peasant."

Michael slowly rose to his feet. He felt unsteady and light-headed. Beside him on the dock, a long concrete walkway stretched up towards thick grey double doors. He saw the words LOYALTY-UNION-SAFETY-SALVATION etched into the archway above the doors and cursed the Union under his breath. The outline of the all-watchful red eagle covered the double-doors. About three metres wide, the concrete walkway appeared to be close to fifty metres long. Huge taser cannons, bigger than a human body, hung mounted on steel turrets outside the entrance.

The short, plump Union advisor in his strange coat began walking towards the steel doors. Nine-Thirteen grabbed Michael with one hand and lifted him up onto his shoulder. Without so much as an increase in breathing or a laboured stride, the soldier carried Michael towards the thick grey double doors.

Impossible, Michael thought. *This man is smaller than me.*

Once inside, Nine-Thirteen carried Michael down a bright concrete corridor into a white-tiled room. Large, square lights flooded the room with artificial sunlight. Dried blood, caked brown, covered the floor tiles. A single yellow tile lay in the centre of the room amongst the pattern of white. Nine-Thirteen dropped Michael on the tiles and left without a word. Once Michael was alone in the room, a steel door slid shut with a beep.

"Welcome to Terra Carcerem," an automated female voice spoke from a speaker in the ceiling. "You are no longer a member of the Empire. You are now the property of the Humanist Union. Stand up straight on the yellow tile and do not move. Failure to comply with my commands will result in surface exposure."

Michael did as he was told.

Quicker than a blinking eye, three holes opened in the ceiling. From two holes mechanical steel arms descended like thick metal snakes, grabbing Michael around the shoulders. From the third hole a mechanical arm descended with a Fosform Five injection gun built into the tip. The colour of the fluid in the cylinder was not the typical blue synonymous with Fosform Five. Instead, it was a yellow, almost orange colour. The mechanical arm slammed the injector gun into the side of Michael's neck. He heard the cylinder compress and felt the cool liquid enter his bloodstream. The injector gun retracted.

"What the *hell* was that?" Michael yelled to the empty room.

Lights flashed and buzzers beeped. The tiles in front of Michael on the floor opened with a slight mechanical hum, exposing a deep cavern the size of the yellow tile where he stood.

"Prepare for induction," said the automated voice. "In three, two, one…"

The mechanical, snake-like arms lifted Michael forward and dropped him down into the blackness of the hole. At first, he was free falling. The light above him shrunk to nothing more than a pinprick speck of light. His back came into contact with wet, slimy steel then he slid down some kind of dark tunnel. As he slid through the darkness, hot, foul tasting water sprayed him from high-pressure hoses within the tube. The taste reminded him of the antiseptic liquid he had used in childhood to treat cuts and grazes.

As fast as the journey through the pitch-black tunnel had been, it was over. The tunnel ejected Michael from its mouth into a pool of warm, viscous liquid.

He came up spluttering, gasping for air. Wiping the warm liquid from his face, he stood and looked around. Three Union soldiers stood at the edge of the pool with taser cannons resting on their shoulders. The short, pudgy guy from outside on the dock was standing amongst the soldiers.

"I am Doctor Wells," he said, staring down into the pool. "Do you have a name?"

Michael gagged as the potent liquid dripped from his chin. "My name is… my name is Michael."

"Well, *Michael*. That is no longer your name. For all intents and purposes, you are now Nine-Twenty-One. Now get out of the pool and follow me."

FIFTY-FOUR

Brie woke, groggy and confused.

It surprised her to be alive. She had been so sure that whatever they had injected into her neck had been to kill her. She was wrong. It was not her time just yet. They would force her to endure the Union's retribution a little longer.

Brie looked around.

She was in another foreign place, stranger, but no less distressing than G-Block. Once again she wore no clothes. She touched her head. During unconsciousness, they had shaved her hair to short stubble. Despite being in much more sanitary conditions, Brie was in a cell no bigger than the one she had grown to know so well in the Northern Sector. The walls, if they could be called walls, were made of thick glass. The room itself was impeccably sterile. No dried blood. No stains on the ceiling. Just shiny, blue tiles on the floor and four glass walls. Beside her cell, a row of other cells the same shape and size as hers continued in both directions as far as she could see. Some cells housed captives similar to her, naked, shaven and bruised. Other cells remained empty. Neat, tidy, and beds made, awaiting future tenants.

A wall-mounted water fountain hung from the corner of her small cell, giving her constant access to drinkable water. She noted that all the other cells had the same fountains. Beside the water fountain was a steel toilet bowl.

Brie stood and walked to the glass between her cell and her neighbouring one. She placed her palm on the cold glass. She looked inside the neighbouring cell. A young woman, no older than eighteen, slept naked on a stretcher bed. A carbon-fibre cast covered her left arm and her left eye was purple and swollen. Brie knocked on the glass to get the young woman's attention.

"*Brie van Bueren,*" said an automated female voice from somewhere in the cell. "Step away from the wall. Failure to comply will result in mild electrocution. We do not permit communication between prisoners."

The young woman woke. She opened her swollen eyes and saw Brie standing there, two metres from her. She offered a faint, defeated smile before rolling over and turning away.

Hours passed.

Hunger rumbled in Brie's empty stomach. At the far end of the corridor two large steel doors opened and in came an entourage of soldiers and Union staff. The soldiers wore grey fatigues typical of surface teams. The Union staff wore aqua-blue suits, the colour of Fosform Five – the same colour as the tiles in her room. The group walked two abreast towards Brie's cell but stopped short beside the neighbouring cell, housing the young woman. Brie watched in frightened awe. One of the Union staff, a tall woman with long blonde hair, pulled a device from the pocket of her blue jacket and typed in something. The seemingly solid glass wall separated, opening outwards on invisible hinges.

The soldiers entered the cell first. Followed by two of the blue-suits, the blonde woman included. Two soldiers lifted the young woman from her stretcher bed and forced her to stand. They exchanged words. Because of the thickness of the glass, Brie could only make out several words.

Time... Operate... Compliant... Bestia...

The young woman tried to wriggle free from the strong grasp of the soldiers. It was to no avail. They held her firm. She yelled in defiance. She pleaded for mercy. She shed tears from her swollen eyes.

Within thirty seconds of entering the young woman's cell, they left, dragging the naked girl screaming down the corridor. The cell wall closed and the entourage left. Silence enveloped the cellblock. Other naked captives had watched the young woman get dragged from her cell. They all sported the same frightened stare of uncertainty. They knew it was only a matter of time until the blue-suited doctors would drag them all screaming from their cells.

Despite the anxiety clawing at her bare skin, Brie drifted off to sleep, exhaustion's powerful grip luring her into dreamless darkness. She woke just as startled as before, but this time less groggy, less confused. She heard the hum of the double doors open at the end of the corridor. The same entourage of soldiers walked in. This time the blue suits were absent. Two of the soldiers dragged a limp and lifeless man towards the empty cell beside hers. From her stretcher bed she watched the soldiers approach. The glass wall separated and the soldiers dragged the man inside the cell and dumped him on the bed. He lay there unconscious.

Too shocked to breathe, Brie's heart rate went into overdrive. Her empty stomach dropped as dizziness consumed her.

The soldiers turned and left the cell. The glass wall closed behind them.

A range of emotions cascaded through Brie's veins.

Hope.

Happiness.

Longing.

Fear.

Utter disbelief.

Tears flowed uncontrollably from Brie's tired eyes. She blinked away the tears. She blinked away her disbelief. She leapt up and ran to the glass barrier between the cells.

"Brie van Bueren," said the automated voice. "Step away from the wall. Failure to comply will result in mild electrocution. We do not permit communication between prisoners."

Brie yelled through the glass, ignoring the robotic woman's warning. She yelled again with no response. It seemed almost impossible to comprehend. Brie stared through the glass at Michael Butcher. *Her* Michael Butcher.

FIFTY-FIVE

EVAN SAT IN HIS USUAL PERCH IN T-TREE.

The residents of T-Town had fallen back into their normal routine. Gabbie had been right. Bruce Chadwick was finally up and about and almost back to his normal self. He would never quite be the same though. With Francis and Michael gone, there was a part of Bruce that had gone with them.

Since breaking free from his strange, post-traumatic mourning, Bruce had ordered double the digging as usual, intending to increase pace and productivity. With Evan helping, Bruce completed a stocktake of Fosform Five. From that, they made the assessment that even with the ration supplies he had brought back with him from Gate Eight, the T-Towners had maybe three months' worth of the anti-corrosive serum, maybe four. They no longer had the manpower or the emotional energy to attempt any more Fosform missions.

Estimated measurements of the length of the tunnel led Bruce to believe that they were within fifty metres of the wall. If they continued with the backbreaking double shifts, they could angle the tunnel up towards the surface in a little over a month. If everything went like clockwork and the workers could continue with the pace, then they would be free from Soteria before the end of Envy, the sixth month of the year.

Evan sat perched in the tree and just watched the jungle. His countless hours of keeping guard enabled him to hear things that others couldn't. The pitch of the birdsong could tell him what hour of the day it was. He could also tell the minute something was amiss by the unusual silence. Evan stood up and looked out west as he took it in.

Something was wrong.

It wasn't long before he smelt it. The wind was barely blowing, so it was difficult to tell from which direction it came but it was unmistakable. It was the thick and claustrophobic smell of smoke. Potent and harsh on the nostrils, the smell intensified with each passing minute.

Evan leaped down from his perch in T-Tree and entered the tunnel bunker. It wasn't long until he located Bruce.

"Hey Bruce, I think you need to come up top. You need to see this."

By the tone in Evan's voice Bruce knew something was amiss. He didn't need to be told twice.

"Should I grab a cannon?"

"No, I don't think that will help us much…"

Evan and Bruce climbed up and out of the main entrance underneath T-Tree. As soon as they left the safety of the tunnel it became apparent. There was a fire nearby.

"Shit," said Bruce. "Where do you think it's coming from?"

"It's impossible to say at the moment. I think we should scout around and locate it. See if it will be a threat."

"No way. With jungle this thick, if the wind picks up you'll be burnt alive. Fingers crossed it doesn't come anywhere near us…"

"Is there anybody outside of the bunker?"

"*Shit!* There is! Remy and Aidan are out collecting fruit. I hope they're not far."

———

REMY WAS UPWIND OF THE RAGING INFERNO. SHE WAS UNAWARE THAT between her and the safety of T-Town was a ferocious blaze consuming every bit of vegetation in its path. She heard the blaze raging before she could smell it. At first it sounded like white noise, a static hum. Then she heard the distinct crackling of wood expanding as it burnt.

"Do you hear that?" Remy asked Aidan as he walked ahead of her with a woollen sack full of root vegetables.

"Hear what?"

"I'm not sure. It sounds like fire."

"Fire…? Man, that's not good. It hasn't rained in over a week either. Let me have a look."

Aidan dropped the bag of vegetables and climbed a nearby tree to get to a higher vantage point. The tree was taller than the surrounding canopy so with each metre he gained, the view of the great green expanse opened up before him. He didn't need to get to the top of the sturdy tree to see it. As the canopy opened up, he saw through gaps in the neighbouring tree's branches.

"Oh, shit!"

Thick, black smoke billowed and churned in unpredictable torrents. It rose high into the cloudless sky, swamping the horizon. Aidan looked east, toward T-Town. From his vantage point he could see flames licking the smoky sky. He looked west. Smoke wafted from the thick canopy of trees.

"We need to get out of here! Right now! There's more than one fire!"

Aidan dropped from the tree, swinging from branch to branch and together with Remy started running south through the thick undergrowth. The going was slow. Several times they backtracked to get around thick, impassable vegetation. They ran into small impassable ravines in the jungle terrain. Visibility was decreasing, the air around them filling with thick, dark smoke.

It became difficult to breathe. Remy pushed through laboured breaths, sweating as she ran as fast as the terrain would allow. No matter how much they ran, the fire and smoke seemed to linger behind them, hot on their heels. Looking back, Remy saw the orange flicker of flames jump from tree to tree. The fire was building in intensity. Trying to outrun a fire in the jungle was madness.

Racing through the thick foliage that littered the jungle floor, Aidan slipped on a fallen, moss covered tree branch. He roared in pain as he tumbled through the moist leaf litter.

"Shit, Remy! I've just done my ankle." Fear filled his words.

Despair.

"Here, let me help you." Remy helped lift Aidan to his feet. "We have to keep going. That fire is right behind us. Can you put any weight on your leg?"

Aidan tried taking a step and winced in pain. He limped, lifting his maimed leg and resting his weight on the other. "You gotta go, Remy. You gotta warn the others. You all need to get underground right now and seal up T-Town. Just leave me…"

"I'm not leaving you, don't be stupid! We are *not* going to die today!"

Remy ripped a branch clean off a nearby tree and stripped it of the smaller branches, creating a smooth crutch about the width of her forearm. She hung it in the air alongside Aidan for measure-ment, then snapped off another foot, making it as close to the height of his armpit as time would allow. She then tore her shirt off, exposing her bare breasts. There was no time for modesty with a raging fire surrounding them.

Remy rolled her shirt into a crude ball. "Here, put this in your armpit and shove the stick up into it."

Aidan did as he was told. The stick wedged Remy's rolled-up shirt in place to make the makeshift crutch more comfortable.

"Now, get the hell up and let's go!"

Aidan got to his feet and starting hobbling behind Remy, trying to keep pace as best as possible. The fire was within eyesight but it didn't appear to be coming towards them. The wind was taking it further east. They continued south, Aidan hobbling behind Remy with every ounce of his will to live. As exhaustion showed itself, they appeared to be putting distance between themselves and the flicker of the flames. They could slow their pace. The fire was no longer flocking at their heels.

Relief.

Hope.

Then they heard it.

Helicopters were a strange sight this far north in the Empire. In all her time at T-Town, Remy had never seen one. Yet there it was, hovering above them, dark and threatening. Before they could react, before they could duck for cover or hide in the thick vegetation, a large canister twice the size of a man fell from the bottom of the Union helicopter. It dropped through the canopy and landed with a thud only twenty metres from where Remy and Aidan stood, watching in frozen terror. The canister beeped three times then exploded in a fierce fireball, consuming everything in a fifty-metre radius. Remy and Aidan didn't have time to blink. No sooner had they heard the three rhythmic beeps than the flame swallowed them, engulfing them in a deathly inferno.

Not even their skeletons remained.

———

BRUCE HAD LEFT EVAN ALONE AT THE ENTRANCE TO T-TOWN. HE had gone back inside the bunker to prepare the others for a lock-down. Evan waited from Remy and Aidan to return. For once he didn't climb the tree to his usual perch. Instead, he paced back and forth, biting his nails with nervousness. The jungle became thick with dirty grey smoke. The birdsong was non-existent, drowned out by the churning and crackling of the approaching fire.

Evan knew they didn't have long.

He could make out hypnotic flames in the distance, flaring up as they danced between trees. He could see the ferocity of the fire swallowing the jungle in its path.

"I'm sorry, guys. I really hope you're somewhere safe," he whispered to himself as he turned and made his way to the trapdoor entrance. "You're on your own…"

As he did so, without so much as the hum of its blades, a helicopter flew overhead, only metres from the canopy of T-Tree. Evan's heart skipped a beat as he watched something fall from the Union aircraft's undercarriage.

Evan stood motionless and watched the canister fall in slow motion. Only two steps from the trapdoor entrance, he knew he didn't have time. He didn't breathe. He didn't scream. As the bomb made impact with the ground beside the thick buttress roots it exploded into a vicious fireball, consuming Evan's faithful T-Tree and everything around it.

Not even his skeleton remained.

FIFTY-SIX

AUGUSTUS CARTER STOOD ALONE ON THE BEACH, STARING OUT across the glassy water.

Eli and I met him on the northern end of the beach after collecting supplies we needed from Carter's basement dwelling. He'd been preparing the RIB to get us safely to our underwater chariot.

We had only been on Lord Howe Island for two days and already it was time to say goodbye. I was enthusiastic. I was excited about the next step of the journey. I think Eli was too. I wasn't as sure about Carter, though. He just stood and stared out into the glassy water. His expression was difficult to read. I think it was fear. I think he was weighing up the practicality of heading east into the Lion's den. Terra Carcerem – the land of imprisonment. It didn't sound like the place one went willingly towards.

Eli broke the silence.

"Are you all right, Gus?"

Augustus Carter looked at Eli with a smirk. "No one has called me Gus since my mother died."

"Well, you look like a Gus. And let's be honest, Augustus is well, you know, so old…"

Carter laughed for the first time since we had met him.

"Gus is fine with me, young man. It's much more pleasant than *Doctor*. And yes, I'm fine. I've just been on this island for so damn long that I'm apprehensive to leave."

"Man… That's exactly what they want," I interjected. "They want fear stopping us from taking action. I had the same feeling in 3rd Sydney West. I was afraid to leave and now, standing here with the sand between my toes, going back to the sub-plaza is the last thing in the world I would do."

"A part of me admires your youthful ignorance, Tyson. Going to Terra Carcerem is not the same as fleeing your sub-plaza. It is a fortified Union compound. I have a few tricks up my sleeve, but not enough to take on the entire Empire. How do you intend on getting out alive?"

"That's something we can work out on the way. But really, Carter, what have you got to lose?"

There was a pause of silent reflection. Then Carter's body language changed. It was clear he accepted the fact we were about to leave his island.

"I suppose you're right. We've got very little to lose. Let us be off, then. Let the ignorance of youth guide us."

We took the RIB through the shallows and around the headland at the northern end of the island. The colour of the water changed from a Fosform turquoise to a deep dark blue. I got a final fleeting image of the beach before we turned east around the headland and Carter's hotel hideaway disappeared from view. I wondered if we would ever be back. Returning would mean defeat. Returning would mean failure. I was confident that was the last we would ever see of Lord Howe Island.

Close to a hundred metres from where the rocky outcrops met the waves we stopped and turned off the outboard engine.

"The submarine is directly below us now," Carter said with a newfound enthusiasm.

"How do we get in there, Gus?" Eli asked.

"I will bring it to the surface via remote piloting."

"Cool…"

Carter opened the bag that still hung from his shoulder. He produced a small tablet device not dissimilar to a registration chip reader and began typing into the touchscreen. At first nothing happened. Then the water beside our little boat started whirling and bubbling. The RIB swayed from side to side. I had to hold the gunwale to stop myself from rocking.

The whirling water turned into a churning mass of violent white water. From the white water a steel object rose. It glistened in the sunlight, dark, metallic and grey. Only about the size of my Block 7 internal transporter tunnel, it underwhelmed me as it breached the surface. It would be a cramped voyage for three people for days at sea.

"Is that *it*?" Eli asked in surprise, clearly as disappointed as me.

Carter laughed. "Patience my boy. I need to remove water from the ballast."

He busied his fingers typing on the small device, giving the remote piloting a few more commands. The vessel rose higher. The small portion that had already breached the surface was nothing more than a turret at the top of the vessel. The bubbling water churned with ferocious force. Out of the deep blue bubbling wash came the rest of the craft. Close to fifty metres long it looked about the length of a turf-ball field. Huge torpedo arms clung to the sides of the streamlined, almost shark-like body. It resembled some mythical underwater creature. It was an intimidating sight. As it broke the surface, I saw those four words etched into the steel along the waterline.

Loyalty.

Union.

Safety.

Salvation.

"Holy shit! This thing is massive."

"Yeah," said Eli with eyes wide. "How do we get in?"

"One thing you will need to learn, young Eli, is patience. You will find out how to get in when it is time to find out how to get in."

Eli mumbled something under his breath and waited.

"First, I need to re-oxygenate the chamber and run the air filtration system. The air that's currently stagnating in this sub is over twelve months old. It would be void of any breathable oxygen and is most probably ripe with Turners Necrosis. The filter shouldn't take more than a few minutes."

After a short wait the device in Carter's hand flashed green as the submarine's side opened with the sound of compressed air being released. It revealed an entrance no bigger than my sub-plaza apartment front door. Below the entrance a small, steel, balcony-like platform extended from the body of the submarine. On the small platform were several rigging points. I steered the RIB over towards the entrance seal and with Eli's help we secured our small inflatable to the entry dock of the sub.

"Okay boys, all aboard," said Carter.

"What are we gonna do with the RIB?"

"We will take it with us. It may be useful in getting us successfully onto Terra Carcerem. We won't be able to get close to the shoreline in the sub. It cannot go in water shallower than eight metres. There's a large loading dock at the back between the two propellers. We can only open it from the inside. Eli, come with me and we will stow all our equipment. Tyson, you take the RIB around the back and wait."

"Roger that, Captain…"

Carter and Eli stepped from the RIB onto the solid steel platform. It was a balancing act for Carter, who swayed with unease as he reached out for the handrail. I handed up our supplies and they disappeared into the darkness of the submarine. Idling, I took the small inflatable boat alongside the huge, intimidating piece of Union technology. I wondered how many of these war machines were scouting the exact waters in which we had been steering the Wife in the days before. Soteria's waters were probably crawling with them.

At the back of the giant Kraken-looking vessel it didn't take long until a seal released compressed air and the loading dock opened. A ramp hit the surface of the water and sent a small wave rolling towards me. As it hit the RIB, the wave cascaded over the side of the small inflatable boat and covered me from the waist down. I looked up to the sound of Eli laughing. He stood at the top of the loading ramp holding a device attached to the wall of the dock via a thick cable. His grin was so big it almost swallowed his face.

"Man, this thing is *so* cool. It's unlike anything I have ever seen. Gus is in the cockpit turning everything on. He said to attach the winch at the top of the ramp to the front of the boat and use this button to winch the boat inside."

He pointed to the green button on the device.

"Sounds easy enough. Here, pass me the winch cable."

Six minutes later the RIB was inside the loading dock and strapped down firm with ratchet straps. Eli used the device in his hand to close the loading dock. The ramp retracted and the seal re-compressed.

"Loading dock seal is secure," said an automated female voice. "You are now safe from surface conditions."

"Okay," I said as Eli hung the device back on the wall in its mount. "Let's go have a look around."

FIFTY-SEVEN

MICHAEL WOKE WITH A SUDDEN JOLT OF DISORIENTATION.

His head thumped. A strong ringing, like a distant alarm, wailed inside his ears. He had been in so many places during his short time in captivity that he no longer remembered where he was. He remembered Aquilonem. He remembered the flight and the sterile room. He remembered the pool of warm, viscous liquid. He remembered defeat.

With heavy eyes he observed his surroundings. He was yet again somewhere different and still; he wore no clothes. Someone had shaved his head, armpits and pubic hair. The room was small but clean. Despite waking up on the cold tiled floor there, a neat enough bed was made in the corner and beside that, a metal toilet bowl. The walls were clear, made of thick glass and, to the untrained eye, there didn't appear to be any doors in or out of the glass cube.

Michael stood up and stretched. He looked into the cell beside his. It was empty, impeccably clean. He could see an endless corridor of glass cubes. Further down the corridor, looking through a series of glass walls, Michael noticed occupied cells. People asleep on their beds, naked, hairless and helpless. He wondered what their stories were. He wondered what crimes they had committed that landed them in such an unusual place. He spun on the spot and looked the other way, to the neighbouring cell beside his.

Confusion.

Michael's heart skipped a beat. At first there was a vague recognition.

Familiarity hit him like a Union soldier's baton. It made him feel dizzy. Michael stared into the small cell beside his. She looked different, almost unrecognisable, but Michael knew it was her. Reacting to his emotions, acting on subconscious instinct, Michael dashed across the aqua-blue tiles and slammed into the glass between cells.

"*Nine-Twenty-One,*" a voice called from invisible speakers within the ceiling. "*Step away from the wall. Failure to comply will result in non-lethal electrocution. We do not permit communication between prisoners.*"

Michael ignored the automated warning. His hands were clammy with sweat. His eyes welled with tears. Less than four metres away Brie Kallas sat on the edge of her institutionally clean bed and smiled at Michael. She looked like a different person than when he had last seen her that night in the jungle. She looked like she had been through hell. She was naked. Purple swelling ballooned around her left eye. They had shaved her head. They had shaved her pubic hair. Her front teeth were missing and her jaw ballooned out on the left side of her face. But it *was* Brie. It was *his* Brie. Michael cried. Brie, too, shed tears. They were tears of defeat, tears of helplessness. But through her bruised and swollen eyes, Michael sensed tears of joy. Through the pain he sensed her compassionate warmth. He felt the butterflies of life flap within his broken spirit. He had followed his instinct; he had ignored logic. Love had brought him back to Brie Kallas.

"I don't believe it," Michael yelled through the glass. "This cannot be real?"

"*Nine-Twenty-One, step away from the wall. We will not remind you again.*"

"How did you get here? Brie, oh my fucking God, I can't believe it's you..."

Brie stood. She tried to get words out but a torrent of tears hindered her speech. She went from crying tears of joy to hysteric wailing in a matter of seconds. She sucked in air between cries. Disbelief crippled her, shattering the strength she had held onto for weeks. She had been so strong for so long. She had held it together through her solitary confinement in the Northern Sector, through the rape and the abuse, through G-Block and her encounters with Master Stephen Haynes. But now as she looked into the calming blue eyes of Michael Butcher, her defences shattered. She no longer needed the strength. She knew, looking into the cell beside her, that she was no longer alone.

Brie dropped to her knees and forced a toothless smile between wailing.

"You're... you're alive," was all she got out as the glass wall between them flashed a quick electric blue, sending Michael flying airborne across his cell. Unconsciousness claimed him before he even hit the tiles.

Brie stayed on her knees. Despite the pain and trauma, despite watching Michael get electrocuted, she couldn't wipe the smile off her face.

Michael was alive.

She was no longer alone.

FIFTY-EIGHT

SUBMARINE LIFE WAS CLASSY.

Compared to the loud, rusty freighter, the Union submarine was like a five star sub-plaza apartment. The mechanisms designed to counteract motion meant that we could travel at thirty kilometres an hour and it didn't even felt like we were moving.

The living quarters were spacious with alpaca-wool couches, large beds, tiled bathrooms and even recreational chambers with 8-ball tables. I hadn't seen 8-ball since childhood. Eli had never played. He was hooked. After the novelty wore off for me, Carter and I would leave Eli alone for hours while he played against himself.

Inside the kitchen, the pantries were less than half stocked. Even so, we had plenty of canned foods. Baked beans, processed meats, tinned vegetables, crushed tomatoes and enough tuna to feed an army. There were whole bags full of rice and rice noodles, pasta, flour – you name it.

While Carter set course on the first night inside the submarine, which Eli named the Whore, on account of it being faster and sexier than the Wife, I attempted cooking. I boiled pasta and added tuna, crushed tomatoes and pepper into a pot. The result was a warm, homely dinner. Despite my lack of cooking skills, after living off out-of-date rations, the pasta dish was a great success.

The Captain's quarters had a hardwood library shelf with books I didn't even think the Empire of Soteria permitted any longer. There were old books, ranging from Homer's *Iliad* to biographies of Australian explorers from the nineteenth century. Eli couldn't read well, but he seemed happy enough to flick through the pages in search for pictures. As Carter set the subma-rine to autopilot using GPS and SLD technology, the journey gave us time to eat, read and attempt to come up with a plan. The days passed. Carter only left the lab down in the bottom deck of the Whore to eat and sleep. Whatever he was working on fuelled his motivation. He became a different person. It inspired him to help plan the demise of the Union. His inspiration in turn inspired me. Although we had set course to the island of impris-onment, to the home of these elite super-soldiers, I had a good feeling.

Four days into our underwater voyage and he appeared from the lab. His beard was more dishevelled than normal. The dark circles under his eyes made it look as if he hadn't slept in days. He looked more like a mad scientist than ever before. He was finally ready to talk us through his plan. The timing couldn't have been better as Eli began to show signs of cabin fever. There was only so much 8-ball and tuna he could endure.

The three of us sat down on the Alpaca-wool lounge suite. Carter told us that during his time working for the Union he had been at the forefront of the initial Bestia design and he was as familiar with the technology as anyone else on Terra Carcerem. He talked us through the surgery and the operating system implanted into the mind of the Bestia to make them compliant. He talked at length about the software that he helped write. The software was uploaded into a portal in the Bestia's neck and with it came instant knowledge and skills.

Carter expressed confidence that if we could get within prox-imity of a Bestia soldier, he could disable the software by implanting a wireless virus, and then he would attempt to reload similar software, one that he had spent the last five days manipulating. The new software would make the Bestia serve him, not the Union.

"If you can implant a wireless virus, why can't you just implant it into all the Bestias and, bang, mission accomplished?"

"Unfortunately, that's not possible. It would be a monumental flaw in the design that I helped create. To implant the virus, we need to get within a few metres of a Bestia so I can let off an electromagnetic pulse through a device I have just finished constructing. It will maim the soldier. It will paralyse them long enough for me to upload the virus via his influx portal. He will be paralysed for maybe a minute at the most. The electromagnetic pulse will only be effective for a ten-metre radius."

"Why don't you make a device big enough so the electromagnetic pulse can shut down the entire island?"

"That would require a source of nuclear power so big that the radiation alone would kill us instantly. To create an electromagnetic pulse of that magnitude, I would need far more power than I can harness in the submarine laboratory."

"What about the submarine itself?" I asked.

"What do you mean?"

"I mean can we use the submarine's nuclear engine to create this electromagnetic pulse when we get there?"

"And what, kill the three of us? That would not be wise. We will not die as martyrs. Not yet, anyway. For the time being, let us try to capture and reprogram a Bestia. That will be a valuable start."

Eli spoke for the first time. "I like Gus's idea. I don't really want to fry our brains with nuclear radiation. It's too soon for the adventure to end."

"Okay," I said. "How are we going to capture a Bestia? If they're these unstoppable super-soldiers, it's not like we can exactly walk right up to one is it?"

"No, you're right. We can't be seen. We must gain access to the island undetected and then we must get within range using stealth."

"I'm good at that," Eli said enthusiastically. "I survived by using stealth. I bet you a million credits that I could sneak up behind one of these things."

"Eli, you don't even have ten credits, let alone a million."

"It's not the point, man. I'm with Gus. When we get there, we will sneak up on a Bestia and zap that motherfucker!"

Augustus Carter smiled. He admired Eli's youthful attitude. "Yes, Eli. Let us zap this so-called *motherfucker*…"

FIFTY-NINE

WE REACHED SHALLOWER WATERS FIVE DAYS AFTER LEAVING LORD Howe Island.

For most of our journey the submarine hovered above the sandy floor of the Pacific Ocean. We averaged a depth of about forty metres. Now, as we neared the cliff-lined island of Terra Carcerem, the submarine hovered at a depth of just twelve metres.

Carter had completed refining the small device we would use to paralyse a Bestia, if we found one, and he stored the software he had coded on a small hard drive about the size of a fist. We planned to plug the hard drive into our maimed captive if A, we got close enough to one, and B, the electromagnetic shock actually worked.

As we inched closer to the island of imprisonment, I became less settled. Nervousness boiled in my belly. Anxiety followed me around the confined quarters of the submarine. Eli seemed excited to be getting on dry land, even if it was a heavily guarded Union facility. He was starting to go a little crazy from the confined space and the artificial air. He played games of hide and seek within the corridors of the vessel to occupy his time. The concern was that he played alone, so he was both the hider and the seeker. I ignored his behaviour. I battled my own nervousness and inner demons.

I thought about 3rd Sydney West. I thought about George and Jonah and my apartment. I wondered how my friends were doing. I wondered if they missed me. By now someone else would have moved into my apartment. It was probably a wealthy surface dweller that had been biding their time on a waiting list. I wondered what they were like. Had they changed Laura's accent? Were they using my database of films? Did they have a wife? I wondered what the Union had done with all my possessions.

Everything had been so crazy since fleeing the sub-plaza that I hadn't had the time to reminisce. But there, on the sixth day inside the submarine, I missed George. I missed coffee. I missed Christie and Fay's morning conversations. In a weird way I missed Father Kassal's Sunday morning speeches. I missed our epic surf sessions on the Second Tier. Freedom was what I had wanted so badly. The grey space had been what I longed for. So why did I have these feelings? Regret is a heavy word. It carries with it a certain burden. It wasn't regret I felt, but it was some-thing similar. Emotions ebb and flow, Carter told me. I suppose I was ebbing.

The submarine came to a complete stop and slowly sank to a quiet rest on the ocean floor. Despite the coral outcrops scattered amongst the sand, Carter moored it smoothly between these. He turned off the engine and silence enveloped the cockpit.

"We will need to wait until the cover of darkness before we ascend."

"So are we gonna bring the Whore to the surface and use the RIB to get to shore?"

"No, after much thought I have decided that wouldn't be wise. The submarine must stay here. The inflatable will also remain. We will ascend with scuba gear. We will need to swim to the island underwater and undetected."

Eli looked puzzled. "Scuba?"

"Yes, Eli. It stands for Self Contained Underwater Breathing Apparatus. In the stockroom there are wetsuits, oxygen cylinders, buoyancy control devices, masks and breathing regulators. It is quite straightforward. You breathe through the regulator, similar to surface soldiers' oxygen conditioners, only designed for water instead."

"Whoa, sounds scary."

"To put in into perspective young man, we are about to storm onto an island where the Union makes the most murderous hybrid robot soldiers on the planet. We will attempt to catch one of these hostile murderous machines and reprogram it as our own, so going for a scuba dive is the furthest thing from scary."

"Well, if you put it like that, I guess you're right."

"It will be fine," I interjected. "But Carter, how are we going to get your device and any weapons to shore if we're underwater?"

"We will carry all that we need in compression dry bags. There are plenty of them in the storeroom. Now let us go prepare."

"Righto, Captain."

Carter led the way down into the storeroom beside the diving dock and taught us the basics on using the diving equipment. It seemed easy enough to breathe through the regulator. It would be a whole different experience underwater and in the dark. Eli didn't look at all happy about it.

We packed three taser cannons, a nuclear shock ball, some drinking water, Carter's strange electromagnetic weapon and the hard drive with the new software into a yellow compression sack and pressed a button. Upon pressing the button, compressed air was sucked from the bag and it formed an airtight seal. A clip on the outside of the bag allowed us to attach the bag to Carters buoyancy vest. The bag was heavy but Carter assured us that once in the water it would more or less be weightless.

When the sun sensors beeped a melodic tune, it indicated sunlight could not be detected above the surface. The sun had set. It was time to act. The three of us put on neoprene wetsuits and our scuba gear and entered the small diving dock. No bigger than an internal transporter cell, the dock was a small, steel room with no features other than a sealed door on both sides and a small touchpad on the wall. Carter handed us foot-long plastic fins to clip to our shoes to help propel us through the water.

"How far do we need to go?" I asked.

"It's about five hundred metres, give or take. Remember though, we want to take our time. The more energy you expel, the higher your respiratory rate will be. That means you will chew through your oxygen too fast and you may not have enough to get back to the submarine. Long breaths are what you need to focus on. Got it?"

"I think so."

"Wait a minute," said Eli. "If we need to use the oxygen to get back to the Whore, how are we gonna get one of these Bestia things back here? Don't we need to take an extra set of diving gear?"

"No, Eli. The Bestia do not breathe. They run on a nuclear core. They do not require oxygen in the same way that mortal humans do. Got it?"

"Sure… Let's do this, Gus!"

Once inside the diving dock Carter typed something into a touchpad on the wall. The internal door closed shut and a green light flashed when the seal became airtight. Carter pulled a small nylon cord from his waist belt and clipped it to all three of our buoyancy vests.

"Visibility will be limited. I will follow a bearing and you two follow me. For safety's sake we are all attached. I wouldn't want to lose one of you in the current. I suggest you get those regulators in your mouths now," he said with a grin. For maybe the second time since meeting him Carter looked excited.

He typed something else into the touchpad as I placed the round regulator into my mouth and took a breath. The air was cold and tasted a little odd, but other than that I felt okay. I looked over at our young accomplice. He was white in the face. Nervousness oozed from his frightened eyes. I patted him on the shoulder and nodded my head. He nodded back. It was not convincing.

Carter finished typing into the touch pad and an automated female voice spoke from speakers somewhere within the dock. She sounded similar to Laura. "Don your breathing apparatus now. You will be exposed to underwater conditions in seven seconds."

My heart rate increased.

I counted backwards from seven.

SIXTY

RIGHT ON ZERO A RED LIGHT FLASHED AND THE OUTER SEAL OPENED.
Water came gushing in through the dock in a torrent of whirling white. It was cold around my ankles. It was cold at my waist. Within seconds it was up to my neck and then suddenly a bubbling wash of moving water surrounded us. It occurred to me as I sat there and held my breath that I was too scared to breathe. I told myself to stop being a coward and took a deep breath in and out through the regulator. Bubbles exited my mouth and collected at the top of the cell. Once the water settled, I looked over at Eli. Through his mask I could see his eyes wide with fear. From the pace in which the bubbles left his regulator I could tell he was almost hyperventilating. I motioned to him to relax and breathe slower. I don't think he understood.

We stayed motionless for a minute, floating inside the dock chamber while both Eli and I adjusted our breathing. I looked out into the open darkness. Visibility was almost non-existent. Moonlight provided the slightest aid in making out features and shapes on the sea floor, but I figured that because of smoggy poisonous cloud, there may not have been a great deal of moonlight on the surface, anyway. We would swim blind.

Carter floated outside the dock chamber in the dark water. I could make out the faint silhouette of his body but nothing more. The thin nylon cord attached the three of us at our waists. It wasn't long until I felt Carter tugging at the cord, urging Eli and I to leave the safety of the dock cell.

I kicked hard with my fins, heading towards Carter's silhouette. Because the nylon cord behind me never went tight, I knew Eli was staying close. The three of us kicked our way through the gloomy water in silence, our bubbles rising to the surface as we approached the island of imprisonment. With no way to communicate, it left me alone with the sound of my heavy breathing through the regulator. I focused on my breathing, using it as a meditative mantra. In the gloomy silence I used my breathing as something to focus on, something to distract me from the fact that I was shitting myself. After ten terrifying minutes of kicking through the darkness, the water became shallower. The underwater noises changed their pitch. I heard the faint rumble of breaking waves. Before long we surfaced between a field of slimy boulders at the water's edge.

"Stay low," Carter said, after pulling his regulator from his mouth. "I just want to make sure this end of the island is safe."

He looked as calm as a sub plaza injection doctor. I on the other hand, was far from calm. I pulled the regulator from my mouth and took a huge gulp of real air. My heart rate returned to a normal pace. I could breathe again. As we waded through the slimy rocks, it felt like I was going to war. It almost felt unreal, like an out-of-body experience. There I was, with two people I had only known for a few weeks, literally about to steal a fucking robot soldier from the Humanist Union. Three weeks ago I was lying in my Third Tier apartment cell in cold sweats dreading my purposeless existence and now I was committing the highest order of terrorism. How life had changed.

"That was fun," Eli said, grinning in the darkness.

"Trust you to find fun at a time like this," I said. "I'm scared shitless."

"Shhhhhhhhh!" Carter gave us both a stern look in the faint moonlight.

We waded through the waist deep water, using the large brown rocks to conceal us in the darkness as we approached the small sandy beach. The terrain above the beach looked lifeless, wild. That was a good sign.

"We have landed at the northern tip of the island. The facility is at the other end, beside the old airport. The safest way to approach will be via the coastline. We will follow the beach around. It's rocky and there are some steep cliffs so be careful."

"And then what?" Eli said.

"And then, young Eli, we will wait for the opportune moment. We will know that moment when it arrives."

"That doesn't tell me anything."

"And what did I say to you earlier about patience? You will know what we need to do when we need to do it. For the time being we need to head south, unseen."

Eli mumbled something I didn't hear.

Under the cover of darkness, we removed our diving equipment and left it hidden in a small cave. Walking in the neoprene wetsuits would have been uncomfortable and horribly warm, so instead, Carter opened one of the dry bags and pulled out our change of clothes. We wasted no time throwing on a pair of pants and a shirt each, replaced our shoes, holstered our weapons and began the slow journey south through the wet boulder field. The three of us had taser cannons fresh out of the wooden crate from the Wife, fully charged and set to their most powerful setting. While carrying a Union-issue weapon lulled me into a sense of security, if the Bestia were as supreme as Carter had described, our weapons would be of little use. I gripped it firmly anyway.

A little over five minutes into our approach we came across a small cliff-bound cove. To get around the jagged cliffs, we needed to ascend a rocky slope and climb up and over the rocks. We scrambled up the loose rocks on all fours, unavoidably sending avalanches of loose debris cascading down the slope. I winced with fretful unease as the rocks crashed and ricocheted down the slope, fearful that someone would hear us. Thankfully, according to Carter, the facility was still quite a distance away.

We reached the top of the cliff with a few new scratches and stood up in the darkness. I wiped the dirt and rubble from my knees and looked south. From our high point, we could see to the other end of the island. We could make out the Terra Carcerem facility for the first time. Lit up like the entrance to 3rd Sydney West, the facility was a large steel square beside a long, overgrown airplane runway.

Carter pointed out that like most Humanist Union facilities, most of Terra Carcerem was underground, split over seven levels and two separate sub-plazas. Each sub-plaza facility served a different purpose. The facility closest to the runway was Inferno, built for induction of new detainees and holding cells. The second facility, not visible from their vantage point, was named Paradiso. Paradiso housed training facilities for new Bestia, laboratories and factories for the design and manufacturing of the hybrid soldiers. Carter had spent most of his time down in the depths of Paradiso laboratories. Two thoroughfares connected Inferno to Paradiso. One was on the surface. This allowed vehicle transfer between the two facilities. The other was on Level 3 and allowed pedestrian access via horizontal transporter cells.

The Union guarded the grounds surrounding Inferno with large lookout towers that rose from the surface like ominous concrete mushrooms. On top of the mushrooms I could make out huge missile launchers, cradling missiles larger than a human body.

"Anti-aircraft weaponry," Carter said, noticing me transfixed on the distant mushrooms. "They're automated, based on radar technology scanning the surrounding airspace. They will not be a threat to us."

"If you say so," I replied nervously.

I shook off doubt and uncertainty. I reminded myself that coming here was my idea. Eli and Carter had followed me. They had supported my ambitious and ignorant desire. Now was not the time to get cold feet.

"What are we waiting for?" I said.

I began the walk off along the rugged cliffs towards the distant runway. Carter and Eli followed right behind me.

SIXTY-ONE

MICHAEL REGAINED CONSCIOUSNESS. AGAIN.

Opening his eyes, he quickly remembered where he was. The constant loss and regaining of consciousness was beginning to take its toll; a dull ache hammered away with each heartbeat. He remembered the induction, the water slide and the glass cell. He remembered the bolt of electric energy that sent him flying across the room. Then he remembered Brie.

Michael looked towards Brie's cell. She sat on the edge of her small bed, smiling at Michael through swollen lips. Despite her shattered teeth there was so much warmth, happiness and love in that broken smile.

Electrical burns had charred Michael's hands. Regardless, he pushed himself off the tiles and stood unsteadily on bare feet. One slow movement at a time, he made his way as close to the glass as he would dare. He worked out the cells were almost soundproof. Instead of pointlessly screaming through the thick glass, Michael attempted to use sign language as he mouthed the words, "I. Came. Looking. For. You."

Brie nodded. She understood. Her eyes were puffy and red from crying. The torrent of tears started again. She lost herself in his

344

comforting eyes. She found herself just as quickly in his inviting smile.

"I miss you," he mouthed again.

"I miss you, too," Brie mouthed, forcing a smile.

"What happened?"

Their bittersweet reunion came to an abrupt end as the double-doors at the end of the corridor rolled open to the familiar sound of a sub-plaza beep. They both turned their heads. Two soldiers entered the corridor followed by two Union advisors dressed in suits the colour of Fosform Five. Brie recognised the two advisors. They had come before. They had dragged the neighbouring cell's previous tenant away. Now they were back. She knew what was coming.

Time... Operate... Complaint... Bestia...

Michael recognised one soldier. Medium height. Black hair. Clean-shaven. He had carried Michael inside Terra Carcerem without breaking a sweat. He had stood at the edge of the warm, viscous pool. The short, pudgy guy with the comical collar had referred to the soldier as Nine-Thirteen. The other soldier was a thin, tall Negro, towering close to seven feet tall.

Nine-Thirteen stood outside Brie's cell as the clear glass slid open with a beep. The female advisor entered Brie's cell with the second soldier right behind her. The advisor stepped in front of Brie and restrained her wrists with a carbon fibre rod as the soldier stood idle, aiming a taser cannon at Brie's face. The advisor pulled a black canvas bag from the pocket of her aqua jacket and placed it over Brie's head, pulling the drawstring tight around her neck. They ushered Brie out of her cell, naked, exposed and blinded by the black bag. They ordered her to stop in the corridor.

Michael stood frozen, crippled by shock.

Where are they taking her?

Defeat rose from the pits of his stomach. Fate was a heartless tease. He had sacrificed so much to find Brie Kallas, and now that he had, she was being taken away at gunpoint to God knows where only moments later.

The female advisor exited Brie's empty cell and left her standing in the corridor with the tall Negro soldier resting his taser cannon at the base of her skull.

Watching in awe, Michael saw the female advisor use a touch-screen device strapped to her arm. As she typed, the glass wall to Michaels's cell slid open on invisible hinges. The advisor entered with Nine-Thirteen right behind her.

"Nine-Twenty-One," she said, looking at Michael. "Place your hands out in front of you."

Michael stood with proud defiance. He kept his hands at his sides. "My name is not Nine-Twenty-One. My name is Michael Butcher…"

"You can call yourself whatever you choose. You can call yourself God if it makes you happy, but you will respond to Nine-Twenty-One. Now, put your hands out in front of you or else Nine-Thirteen here will cut your little penis off."

As she spoke, she looked down at Michael's naked body, pointing to his manhood hanging exposed between his thighs. Michael looked at Nine-Thirteen. The man showed no expression. He stared at Michael with abnormally large pupils, almost inhuman. A cold shiver ran down his spine as he looked into those callous and cold eyes.

Defeat.

Michael raised his hands out in front of him as the woman pulled a restraining rod from the pocket of her jacket and connected it around both his wrists.

"Now, that's a good little boy," she said as the device locked firm.

She grabbed the rod in the middle of Michael's wrists and dragged him from the cell. Nine Thirteen stood a metre behind Michael with his taser aimed at waist height.

Everything happened so fast. Michael was still coming to terms with the fact that he had found Brie. The chances of being thrown into a cell beside hers were almost too much of a coincidence.

Michael had given up everything to find Brie, and now he stood right beside her in the corridor of a Union correctional facility, helpless. She stood less than a metre from him. She stood still as the Negro's taser rested on her shoulder. Michael wanted nothing more than to reach over and hug her, to pick her up and embrace her, to kiss her cracked lips. He wanted to feel her skin. He wanted to smell her hair. He knew that if he made any quick movements, he would receive a blast to the spine. Brie didn't even know he was there. Blinded by the canvas bag, she was oblivious to the fact that Michael Butcher stood right beside her.

"It'll be okay," he said as reassuring as he could. "I'm here now. I'll get you out of here…"

"I can't believe you're here," Brie said, her voice muffled from the canvas. "How did you…"

"Shut up, pit whore," the advisor interjected.

Now with such proximity, Michael could get a better look at Brie and her wounds. She'd been through hell. Michael noticed the bruises and swelling covering a good half of her body. Her skin looked like bluish army fatigues, blotches of different colours scattered over her bare body. It pained him to see the agony she had endured. By the state of her wounds Michael could see that somebody had taken Brie to the verge of death.

"What have they done to you?" Michael asked as his eyes welled.

"I…"

"I said shut up, *swine!*" yelled the advisor. "No communication between inmates. Another word from either of you and I'll take out your tongues. We don't require your tongues to make useful Bestia."

Brie rotated her head towards Michael but said nothing. Michael looked at the blank black canvas, imagining her sweet features, frightened and trapped inside the bag. He wanted nothing more than to look into her eyes, to reassure her that everything would be okay. There was a part of him that doubted that. Things didn't seem to be going in their favour at all.

Chance was an unusual thing. As Michael stared at the black canvas concealing Brie's bruised face, he thought about chance. What was the chance of him ending up in the same facility at the same time as Brie? What was the chance of him ending up in the cell next door? What was the chance of both of them being taken to wherever they were being taken to at the same moment? It wasn't chance. It couldn't be. It was fate. Michael thought about fate. Whatever happened next, Michael was content knowing that fate had brought Brie Kallas back to him.

The tall Negro soldier pulled a metal rod from a bag over his shoulder. No thicker than Brie's wrist, the rod was close to a metre long and had a wire cable loop at either end. While Nine-Thirteen aimed his taser, the Negro fastened the first waist loop around Brie's waist, followed immediately by Michael's. They were joined at the hip with the rigid pole. Trying to flee would be impossible. The last thing Michael saw was the black canvas come over his head and the cord pull tight.

"Okay," Michael heard the woman say. "Walk. We're going to Paradiso…"

SIXTY-TWO

BRUCE CHADWICK SAT IN THE T-TOWN COMMUNAL ROOM WITH HIS fellow outlaws.

The mood was beyond sombre, shifting through various stages of shock, hysteria, fear, acceptance, mourning and now helplessness. Bruce knew Evan was dead. Bruce knew Remy and Aidan were dead, too. It had been three days since they dropped the bombs, three days since the raging blaze on the surface had confined the T-Towners to their underground bunker. As Bruce sat in silence, he questioned the timing. They had taken Brie a little over a month ago. Michael had gone not long after. Now, somehow, the Union knew about T-Town. The bombs had been dropped strategically, not by chance. Bruce Chadwick didn't believe in chance. Bruce didn't believe in coincidence. He knew that either Brie or Michael had given them up. Tortured, no doubt. Beaten into compliance. If it weren't for Brie, Michael would still be there with them. In Bruce's eyes this was all Brie's fault.

"Damn you, woman."

Robin and the rest of the digging team tried to find a way out of their underground bunker. They had little success. The explosion blocked the main entry under T-Tree. Either the tree itself had burned and toppled over, restricting the trap door from being able to open or debris has fallen around the thick buttress roots, blocking the exit.

The other two exits beside the hover-bike compound were the same. Something on the surface blocked the thoroughfare. Robin couldn't determine whether fallen branches, debris or even large amounts of ash were the cause. What he knew was that they were trapped in their own hideout. The fires on the surface had turned T-Town into one giant grave.

"What are our options?" Gabbie asked, tired from stress.

"Well, we need to dig our way out," Bruce said, rubbing dirt from his temple. "We don't have enough food in here to last more than a week. Water probably less. We need to put the bloody tunnel on hold and dig our way up and out. Robin thinks digging out the back will be easiest. If T-Tree has come down, that will be impossible to dig through."

"When do we start?"

"We already have, Gab. The boys were onto it this morning. I bloody well hope they make some progress. If we all fucking suffocate in this damn place because of Brie bloody Kallas, I'll be kicking myself in Hell for bringing her back here. I should have let her explode beside the wall…"

"Hold on, Bruce. That's unfair. You don't know that Brie had anything to do with this."

"Come on, Gab. Use your bloody brains. Brie disappears, taken hostage, right? Not long after she's gone and the bombs drop. That's no coincidence. She ratted us out, mate. She gave away our location. Probably made a deal or something. Useless bitch. Absolutely fucking gutless."

"It is a possibility, but Michael has also left. Or, it could be something different. Maybe it has something to do with what happened at the wall? Maybe they're taking more precautionary measures now that we breached their facilities? You can't blame Brie for all of it."

"I can and I will. It *was* Brie. I can feel it in my guts. We made a big mistake the day we took her in. She fucked everything—"

"Well, even if you're right, sitting here being aggravated won't help us get food and water. Even if it was Brie, which I'm not saying is true, what difference does that make? You will never see her again. She's gone. Holding grudges will just make you bitter. You're far better off using your energy to pray for the dear friends that we have lost. Pray for Evan. Pray for Francis and Remy. Pray for Caleb, Milly, Krit, Tinker and Tom. And wherever Michael may be, pray for him too. We need to survive. We all need to dig. We need all hands on deck if we plan to survive."

"You're right, Gab. Let's go round up the gang."

Twenty-two hours later Robin poked his head through a small hole above T-Town. They had dug through bedrock and soil above the storeroom, working around the clock in teams of four. Dig, rest, dig, rest and rotate. Everyone helped. Even Gabbie had blistered fingers and dirt under her fingernails. The task had brought the group back together. It had given the group a collective purpose. Gabbie felt the strong sense of community that had been missing from T-Town for weeks.

Climbing out of the hole, Robin brushed off the dirt, stood up and breathed in the outside air for the first time in days. Bruce followed behind him.

"Well done, mate. Feels good to be out of that tomb, hey?"

Robin said nothing. He just looked around in silence, taking in the barren destruction that surrounded them. The jungle was gone. The thick canopy of moist green leaves was gone. The sound of birds singing through the forest was gone. Their secrecy was gone. All that remained was a bed of grey ash and the withering skeletons of dead trees visible in every direction.

"Jesus Christ," Bruce said. "This is not bloody good."

"No jungle mean no food," Robin said in his broken English.

"No shit, Robin. I get it, mate."

"What we do?"

"You know what, mate. I have no bloody idea…"

351

SIXTY-THREE

THE SUN ROSE ON THE EASTERN HORIZON AND A SPECTRUM OF EARLY morning pinks glowed across the island of imprisonment.

Eli, Carter and I sat huddled behind a small mound of grass less than fifty metres from the arched concrete bridge that joined Inferno to Paradiso. Carter and I held taser cannons. Eli held the small device that Carter had made in the depths of the Whore. Smaller than a registration chip reader, the device was a black cube with a small plutonic battery connected to a series of charges. There was a square orange button on the top of the cube. The plan was to get Eli within fifteen metres of a Bestia and compress the orange button.

According to Carter, the pulse would charge and the Bestia would lose function for a minute, maybe two, collapsing on the spot. In theory, this would allow time for Carter to upload his tailored software via the influx portal on the Bestia's neck. We didn't dare enter the facility, so we waited, biding our time until something happened. For a long time, nothing did.

Hunger and thirst were becoming a problem. We had a few snacks in Carter's dry bag but not enough to silence the cravings. We couldn't just sit behind a pile of native grasses all day. If something didn't happen soon, it would force us to either retreat to the safety of the Whore or make another plan. I hoped that plan didn't involve trying to find our way into the steel labyrinth of Terra Carcerem. That would be suicide.

As if on cue, triggered by my growing restlessness, a short blast of beeps sounded from above the steel doors leading into Inferno. I held my breath with anticipation. The large doors opened as the beeping ceased. At first I couldn't see within the darkness of the facility, but as I strained my eyes, I made out shapes. Five people emerged from the doorway and out onto the bridge.

"Holy shit, it's happening," Eli said, his voice rich with fear.

"It's up to you now, Eli. Do what you do best and sneak up beside them. You need to get within ten metres."

The colour drained from Eli's face. He looked frightened.

"I don't think I can do this…"

"Look man, I know you can. Just pretend you're back at Collaroy trying to sneak around to find Fosform. You said it yourself; you spent every day being stealthy. This is no different. I believe in you. Go zap one of those *motherfuckers*."

"How do we even know if one of them is a Bestia?"

Eli and I both looked at Carter. It was a valid question.

"Patience," was all Carter said. "Once we can see them, I will know if they are Bestia or not. It will be clear in their stride, in their posture. And worst case, if they are not Bestia, the device will have no effect on a human and they won't even know you're there."

"You can do it, man. I'll be right behind you with this taser cannon ready to drop them dead."

"Tyson, they're robots… They're taser proof."

"Shit…"

"It's okay, I'm doing it. We didn't come here for nothing. It'll be a walk in the park. You two just be ready."

And with that, Eli rolled forward onto his stomach and started crawling through the tall grass. Except for the barely noticeable swaying blades, Eli was invisible, hidden even from us. I waited in silent anticipation. I gripped the rubber handle of the taser tighter. I felt sweat forming on my brow. I looked up on the bridge. The five people had left the shadows, now visible in the early morning light.

"Carter, look up there," I whispered.

What we saw were two soldiers dressed in grey fatigues, one was an average height and the other was the tallest man I had ever seen, a Negro towering seven feet tall. A blonde woman in a strange aqua trench coat accompanied the soldiers with what appeared to be two prisoners, naked and bound, their heads covered with black bags. The blonde woman wore a small portable oxygen conditioner.

"They're moving prisoners. They're preparing them for the Bestia update," Carter said. "The woman is Eileen Myers. I worked with her for a long time. She is a dreadful woman. She's as ruthless as anyone I've ever met."

"And are the soldiers Bestia?"

Carter watched in silence as Eileen dragged the prisoners forward by the rigid rod. The two soldiers walked in perfect synchronisation behind the prisoners. Their posture was flawless. They showed no emotion and most importantly, they wore no oxygen conditioners.

"They certainly are."

"Okay, so what are we going to do with the woman when Eli uses your thing?"

"Don't worry about that, Tyson. Leave Eileen to me."

By the time Eileen Myers had escorted the prisoners halfway across the bridge I felt sick with worry. I couldn't tell where Eli was. There was no movement. There was no swaying grass. The sweat on my brow dripped down the ridge of my nose.

Surely he must be close by now.

I looked at Carter. For the first time since meeting him I saw rage in his eyes. He was passive by nature. He was the sense of calm that helped ground the storm that Eli and I harnessed, but behind that mound of grass he looked fearsome. He looked driven.

Then it happened.

Without a sound the two taser-wielding soldiers dropped to the ground, lifeless on the walkway. Eileen Myers stood in shock, staring at the soldiers, unable to comprehend what was happening. The two prisoners stood still, unaware of what was occurring, oblivious to the fact that shit was about to hit the proverbial fan.

"Go!" Carter yelled.

Despite the anxiety pulsing through my veins, I was up and running in half a heartbeat. Carter ran right beside me. We reached the steel stairwell in less than ten seconds. As we made it to the bottom stairs, Eli appeared from the bushes underneath the bridge. He wore a grin from ear to ear. "It worked," he said as he dashed up the stairs, taking three steps at a time. Carter was not quite so agile. Eli and I were already on the bridge as Carter struggled with the first few stairs. I reached Eileen Myers first. Raising my taser cannon, I leapt out in front of the surprised Union advisor. "Don't move, bitch," I yelled, shoving the taser up into her ribs.

"What in all of Soteria is going on? Do you know who I am? Do you have any idea what you're doing?"

Carter reached the bridge, panting. Rage radiated from his driven eyes. "Hello Eileen," he said between gasps of air. "It has been a while…"

It took about three seconds for Eileen to recognise Carter under his scraggy beard and unkempt hair.

"Augustus? What on Earth is going on? You filthy traitor! You're an embarrassment to the Empire."

Carter was well aware of our time restraints. He didn't have the time or the patience to discuss morals with his ex-colleague. Without a word he raised his taser cannon and fired a shot of compressed electricity at Eileen's surprised face. The close-range impact burnt a hole through her oxygen conditioner and right through her skull. Chunks of brain leaked out over the bridge as she toppled forward.

"Who's the embarrassment now," Carter whispered with a crazed cackle.

He wasted no time. Carter moved with haste beside the two lifeless soldiers, knelt down and pulled a small hard-drive from his dry bag. I turned my attention to the naked prisoners. They knew something was happening. They had heard the taser blast. They would have smelt Eileen Myers' burnt flesh.

"Hey, you two," I said. "It's all right. We'll get you out of here…"

"Who *are* you," the bound woman said, muffled through the black bag. "What's going on?"

"Just give us thirty seconds and we will explain everything…"

"We can only upload the virus once," Carter said, interrupting me. "It means we can only take one Bestia. The other will need its plutonium drain opened. Quick, see the black plug beside his influx portal. We need to unscrew it. It is difficult but with a multi-tool you should be able to release the plug. Turn anti-clockwise."

Carter threw me a multi-tool. I squatted down beside the closest Bestia, ready to open up his plutonium drain and disable the robot permanently. For the first time since arriving on the bridge I looked at the soldier's features.

What.

The.

Actual.

Fuck.

SIXTY-FOUR

MY HEART WENT INTO OVERDRIVE. THE WORLD AROUND ME SWAYED with uneasiness. I think I almost fainted.

"This cannot be," I said, gasping between words. "This… is… *impossible.*"

"What is it, Ty? Hurry, man. Drain that motherfucker!" Eli was bouncing with nervous impatience.

"I can't. Not this one…"

I hesitated. We didn't have time to hesitate, but I did.

I looked down at my closest friend. I looked down at George Clarkson lying lifeless on the bridge. Somehow George was a Bestia. Somehow George was there on Terra Carcerem. I didn't have time to consider how. I didn't have time to analyse the situation. Whether it was chance or fate or coincidence was not of importance. I was about to permanently disable my closest friend.

"We need to drain the other one," I barked at Carter. "You need to upload your software to this one. Now…"

I hurried, fighting the overwhelming feeling of shock and disbelief. I squatted beside the other lifeless soldier, the giant Negro, and used Carter's multi-tool to unscrew the black plug. Slowly it turned, then after five or six rotations it pulled free. A thick, foul-smelling Fosform coloured liquid oozed out from the hole.

"He won't be going anywhere," I heard Carter say. "He's as good as dead."

I looked over to Carter, now kneeling beside George. He had plugged his hard-drive into a small port under a flap of synthetic skin at the base of George's skull. Carter referred to this as the influx portal. Sweat dripped from my eyebrows. My heartbeat hammered like a wall construction tool. We hadn't even been on the bridge for sixty seconds. My eyes bounced from Carter and George to the large steel doors at the end of the bridge. I half expected them to open and face an army of Bestia.

"We need to be faster," I yelled, verbalising the voice in my head.

"This will take another thirty seconds," Carter said to me with a chilling calmness. "Get the prisoners ready for a quick retreat."

I was so overwhelmed by George's presence I had almost forgotten about the two prisoners standing only metres away, naked, bound and oblivious to what was taking place. I loosened the cord on the man's black canvas bag then pulled it free from his head. He squinted in the gloomy morning light. He looked me up and down with caution.

"Thanks," he said. "What are you guys doing?"

"We'll explain everything as soon as we got off this bridge…"

I repeated the process on the woman's canvas bag. She, too, squinted. She looked like she'd been through hell. Her naked body was a patchwork of bruises. Her jaw was swollen. Her eye socket was purple. I looked into her green eyes. They were captivating, magnetic.

"Here, stand still," I said to them both as I pulled my taser cannon from its holster. At first the woman flinched with fear. "Relax," I said. "We're here to help."

I aimed my taser at the carbon fibre rod joining them at the hip. Firing a short blast, the rod melted, turning into a pile of liquid gloop on the concrete. They were no longer bound to each other. I helped them both slip free from the cables looped around their waists and then discarded the cables over the side of the bridge.

"Thanks," the woman said with sincerity, rubbing the red and blistered skin above her hipbone where the cable had been.

Carter said something behind me. He was talking to George. I turned my attention to them.

"What's your name, soldier?"

Short silence.

"My name? My name is George… I think…"

"Who do you serve?"

There was a blank stare.

"I'm not sure, sir."

"*Excellent*! It has worked. George, come with us." Carter looked at Eli and me. "We need to leave. Right now!"

Without another second wasted, the six of us fled down the stairwell and out into the open grass beside the airport. We had been on the bridge for two minutes, maybe less. The naked prisoners did not need convincing. They ran alongside us with newfound enthusiasm. Hope powered their weary muscles as they ran barefoot over thick scrub and rocky terrain.

We didn't stop until we had made it halfway back to the seaside cave. Only when we could go no further did we slow the pace. And it was only then that I made eye contact with George. At first he looked through me, unsure who I was. He looked different, emotionless. His eyes looked like death in the flesh. All black, no iris. Just like the woman that had haunted my dreams.

"George, it's me. Don't you recognise me?"

"I have memories of you," he said in a monotone response. "I have seen you before but I am unaware who you are."

"Tyson, you *know* this Bestia?" Carter interjected with a voice of disbelief. I nodded. "That is uncanny. How do you know this machine?"

"He's my best friend," I responded, tears welling in my eyes. "He was like a brother to me. He's from 3rd Sydney West."

"What are the chances of that?" Carter responded. "Unbelievable… Chance is such an incredible thing. Worry not, his memory will return, Tyson. Give it a few days and his memory from before the operation will come back. For the time being, we need to get off this island."

As if the reunion with George wasn't hard enough to bear, I had only turned away from his black stare for less than a second when I heard tears. Hysteric tears behind me. I spun around to see the two prisoners locked in a firm embrace. They hugged each other like the world was ending. They kissed like no one was watching.

"I knew I would find you," the man said between kisses, tears rolling down his face. "I knew that you were alive. I knew if I came looking that I would find you. I love you, Brie. God, I love you so much."

"What on Earth is going on?" Eli said. "Is anyone else as confused as I am?"

"Sorry to interrupt," I said to the prisoners. "But we need to get out of here *right now*. You two can do that later."

SIXTY-FIVE

WE MADE IT BACK TO THE SMALL CAVE ON THE NORTHERN END OF the island without incident.

Our presence on the island was well and truly known. What had been a lifeless island in the morning now had its sky swarming with activity. Helicopters scouted the coastline at the southern end of the island, searching the area surrounding the Terra Carcerem facilities. It wouldn't be long until their search extended further north. We needed to get off the island. We didn't have long.

The prisoners introduced themselves as Brie and Michael. By the sounds of their continuous conversation they both had quite the story. Now was not the time.

We collected the diving equipment from the back of the cave and readied the oxygen cylinders. We didn't have time to get into the neoprene wetsuits. Instead, we would just enter the water in our clothing. We thought it wise to take the wetsuits with us in the dry bag, as we didn't want to draw any attention to our location or our means of escape. We didn't want to leave clues behind.

Black rods still bound Brie and Michael at the wrists. They would require the use of their hands to swim. Using delicate precision, I blasted the small rods between their wrists, fearful I would take their thumbs off. I removed Brie's restraint flawlessly. She thanked me with a toothless smile. I miscalculated the angle as I shot the rod connecting Michael's wrists though. Radiant energy burned the back of his hand as the carbon-fibre rod melted. He swore in pain and ran to the water's edge, submerging his hand in the small waves.

"I guess a burnt hand is better than being turned into a robot," Eli called out.

Michael didn't respond.

"Now this will be a little more difficult than getting onto the island," said Carter. "We will need to share the oxygen tanks. There are three regulators and five of us. We will all need to stay together and we will use signals. One finger means you are okay holding your breath still. Two fingers means you need to breathe. We will rotate the regulators in a clockwise direction. Understand?"

I nodded. Brie nodded. From the water's edge, Michael nodded.

"Not really," Eli said, confused.

"Just follow my lead," I said, reassuring Eli with a pat on the back.

"And what about me?" George asked.

"George, you do not breathe. You can swim beside us or walk along the seafloor. In fact, it would be helpful if you could go ahead of us and prepare the dock for entry."

"I don't know how to do that."

"You will know when you get there. I have programmed you with the knowledge and skills for all Union vehicles and vessel operation. If you head off now, follow a bearing of 282 degrees and you will come across the submarine."

"Right away, sir. 282 it is."

With the calm approach of a sea turtle, George entered the water, walking through the small rocks one slow metre at a time until he disappeared from sight into the small lapping waves. It was a strange feeling, watching my friend walk into the water without the necessary diving equipment we all needed. It made me feel sick in the stomach. I was still coming to terms with the fact that George Clarkson didn't breathe. It was already proving to be the strangest and most intense day of my life and it hadn't hit 10:30am.

Carter produced the nylon cord from the dry bag. The three of us with buoyancy control vests clipped the cord onto small brass loops attached to our vests. We needed to tie the cord around the waists of Michael and Brie to ensure they stayed close during the swim. I handed them both the tail of cord and noticed Brie's discomfort, standing in the shallows baring all, naked and vulnerable.

"Don't worry," I said to them both. "There are plenty of clothes for you back on the submarine."

The noise of distant helicopter blades shifted my attention from Brie's nakedness to our impending doom. We saw a third chopper in the skies to the south. It had changed its direction of travel and swerved north through the centre of the island. Soon there would be more. Soon there would be infantry. Soon there would be Bestia swarming the island by foot. We had no more time to waste.

"We're going," Carter said. "Right now."

All connected by the cord, the five of us entered the water, dodging slimy boulders as we approached the small waves.

"Have you ever done this before?" Eli asked Michael and Brie. They both shook their heads. They looked calm though, much calmer than I had felt only hours before when I left the safety of the Whore for the first time. Calmness is subjective, I suppose. I wasn't sure what they had endured during their captivity. Maybe walking into the deep, cold, poisonous water without breathing apparatus was less fearful than what they had gone through. We would know soon enough.

As I entered the water I breathed in the metallic air through my regulator. My heart rate increased. I looked over at Michael and Brie. Only fifteen seconds into our underwater escape and Brie raised two fingers. As Carter was closest to her, he removed his regulator and handed it over to her. She bit down on the breathing device and bubbles appeared. Another fifteen seconds after that Michael raised two fingers.

This would be a slow and frightening process.

Two minutes in and we were getting into a rhythm. Rotate and breathe, rotate and breathe. From the sun's playful reflection bouncing off the surface of the water I estimated that we swam at a depth of about five metres. I hoped it was deep enough to be unseen from the sky.

We had a long way to go. As Michael and Brie didn't have fins to kick with, our pace was half what it had been getting to shore. I prayed there would be enough oxygen in the cylinders to last the journey. Doubt returned. Running out of air would mean serious trouble. Our pace was working against us.

Suddenly I saw something moving in the water ahead of us. The others saw it too. I froze. It was faint and distant but something moved towards us in the murky depths with a frightening pace. At first I thought it was a shark. I envisioned the five of us being ripped to shreds by a hungry underwater predator. I started breathing with manic fear, sucking the dwindling oxygen supply from the cylinder at a selfish pace, waiting to be eaten. Tied together, we simply couldn't out-manoeuvre a shark. We were literally sitting ducks.

It came closer.

I saw limbs. Legs.

Relief.

It definitely wasn't a shark.

Confusion.

It was human.

It was *George*.

He walked across the seafloor with ease, carrying a thick steel cable over his shoulder. He approached us with an emotionless visage and handed one end of the cable to us as casually as a food court hospitality worker handing someone a takeaway burger. Carter and I, being in the middle of the group, held the cable firm. George then started pulling us through the water with the speed of a turfball player. Bundled together by the nylon cord, George pulled all five of us through the water. He ran across the sandy bottom dragging us at a pace five times what we would have been able to swim.

Impossible, I thought to myself. It was almost comical.

This is ridiculous.

As George dragged us through the water with superhuman strength, we rotated the regulators with difficulty. At one point my regulator slipped from my grasp and I left it trailing behind us. Brie reached back and snatched the trailing oxygen hose, shoving it in her mouth. She breathed deep, laboured breaths.

Within a minute I saw the dark outline of the Whore in the water ahead of us. As George dragged us closer, I saw the entrance dock was open and ready for our arrival. He dragged us right to the open seal of the dock and the five of us crammed inside, followed by George. He typed a sequence code into the touch pad beside the door and the outer seal closed. Several beeps sounded, followed by flashing lights, then the water began draining from the dock. The churning white water bubbled around us until the five of us sat there in the conditioned air, wet and fatigued. Eli pulled the regulator from his mouth and looked at Michael and Brie.

"Welcome to the Whore."

SIXTY-SIX

IT WASN'T EVEN MIDDAY YET AND THE WHORE WAS ALREADY ON ITS way north through the dark water.

I had searched through the bunkrooms and found clothing for our new companions easily enough. Finding clothing for Michael had been simple, but as the Union army enlisted no women, finding clothing of a suitable size for Brie proved difficult. She wore the smallest pair of Union trousers and shirt that I could find, yet they still hung from her malnourished frame, making her look like childlike.

George was on the bridge with Carter. At that moment I thought it best to give him space. I wanted his memory to return so I could speak with the real George Clarkson, not a software update. It broke my heart to see what the Union had done to him. He was no longer the man that I had grown to call my friend. I wanted nothing more than to know why he had ended up in the Bestia program. It pained me to sit there without the answer. I prayed it had nothing to do with my escape. Surely it didn't. I convinced myself it couldn't. I wasn't sure I could carry that burden.

In the recreation room, Michael and Brie spoke at length as Eli and I sat and listened intently. Their stories of hardship, escape,

366

treason and murder were far more outlandish than my simple escape from 3rd Sydney West. They spoke of T-Town. They spoke about their tunnel. They spoke of stealing Fosform during missions of ambush. Michael told us about breaking into barracks on the wall using the registration chips of surface soldiers. He told us about Aquilonem and his plan to find Brie. His story was almost too farfetched to believe.

Brie told us of her capture. She told us about G-Block and her meetings with Master Stephen Haynes. She spoke about being captured in the jungle the very night they took her from Michael. He added to the story. He told us about transporting Bruce Chadwick unconscious back to their underground hideaway.

It was all so much to absorb. It was crazy to think they had endured so much and somehow found their way back to each other. Maybe holding onto hope was worth it after all? Maybe fate was real? Maybe God did exist? Whatever you want to call it, fate, hope or God, it had to be more than pure coincidence that brought them back together and landed them on the Whore with us heading northeast towards the wall. I put it down to the power of hope. Hope could be the triumphant winner. Hope had brought them back together.

Eli and I spoke of our journey. I spoke of the Marriage Lottery I fled from. We spoke of the hydro-harbour and our commandeering of the Wife. We spoke of Lord Howe Island and finding Carter. Michael listened with wide eyes, asking us questions and commenting on our narrative. Brie stared off into the blank space behind me. She seemed distracted, haunted by her horrific experience.

———

BRIE BLINKED AWAY DARK MEMORIES AND LOOKED AROUND AT HER new crew mates. She had deliberately left out parts of her story. As far as she was concerned, although these young men had saved her, they were still strangers. They had access to a Union submarine. They had access to Union weapons. Her time in captivity had made her cautious. It would take a little more than a gallant rescue mission for her to trust them. After everyone's stories of courage and adventure had ended, Brie stood.

"I would like to be alone with Michael for a moment. There are some things we need to discuss."

"No worries. There's a room for you at the far end of the corridor, down the ladder and to the left. I'm sure you guys want to rest for a bit. By the sounds of it, you could both do with it."

"Thanks, Tyson," Michael said as he stood up and patted me on the back. "Man, am I glad you guys stole one of these crazy robot dudes when you did. An hour later and things would be very different right now."

Brie and Michael left the recreation room and headed off down the corridor. They found an empty bunkroom with four single beds, a wall screen and a few cupboards for clothing. Brie pressed the touchpad beside the door and the thick steel rolled closed. She looked deep into Michael's eyes. At first she was smiling. Her smile faded, replaced with a torrent of tears. She hugged him, pressing her face against his hard chest. He held her and said nothing while she cried. She needed to get it out. For several minutes they both just stood in silence. Michael wrapped his strong arms around Brie's thinning frame while she cried hysterical, broken tears. For the first time in a month Brie felt somewhat safe again. She had held on to hope for so long. For so many hours of torment and solitude she had envisioned Michael's smile, wondering if she would ever see him again. Now she stood with him and kissed his neck. She cried between laboured breaths. She hugged Michael tight, fearful to let go.

Once the tears had ended, Michael wiped Brie's cheeks with his thumb and kissed her softly.

"God, there is so much I didn't say up there," she said as she wiped her face. "I don't quite know what to make of these guys, though."

"I think they're on our side, Brie. Tyson bares the same scar on his neck as we do. Remember what you learned at T-Town? Sometimes you need to trust people. We let you in to our underground home, didn't we? You were a stranger to all of us…"

At the mention of T-Town, Brie broke down again. She wailed hysterically, crippled with guilt and trauma. All Michael could do was hold her.

"Michael, they made me tell them where T-Town was. I didn't do it. I couldn't do it. So, I lied. They found out I lied. They said they would bomb the entire northern jungle. Michael, I think T-Town may be gone. I think they might all be *dead*."

"You don't know that for sure, Brie. It could have just been a scare tactic. It could have been a threat to make you compliant."

"I don't think so. They had Francis' head. They have camera footage of Bruce and Francis stealing Fosform. Did you know Francis was a Union soldier before he joined Bruce?"

Michael shook his head.

"And," Brie continued. "They had footage of *you* in the wall barracks. They knew that T-Town was up in the jungle. They knew we were stealing Fosform. I can feel it in my guts. T-Town is gone."

"Well, I'll hold on to hope, Brie. Holding on to hope got me back to you, didn't it? We will know for sure what happened to T-Town when we get back there."

"Get back there? You want to go *back*?"

"Bloody oath, I do. Why wouldn't I? I have you back, now it's time to return to our friends, our *family* and finish our tunnel and escape this fucking place."

Tears welled in Brie's red and swollen eyes again. She leaned over the bed and kissed Michael passionately. He kissed her back, long and hard and full of love. He pulled her oversized shirt off in a swift action of erotic longing. He kissed her neck. He kissed her breasts. He repositioned himself and went to remove her pants. Despite fatigue, insatiable animalistic instinct took over. He wanted to feel her naked skin against his. He wanted to love her.

"Wait," Brie said, taking Michael's hand off the waist of her trousers. "I can't. Not just yet, Michael. Please understand."

Michael sat back and looked at Brie with compassion. She slipped her loose shirt back over her head. and shuffled back.

"Michael..." The words couldn't come. Brie took a deep breath and wiped the tears from her cheek. "Michael, they raped me," she said, her voice rich with shame. "They raped me every day for a week. The Union ordered them to do it. Eric van Bueren made them..."

More tears, more hysterical breathing.

"Those weak *bastards*," Michael yelled, standing up and punching the bed frame with a clenched fist. "I'm going to murder those *motherfuckers*. How dare they..."

"Anyway, look at me," Brie said as she took Michael's hand and held it in hers. "I want to be intimate with you, I do. I have dreamt about it for so long. But it will need to wait a bit. I haven't healed properly."

Michael leaned forward and hugged Brie. He kissed her on the neck. He ran his finger slowly up and down her arm. "You take as long as you need to, Brie. Don't feel pressured by me. I will wait until you're ready, however long it takes. I'm just happy to have you back..."

They sat in silence on the edge of the bed, embraced in each other's arms. Brie rested her shaved head on Michael's shoulder. Michael kissed Brie on her forehead. They didn't need to speak. Each other's company was enough. It was surreal. Both of them had accepted death. Both of them had looked it in the face. And now they both had what they had longed for.

"Oh, by the way," Brie said with a giggle after a long and beautiful silence. "I had to go down on a woman to pay for protection in jail."

Michael's eyes lit up, his libido surging like a high tide. "You went down on a *woman*?"

"Yep," she said, laughing. "And you know what? It wasn't even that bad..."

SIXTY-SEVEN

It was unusual for Master Stephen Haynes to leave Brisbane.

He rarely needed to. That's what his advisors were for. But on hearing the news of a catastrophic security breach on Terra Carcerem he boarded his personal jet along with his trusted colleague Eric van Bueren and together they headed straight to the island of imprisonment.

He was more than displeased. He was furious. They had notified the Master of the breach about twenty minutes after it had occurred but given him very few details. He had been told it was a category five breach. There were only five categories.

Landing on the airstrip beside Inferno, three Bestia escorted the Master and van Bueren from the jet. As they left the aircraft, they donned oxygen conditioners and followed the soldiers to the bridge between Inferno and Paradiso. Already standing on the bridge was the chief Bestia official, Doctor Wells, along with several staff and soldiers from the Paradiso facility. Doctor Wells was pale and clammy. He looked nauseous, scared. As he stepped forward to greet the leader of the Empire, his words shook with fear.

"I'm so sorry you had to come out here, Master. We are still trying to analyse how this happened."

"Would you mind telling me what *this* is?" the Master asked impatiently, looking down at two bodies on the concrete. One body was female, dressed in the standard issue aqua-blue uniform for Terra Carcerem doctors. She had a charred hole where her face should have been. Liquefied brain pooled beside her lifeless body. The other body was that of a tall Negro. A thick, blue liquid pooled beside him. There was no blood, no obvious wounds, just the pool of the blue, sticky chemical.

"It appears that outlaws have snuck onto the island and taken two prisoners. They killed Eileen here during the attack. They also appear to have opened the plutonium drain on this Bestia."

Master Stephen Haynes' face reddened. His jaw muscles flexed. "This nigger here on the ground is a Bestia?"

"Yes, sir…"

"I thought they were un-fucking-killable?" He raised his voice. "I thought we made the ultimate soldier and you're telling me that some surface-dwelling outlaws killed one?"

"Well, not exactly, sir. The Bestia is not dead. He is suffering from radiation poisoning. He's in toxic shock. With a bit of surgery we should be able to resuscitate him. It was not just any surface-dwelling outlaws though, Master. We have footage. It was Augustus Carter, the Bestia doctor that absconded from Terra Carcerem a year ago."

"Doctor Wells, you're telling me you not only let your colleague escape a year ago, but he came back to kill Eileen and rescue some prisoners?"

Doctor Wells hesitated. He nodded nervously.

"Who were the prisoners?" van Bueren asked, speaking for the first time.

"Well, sir. It was the man sent to us from Aquilonem, the one that raided Gate Eight."

"And…"

"And, well… it was your niece, sir. Brie van Bueren."

"You've got to be shitting me!" van Bueren said, raising his voice. "You let Brie escape? You incompetent piece of shit! How on

Earth did Augustus Carter know they would be here? God, this is a cluster-fuck. How was it timed so flawlessly?"

"And how is this a category five incident?" Master Haynes asked. "The death of a Union doctor and the injury of an expendable Bestia? This is category three at the most."

Doctor Wells hesitated again.

"Well, reviewing the footage, we can see that Augustus Carter had two accomplices, two young men, in fact. Facial recognition software identified one of the young men as Tyson Anderson. He fled from 3rd Sydney West nearly a month ago on the day of his Marriage Lottery. He is a wanted outlaw. The other is not a registered citizen."

"How does a young man escape a sub-plaza in Parramatta and end up on Norfolk Island? And what does that have to do with Brie van Bueren or the fact that this is a category five?"

"Well, Master, the thing is, I don't think they came here for Brie or the Gate Eight man. They came here... for a Bestia..."

"What in God's great Empire do you mean they came here for a Bestia? The Bestia is lying dead on the bridge beside Doctor Myers."

Doctor Wells hesitated, yet again. It was clear he was stalling.

"Talk, you useless sod," Master Haynes yelled.

"Master, they have a device with them. Augustus Carter did something to the influx portal of the other Bestia."

"The *other* Bestia," Van Bueren interjected.

"Yes, sir. They seem to have reprogrammed one and taken it with them. Based on the footage, it seems to answer to Carter now."

Intense silence.

"You mean to tell me, Doctor, that treasonous outlaws now have one of *my* Bestia and that it is now a potential threat to *my* Empire?"

"Well... yes, sir. That's why we called you here. It's a category five breach because there are no Bestia in active duty yet. We've stationed no Bestia outside of Terra Carcerem other than the ten prototype trials. Therefore, it may be difficult for current soldiers to stop him. It could be quite a problem."

"You don't fucking say."

"The other bit of information, which I only just learned, is that the hijacked Bestia, Nine-Thirteen, was also a resident of 3rd Sydney West. Nine-Thirteen was a close associate of Tyson Anderson, the Marriage Lottery deserter."

Master Stephen Haynes stared at Doctor Wells and said nothing. Fire burned from the anger in his eyes. He looked at Eileen Myers, lifeless and stiff. He then looked at the Bestia lying in silent agony.

"Doctor Wells, what is the name of the Bestia standing beside you?"

"This is Six-Twenty Two, sir."

Master Haynes looked at Six-Twenty Two. He was of average build. He had a shaved head and a defined jawline. "Six-Twenty Two," the Master said. "This is my Empire. I am the leader of the Soteria Humanist Union. I am the owner of your worthless existence. Who do you serve?"

"I serve the Humanist Union, sir. I serve you."

"Excellent. Six-Twenty Two, I order you to remove Doctor Wells' left arm."

"Right now?"

"Immediately."

"Without question, sir."

"*No*," Doctor Wells screamed. "Please Master, *please* don't do this."

The Doctor's pleas were futile. Six-Twenty Two stepped towards Doctor Wells with the swift efficiency with which he had been designed. In one rapid movement he grabbed underneath the armpit of Doctor Wells, locking his thumb over the doctor's clavicle. With his other hand he gripped tightly on the doctor's forearm and pulled. Bones cracked and ligaments tore as the doctor screamed in agony. Without so much as a change in Six-Twenty Two's facial expression, he removed Doctor Wells' entire arm and held onto it. Blood spewed from the doctor's shoulder as he dropped to the concrete bridge. He passed out from shock as blood pooled around him.

"Leave him there," ordered Master Haynes. "No one is to touch him. Six-Twenty Two, in five minutes, *if* he is still alive, I would like you to remove his right arm."

"Without question, sir."

"Now to fix this fuck-up, Eric, I would like you to question the staff here. Find out how Augustus Carter escaped twelve months ago. Find out what sort of person he was. Find out where he's been hiding all this time. There is a very high probability that they will return to whatever rock they have been hiding under. I would also like a team of twenty Bestia ready for dispatch *tomorrow*. They will search this entire Empire for Augustus Carter and this Marriage Lottery deserter. I will get my Bestia back, Eric. And you will get that whore of a niece back, too. We should have killed her when we had the chance."

"Absolutely, Master. I will take up residence here on Terra Carcerem. I will not leave until this comedy of errors is rectified. I will begin my interrogations immediately."

"Splendid. I need to return to Brisbane for other matters. I will be back here in two days. I have faith in you, my friend."

"I won't let you down, sir."

SIXTY-EIGHT

ALTHOUGH WE HAD ONLY BEEN ON TERRA CARCEREM FOR THREE hours, the whole process had been draining.

After showing Michael and Brie to their room, I went to lie down and woke up six hours later to the smell of something cooking. I left my sleeping quarters to find Brie in the kitchen alone. She was stirring a range of ingredients in a large pot with a wooden spatula. Her eyes lifted from the pot when I entered.

"Hey," I said as I sat on a steel barstool bolted to the floor beside the kitchen bench.

"Hey, yourself. I hope it's okay that I cook something for everyone. There wasn't really anyone around to ask?"

"Oh, that's fine. Make yourself at home. It's as much mine as it is yours. Where is everyone?"

"Well, I found Eli snoring like a chainsaw in the room beside yours. George is in the bridge doing something with the submarine controls. He frightens me so I left him be. And the old guy…"

"Carter," I interjected. "You can call him Carter. Or Gus."

"Okay. Carter is nowhere to be found in this underwater maze."

"Did you check the lab at the back?"

"I didn't know there was one."

376

"Yeah, he's probably in there creating some outlandish contraption to help bring the Union to its knees."

"What's his deal?" Brie asked. "Like, why is he here with you two? It's an odd match. A young kid, you and this old guy…"

I told Brie what I knew about Carter. I told her about his depression and guilt and his involvement in the Bestia programme. I told her about his solitude during his time on Lord Howe. Brie listened with genuine interest. We spoke at length. We spoke of the Marriage Lottery and sub-plaza life. She told me of her escape from a Brisbane sub-plaza, which in many ways, was not dissimilar to my story. She spoke at length of her friends at T-Town. It sounded like a great place filled with kindness and humanity. It sounded like just the place I had been searching for. Then she told me how the Union had threatened to flatten the jungle to destroy their outlaw community. I told Brie I admired her courage. Brie was a compassionate woman. It was clear in her tone. She had endured so much at the hands of the Union, but it somehow hadn't broken her. She was strong. She was driven. She was admirable.

"It's funny," she said after we had spoken for what felt like a good hour. "At first I wasn't sure about you, Tyson. I mean, you have to admit, you guys being on that island at the exact time we were being dragged naked across to God-knows-where is a strange coincidence."

"The world is full of strange coincidences," I said.

"I suppose so. But when you've been through what I've been through, it's not so easy to trust people. You're actually very much like me. Hopefully, one day we both find our freedom."

"We will, don't you worry about that. We're on our way to our freedom as we speak. We have a Bestia to help us. And I'm sure Carter has a plan. We will be on the other side of the horrible wall in no time. We've made it this far…"

"I really hope you're right."

Carter appeared from the hallway moments after I said his name. He looked even more like a crazed madman than ever before. His grey hair was more dishevelled that it had ever been, most probably from the salt water. His white beard was matted and scraggy. The dark rings under his eyes looked like a strange war paint.

"I have a plan," Carter said with a strange smile. I looked at Brie and grinned.

"I told you he would."

"Where are the others? Where is young Eli? Where is Michael?"

"They're sleeping, Gus."

"Well, go wake them up. We will talk logistics while we eat whatever it is that smells so fantastic."

I offered to round up the others while Brie finished preparing the meal. As I walked down the small corridor towards the bunkrooms, I thought of George alone on the bridge. Instead of turning left towards the bunks, I went to find him.

Pushing open the door I found him playing with the complex touchpad beside the 3-D screen. The submarine controls looked like a random display of lights and buttons. George seemed to be able to navigate through them with ease.

"Hi George," I said timidly, standing behind my robot friend.

He turned with robot rigidity and stared at me with his large black eyes. He said nothing. His emotionless stare intimidated me. The blank facial expression turned to a confused frown, then just as quickly, to a small smirk of familiarity.

"I know you," George said. It was a statement, not a question. "I remember building the wall with you. I have memories of attending church with you. Did we ever surf together?"

I smiled and nodded. "We sure did, man."

My friend was in there somewhere. He continued to look at me, boring into me with those dark, intimidating eyes.

"What is your name?"

"It's me, man. It's Tyson. I can't believe what they have done to you. How did they get you? Why did they take you?"

"I do not have the answers to these questions. There is a great deal of nothing when I try to remember recent events."

"Hey, George, look. For what it's worth, I'm sorry for leaving you behind, man. I know that you don't remember but if I could do it again, I would've asked you to come with me."

"Do what again?"

"Don't worry. Just know that I thought about you a lot. I felt shitty abandoning you like I did. Now anyway, do you want to join us all in the mess? I think Carter wants to talk with all of us."

"Sure. Let me just set our course and activate autopilot. I will be in the messroom in three minutes."

Shortly afterwards I was in the mess with the others. Michael was easy to wake. At the mention of hot food he bounced right out of his bunk. Eli was not so sociable; he was over-tired and short-tempered.

The six of us sat around a large steel table bolted to the floor of the mess while Brie served us large portions of the rich-smelling stew. While the rest of us wasted no time shovelling the food into our mouths, George sat and watched with indifference. He would never again know hunger. He would never know thirst. He would never know fatigue. Oddly out of place but too compliant to say anything, my best friend sat with disciplined rigidity and said nothing.

"So," Carter finally said between mouthfuls. "I have done some basic mapping and I believe we should be able to reach the wall just south of Fiji within three days. The Union mapping software shows there is a maintenance storage facility at the latitude and longitude I have set a course for. From there we can penetrate the wall and head to the island of Hawaii to find salvation."

"Penetrate the wall? How do you propose we penetrate the wall?" Michael asked.

"This question coming from a man who did just that very thing at Gate Eight? Worry not, my new friend. George will sort out the difficulties. As long as you all do what I ask, George should be able to open the maintenance storage facility without too much trouble. It will be guarded, but Union soldiers will be no match for George."

"Hold on a minute," I said. "I thought we would flatten Terra Carcerem? I thought we would stop the Bestia and do our part to stop this evil Empire?"

"Tyson, that would be suicide," Carter responded. "As I have already stated, there is no safe way we can cause damage to that facility without causing harm to ourselves."

"What about the Whore? We can still use it as a giant explosive device, can't we?"

"Not without someone driving back to the island and closing the circuits in the engine. That needs to be done manually. That needs to be done once the submarine is in location. And then we would have ninety seconds to get clear from the impact zone. That is just not possible. What is it we want? What is it you want, Tyson? Do you want freedom? Do you want to know what's on the other side of those walls or do you want to die blowing up Terra Carcerem?"

"I want to stop the Union."

"Boy, I admire your youthful ignorance but think wisely. If we were to destroy Terra Carcerem would it actually change anything?"

"It might. How can you know for certain that it won't?"

"And how can you know for certain that it will?"

"I don't. All I know is that I don't want people being forced to marry strangers. I don't want people living day to day on the surface waiting to die while their superiors eat six course meals. I don't want people being beaten and raped by a corrupt system. I don't want children to grow up in this Empire."

"Tyson, that's very noble of you," Brie said, interrupting. "But these things you speak of have occurred in human civilisations for centuries. Inequality has existed forever. It always will. How about we see if we can get through this maintenance facility and if so we can work out a plan? One step at a—"

"I will do it," George said out of nowhere, speaking over Brie.

"Do *what*?" Eli and I asked in unison.

"Once we have successfully penetrated the wall, I will return with the submarine and close the circuits. I will destroy Terra Carcerem."

I looked at my best friend. Not a single ounce of emotion radiated from his frightening black eyes.

"No one is doing anything of the sort," Carter scolded. "We will continue on course until we're about to approach the wall. Then

George will sneak in for us and disable the security system. Does anyone have a better idea?"

Silence enveloped the table.

"Splendid. Then for the next three days let us rest. We will discuss Terra Carcerem when, and *if*, we get through the wall."

SIXTY-NINE

Master Stephen Haynes sat at the solid mahogany desk in his Brisbane sub-plaza office. It was an antique he had taken from the Governor General estate when the Union rose into power and they introduced martial law.

He had been back from Terra Carcerem for a day and in that time he hadn't stopped thinking about the events that had occurred. His system was failing. Either fear no longer seemed an appropriate motivator for compliance or people were no longer afraid. He had registered sub-plaza citizens removing chips and skipping the lottery. He had outlaws breaking into secure wall facilities. He had prisoners being rescued and Bestia being rewired and stolen. It was time to bring a little fear back into the citizens of Soteria.

The Master's mood was foul. He ordered one of his chief advisors to his office without delay. Hincks arrived only minutes later. As one of the original members of the Forward Foundations Party, Hincks had been a loyal servant of the Master since before the Union came into being. He was on the verge of fifty years old with a poor posture and a round belly. He stood before the mahogany desk and waited for the Master to speak.

"Why has there been so much civil disobedience of late?" the Master finally asked.

"I do not know, Master. I am not privy to what has occurred in other parts of the Empire. I only know of what has occurred in the Eastern Sector. The crime rate percentage still shows ninety-six percent compliance."

"Ninety-six…" The Master was silent. He massaged his beard with his fingers before speaking again. "Do you think citizens still fear the Union? Do you think we have become too soft?"

"I believe the Union creates a sense of fear, sir. I believe that there will always be a small percentage of the population that will try to rise against those that command them. It is part of human nature. A part of the human spirit wants to be free. It is natural."

"To *hell* with the human spirit," the Master said, his tone darkening as he raised his voice. "*To hell with human nature*. Hincks, today we will remind the masses why I am in control and they are not. Today we will show Soteria that compliance is paramount. We don't *need* the citizens. They *need* us."

"Certainly, sir. What do you propose?"

"I want you to shut down the oxygen conditioners to Block 7, Tier Three, 3rd Sydney West. I want you to disable the transporter tunnels and close the seals."

"That will kill over five thousand residents, sir. Many of them being Union employees."

"I am well aware of that, Hincks. Like I said, we do not need them. It is time to remind them of just why they need us."

"Okay, sir. I will see to it immediately. Before nightfall this evening Block 7 will be a tomb."

"Wonderful. Now leave me."

Once the Master was alone in his office, he sat and stared at the wall. Power was like an addiction. He felt adrenalin coursing through his aging veins. He felt like he wanted to order more death and destruction. He wanted to let the Bestia loose on China. He wanted to go on a culling mission of unregistered surface-dwellers. He wanted to bathe in his own self-righteous power.

He wiped sweat from his forehead and walked towards his wall screen.

He wanted to see what the jungle of the Northern Sector now looked like after the bombing. He wanted to make sure his act of cleansing had served its purpose. He wanted to be certain that the chance of another breach of the northern wall was non-existent.

Pulling the Northern Sector up on the large SLD, he used his fingers to drag and zoom across the large screen. The video feed was live, delayed only by a few seconds. To his great pleasure, he looked at the scorched, lifeless earth as he scrolled across the footage of the once-dense jungle. He smiled, sadistic and cruel. Nearing the wall itself, he stopped. His smile dissipated. The satellite image hovered over a small clearing. He zoomed in again.

"What in Satan's Hell!"

The Master stormed over to the monitor on his desk and dialled furiously, muttering insults under his breath. He demanded Hincks return along with two other advisors, Jane Ahrens and Elliot Pews. Both Ahrens and Pews were loyal members of the Union. They shared the same status as Eric van Bueren.

Four minutes later Hincks, Ahrens and Pews stood side by side before him. He was red-faced and pacing back and forth beside his large wall screen.

"I want you to look closely," he said through clenched teeth. "I want you to tell me what you see."

The Master zoomed in on what appeared to be a patch of blackened jungle, one kilometre south of the northern wall. The three advisors stepped towards the screen to get a clearer view. There was obvious movement. There were people moving between the scorched trees. On closer inspection they saw someone appear from a small hole in the ground. It appeared to be some kind of trapdoor in the dirt beside a large blackened tree stump. The person appeared to be holding a Union-issue taser cannon.

"It appears there are surface dwellers moving through the bomb site," Jane Ahrens said, the first to speak. "They appear to have Union weaponry."

"Yes, Jane. That is what it looks like. How on Earth did people survive our *cleansing* of the jungle? This is unacceptable!"

"Sir, if I may. We…"

"Jane, you *may not*! My patience has run thin. I no longer have time for failure."

Without another word Master Stephen Haynes walked behind his grand antique desk and removed a small steel blade from the bottom drawer. The blade had a hand-carved ivory handle. He stepped towards his loyal staff and threw the blade at their feet.

"Unacceptable behaviour requires disciplinary action," The Master said with a sadistic scowl. "One of you may leave my office today. The other two will not."

"But Master, we—"

"You think I am interested in your *pathetic* opinions? You have *all* failed me. Everyone has failed me. Now, who has the courage to remain a Union advisor? Who has the courage to spend another day in *my* Empire?"

Without a word, Hincks dived at the floor and scooped up the blade in a swift motion. He knew how this worked. He turned to ready himself as Pews punched him with a quick right jab to the bridge of his nose. Hincks felt his nose shatter as blood spewed from his nostrils. He dropped the blade just as quickly as he had gained it. Swinging blindly, Hincks began connecting with Pews' body. A few lucky rib shots dropped Pews to the ground. He wheezed in pain as he inhaled, a broken rib making it difficult to breathe.

Hincks wiped the tears from his eyes and the blood from his face just in time to see Jane Ahrens come up beside him and shove the four-inch blade right into his throat. She pushed it all the way to the ivory handle and yanked it out as she roared with animalistic rage. Blood gushed from the gaping hole under his jawline. He tried to speak but fell forward as he attempted to get a word out. He was dead before he hit the floor.

Jane Ahrens spun on the spot. Hincks' blood covered her polyester and latex Union uniform. Her blonde hair was stained red. Pews stood up. He was only a metre away. He clenched his right fist and supported his ribs with his left hand. He stared hard at Ahrens.

Before she could swing the blade Pews stepped forward and with a large backswing, he kicked Ahrens so hard in the groin it lifted her off the ground.

Jane Ahrens screamed as she dropped to the carpeted floor of the office. She curled into the foetal position, clutching between her legs. Pews wasted no time. He dived on his injured colleague and started swing punches, connecting with Jane Ahrens' pretty face. Rage took over and he continued to rain blows. Bone shattered and blood spewed. Ahrens was unconscious after eight or nine punches yet Pews kept them coming, hammering down on her bloodied face. By fifteen punches she was dead. Just to be safe, Pews grabbed the blade from Jane Ahrens' stiff fingers and rammed it into her swollen and bloodied left eye. He sat back and looked at the chaos. He looked at his dead colleagues. He looked at his broken and blood covered knuckles. He looked at Master Stephen Haynes.

"Splendid," the Master said as he raised a micro taser and aimed it at Pews' face.

"Wait, please… Master, I—"

Master Stephen Haynes pulled the trigger and burned a hole right through Pews' surprised face. He slumped forward and collapsed, sprawling over the dead body of Jane Ahrens.

With the calm graciousness of someone attending Sunday morning Mass, Master Stephen Haynes stepped over his dead employees and avoided the pooling blood on his office floor. He made his way to the wall screen, noted the coordinates of the blackened tree stump and dialled Saviour, his chief advisor at Aquilonem.

"Sav," he said through a small microphone built into the screen. "I have just sent you specific coordinates. I believe the men who raided Gate Eight came from this location. I believe the man you captured has friends here. Make sure they all die. If I find even one survivor, you will be accountable. Have I made myself clear?"

"Clear as crystal, sir. Zero survivors."

SEVENTY

Bruce Chadwick sat with Gabbie and a few of the other remaining T-Towners.

They had completed a stocktake of their supplies and the news had crippled the outlaw community. There wasn't enough food and water to last more than a week. Finding more would not be easy. In all directions the jungle above T-Town was charred and lifeless. Blackened vegetation and scorched dirt filled the creek beds and streams. Getting food and water within proximity of their bunker would not be possible.

They knew they couldn't stay at T-Town much longer. Even with that knowledge, it was a difficult truth to accept. They had put their blood, sweat and passion into their small underground home. They had lost so many of their friends for that tunnel and now it was looking as though their only real chance for survival was to abandon their dreams.

"Where do you propose we go?" Gabbie said.

"I've got no idea Gab… Walking around up there with no jungle for cover will be suicide. The sun will bloody-well kill us."

"Can we head south and find somewhere to settle down? Take the Fosform supplies and seek refuge somewhere?"

"What for? To bide our time while we wait to die? Screw that! We're gonna finish this bloody tunnel. It's the only option. We need to send a small group south to find food and water and bring it back. We can make this work."

"How, Bruce. We have no hover-bikes. We have no mode of transport. Even if we were to send people, how will they bring food and water back? With their hands? Enough to feed all of us? No, that's madness. I think we need to evacuate T-Town."

"We're not leaving, Gab."

"In fairness, Bruce, that's not a decision you can make on your own. I feel we need to address our friends and call a meeting. It needs to be democratic. If not, then we are no better than the Union."

"Okay, okay. You're bloody right, Gab. Let's do this. I can feel it, though. People are bloody scared. People will want to leave. I tell you what though. We can never dig another tunnel like this. We will never have access to Fosform like we have had before. Something happened when Brie Kallas left. The Union are onto us."

"Save your speech for everyone else, Bruce."

Gab got up and disappeared down one of the dimly lit corridors. Bruce sat alone and poured himself the last cup of Whooze. He knocked it back in a quick swig and shivered from the potency.

Minutes later Gabbie reappeared with a small crowd of dirty, frightened T-Towners. She had asked them to join Bruce in the communal room to discuss their limited options. Silence and fear replaced the once vibrant homely atmosphere of their outlaw community. The inescapable smell of burnt wood and smoky air had replaced the hearty smell of stew bubbling over the stove.

T-Town's total population had dropped to nineteen. They could all fit on the crude wooden benches beside the food preparation tables. No longer did the T-Town community need to squeeze from wall to wall to meet in the same place. The situation was dire. Everyone in the room knew it. No one had even bothered to dig the tunnel for the last two days. They knew there was no point.

"So guys, it pains me to say this but..." Bruce paused,

distracted. He looked down the dark corridor towards the entrance where T-Tree had once stood, straining to listen.

"Is anyone up top?" Bruce asked the room.

"No one," Robin replied. "Everyone here."

Then they appeared.

Out of the darkness of the corridor, Union soldiers flooded into the room. They wore full-face oxygen conditioners and brandished shiny new taser cannons. T-Town residents shrieked. Screams echoed around the small room as the outlaws tripped over themselves trying to get away. Seven soldiers had stepped through the dark hallway and formed a semicircle at the southern end of the cavern. It was a bottleneck at the other end of the room. Nineteen people trying to fit through a narrow hand-dug corridor was impossible. Bruce Chadwick stood still and stared across the room.

"Come and get it, you filthy Union dogs," he whispered through clenched teeth.

The soldiers made their move. In unison they took two steps forward and fired their taser cannons in precise synchronisation. The room lit up with bright blue blasts. Bruce was the first to get hit. A taser blast took his left cheek clean off, melting half his face. It gave the appearance of a sadistic grin. The second blast caught him in the chest. He dropped to the ground with a fist-sized hole going right through his torso.

Chaos followed. Manic screaming accompanied the dropping bodies. Taser blasts fired in rapid succession as T-Towners died on the dirty ground. Most of the outlaw community was shot trying to escape down the corridor. It was a heartless massacre, a perfectly executed Union cleansing.

Robin was one of the first down the corridor. He escaped the onslaught. Sprinting through the dim tunnel, he reached the equipment store unharmed. He grabbed an AR-15 assault rifle and slammed a magazine in, loading the weapon. His heart pounded. His forehead was wet with sweat. He knew all of his comrades were dead.

It was now or never and never wasn't an option.

Leaping out of the storeroom, Robin began firing the rifle. The bullets ricocheted off the walls, bouncing with unpredictability. Running down the corridor, he sprayed bullets at the semi-circle of soldiers. Two dropped to the ground, blood spewing from gaping holes in their stomachs. Robin fired maniacally, spraying the intruders with bullets. He made direct contact with two soldiers. They remained standing, unharmed. It was almost as if the bullets bounced right off them.

"Impossible," Robin whispered as he continued to fire. He raised the rifle and aimed at a soldier's face. He fired the weapon and shattered the full-face conditioning mask as bullets impacted the soldier's smug grin.

There was no blood.

There was no screaming.

Chunks of skin hung from the soldier's jaw, yet he remained standing, staring back at Robin with a callous smile. The grinning soldier stepped forward and threw a nuclear shock-ball across the body-filled room. It landed within a metre of Robin's feet, wedged between two bodies.

Robin didn't even have time to flinch. The shock-ball exploded, swallowing the hallway in a thick fireball. Robin was blown from his feet, thrown across the room and engulfed by white flame. The smell of burning flesh filled the corridors of T-Town.

The human soldiers made their way back up to the surface to scout the surrounding area. Two Bestia walked through the smoky halls looking for survivors. They fired taser rounds at every lifeless body, just to ensure no one lived through the onslaught. After fifteen minutes of searching the underground bunker for survivors, they joined their comrades on the surface.

T-Town was a tomb.

There were no survivors.

SEVENTY-ONE

I stood on the bridge with George.

In the two days since leaving Terra Carcerem I had endeavoured to make an effort with him. I wanted him to remember our friendship. I wanted him to feel something. There on the bridge, as his memories slowly seeped back, he finally felt something. It wasn't what I had expected, though. I wanted him to feel friendship, compassion. I wanted him to feel happiness. He felt neither.

"I remember now," he said, monotone and quiet. "It was your fault."

That took me off guard. "What was *my* fault?"

"This! You're the reason they took me. You're the reason they made me this way. I remember now. They tortured me to find you. You escaped on the day of your Marriage Lottery. They left me in a cage on the surface. They wanted answers from me…"

"Man, I'm so sorry. Like I said, I wish I had asked you to come."

"Well, you didn't, Tyson."

George's face still lacked expression. Despite the eerie lack of emotion, I could sense resentment tainting his words. Despite the monotone, he sounded bitter.

"I wish you could see it from my perspective, George. I needed to leave. I took a huge risk. Hell, I didn't even know if I would survive the night. I couldn't put that burden on you. It was my demons I ran from. I thought it was selfish to ask you to come. I thought it was selfish to make you an accomplice to my treason. I thought it was selfish to bring you into my shit."

"And look what happened, anyway. I would have been better off coming with you. If only you knew what I went through. If only you knew what I felt."

"So, tell me, man. Speak to me. We are best friends. You can confide in me."

"You say that. I believe I cannot confide in you. I believe I cannot confide in anyone. I follow orders from Augustus Carter. That's it. I am a Bestia now. I remember everything now. Bestia do not require friendship."

"Who says?"

"My software, Tyson. We do not require social interaction to perform duties."

"Fuck your duties," I said, tears welling in my eyes. "And fuck your software. We were friends. We spoke about everything. You said you have those memories back so surely there is a part of you that remembers the feelings?"

"I said I have the memories, not the feelings. It is difficult for me to feel anything. It is not part of my programming to *feel*. That is a human trait. Humans are obsolete. Humans will soon be irrelevant."

"So... what? You're not my friend anymore?"

"I didn't say that."

"So you are?"

"I didn't say that either. I remember it was because of you they tortured me. I remember it was because of you they turned me into this. I remember I was angry. I cursed you. I blamed you. I still blame you, but what's done is done. I am Bestia. I will no longer be the George Clarkson that worked with you building the wall. I have those memories, yes, but they are just images. They are not connected to any emotion. If you are waiting for me to re-learn emotion, then you will wait forever. I am Bestia."

"So what does all that mean?"

"It means I am here with you now. It means I will help you find your freedom. I will serve Augustus Carter loyally but we are not friends. Friend is the incorrect word. We exist together. That is all."

The sealed door behind us beeped as Carter entered the bridge. He looked at me and noticed my distress. He looked at George and saw the same expressionless gaze we had all come to know.

"Everything okay?" Carter asked.

"Everything is fine," George responded. "Submarine functionality is at ninety-eight percent. The ocean current is six knots easterly. Distance to target is four hundred and eighty-three kilometres."

"I meant is everything okay with you two? I'm sure there is some catching up to do."

"It's fine," I said, my words thick with bitterness. "I'm just leaving."

I walked past Carter and wiped a tear from my face. I didn't want him to see me upset. It embarrassed me. It annoyed me. The burden of guilt was hard to bear and feeling so emotional when George didn't feel a thing, made me feel even worse. Carter sensed my sorrow and followed me out into the corridor, leaving George alone to control the Whore.

"Tyson, what pains you?"

"Man," I said shaking my head. "You said George would come back to his normal self. You said reprogramming him would make him the same. He's a fucking computer. He cannot feel anything. He said they do not program him to have emotions, ever!"

"Yes, I knew this may happen. Tyson, you need to understand that I wrote that software in primitive conditions. At least I could override the Union programming. Is it not better that he is here? Even if he is not the close friend you once had?"

"I'm not so sure, Carter."

"Well, think of it this way. He may never share the same bond with you he once had, but at least he is here. There must be a part of you that's content knowing where he is, knowing he is safe. You will not lose sleep wondering about his fate."

"Yeah, but the whole reason they took him and turned him into a fucking machine is because they were looking for me. If I hadn't left, then he would still be the George that I knew."

"You can't look at it that way. If you had not left, everything would be different. If you had not left, you would be married and depressed. If you had not left Eli might be dead. If you had not left, Brie and Michael would be Bestia by now. I'm not saying things happen for a reason but what's done is done. I empathise with you, I do, but George is a Bestia. At least he serves us. I understand it pains you to know that your relationship will never be the same but to put it in perspective, you abandoned him. You accepted the fact that you would never see him again. You knew the day you left that you said goodbye to everyone in your life, George included. You cannot now turn around and feel upset that your bond is gone. It was pure chance that he was on Terra Carcerem at the same moment as us. I would take that for what it is."

Carter was right. The moment I left the sub-plaza I abandoned George. That was my choice. Not his. I couldn't pick and choose the amount of weight I wanted to place on our friendship. Friendship didn't work when it was convenient for one person. I could see that now. I guess, like always, I was being selfish. My whole dash for freedom was selfish. Leaving 3rd Sydney West was selfish. Asking Eli to come with me was selfish. Being upset because of what has happened to George was selfish. And you know what? I was okay with it.

To add to my selfishness, a part of me wished George wasn't there. A part of me wished we had hijacked some other Bestia. It was harder on me knowing that my friend was in there behind those black eyes. It was harder on me knowing it was my fault. This was Soteria. This was a world where you needed to be selfish. Being self-less didn't help anyone. Being selfless would not get me on the other side of those walls. I needed to keep my priorities in line. I needed to get on the other side of those walls.

I left Carter standing in the hallway and went off to be alone with my selfishness.

I didn't want to talk to anybody.

SEVENTY-TWO

THE NEXT DAY WENT BY WITHOUT INCIDENT.

I had shaken my selfish blues. George was fine. He didn't have emotions, so it's not like he would hold a grudge. He was ambivalent. He always would be. If I learned that and accepted it, then we would get along fine.

I spent more time with Brie, Michael and Eli. Brie's swelling had subsided. Even though she still had purple bruising covering much of her face and short stubble for hair, I could now see how attractive she was. It was also clear she was head over heels in love with Michael Butcher. I mean, why wouldn't she be? He was strong, handsome and tall. He was a genuine guy, polite and thoughtful. He kept asking what he could do to help. He wasn't the kind of guy that was there for a free ride. The two of them grew on me. While I got along well with Eli and we had formed a brotherly bond, it was good to have a few other people around. It broke up the monotony and changed the dynamics of our group.

With or without monotony, the mood had shifted by mid afternoon. We knew we were only hours away from the wall. Brie paced back and forth with a gleam of hatred in her eyes. She wanted vengeance, pure and primitive. Eli needed to get on solid ground.

His cabin fever had well and truly set in. There was only so much conversation and 8-ball that could keep him from slipping into insanity.

As we neared the wall, Carter had collected all the weaponry available on the Whore and laid it on the table in front of us. We had three taser cannons, two micro tasers and a handful of shock-balls. We set all taser cannons to maximum power.

Just after we packed the weaponry and supplies into waterproof dry bags, the Whore came to a stop half a kilometre from the main-tenance dock bordering the eastern wall. Carter didn't want to get much closer. He knew that certain Union facilities had a range of security measures including underwater motion detectors and surface level weaponry. It would be easier for George to sneak through the motion sensors alone. Now was his time to shine.

Carter's plan seemed simple enough. George would enter the facility via the water and disarm the security system, thus allowing us to take the Whore right up to the facility's dock. Once George had successfully neutralised the guards, we were on the home stretch. That was it. George seemed calm. Adrenaline already coursed through my veins.

"Let's do it," George said with indifference.

Entering the divers' dock, George looked back at the five of us huddled together in the steel hallway. He had received a radio code from Carter. When he had breached the facility, he would notify us via a closed channel.

His black eyes stared at us. He almost smiled. "See you soon," was all he said as he closed the inner seal to the dock. Once closed, he typed in the sequence for the outer seal and the dock filled with murky and poisonous tropical water.

The five of us watched in silent awe as George continued to stare back at us until the cell had filled with water. He raised his hand and waved before typing the outer seal code into the wall-mounted touch screen. Through the reinforced glass we saw the outer seal open and watched George calmly step out into the gloomy depths. The outer seal closed, leaving us staring through the glass at an empty cell.

"Now what?" Eli asked.

"Now we wait," Brie responded with vengeance in her words.

The time went slowly. Brie paced back and forth. Michael seemed calm. As usual, Eli fidgeted and Carter was off somewhere else. An hour had passed since George had disappeared into the murky blue ocean and still nothing.

———

SITTING INSIDE THE FACILITY, ATKINS, A TIRED AND AGEING SOLDIER watched the satellite feed before him on several screens.

He yawned and sipped a cold coffee. The Union had built the maintenance facility to store machinery and equipment capable of fixing and replacing sections of the wall without the need to transport equipment to the wall by boat. It was a measure designed to save time. The wall-builders could fly out to the facility to find all the equipment already on site. There were over two hundred of these facilities at various intervals along the wall.

Most citizens of Soteria had no idea the maintenance facilities existed. Augustus Carter wouldn't have known the facility existed if it wasn't for the software already loaded into the mapping system on the submarine. Because of the secrecy of the facilities, being rostered on for security was one of the most monotonous tasks in the Union Army. Nothing ever happened. Soldiers did ten-day rotations and in those ten days the soldiers sat around, drank coffee and played cards. Because the role was low impact, The Union rostered soldiers unfit for active duty elsewhere. They were the older registered soldiers. Often with injury or illness.

Ten soldiers manned the facility. Atkins included. As he refilled his coffee mug, a red light started flashing in the bottom corner of one of the many screens before him. It was a motion sensor. It was not uncommon for the motion sensor to go off, often the cause being curious sea life. Atkins rotated the camera feed to bring up the images from the underwater camera facing dead west.

He knocked over his coffee mug as he lunged to his feet.

"What in God's name...?" Atkins roared as he slammed down

on the alarm. "Guys, get here now!" he yelled down an empty hallway.

As his peers joined him in the control room, they stood in silence and watched a man wade casually past the camera lens underwater. He wore no diving equipment. He wore no oxygen cylinder. He just walked along the sea floor, calm and frightening.

"Impossible," Atkins said. "What in all of Soteria is that thing?"

"Who knows, who cares," one of the youngest of the stationed soldiers responded. "They're out there and we are in here. He cannot get inside."

"What makes you so sure?"

"Because we built these facilities to keep intruders out."

"Yeah, but the weapons are on the *surface* of the water. The turrets are to keep boats away. We have nothing for the sea floor. Just to play it safe, I'm sending an alert back to the Eastern Sector. I'm sending the video footage. Maybe someone back in Brisbane can tell us why there is a human being walking around under water. This is madness…"

As Atkins sent the alert to the main control centre back in Brisbane Central, the group of soldiers heard a deafening crunch as another alarm sounded. An orange light flashed in the concrete ceiling above them, accompanied with the high-pitched wail of a siren.

"Shit," one of the older soldiers said to Atkins. "There's been a breach. That fucking thing is inside. Get the tasers!"

———

GEORGE SWAM UP UNDERNEATH ONE OF THE DOCKING CELLS BUILT into the wall and pulled himself onto the docking platform. He studied the design of the intruder-proof entrance. The blueprints of the door's design were on file in a Union database, so he too had that blueprint uploaded into his software. He therefore knew its weakness. With little effort, he pulled the steel door straight off its hinges. He let go of the heavy chunk of bullet-proof metal and watched it sink to the sea floor.

George stepped inside the dim corridor. Four armed soldiers stood at the far end of the corridor waiting. They were frightened. They looked down the corridor at George, their taser cannons trembling in their hands. Water pooled at George's feet, dripping off his Union clothing. He displayed an eerie smirk.

"Hello," he said.

Without waiting for a command, the frightened soldiers fired. Taser blasts hit George in the chest with little effect. He didn't even move from his path. With the speed of a turf-ball athlete, George ran forward through the oncoming blasts of compressed electricity and was on the first soldier before he could react. With one arm, George threw the frightened soldier fifteen metres down the length of the corridor. He slammed against the concrete wall with such velocity that his neck snapped on impact. The other three stopped firing for a moment in shocked disbelief. Then George was on them. He kicked hard at the knee of one, snapping the soldier's leg in half, while lunging at another. With one hand George grabbed the soldier at the throat and snapped his neck with the flick of his fingers.

Two were dead. One wailed on the floor with his leg dangling from the knee and the other turned to run. George picked up a dead soldier's taser cannon and fired two shots to the back of the retreating soldier's head. He fell forward as brain oozed from the hole in his skull. Calmly, George walked over to the screaming, defenceless soldier with the dangling leg and stomped on his head. Skull crunched and brain mushed under the power of George's inhuman strength.

SEVENTY-THREE

Six remained.

Atkins watched the slaughter take place through the video feed in the control room.

"We're in deep trouble," he said to his peers, staring in awe beside him. "That thing is no human. We need to get out of here. Now!"

"How? The next boat isn't due back until Tuesday. The life rafts are at the dock. How can we get past that... *thing*? Man, we are in trouble."

"Well, let's blow that fucking thing up. Quick, get a shock ball and throw it down the corridor..."

The younger soldier ran behind them, his steps nervous. He reached the gun cabinet and withdrew two small nuclear shock balls. He entered the universal Union arming code into each one and ran to the control room door. Through the camera monitors, Atkins watched the beast walk casually down the quiet corridor, leaving a bloody footprint in his path from the chunks of brain clinging to his shoe.

Opening the door, the young soldier launched both shock balls in George's direction and just as quickly closed the door. George saw them approach. As they rolled towards him he kicked one back towards the control room, his motor skills and hand-eye coordination being better than even the most talented sportsman. He was not fast enough for the second. White-hot light exploded metres from him. The resulting fireball swallowed the hallway and wrapped itself around George's expressionless face.

The shock ball he had kicked fell short of the control room and exploded in the hallway. The entire facility shook as orange flames danced down the corridor. A large section of steel ceiling collapsed and wedged itself between the hallway wall and the control room door, trapping the remaining six soldiers inside the control room.

Atkins and his colleagues had nowhere to go. Smoke oozed into the control room through the seals in the doors. Through the camera screens Atkins saw George appear from the grey smoke.

"How in God's name can that thing still be alive?"

George's clothes were now nothing more than burnt rags. Chunks of his skin were either charred or missing. His hair was charred. His boots had melted. Yet he continued walking down the corridor with the same expressionless face.

Reaching the fallen debris, George looked around the damaged corridor, analysing the situation. The solid steel beam blocked the opening seal to the control room. The beam had trapped any soldiers inside the small room.

George looked up at the ceiling. He knew what he needed to do. On his tippy toes, he reached up and tore open the alloy housing that concealed all the facilities circuitry entering the control room. Once open, George looked at an intertwined bunch of cables, pipes and wires, no doubt providing power and oxygen to the control room. He grabbed hold of the bunch of cables and tore them all from their position in the alloy housing.

The control room went black.

George then grabbed the large cylindrical pipe and snapped it in half. Compressed air bellowed out into the surrounding corridor, forming a thick mist that hovered below the ceiling.

The control room lost its supply of conditioned oxygen. The six remaining soldiers were trapped in the pitch-black, stale air. With no conditioned air they would be dead before the day was through.

George turned back down the hallway. He reached the only dead soldier the flames hadn't consumed and calmly removed the clothing and boots. Just as calmly, he dressed himself, leaving a lifeless corpse sprawled naked in the corridor. Despite his lack of emotion, as a programmed soldier of the world's proudest army, somewhere in George's software was a modicum of modesty. He wouldn't walk around naked if he did not need to.

Finding his way back to the damaged dock, George logged into the wall screen beside the door and dialled into the right frequency with the radio code supplied by Carter.

"Carter," he said in his deep, monotone voice. "Carter, are you there?"

"Yes, we receive you, George. Loud and clear."

"I have neutralised the facility. You may bring the submarine to the south dock door. I have disabled the weaponry."

SEVENTY-FOUR

Eric van Bueren had made himself at home in the few days he had been at Terra Carcerem.

He walked around the facility with a sense of importance and self-righteousness. He had interviewed all of Carter's colleagues and previous associates, and studied Carter's diary entries and laboratory findings.

He was on his way to Carter's old room when his presence was requested in the Paradiso control room. They told him to hurry. By the time he arrived, three Union doctors stood beside the control panel with sullen faces. Their cheeks were drained of colour. It was clear they knew something Eric van Bueren did not.

One of the Union staff pressed a small green button beside the large wall screen and a live image of Master Stephen Haynes came up on the screen. He looked furious, crazed. His sunken eyes were bloodshot.

"Eric, I trust you have found some answers?"

"Well, sir. We have made progress. I have learnt a great deal about this Augustus Carter."

"Eric, I am on my way to Terra Carcerem as we speak." Impatient fury tainted his words. "I am in the jet. I'll be there within the hour. I want a team of Bestia armed and ready to go. This will stop right now!"

"What will stop, sir?"

"Watch this footage. You tell me what you see."

The image on the wall screen of Master Haynes was replaced with grainier, black and white security footage. It showed a person walking calmly through murky water without breathing apparatus. The feed then jumped to another set of images. The same person walked through the corridor of an unknown Union facility and took taser blasts to the chest, only to disarm and graphically execute several Union soldiers.

The Master returned to the screen.

"Don't you know what this is?"

"I assume it is most probably the missing Bestia, sir. Where is this footage from?"

"This is from a maintenance facility on the Eastern Walls. Dock Sixty-Three. South of Fiji!"

"Shit."

"Shit, indeed. I believe they will attempt to escape Soteria. With a *motherfucking Bestia*!"

"Sir…"

"I want a team of ten Bestia ready to board my jet when I get there. We need to stop these traitors…"

Van Bueren attempted to respond and was met with a blank screen and radio silence.

Fifty-three minutes later the Master's personal jet came to a silent landing on the runway beside Paradiso. Eric van Bueren emerged from the large double doors at the entrance to the facility with an oxygen conditioner strapped to his face. An entourage of doctors followed him out into the open air. They too all wore portable, single use oxygen conditioners.

Master Stephen Haynes appeared from the side of the jet without one. He looked furious. He looked stressed. Worry was etched into the creases on his forehead. Dark rings bordered his angry eyes.

"Sir," van Bueren called out from the walkway. "You cannot be out here without a conditioner."

"Shut up, you fool," The Master snapped back at his trusted friend and colleague. "Right now, I don't have time to die. Now where in God's name are these Bestia? I want blood…"

"Come this way, sir."

SEVENTY-FIVE

Michael and Brie entered the maintenance facility first.

Armed with Union weaponry, they jumped across the void between the open submarine docking cell and the damaged facility dock. Murky seawater lapped at their feet as they landed on the warped steel platform before entering the facility. The platform was bent out of shape from George's forced entry. The thick steel was twisted, morphed like abstract art. Eli and I bounced across the void between docks. Gus wasn't quite so nimble. He attempted to clear the void between the submarine and the dock and fell and few inches short. Eli and I grabbed him by the shoulders as his feet slipped into the cold water beneath us.

George greeted us in the hallway. He looked grotesque. Charred skin. No hair. Exposed titanium reinforcements. Brie flinched as she looked him up and down.

"It's okay," he said with indifference. "Do not let my appearance concern you. I am the same Bestia I was an hour ago."

Despite his attempt to comfort us, Brie seemed wary of George. She had justifiable trust issues.

"Can you smell it, guys?" I said with excitement.

"What? The smell of burnt flesh and death," Eli responded.

"No, dickhead. The smell of victory! The smell of freedom! We're so close now. We just need to get on the other side of this facility and we're no longer in Soteria."

Those words were heavy. Just saying them gave me goose bumps.

No longer in Soteria.

What I had dreamt of for so long was now only metres away.

The six of us gathered in the small corridor. Like Brie, I think George's appearance unnerved the rest of us. His charred flesh was unsightly. As usual, Eli seemed to bounce off the walls. He was fidgeting. He was pacing. I wasn't sure if it was nervousness or excitement, but I knew we needed to act fast. Idle time was something we did not have.

"So," Carter said. "From here we need to locate the escape rafts. All facilities have them. The only issue is that they're stored on the dock to gain access to Soteria waters on the western side of the wall. There will be no dock on the outside wall."

"So how do you intend on getting this escape raft on the other side?" Michael asked. "There's no point escaping back into the sea we have just come from."

"I hadn't worked that out yet. I'm open to suggestions?"

Silence filled the small corridor. Then Eli spoke. "Hey Gus, is there any way we can get to the top of the wall?"

"Possibly. I daresay that there is a helicopter pad on top of the wall to transport staff in and out. Why, what do you propose?"

"We need to find a rope or a cable long enough to attach to the raft on the dockside and we can pull the raft up and over the wall, then lower it down the other side."

"And how do you propose we lift a life raft for thirty metres? The thing probably weights half a ton."

"We have him…" Eli pointed at George.

He had a point. George could help us pull the boat up and over the monstrous wall.

"Okay," I said. "Good idea, Eli. We need to split up. I'll go with Brie and Michael and find the raft. You go with Gus and George and find the top. Hopefully, on route you come across something that's long enough."

"Cool," Brie said, smiling through broken teeth. "Let's do it."

Endorphins coursed through my veins as I took off down the corridor with Brie and Michael. Although there were still several Union soldiers trapped inside a small room only twenty metres from me, I felt like we were on the home stretch. I looked at Brie. For the first time since meeting her I saw a different look in her eyes. She was glowing with excitement. The desire to succeed had energised her. Like me, she knew the end was close.

It didn't take long for us to locate two small escape rafts hanging from pulley winches in a storage room beside the docks. I use the term *escape raft* loosely. The boats were identical; about four metres long, made of a lightweight alloy and each had an outboard motor with a propeller. They even had a small canopy over the seating to protect passengers from the damaging sun's rays.

It was clear no one had ever used the rafts as a thick layer of dust coated the shell. I read those four infamous words printed onto the side of the hull.

"Fuck the Union," Brie mumbled, noticing me read their slogan.

"Yep. Pretty soon the Union will all be in the past."

"I really hope you're right," Brie said, smiling at me through cracked teeth.

Michael located the electronic device used to lower the winches. He opened the control pad on the dock wall and started lowering the closest boat. The cable groaned under the weight of the boat as it came down to the water's surface. Once down, we inspected the interior of the craft. There were some buoyancy devices, rescue flares and some Union ration packs stored in a steel box bolted to the back of the craft. Brie opened the box and pulled out some tinned food, water canisters and a few shots of Fosform Five.

"I think we should lower the other one and take the rations from both. Better to have as much shit as we can. We don't really know how long we will be out there."

Ten minutes later and we had the rations from both boats

secured inside the steel storage box. Pulling the chain at the front of the boat, the three of us guided it along the concealed internal waterway and out into the open water beside the wall that kept us from our freedom. Now it was time to wait.

———

Eli bounced up a steel stairwell at the far end of the facility. It didn't take him long to locate the door that opened out onto the top of the wall. By the time he reached the outside air he was panting. Sweated beaded on his brow. Augustus Carter was quite a way behind the excited youth.

Eli looked east, admiring the waters outside of Soteria for the first time in his life. He looked beyond what he had previously accepted would be the walls that would surround him until his death. The great blue expanse and wide unknown was right there. He breathed in the poisonous air and grinned.

"We're coming your way," he whispered to the open ocean.

George and Carter appeared behind Eli. He turned to see George with a coiled cable hanging over his shoulder.

"This will be adequate," he said.

Eli ran past the helicopter pad and leaned out over the edge of the railing. He looked down thirty metres below at the seawater lapping against the cold concrete wall. He could make out the broken dock entrance where George had ripped the door off. He saw nothing else.

"They're not there," said Eli with concern.

"Patience, young man. Give them time."

"Okay, let's see if that cable will be long enough. George, lower it down the wall. Hopefully, it will reach the bottom."

George stood beside Eli and while holding one end of the cable he let the coil go. It slid down the wall and untangled itself as it fell. The other end of the cable stopped about a metre short of the waters surface.

"Shit! Do you think that will be enough?" Eli asked. Doubt dampened his excitement.

Before Eli got a response, he watched Michael and Brie emerge from the dock seal, pulling the boat out through shallow water as they traversed the warped steel platform.

———

I held the back of the vessel in place and looked up. The cable seemed a little short. It needed to attach to a welded tie-down handle at the bow of the boat. As we pushed the boat closer it became apparent that the cable would not reach.

"It's too short," I yelled up to the others above. "We need another half a metre. Maybe more."

George looked around. He examined the lip on the concrete edging. He clenched his fist and punched the lip to determine its strength. With a light punch, the concrete didn't budge. He punched it harder and the concrete cracked under his inhuman force.

"It should hold," he said.

George hung out over the edge of the concrete wall and lowered himself, head first towards the lapping water below. He hooked his feet on the lip of the concrete edging and extended his arms below his head. Hanging upside down, with only his toes clinging to the edge of the concrete wall, the cable reached the water. I couldn't believe it. I watched with nervousness, half expecting his feet to slip and see George plummet head first into the water below.

George's upside-down body length gave us the extra cable we needed. Michael tied it around the handle and looked up. "It's good to go," he called out.

With as much effort as it took to tie a shoelace, George pulled the boat out of the water. Still hanging by his toes, he dragged the boat up the wall. The grinding noise that the hull made as it slid its way up the concrete sent my body into goose bumps.

I looked at Michael and Brie. They too stood in awe, captivated at the sight. They too held their breath with nervous anticipation.

"Come on guys," I said. "Let's get up there. Time to leave this rotten place for good."

SEVENTY-SIX

MASTER STEPHEN HAYNES HADN'T EVEN BEEN ON TERRA CARCEREM for an hour.

Before him stood a team of ten brand new Bestia, fresh out of software updates in Paradiso. They were all dressed in Union combat uniform and equipped with taser cannons slung over their shoulders and combat knives in the sheaths on their belts.

"Listen here," Master Haynes said to the emotionless warriors. "You're about to board a helicopter. We're sending you to a facility overrun by traitors. They are the enemy. You are to destroy all enemies. I want to see blood. I want to see victory. I want you to bring back their heads!"

On a large control screen before them an image of Augustus Carter appeared. He looked younger. He looked healthier. He had shorter hair and a manicured beard.

"See this man," Master Haynes said. "I want his head!"

The image changed to an employment photo of a young Union administrator.

"See this man. Tyson Anderson, 636-124. He abandoned the Empire on his day of the lottery. I want his head!"

The image changed to a recent photo of George Clarkson after his Bestia update.

"This one will be interesting. He is one of you. He is Bestia. He is Nine-Thirteen. He is a treasonous traitor, a disgrace to the Empire. I want his head!"

The image switched to a photo of Brie van Bueren, taken some time ago. She looked young and fit. She looked healthy and happy. Her smile was captivating, her eyes hypnotic.

"See this woman. I want her *alive*. We will teach this treasonous whore the meaning of pain. We will show her what betrayal feels like. I say again, I want her alive... Now get out of my sight and go protect my Empire."

In perfect synchronisation, the ten Bestia left the facility and made their way outside to the aircraft terminal. A large combat helicopter idled on the pad, its blades already spinning. They boarded the aircraft and harnessed themselves. There was no tension. There was no pre-battle anxiety or nervousness. There was no ferocity or anger. All ten sat in silence with a resting heart rate. They were about to do exactly what the Union had programmed them to do. They were about to destroy the enemy.

Back inside Paradiso, Master Stephen Haynes sat with Eric van Bueren. He poured a glass of malt whisky for each of them into crystal tumblers. Without a toast he put the tumbler to his lips and tilted the glass.

"Eric," he said, pouring another glass straight away. "I will not leave this place until I have their heads. Neither of us are leaving until your niece is begging for mercy. I don't care if we cut off a finger at a time. She *will* beg for mercy. These last few weeks have drained me, Eric. Your niece has drained me. These traitors have drained me. If word gets out that registered citizens are abandoning their registration chips and fleeing the Empire, there could be a revolt. There could be an attempted revolution. I don't want the news of this wall breach leaving this island."

"Absolutely, sir. We will stay right here until we're satisfied with the result."

They both swigged their whisky and poured another glass.

"To victory!"

SEVENTY-SEVEN

BRIE, MICHAEL AND I REACHED THE TOP OF THE WALL AT THE SAME time George pulled the boat up and over the inside rail.

I sucked in large mouthfuls of much-needed air. The muscles in my legs burned from the stair climb. Michael and Brie looked equally fatigued. Eli stood beside George, watching in awe as he carried the four-metre vessel on his shoulder. He paced across the helicopter pad and hung the boat over the outside rail of the wall. Without changing his facial expression George lowered the boat towards the water below, gripping the cable with one hand and feeding the cable one slow metre at a time through his inhuman grip.

I looked out to the waters I had longed for. I looked at the eastern horizon. For the first time since building the walls when I was seventeen, I looked at freedom. I looked at neutral waters. I looked at hope. I looked at a horizon that the Empire didn't control. I looked at my future, my grey space. I realised I was grinning from ear to ear. Tears welled in my eyes as my heart rate pounded with excitement.

We are going to make it.

Then I looked at the others.

413

Eli had been so strong throughout everything. I wouldn't be standing there on top of the wall if it weren't for him. I thought of our escape from Sydney. I thought about the massacre we left on the Wife. I thought about his infectious sarcasm and his will to survive. He stared at George, watching him closely as he lowered our getaway vessel.

I looked at Michael and Brie. Michael had his arm around Brie's waist. He was her rock, her desire to survive. Her bruises, her shaved head and her broken teeth were a testament to that desire. They looked at each other and smiled with sincerity and warmth.

Then I scanned the helicopter pad for Carter.

"Hey, Eli," I said, looking at the empty concrete beside us. "I thought Carter was up here with you."

Eli took his eyes off George for the first time. "He was. He was here just before you guys arrived."

I looked at Brie. "Did you see him on your way up?"

"No, not at all. I was with you."

"What the hell? How can he just disappear?"

"He hasn't disappeared, Tyson. Let's just go find him."

I left the helicopter pad and made my way back down the steel stairs with Eli right behind me. I had a strange feeling that something wasn't right. My excitement waned. Concern rose from the pits of uncertainty.

"Maybe he's just gone to the dunny," Eli said, unconvincingly.

We reached the corridor at water level. There was an eerie silence. Eli called out his name only to hear his own voice echo down the damaged corridor.

"Surely he's just getting provisions out of the Whore. He must be in there."

We ran down the corridor, leaping over dead soldiers as we went. We reached the warped metal platform by the dock. I turned the corner to step out over the small void separating the platform and the Whore.

I stopped.

I stared out into a great expanse of still blue water. Scanning the horizon, I saw nothing but the open ocean. Fear clawed at my back.

"The Whore has gone," I whispered, as much to myself as to Eli, who stood beside me in silent shock.

"It can't be. Gus wouldn't leave us. Something is wrong."

I stood for a moment, unsure what to do next. Surely Carter wouldn't abandon us? We had been through so much with him. He had become an integral part of our group. He had provided the words of wisdom. He was the voice of reason.

"Something's not right."

Unsure what to do, we turned around and ran back along the length of the death-filled corridor and up the flight of stairs. Brie and Michael were standing with George, all looking over the edge of the concrete rail.

"The boat's down," Brie said with a smile. Her smile faded as soon as she saw the concern etched across our faces. "What is it?"

"The Whore has gone," I said. "Carter has taken the submarine and left."

"What? Why on Earth would he do that? We are right here? Freedom is at the bottom of this cable."

"Let us speak with him," George interrupted. "The radio control panel in the dock allowed me to communicate with the submarine when I first breached the facility. He is likely still on the same channel."

I looked at my best friend. His grotesque, charred and melted face was a hard sight to bear. His lack of expression was unusual but I could tell now that despite the monotone and never-changing facial expression that his intentions were pure. He was on our side.

"Good idea, George. Lead the way."

Down in the dock the five of us stood huddled around the wall-mounted radio panel. Our mood had gone from triumphant excitement to distress and trepidation in a few short minutes. My sense of success had deflated in one quick moment of realisation. For whatever reason, Carter had abandoned us.

George turned on the radio device and selected the right channel. I pressed down on the receiver.

"Carter! Carter, are you there? Where have you gone?"

Silence.

415

We waited for what felt like forever.

I pressed down on the receiver again. "Carter, where the *fuck* have you gone?"

"Just leave him," Eli said. "He's a damn *coward*..."

After a few silent seconds we heard the crackle of radio static. "If only that was the case, young man," we heard Carter say. "Being a coward would make this infinitely easier."

"What does that mean? Where are you?"

"There is something I need to do and I need to do it alone... You all deserve your freedom and you have it right there in front of you. I, however, do not deserve it."

"Yes, you do. You deserve it as much as we do."

Carter laughed. There was no happiness in it. There was guilt. There was anguish. There was loneliness. "That's kind of you to say so, but unfortunately that's untrue. I'm taking this machine back to Terra Carcerem and I will destroy that God-awful island. I will do what I didn't have the balls to do a year ago."

"You're going to blow up Terra Carcerem? But wait, freedom is here, Carter. It's right here. You don't need to do that."

"*Your* freedom is right there, Tyson. But what about the tens of thousands of other people who have no understanding of what freedom is? You said it yourself only two days ago. What about the innocent citizens that will become victims of the Bestia? Where is their freedom? I can change the course of the future of Soteria. I can help the people find freedom. And by doing this, by blowing up the island of imprisonment, hopefully I will find mine..."

Brie said nothing. Michael said nothing. Maybe a part of them thought it was a noble endeavour. Maybe a part of them thought he was right. I looked at Eli. Tears welled in his eyes. The colour had drained from his face.

"But Gus," Eli said with youthful anguish.

"Look here, young man. There is nothing that any of you can say to make me turn around. I need to do this. By tomorrow you will all be in a safer place and Terra Carcerem will be nothing more than a pile of ash and rubble..."

I didn't know what to say. I took a breath and said the only thing there was to say.

"Thank you, Carter. Thank you and good luck." I began to cry. "We wouldn't have come this far without you."

"No, Tyson. Thank you. It was you and Eli that gave me the confidence I needed to get off that island. Without knowing it, you two have given me the confidence to do this, the confidence to make a change. No longer will we let fear and power govern us. Now get out of that damn facility. You won't have much time... Travel safe. I'll see you on the other side..."

The static returned then the channel went dead.

Carter had gone. We didn't even get to say a proper goodbye.

If I thought our mood had deflated before that conversation then we were at a whole new low. The four of us had tears in our eyes. It had drained our energy. Fatigue had mixed with negative energy, creating an ache in my muscles. I wiped the tears from my face.

"Carter was right," Brie said. "We won't be safe here for too long. It's time to get the hell off this wall!"

SEVENTY-EIGHT

It was now or never and never wasn't an option.

We needed to do this for Carter.

The escape raft floated calmly at the base on the concrete monolith. George had lowered it down the wall with ease. Although the cable still held the bow of the small boat in place, there was nothing adequate on top of the wall to tie the other end of the cable to so we could climb down it.

George agreed to hold the cable, acting as an anchor, while the four of us took turns lowering ourselves down the line. Eli went first. With the agility and wiry strength of a primate, Eli wrapped his feet over the cable and lowered himself down. He made it look too simple. Within four minutes he stood in the small boat looking back up at us with excitement. I knew why. He was officially outside of the Empire. His excitement was infectious. Realisation hit me that this was actually happening. My hands began to sweat. My heart rate increased. I replaced my sad thoughts of Carter with the understanding that we were leaving Soteria behind for good. No more sub-plazas, no more dosage day and no more Union. No more life, loyalty and salvation propaganda. The grey space that I longed for was literally at the bottom of the cable. I took a deep breath to placate my eagerness.

We're not there yet.

Brie grabbed the cable next. Through her broken teeth she smiled at Michael and me. She deserved this as much as any of us. Probably more. She was mere metres from freedom, the freedom that she had fought so hard for. It empowered me to know that we had helped her gain it.

She was halfway down the cable when I heard it.

Then George and Michael heard it.

Goosebumps enveloped my sweaty skin. The three of us turned to look out over the vast western horizon. The position of the lowering sun made it impossible to see. I squinted into the sunlight and saw nothing.

The noise became louder. It was unmistakable.

"Holy shit," Michael said. "It's a damn helicopter. They're here already."

Fear.

Doubt.

Nausea.

I leaned over the edge of the concrete wall. Brie still hung a good fifteen metres above the lapping water, taking her time to lower herself down the line safely. We no longer had time. With Brie still on the cable, George was immobilised. Acting as an anchor for our escape cable, he remained at the mercy of Brie's pace. Down on the eastern side of the wall, out of view from the west, Eli and Brie were oblivious to the approaching chopper.

"Brie," I called out. "You need to hurry. There is a Union helicopter coming. They are nearly here!"

Michael grabbed a taser cannon strapped to his bag and turned the setting to high. I did the same. We waited as each painful second brought the helicopter closer to the wall. Time slowed down. The moment seemed locked in a strange dreamlike state. Brie was taking too long.

Shit. We're not going to make it.

The chopper was upon us. It hovered fifteen metres above the wall. The deafening sound made communication with Eli and Brie impossible. I fired my taser cannon at the underside of the chopper. Michael did the same. The compressed electricity seemed to bounce right off the reinforced shell with no effect.

We continued firing. Then the impossible happened. Frozen in utter disbelief, I watched as three men jumped fearlessly from the side door of the chopper.

Impossible.

They landed on their feet with barely a bend in their knees. From that height a normal human would have been dead. They looked across the helicopter pad at us. They bore the same expressionless stare that I had grown accustomed to with George. Their eyes were the same deathly black.

"Oh shit," Michael yelled. "They're Bestia!"

Acting on impulse, the two of us fired our taser cannons at the three Bestia. I roared as adrenaline coursed through my frightened veins. As calm as an injection administration officer, the three Bestia walked towards us through our assault of taser blasts, unharmed.

George did what he needed to do. He let go of the cable, throwing it over the eastern side of the wall. Brie fell the final ten metres and landed in the water beside the boat with a surprised splash.

The Bestia stood metres away. They began walking through our relentless onslaught. George stared at me. Somewhere in that stare, for the briefest second, I saw the friend I used to know. It was in the smirk. It was in the slight tilt of the head. Something he usually did before laughing. My heart warmed with reminiscence. The George I thought I had lost was in there after all.

"Leave this to me," he said. "You are so close. You can be free. I will *never* be free. I forgive you, Tyson. But you need to go. *Now!*"

Without another word, George turned and ran at the three oncoming Bestia with inhuman pace. I froze, crippled with disbelief. I watched as George leaned back, dropped and slid across the ground towards the closest Bestia. In one quick movement he disabled the Bestia by ripping his leg off at the knee. The other two dived on George with the ferocity of a carnivore hunting its prey.

Michael grabbed me by the collar. "We need to jump. *Come on!*"

It was hard to leave George behind. It was the second time I would abandon my friend. This time I knew I would never see him again. This time he was saving our lives. This time it was for good. So many emotions flooded my manic mind that I felt dizzy. I felt nauseous and lightheaded. Now was not the time to pass out.

Michael, clutching me by the shirt, stepped up on the edge of the concrete wall as George wrestled with the two Bestia. I stepped up beside him and looked down. It was a frighteningly long way. My stomach tightened. I thought for the briefest second that if the jump didn't kill us, then the Bestia surely would.

It's now or never and never isn't an option.

Without counting down, I leapt. The free fall felt like a gut-wrenching eternity. With shattering impact I hit the water beside the boat. I surfaced just in time to see Michael hit the water beside me. I was dizzy, disorientated. My left eardrum ached. The palms of my hands stung from the heavy impact.

"Get the motor going, Eli. *Right now!*"

Brie was already in the boat with Eli. She looked like a drowned lab rat. Coming to the side of the gunwale she helped pull the two of us in the boat as Eli ran to the back and pulled the starter cord. It did nothing. He pulled it again. Nothing.

"Turn the choke on," Michael yelled, wiping water from his face.

"I don't know what the fuck that means!"

"Here, get out of the way. Let me try."

BANG!

Startled, the four of us nearly dived out the vessel from shock as something landed inside the boat with a deafening thud. I looked forward.

Fear.

Doubt.

Nausea.

George's detached head lay lifeless and crushed in the front of the boat beside our rations. Circuitry, brains and a blue fluid leaked from the gaping hole under his jaw. The Bestia had been victorious.

The Bestia had done exactly what the Union had trained them to do. George was no match for two of them.

I looked up and saw the two Bestia standing on the edge of the concrete wall. The chopper had now landed on the helicopter pad, the rotor blades slowing down. More Bestia joined our two observers on the wall's edge. A team of six or seven man-made soldiers stood together in perfect stance, staring at us below with the same frightening expression. One pulled a taser from his holster and began firing. From the height of the wall the taser cannon was inaccurate. The electric blasts flailed off and hit the water beside the boat. It was only a matter of time until one of the flailing shots hit us by chance.

My heart rate hammered.

Brie mumbled blasphemous remarks.

Staying focused under the intense pressure, Michael manually pumped the choke getting fuel into the line. He pulled the starter cord. The engine purred and coughed. Black smoke bellowed from the outboard motor. Still, it did not start.

"Guys..." Brie yelled as she looked up in frozen terror.

We all looked up. As we did, four Bestia jumped in unison, freefalling with precision as they rolled into a dive position.

Michael pulled the starter cord again. The engine coughed and spluttered.

I held my breath as I watched the Bestia hit the water on both sides of the boat. They surrounded us. We bobbed in the water, defenceless as a team of killing machines encircled us. As they surfaced, they swam towards our defenceless vessel with the stone-cold confidence that only comes from orchestrated algorithms of computer software.

They were two metres and closing.

I will not die today.

"WE WILL NOT DIE TODAY!" I leaned over Michael and with every ounce of rage, fear, doubt and will to survive I grabbed the starter cord and pulled. I pulled it back so hard I went tumbling forwards in the boat, sprawling beside George's crushed head. The engine coughed to life. The choke was still engaged, so it revved high pitch and fierce.

The Bestia were an arm's length away.

Michael grabbed the throttle and cranked it down. Our escape boat pulled forward through the water at the same time the closest Bestia reached the port side gunwale. He gripped the rail and held firm as we dragged him through the water. Eli pounced to the side of the boat, brandishing a taser cannon. He leaned over the side and shoved the barrel in the Bestia's open mouth.

"Go back to the Hell from where you came from," he yelled as he pulled the trigger. While not fatal, the mild electrocution caused the Bestia to let go of the gunwale for a moment. That was all we needed. Michael held the throttle firm as the boat increased pace and we took off east.

We looked back and saw all four Bestia treading water at the base of the wall, bobbing in our wake.

We sat in silence. We sat in disbelief. We let realisation sink in and let our heart rates subside. The dreamlike state of victory was our new reality. The wall became smaller and smaller until it was nothing more than a darkened strip on the western horizon. Soteria was now behind us for the first time in our lives. The helicopter didn't follow. The pilot was probably preoccupied with retrieving the Bestia.

I glanced at my peers. They looked exhausted. I smiled and they all smiled back. Then I laughed. Eli, Michael and Brie joined in and there in that small boat, over the hum of the outboard engine, was a beautiful symphony of victorious laughter.

Someone once told me that freedom exists in the mind. Someone once told me that people are as free as they allow themselves to be. I know now that it wasn't about what we were allowed. It was about what we fought for. It was about how much we wanted it, how much we would sacrifice to taste that freedom. Sitting there in that small escape boat, staring east towards our future, I finally understood what they meant. We had given it our all. We wouldn't take no for an answer. We had pushed ourselves to the brink, and past it.

As we put distance between the wall and our escape vessel we sat in intimate silence. I looked at my friends. I looked at Eli and smiled. His youthful grin was infectious. His courage was admirable. His loyalty was admirable. I looked at Michael and Brie. For the first time since knowing her, Brie looked at peace. Maybe she had finally beaten her demons.

Then I looked east towards the great unknown, towards that grey space I longed for. I looked out towards our freedom. I wanted to scream at the top of my lungs. We had broken the system. We had created our own system. We had freed ourselves of the Humanist Union. Brie looked at me with a smile. She could sense my overwhelming happiness. "Where to now?" she asked, baring the same infectious smile.

I pointed to the blank eastern horizon before us and laughed again. "That way…"

EPILOGUE

MASTER STEPHEN HAYNES STOOD INSIDE THE MAIN CONTROL CENTRE of Terra Carcerem's Paradiso facility.

He paced menacingly between control booths. Two days had passed since the helicopter's return. The pilot had spent the better part of an hour locating something inside the facility to hang over the wall and retrieve the Bestia floating patiently at the base of the concrete mass.

The Bestia had used their superhuman strength to remove the fallen steel frame from the corridor in the maintenance facility, freeing Atkins and his colleagues from the pitch-black control room.

Atkins and the helicopter pilot now hung chained to the wall in front of Master Haynes. They were naked. They were bloodied and bruised. Atkins was missing his right hand and the pilot was suffering blood loss from a serious wound to the abdomen.

"I'm displeased with your efforts," the Master said with a look of disgust. "How four mortal humans can outrun a team of Bestia is beyond me. Two of them were nothing more than children. One was a *woman!*"

"I'm so sorry, sir," Atkins whispered. "We did what we could."

"I don't believe that. One can always do more. One can always try harder. You had a simple job. Protect the maintenance facility. You failed…"

Master Stephen Haynes looked to his left. Eric van Bueren stood to his side but said nothing. Even he knew his place.

"Eric, I want you to do something for me."

"Anything, sir."

"I would like you to kill these two for me. They are failures. They do not deserve a place in our Union."

"Without question, sir."

"And then we are to launch the Bestia. There are two hundred of them downstairs ready to go. I will put it off no longer. The first thing we will do is take them east. We will find that boat. We will find your niece. We will find Augustus Carter and finish this."

Van Bueren stepped forward to fulfil his loyal duties. He had never killed with his bare hands before. He had always ordered others to do it for him. He swallowed his apprehension.

Before he could lift the combat knife from the table beside him, the room shook like the hand of God himself had rattled it. The wall-mounted security screens went black. Then all power to the facility shut off as blackness shrouded the control room. There was the briefest moment of panic in the darkness. Master Stephen Haynes didn't get a word out before a nuclear fireball engulfed the entire island with such intensity the impenetrable facilities crumbled to powder. The all-consuming power of the atomic explosion swallowed Eric van Bueren and the Master of The Humanist Union, along with his squad of hybrid killing machines. The penetrating heat and ferocity was so extreme that human and Bestia alike disintegrated on the spot.

Not even their skeletons remained.

Burning debris and chunks of the Terra Carcerem facility rained down on the calm surface of the water surrounding Norfolk Island. Putrid black smoke scarred the skyline. The smell of death, fire and destruction lingered in the fading daylight. The fire continued to burn as silence enveloped all that remained of the island of imprisonment.

Augustus Carter had found his salvation.

Made in the USA
Middletown, DE
20 January 2024

48170488R00255